EYE OF THE LAW

EYE OF THE LAW

Cora Harrison

This first world edition published 2010
in Great Britain and in the USA by
SEVERN HOUSE PUBLISHERS LTD of
9–15 High Street, Sutton, Surrey, England, SM1 1DF.
Trade paperback edition published
in Great Britain and the USA 2010 by
SEVERN HOUSE PUBLISHERS LTD

British Library Cataloguing in Publication Data

Harrison, Cora.
  Eye of the Law.
  1. Mara, Brehon of the Burren (Fictitious character) –
  Fiction. 2. Women judges – Ireland – Burren – Fiction.
  3. Burren (Ireland) – History – 16th century – Fiction.
  4. Detective and mystery stories.
  I. Title
  823.9'14–dc22

ISBN-13: 978-0-7278-6873-2   (cased)
ISBN-13: 978-1-84751-232-1   (trade paper)

Severn House Publishers support The Forest Stewardship Council [FSC],
the leading international forest certification organisation. All our titles that
are printed on Greenpeace-approved FSC-certified paper carry the FSC logo.

Mixed Sources
Product group from well-managed
forests and other controlled sources
www.fsc.org Cert no. SA-COC-1565
© 1996 Forest Stewardship Council

Typeset by Palimpsest Book Production Ltd.,
Grangemouth, Stirlingshire, Scotland.
Printed and bound in Great Britain by
MPG Books Ltd., Bodmin, Cornwall.

One

Guchbrecha Caracniað
(The False Judgements of Caratniad)

The oath of all persons on their deathbed must be believed, for who would lie when faced with eternity?

Most sacred of all deathbed oaths is the sworn testimony of a woman as to the father of her child.

St Patrick's Day, on the 17th of March in the year 1510, was fine and dry, but an icy wind from the north-east funnelled through the gaps between the small mountains surrounding the kingdom of the Burren and then swept across the stone pavements.

The few trees in the rock-strewn land bent and cracked under its force. Under the ground their roots had braced themselves, year upon year, against the continual winds from the west and the south-west, but now the trees were exposed and vulnerable to this unaccustomed onslaught from the opposite direction. Here and there, in the valleys, they lay on their sides, their crab-like roots still with pieces of broken limestone attached, now clutching nothing but air. The wind had stripped the last blackened seeds of the stately oak and ash from the branches, casting them down on to the fertile earth below, and small green buds, destined to die before maturity, pointed skywards from the uprooted gnarled willows outside the caves at Kilcorney. The dry, bleached grass was flattened by the force of the gale, but in the sheltered valleys and under hedgerows, emerald-green blades showed that the sun's strength was enough for new growth.

Within the shelter of the high walls around Lemeanah Castle's courtyard, where the O'Brien clan and their neighbours were celebrating the marriage of Maeve MacNamara and Donal O'Brien, eldest son and heir to the *taoiseach*, Teige O'Brien, there was enough warmth for the young people to stay outdoors even as sunset approached. Not just the O'Brien clan, but also many of the O'Lochlainns, the O'Connors and the MacNamaras were present.

Even King Turlough Donn, ruler of Thomond, Corcomroe and Burren, attended the wedding celebrations of his cousin's eldest son and so did Mara, his new wife.

Mara was not just the king's wife, but also the Brehon of the Burren, responsible for law and order within its one hundred square miles, so she knew every family in the kingdom; their history and secrets had been part of her life since she had become Brehon of the Burren fifteen years ago when only twenty-one years old.

She stood at the gate and looked around at the frolicking crowd with affection and amusement. It was almost like a fair. In a sheltered corner by the kitchen house, one of the Lemeanah servants was rapidly baking griddlecakes over a fire, and as fast as the cakes were taken off the flat piece of iron and spread with a lump of yellow butter and a spoonful of golden honey, they were swallowed down. In another corner, a juggler performed his tricks, watched by an appreciative audience of small children, and a wandering bard told a story in a sibilant whisper to a wide-eyed crowd outside the gatehouse.

Mara stopped to listen to him for a minute. He had only been in the Burren for a week but already he seemed to know the place well. Mentions of Balor's Cave at Kilcorney, less than a mile away from Lemeanah, were interwoven with the story of the malevolent one-eyed god who could kill those he looked at. She hoped the bard would stay. They had many good musicians and singers in the Burren, but a man who could tell a story like that would be an asset to any community.

'You're very welcome, Brehon!' Teige O'Brien came bustling up. 'The king has already arrived. He's waiting for you upstairs. You're looking very well.'

'A new gown for the wedding,' said Mara gaily. 'Turlough chose it. I usually wear green so this red wool is something new for me.' Her well-fitting gown was stitched at the neck and sleeve cuffs with gold thread and her *léine* was of bleached linen embroidered with delicate lace.

I must wear red more often, she thought. She knew that it suited her dark hair and olive complexion, knew too that the bloom of early pregnancy lent her an extra beauty, so in high good humour she followed Teige as he escorted her up the steeply winding spiral staircase and into the Great Hall of Lemeanah Castle.

'A great feast,' said the king with satisfaction, greeting her with a kiss when she joined him at the window of the Great Hall.

After the month's honeymoon at Ballinalacken Castle they were both back to their busy working lives, meeting for a few days before parting again. He was due back in his own kingdom of Thomond tonight, she knew, but they would spend the weekend together. She squeezed his hand and he kissed her again. Then he smiled down at the animated scene below. Three men with fiddles were playing a sparkling tune and the young people were rapidly taking hands and lining up for a set dance.

'It looks as though the whole of the Burren is here,' he said with satisfaction. He was a man who loved a festival. 'There's the O'Lochlainn and his brother, Donogh. And the MacNamara! And the O'Connor! And there's Malachy the physician with his daughter Nuala. Who's that woman with Malachy?'

Mara did not reply. She didn't quite know what to say about Malachy. Her eyes were anxious as they looked at fourteen-year-old Nuala. The child looked depressed, she thought, noting the slumped shoulders and the hanging head. She turned to beckon to her six law-school scholars, who had just finished proffering small gifts to the wedding couple.

'You can take the boys down to the courtyard now, Fachtnan,' she said to her eldest scholar.

This would cheer Nuala up; she idolized Fachtnan, and the other boys were like brothers to her. Mara watched from the window until she saw Fachtnan take Nuala by the hand and lead her into the dance. Sighing with relief, Mara had begun to turn back to Turlough when suddenly she noticed a pair of unfamiliar faces.

'Who are those two men?' she murmured, knitting her dark eyebrows.

'Don't know,' said Turlough laconically. 'Which men?'

'The ones at the gate.' Mara pushed the window ajar and leaned out with one hand on the stone mullion that divided the window space into two. The westerly sun shone brightly on the entrance gate and lit up the figures of two strongly made dark-haired men. 'I've never seen those two in my life before.'

'Teige will know. Teige, who are those two men down there talking to your porter?'

'Blessed if I know.' Teige, the king's cousin, joined them. He was a man of about fifty, the same age as Turlough and a great friend of his. He leaned out of the window and then turned back.

'Seem to be friends of the O'Lochlainn,' he said. 'The porter is bringing them over to him.'

'Hardly friends, he obviously doesn't know them.' Mara watched with sharpened interest as the porter steered the two men through the groups and brought them up to the O'Lochlainn *taoiseach*. Ardal O'Lochlainn was looking puzzled, she noticed. He bent his handsome head of copper-coloured curls down towards the elder of the two men and listened to him courteously. His blue eyes had a startled look after the first few words and he made an abrupt signal to his steward, Liam, and then the four of them moved away from the crowds towards a deserted spot on the outer wall.

'I wonder what all this is about.' Her comment was directed at Teige; he should know whether those strangers had been invited to join the wedding party. After all, the king was present and there was at best an uneasy peace between the O'Briens of Thomond, Corcomroe and Burren, and the O'Kellys from nearby Galway. Teige took the hint and moved away instantly. Mara heard him calling down the stairs.

'You're just a gossip.' Turlough's voice was affectionate. 'Anyway, you haven't told me who that woman with Malachy is. Look, he's partnering her in the dance now. Pretty woman. A bit on the plump side.'

'Her name is Caireen and she is the widow of a physician from Galway.'

'From Galway. How did he meet her?'

'Her husband was some sort of distant relation of poor old Toin, the *briuga* from Rathborney. I think he came to see Malachy after Toin died and when it became known that Toin had left Nuala a legacy. The physician from Galway was ill himself then and he died soon afterwards. Malachy went to the funeral and apparently he and Caireen became friends.' Mara's tone was reserved, but Turlough immediately pounced.

'And you don't like her?'

'Nuala doesn't like her.'

'Well,' said Turlough tolerantly. 'It must be nearly two years since Nuala's mother died. The poor fellow can't remain single forever. Nuala is well provided for. It seems ideal.'

'It's not too ideal,' said Mara curtly. 'This widow has a son of eighteen years who has almost finished his training to be a physician and another son, a year or two younger, who is well on his way to qualifying. And there is a third son about Nuala's age who, also, had been his father's apprentice.'

'So she's going to feel crowded out.' Turlough sounded sympathetic.

'The O'Lochlainn is leaving those men now and coming indoors. But Liam is staying with them.' Mara didn't want to discuss Nuala with so many listening ears around. Her sympathy was with the girl. She closed the window and turned back into the room to cross over to where the young couple sat. The bride, Maeve, had been under her care after the death of the girl's father and Mara was touched by the bliss that she could see on the small kitten-like face.

'I wish you all the happiness in the world,' she said, kissing the girl and patting the young man on the shoulder. 'You are having a lovely spring day for your wedding. Have you all the alterations finished to your house at Shessymore?'

'We have, Brehon,' said Donal, standing up respectfully. 'We hope that you will be one of our first visitors.'

'I certainly will,' said Mara heartily.

The door to the stairway opened and Ardal O'Lochlainn entered. Ardal was always the soul of courtesy, but it was obvious from the way that he stood there, with his eyes fixed on Mara, that he wanted a word. With a few more expressions of goodwill, Mara left the young couple and made her way across the room.

Ardal didn't look well, she noticed instantly. In fact, he looked like a man who had received a bad shock.

'Brehon, I'm sorry to disturb you,' he said quietly, 'but I wonder whether you could spare me a few minutes.'

'Of course, Ardal. Shall we go somewhere private?'

She observed that quite a few of the guests were eyeing him with curiosity. Teige's steward came in and murmured to his master; Mara noticed how the O'Brien *taoiseach* seemed to stiffen with alarm or perhaps it was astonishment.

Ardal bowed. 'You are very good.' He turned to go back out of the room, holding the door open for her.

Mara saw Turlough take a step forward, but she deliberately did not look at him, or beckon him to join them. This was a problem that she had to deal with on her own. Ever since their marriage, and especially as he knew that she was expecting a baby, Turlough seemed to want to share all of her burdens, to treat her like a piece of precious Venetian glass, but she was determined to carry on doing her job for as long as she could. The baby was due in July; her scholars would have departed for the summer holidays by then and Fergus, the Brehon of the neighbouring kingdom of Corcomroe, would look after Burren as well during July. By September she would be fit and well again and would be able to resume her duties as Brehon and as *ollamh*, professor, of the law school of Cahermacnaghten.

After closing the door quietly behind them both, Ardal led the way downstairs. Next to the main doorway there was a small room with an iron brazier filled with glowing pieces of turf burning on the floor under the window. Usually it was occupied by a couple of men-at-arms, but today these were enjoying themselves outside in the courtyard. They would be quite private in here with the door closed against the noisy crowd.

'What's the trouble, Ardal?' Mara looked anxiously at his troubled blue eyes. She had never seen him look like that. He always seemed to go through life with an air of serene unconcern.

'I've had a bit of a shock, Brehon.' He ran his hand rapidly through his red-gold curls and turned a bewildered face towards her.

'Has it something to do with these two men I saw come up to you in the courtyard?'

He nodded. 'They come from the Aran, from Inisheer, the eastern island.'

'A long and difficult journey in a wind like this.' Mara eyed him carefully.

'They set out yesterday and they had to turn back. The weather was a bit better today so they tried again. They've been rowing since dawn.' Ardal seemed to be talking for the sake of talking. That was unlike him; he normally said little unless it was to the point.

'So they must have had a strong reason for coming?'

'They brought a letter . . .' Ardal hesitated. 'Would you like to see them, Brehon, and hear the story that they have to tell?'

'Perhaps it would be better for you to tell me what it's all about first, Ardal. Then I could talk with them if that's what you would like me to do.' Mara's voice was firm. It was obvious that Ardal had been told the reason for the errand and it would be quicker to get the information from him than from two strange men.

Ardal squared his shoulders. 'Well, to make a long story short, Brehon, they came to tell me that the younger man, Iarla is his name – he'd be about twenty, I'd suppose. Well, they came to tell me that he is my son.'

'What!' Mara was startled out of her usual calm.

Ardal nodded. 'That's right, my son.'

'But how?'

'Oh, they can give chapter and verse all right,' said Ardal bitterly. 'This boy was born in December 1489 and I visited Aran in the Easter of 1489. I went with King Turlough, God bless him. Of course, he wasn't king then, not even *tánaiste,* but King Conor, his uncle, had sent him to collect the rents and I went with him and so did Teige. We were just three young men – I was under twenty myself – and, like all young men, we were out for a good time.'

'And you found the island women accommodating.' Mara's grin was tolerant.

Ardal nodded. 'I remember his mother all right,' he said uncomfortably. 'She was the blacksmith's wife. The blacksmith was drunk, completely drunk; he looked as if he wouldn't wake up for an age.'

'Was she pretty?'

'Very. She had hair redder than my own and a pair of lovely grey eyes. I remember her well,' admitted Ardal. 'So will Teige, I'd say, but don't mention it in front of his wife. He was already married at the time.'

'So you had intercourse with her.' Mara's tone was brisk. She had to establish the facts, though she knew that he was taken aback at her directness.

'That was the way of it.'

'But you heard no more from her?'

Ardal shook his head. 'I forgot all about it a few days later,' he confessed. 'I was just a lad and I suppose I hoped that nothing would come of it.'

'But why turn up now? Let me guess. The blacksmith has died.'

'He died a few years ago. No, it's the mother who has died. She made a deathbed confession.'

'Naming you as father of this boy, Iarla?'

'Naming me as father.' Ardal bowed his head and repeated dully, 'Naming me as father in her confession to the priest. The priest has sent me a letter. He writes down the date of the boy's baptism – just about nine months after I lay with the mother.'

'I see,' said Mara. 'Of course the law does say that if a woman names a man as father to her child on her deathbed, then her word should be believed. The idea is that no one will tell a lie to a priest on his or her deathbed. I must say that it is something that I have always had difficulty with. My experience is that a mother's love for her first-born may be stronger than her fear of hell. She might even reason that God would forgive a mother for doing the best for her son.'

And, of course, she thought, this would be a splendid prize for any boy to inherit. Ardal was by far the richest *taoiseach* on the Burren. The O'Lochlainns had been kings of the Burren in the past, before it was conquered by the O'Briens of Thomond. The land, of course, was clan land and should go to the *taoiseach* of the clan as well as many of the sheep and cattle. Ardal, however, had a large personal fortune amassed by breeding and selling horses and by his efficiency as a farmer and this would be a rich prize for any heir, even if Iarla were not declared to be the *tánaiste*. Ardal, of course, would be aware of all this.

'But does the law say that I must recognize this boy as my son?' There was a note of deep distaste in his voice.

'I would be cautious for the moment, Ardal. Admit nothing. Say little. Leave this to me. Now, I think, since I know the facts about the matter, this might be the moment for me to meet this Iarla.' Suddenly a thought struck her. 'But who is the older man? You said that the blacksmith is dead.'

'That's the present blacksmith from Inisheer. He's the brother of the boy's father, or previously acknowledged father.'

'I see,' said Mara. 'Interesting that he comes here with the boy! You would not imagine a man would welcome his brother being known as a cuckold.'

'Shall I bring them in so that you can speak with them?' Ardal winced slightly at her plain speaking, but tried to sound detached.

'Yes, do that, Ardal.'

This should be interesting, she told herself. There seemed to be something odd about the story.

When Ardal returned, Mara was not surprised to see that he was accompanied by Liam as well as the two strangers. Liam had been steward to Ardal, and to Ardal's father before him. He was a strong, active man, reputedly about sixty, though he looked a good ten years younger. Ardal relied on Liam, not just for managing his estate and its revenues, but also for companionship.

What a shame that Ardal had not remarried, thought Mara. If he had married again ten years ago, after the death of his young wife, and now had a string of sons ready to inherit his lands and fortune, then this young Iarla might never have bothered turning up on his doorstep. No doubt the story of Ardal's wealth and his childlessness had penetrated to the Aran Islands.

'This is Iarla, Brehon, and this is his uncle, Becan.' Liam made the introductions with aplomb, but like his master, he looked shocked.

'Sit down, Iarla, and you, Becan.' But before she could move, Liam, efficient as always, proffered the only chair in the room to Mara and pulled out two stools for the men. Then he went and stood quietly beside his master who was leaning against the wall.

'I've heard the purpose of your arrival,' said Mara, addressing Iarla directly. 'When did you first hear this tale?'

He flushed angrily. The word 'tale' had stung.

'Three days ago,' he said briefly.

'At the deathbed of your mother?' Mara softened her voice. It was not for her to take one side or the other, she reminded herself. The fact that she was fond of Ardal and had known him since they were both young should have no place in this enquiry.

Iarla nodded.

'Tell me about it.' As he launched into the explanation she studied him carefully. There was no look of Ardal about him. He was below medium height, with dark hair, a swarthy skin, heavy nose and a full-lipped mouth.

'Thank you,' she said as he finished. 'Now, can I see the letter from the priest?'

He fumbled under his arm. Over the *léine* he wore a short jacket of unsheared sheepskin. It seemed to have some sort of pouch sewn to the inside of that. The package, when he finally extracted it, was completely wrapped in oilskin and he took some time to unfold this, putting the skin carefully aside before handing the sheet of vellum to her. A fisherman, obviously, well used to protecting import-ant goods from the damage of the Atlantic salt water.

And this document was important. Mara read it to herself and then aloud. The letter was well written and referred to the 'ancient law of the land of Ireland' and stated that a woman had confessed her sin on her deathbed and had named Iarla as the son, not of her husband, but of Ardal O'Lochlainn, *taoiseach* of the O'Lochlainn clan of the Burren. The priest, in priest-like fashion, was 'confident that this young man would be instated as the only son of the *taoiseach* and given all of the rights and privileges that came from that position.'

Mara folded the letter and looked up. Ardal's face was now well under control and showed no emotion. Liam looked openly suspicious.

'How did the priest know that the O'Lochlainn had no son yet?' he demanded truculently.

Mara bit back a smile. The whole of the Burren had been trying to marry off Ardal for the last ten years. It was indeed possible that the story of his childlessness had penetrated as far as Aran. Liam, however, had not finished.

'I've seen you before,' he went on, pointing to Becan. 'You were selling fish at the Imbolc fair, here on the Burren, six weeks ago. I remember your face.'

'No crime in that.' Becan's voice was deep and hoarse.

'But you said you were a blacksmith.'

'I do a bit of this and a bit of that.' Becan shrugged, spreading his hands out in the island fashion.

He had more of a look of a blacksmith than of a fisherman, thought Mara. His hands and arms were huge and he had several burn marks on his face as well as his hands. She decided to say nothing though, just to watch and listen.

'And if you are a fisherman,' continued Liam, jutting his chin aggressively, 'why sell fish here in Burren? Why not in Corcomroe – wouldn't that be nearer for you with a long journey to go back to the island? Why walk all the way to the Burren? You had no horse, not even a donkey. I remember seeing you on the road near our place.'

'Why not?' Becan stared back.

'I know why,' said Liam triumphantly. 'You had heard about the O'Lochlainn and you decided to come to have a look for yourself. You picked up all the news and you went to have a look at the O'Lochlainn's tower house. Don't deny it. It wasn't on your road back to Doolin. You were having a good look around Lissylisheen when I saw you.'

I wonder whether this is a fraud, thought Mara. It's beginning to look like that. Aloud she said gently, 'What was wrong with your mother, Iarla? Why did she die? She was still a young woman, wasn't she?'

'She had a lump in her breast,' said the young man sullenly.

'So she knew for quite a while that she was going to die,' said Mara quietly.

She cast a quick glance at Iarla. He had the massive shoulders and well-developed arms of Becan, but he did not look as if he had recently worked at the forge. There were no burn marks on either hands or face. Of course, there would have been very little work for a blacksmith in Aran. As far as she knew there were no deposits of iron in the limestone. Even in the Burren itself there was no iron: Fintan MacNamara, the blacksmith, had to get his from Corcomroe. Mara hadn't been to Aran for several years, but she remembered it very clearly. Everything there was made from stone; there were no gates anywhere; the field gaps were opened and closed by the simple method of moving some of the large stones from the slanting herringbone pattern of the walls. The blacksmith's work would consist purely in making cooking pots and perhaps shoes for the few horses that existed on the island.

'So the blacksmith business belonged to you and your brother?' she addressed Becan.

'That's right, Brehon,' he said gruffly. 'And our father before him.' He looked at her suspiciously, and, when she didn't reply, he said aggressively. 'So what's going to happen now? I have to go back to Aran as soon as possible and I want to see this affair settled. The priest said that Iarla would have to be taken in by the O'Lochlainn. There's nothing for him on the island; his three sisters have their own families to look after and so do I.'

So it was as she suspected. If there were a suspicion that the boy was not his brother's son, then Becan would feel no duty to share the meagre income of the blacksmith's business with him. Mara glanced at Ardal. He was a man of principle and of honour. His own convenience would never form part of a reason for a decision. His eyes met hers, but there was doubt in them. He glanced over at Iarla, looking at him curiously and intently. Iarla flushed, a warm tide of red flooding under the sea-tanned skin. He was a handsome lad in a dark swarthy way, thought Mara, eyeing him with interest. His eyes stared defiantly back.

'What is the position now, Brehon?' Ardal addressed her with his usual courtesy.

'Two things have to be taken into consideration,' said Mara, mentally scanning through the dusty piles of law texts and judgement scrolls that filled the shelves and wooden presses of Cahermacnaghten. 'The first is the sworn deathbed testimony of the mother, witnessed by a priest, that Iarla, here, is the son of Ardal O'Lochlainn. However, secondly, it must be borne in mind that this was a married woman. No doubt during the Eastertide and the weeks that followed, this woman had intercourse with her lawful wedded husband. It would have been strange if she did not do so. She herself might honestly have believed that Iarla was the fruit of her brief intimacy with the O'Lochlainn; a *taoiseach* – and you were already *taoiseach* at the time, were you not, Ardal? – would seem a romantic father for her son. This does put a doubt in my mind. As well as that –' Mara looked very directly at the young man – 'there is no physical likeness between Iarla and Ardal. In fact, I can say, since I know all of the O'Lochlainn's family, that I don't think that I have met any dark-haired members. The red hair seems to persist. What was the colour of your mother's hair, Iarla?'

'It was red,' he muttered.

'I see,' said Mara, 'and of course, two red-haired parents would seem to forecast a red-headed child.'

She looked at him carefully. No, he had no resemblance at all to Ardal: the features were quite different. Ardal had a white-skinned face with a straight, well-cut nose, a high forehead and thin, fastidious lips, whereas Iarla was dark with a swarthy skin, dark eyes and a blunt, fleshy nose. However, she knew that this would only be enough to cast a doubt. The law was very clear; a deathbed confession had always to be believed.

'I think I need some time to decide on this question; perhaps I could appoint a time in two weeks at Poulnabrone. Poulnabrone is our judgement place,' she informed the two men from Aran.

'And in the meantime, perhaps you would like to stay with me at Lissylisheen,' said Ardal, trying to force a note of hospitality into his voice. 'And you, Becan, until the high seas die down.'

The two men looked at each other and then Becan nodded an off-hand acceptance.

There was an awkward silence for a moment. Becan looked from one to the other. 'Well, perhaps in the meantime we'll go back and join the party and let you talk it over,' he said, grabbing the young man by the sleeve and leading him from the room.

'I think it might be an idea to send someone over to Aran to investigate,' said Mara as the door closed behind the two. 'I could send Fachtnan and Enda. They would do it very well and it would be good experience for them. I'd be interested to hear whether the mother ever spoke of the possibility that Iarla was not her husband's son, or indeed, whether she had ever mentioned any other possibility for a father.'

'I'll go with them, Brehon, if you like,' offered Liam. 'We're not too busy at the moment.'

'Thank you, Liam, but I think that I will send Cumhal. He'll enjoy the trip.' Cumhal was her farm manager. He was an immensely busy man supervising and planning all the work on the farm and assisting the Brehon with the scholars' out-of-school activities, but she would feel happiest to entrust nineteen-year-old Fachtnan and seventeen-year-old Enda to him. It was kind of Liam to offer, but she felt neither Liam, nor any of the O'Lochlainn clan, should be involved in this fact-finding mission. Justice had to be seen to be impartial.

'I just don't feel that he is my son,' said Ardal thoughtfully. 'There is nothing there when I look at him, no gesture, no expression, no feature.'

'He looks more like his uncle, the blacksmith.' Liam eyed her hopefully.

'I'll study my law texts,' promised Mara.

'And if the worst comes to the worst,' said Liam with a grim smile on his lips, 'I can always take him back to the island and toss him to the fishes.'

Two

Qudacht Morainn
The Testament of Morann

'Let him (the king) not elevate any judge unless he knows the true legal precedents.'

One of the most important decisions that a king must make is in the appointing of a Brehon (judge) to administer justice in the kingdom.

A Brehon must be a person of virtue and integrity as well as having a deep knowledge of all things pertaining to the law.

'**B**rehon!'
'Mara!'

The two voices almost blended. Mara stood up rapidly. Already her magnificent white wolfhound, Bran, had bounded to his feet and with head raised was sniffing the air. Mara put her hand on his collar and then released it. In the distance she saw Fachtnan, her eldest scholar, and Nuala, the physician's daughter, crossing the clints of shining limestone. She waved and then heaved a sigh. There was some crisis for her to deal with. Her peace would soon be at an end.

'Wait, Bran,' she said, signalling to him to lie down again.

It was Thursday. School had finished, the day was fine and she was snatching a half-hour's gardening, moving some eight-petalled celandines to fill in the gaps in the shining ribbon of gold that wove its way through the hazel wood beside her garden.

Mara's garden was her pride, her joy and the place where she did her thinking. Today as she placed soft piles of vivid green moss around the clumps of butter-pale primroses, shortened the thorny branches of the pale-pink dog rose, dug up the scattered brass-coloured celandine plants, and cleared the dead leaves from where the bluebells had begun to spear their way through the woodland soil, her mind had been busy with the problem of Ardal and these sudden and unexpected visitors from the Aran Islands.

Becan, according to Brigid, her housekeeper, had left Lissylisheen yesterday afternoon. The wind had died down and he'd planned to spend the night at Doolin and make the sea crossing this morning.

Iarla was staying on at the tower house of Lissylisheen, and was, according to Brigid, making a nuisance of himself, following Liam around from barn to farm. Ardal had taken some horses to sell in Galway so Liam had been left to play the host. Possibly not the best of arrangements, thought Mara. Perhaps she should have invited the young man to stay at the guesthouse at the school. However, Ardal had issued the invitation, and maybe it would be good if he were to get to know the boy for a week or two before judgement was announced at Poulnabrone.

By the time that Mara reached her own gate, Fachtnan, closely followed by Nuala, had just vaulted the last low stone wall before the road that ran in front of Cahermacnaghten Law School and the Brehon's house, a hundred yards away from the school. The news was not too serious, she thought, looking at the two young faces. For a moment she had been afraid that something was wrong with Malachy – Fachtnan had gone over to the physician's house after school to deliver a request from Brigid to Malachy for some ointment for a farm worker's arm. However, though their faces were serious, neither looked particularly distressed.

'What's the matter?' asked Mara, opening the gate and standing back to allow them to come in.

'You'll be shocked,' warned Nuala.

'We got a shock,' said Fachtnan. 'Nuala was great. She just got straight down on her knees and started to examine him.'

'What! Has there been an accident?' Mara's mind immediately flew to her six scholars. Ten-year-old Shane and thirteen-year-old Hugh had gone to help her neighbour, Diarmuid, with the lambing; Enda was studying in the scholars' house; Aidan and Moylan were sowing oats with Cumhal. All should be safe.

'Not an accident.' Nuala was watching her face carefully. 'Definitely not an accident.'

'Who is it?' Mara was getting exasperated and it showed in her voice.

'We were just trying to break it gently,' said Nuala reproachfully. 'It's that fellow from the Aran Islands.'

'Iarla,' added Fachtnan. 'The lad who claims to be O'Lochlainn's son.'

'And he's been injured?' But Mara knew it was more than that. 'Killed?' she queried.

Nuala nodded. 'Not recently, either. He's cold and stiff. He's lying in front of Balor's Cave at Kilcorney.'

'I see,' said Mara. Her heart sank. Mechanically she went back and put her trowel and her leather gloves into her small basket and replaced them in the small stone cabin beside her house. She took her fur-lined cloak from the peg behind the front door of the house, but kept on her heavy boots. The way across to Kilcorney was rough with great slabs of stone and tumbled rock; it was no place for fine leather shoes, especially for a woman who was five months pregnant.

'Don't take Bran,' said Fachtnan suddenly and she understood his feeling. She vividly remembered the other occasion when Bran's howls had signalled a dead body and the repercussions for the law school from that discovery.

'Put him back in the stables, then,' she said. 'Oh, and just run and tell Brigid that I am going over to Kilcorney, Fachtnan. Tell her that I should be back for supper. Nuala and I will start going and you can catch us up.'

'Father is with him. He said that he would wait until you came,' said Nuala as they crossed the field, stepping over the grykes where the violets and primroses were blooming in the small crevices between the slabs of stone. Her face grew angry when she mentioned her father, but cleared when Fachtnan came bounding across the clints, his nail-studded boots striking sparks off the huge slabs of limestone.

The body of the young man from Aran lay half concealed by an upturned willow just beside the entrance to Balor's Cave. Mara could understand why no one had seen him before now; he was quite hidden from the lane and, in fact, the lane itself was a deserted one, running along for about a hundred yards with only a single cottage on it and ending at the cave.

'How did you find him?' she asked Fachtnan, after a murmured greeting to Malachy.

'Nuala saw a flock of ravens and she thought that they might be attacking some newborn lambs so we turned down,' he said. 'They hadn't attacked the body yet; probably the branches of the willow made them worry about a trap, but I stayed while Nuala went to fetch Malachy. Then when he arrived, we both went to fetch you.'

'He was killed by someone thrusting a knife or a sharpened stick into his eye,' announced Malachy. 'Look.' He pointed to the mass of blackened blood that crusted over one of the eyes. He gave a quick look around. 'Strange, isn't it, to find a man with only one eye outside Balor's Cave? This will get people scared.'

'No,' said Nuala sharply. 'No, it wasn't like that at all. You've got it all wrong.'

'What do you mean?' Malachy rounded on his daughter angrily.

'Explain yourself, Nuala.' Mara's tone was crisp. Obviously relationships between father and daughter were poor, but the first consideration now had to be this murder. Let them fight it out afterwards, thought Mara irritably. Malachy's half-suggestion that this death was due to supernatural powers was a particularly silly one, she thought, looking at him with disfavour, and then turning back to Nuala.

'There's not enough blood,' said Nuala in a matter-of-fact way. She knelt on the ground beside the body. 'If he had been stabbed in the eye while he was still living, the blood would have poured out. It would have stained his face, soaked his clothes right down the front and probably soaked the ground too. Look, this is what killed him.'

Carefully she put her hand on the shoulder and eased the stiff body over until it lay on its front and then pointed to a large circular wound on the back of the head. There was sticky black blood on the back of the neck and it had soaked into the sheepskin jacket and the white *léine* below.

'I'd say that was done with a heavy club or stick,' continued Nuala. 'The only strange thing is that I would also have expected blood to be on the ground, but I suppose it all bled into the clothing.' She gave a slightly dissatisfied look at the corpse and at the earth around it and then rose to her feet, dusting her hands. 'But it has to be the head, it couldn't be the eye. That was done after death.'

Malachy said nothing. He compressed his lips and his dark eyes were angry, but he did not disagree. Mara felt convinced by Nuala's explanation, but thought it would not be tactful to take sides. There was enough trouble between the two of them at the moment and, although her sympathy was with Nuala, in a way Turlough was right. Why should Malachy not get married again after mourning his dead wife for two years? It was just a pity that the woman he chose had one son ready to finish his medical apprenticeship, another nearly ready and a third coming up. This would make three physicians in the family before Nuala was able to qualify.

'I wonder whether the basket maker would lend us a cart?' she said aloud.

She looked towards the solitary cottage; Dalagh the basket maker had a large family of children; it was surprising that neither they nor he, nor his wife, had arrived to see what was happening.

'There's no one there,' said Fachtnan. 'I went straight to the cottage when we found the body. I thought he might take a message, but he was gone and his cart is gone too. I shouted across the field to Fiachra O'Lochlainn – he's ploughing over there – and he told me that Dalagh set off at about midday with the cart loaded up with baskets and the children went with them.'

'I see,' said Mara. 'Well, we can't disturb Fiachra in the middle of the ploughing so you'll have to be messenger again, Fachtnan. I think Lissylisheen is the nearest place. Would you go and ask Ardal or Liam to send a cart. Just say that there's been an accident and that I sent you. Nuala, would you like to go with Fachtnan?'

'You haven't asked for the time of death.' Nuala's voice was sullen and she gave her father a challenging look.

'What's the time of death then?' Mara hadn't forgotten, but thought that it might be more sensitive to ask that of Malachy once Nuala had departed. Nuala in her present mood was bound to disagree with Malachy, and it was always a difficult point to know how long a murdered person had lain there by the time of discovery. There were so many factors to take into account such as the heat of the sun, the cooling properties of a wind, the stiffness of the body.

'Early this morning,' said Nuala promptly.

'I agree,' said Malachy in an off-hand way.

Nuala shot him a suspicious look.

'Good. Well, off you go, you two,' said Mara hurriedly. 'I'll stay here with the body. Malachy, would you be kind enough to go over to Kilcorney Church? Ask Father O'Byrne if we may bring Iarla over to lie in the church.'

In a moment, all three had gone and she was left alone with the body. A solitary raven flew back and perched overhead, but she ignored it. It would not attack while a living person was present. She bent down and examined the eye injury. She was inclined to think that Nuala was right. There was not a lot of blood; nevertheless, the eye was completely destroyed. Like the god Balor, Iarla was now one-eyed.

There would be a certain amount of superstitious awe about this death, she thought. Balor was an ancient Celtic god, notable for his one eye, who could kill anyone it looked upon. He lost his second eye as a child when watching his father's druid preparing poisonous spells, the fumes of which rose into one of his eyes, but as he grew the remaining one took on strange powers. His eye was normally kept closed; it could only be opened on the battlefield by four men using a handle fitted to his eyelid. It was prophesied that he would be killed by his own grandson so he imprisoned his only daughter in a crystal tower. However, her lover climbed in, released her and she gave birth to triplets. When Balor heard of this he ordered the triplets be thrown into the ocean. One, Lugh, was saved and he defeated Balor on the battlefield. At the moment of death, Balor's eye opened and it burned through the ground and formed a series of underground lakes and caves. This was thought to be the origin of the underground lakes and caves that lay beneath the surface of the Burren.

When Mara was a child, no one would go near Balor's Cave. The lane was deserted and the low-lying marshy acres around it were filled with nothing but old gnarled willows. As soon as Ardal O'Lochlainn became *taoiseach* he set to work to reclaim this part of his inheritance. He and his steward Liam started to clear out the cave of the boulder clay that had been deposited there and when his men saw that no harm had come to them, they joined in. The boulder clay had been deposited in ridges; cabbages, leeks and onions grown on the ridges; and the cave itself, with its constantly cool temperature, was used for storage of the vegetables. The swampy ground around had been turned into a garden for sallies, or willows, and Ardal had built a cottage and installed a basket maker there. This had all happened almost twenty years ago.

And now a foul murder had taken place at this spot.

But why did it happen?

Mara sat on the rough bark of the upturned willow and looked with pity at the body of the young man. No one deserved a sudden violent death like this, least of all a young man on the threshold of adulthood. If any sin was committed, it lay at his mother's door. He could not be blamed for trying his fortune once the opportunity presented itself. He had arrived, told his story and within three days he was dead.

But who had killed him?

And was that story the reason for the murder?

For the moment only one name presented itself and that thought was so shocking and so unlikely that she felt reluctant to grapple with it. She got to her feet and began to pace up and down, but the name could not be dislodged. Only Ardal O'Lochlainn bene-fited from this death. He had not wanted this young man, had not believed that Iarla was his son.

'No sign of the priest, but the church is open.' Malachy had approached quietly. 'I had a look,' he continued, 'and the trestle and planks are there since the burial of old Pádraig last Tuesday. We can still bring the body to the church and perhaps get someone to stay until the priest arrives.'

'There's the cart coming now.' Mara went to the head of the laneway and stood watching. One of Ardal's workers drove it; he and Liam followed on horseback.

'This is a shocking thing, Brehon.' Ardal swung his leg neatly over the horse's back and tossed the reins to Liam. His face looked concerned, not devastated, but then he had no real reason to mourn the death of this unexpected new arrival.

'What happened? Was it a fight?' He walked straight over and stood looking down. 'Poor lad,' he added, not waiting for an answer to his questions. There was a genuine-sounding note of pity in his voice.

'Shall we bring him to Kilcorney Church, Brehon?' Liam had now dismounted. 'There's no reason to bring him over to Noughaval, is there? What do you think, my lord?'

'What do you think, Brehon?' Ardal looked at her doubtfully.

Noughaval was the church where the O'Lochlainn family were buried. No, thought Mara, there was no real reason to bring this young Iarla to Noughaval. Nothing had been ratified about his birth and his birthright. That would have been done at Poulnabrone. Now there was no necessity to send Fachtnan and Enda over to Aran on a fact-finding mission, no necessity for Mara to consult her law texts and, perhaps, to be forced into giving a verdict that went against her commonsense and intuition. Things had worked out well, except for the awful reality of a brutal and unacknowledged killing and a young life cut short.

'Kilcorney seems the obvious place,' said Malachy quietly.

Liam looked at him with an approving nod. Ardal glanced from one to the other and then back at Mara, waiting for her consent.

'Yes, I agree, Kilcorney is the obvious place.' Mara looked keenly at Ardal as she said that, but his handsome face showed no strong emotion, whether of relief or regret; Ardal was his usual sensible, practical and energetic self, prepared to do anything that would help to tidy up this situation.

'Why do you say a fight?' she asked quietly.

Ardal looked startled. 'Well, I assumed that was what had happened. It looks like that. Someone has stuck a dagger into him.'

Malachy, she noticed, did not mention Nuala's assertion that the man had been killed by a blow to the head. Mara had found Nuala's argument convincing, but she said nothing; it was for her, as Brehon of the Burren, to gather the evidence and to find the truth. For the moment she would just listen and observe. After all, it was a reasonable guess that it had been a fight. Most deaths in the kingdom occurred as a result of fights between hot-headed young men from rival clans.

'There was some trouble at the wedding the other day.' Liam joined them at the side of the body. 'You remember, Brehon – the wedding at Lemeanah on Monday. This lad got very drunk. He was fighting mad. I saw him myself. The O'Brien steward told me that a couple of them had to hold him down. They doused him with a pail of water . . .' His voice tailed off and he dropped to his knees beside the body.

'Jesus, Mary and Joseph.' Liam's voice was loud and harsh. He crossed himself rapidly. 'Lord save us and bless us. Here we have a man lying outside Balor's Cave and him with only one eye. It couldn't be . . .'

'You mean Balor, don't you? Just what I was thinking myself,' said Malachy with a quick sideways glance at Mara.

'Not that I believe in these old stories or anything . . .'

'No, I wouldn't either, but . . .'

'Strange things happen though,' said Liam with relish. 'There was a fellow down at Ballymurphy – this was a long time ago. Anyway, this man dug up a thorn tree in the centre of a field, a lone thorn tree, and, you wouldn't believe this, but he was found dead in the very same field seven days later.'

'That's right,' said Malachy. 'I've heard that story. Of course you've heard the story about the man who was so drunk going home. He was seen going down this lane. People thought afterwards that he went down the cave thinking that it was his own house. Whatever happened, he never was seen again in the parish. Nothing was found of him, but two months later the pouch that he was wearing was found in the churchyard at Kilcorney.'

'Tell me about the fight.' It was time to put a stop to this, Mara thought, though even as she said the words, she was conscious that this fight had taken place on Monday and now it was Thursday.

'Some of the young lads.' Liam's voice was off-hand, but he cast a swift glance at Ardal. 'Not sure who they were,' he finished.

That's probably a lie, thought Mara. Liam knew everyone on the Burren and he was the greatest gossip in the kingdom. He would make it his business to know. And why was he looking at Ardal like that? It seemed very unlikely that Ardal would have lowered his dignity to fight with Iarla. She made a mental note to ask her scholars. The four older ones, Fachtnan, Enda, Moylan and Aidan had stayed on at the party after she had taken young Hugh and Shane home with her. Turlough had wished to ride to Thomond that night so Mara had not wanted to stay late. She had confided the four older scholars to Cumhal and had taken the two youngest and departed at the same time as Turlough.

'So when did you see Iarla last?' She addressed her question to both men, but Ardal looked enquiringly at Liam.

'I had supper with him last night,' said Liam. 'Himself –' he indicated Ardal with a nod of the head – 'was still in Galway so we didn't hold the meal for him.'

'And what time did you get back, Ardal?'

'Shortly after compline; I know I heard the bell from the abbey when I was near to Poulnabrone.'

Ardal's reply was quick and decisive. Mara had a feeling that he had been ready for this question.

'Must have been quite dark,' she commented.

'A great moon last night.' Liam had the answer before Ardal said anything.

'And neither of you saw him this morning. That was strange, surely?'

'Not really: we saw little of him in the morning, isn't that right, my lord? He didn't leave his bed too early. Of course he had nothing much to do during the day so he could afford to lie on. Eating, drinking, sleeping, that's how he's spent the last few days.' Liam's tone was dismissive and contemptuous. He was not going to mourn the dead boy, that much was obvious.

'Should the uncle be told?' asked Ardal. 'I can send a message by the ferryman. He'll be making the crossing first thing tomorrow morning.'

'That would be best,' said Mara. An enterprising man in Doolin, in the kingdom of Corcomroe, ran a ferry a couple of times a week between Aran and the mainland. This enabled the Aran Islanders to barter fish and wool for turf, fuel that their island lacked.

'We can delay the burial mass until he arrives,' she added. 'Now I think I'll let you bring the body to the church while I go and have a word with Fiachra.'

She waited while the four of them lifted the body on to the cart and then walked briskly down the road. There was no sign of life from the basket maker's cottage, but perhaps Fiachra might have some information.

Fiachra was in the centre of the field when she reached the hedge. He was holding the bridles of the two heavy horses that were pulling the plough through the fertile brown soil, leaving long shining ridges behind. She noticed how straight the ridges were, almost as if a ruler had made the glistening lines. She doubted whether Fiachra had seen much; work like this needed concentration, but she would wait until he came back to the edge of the field and then ask him.

'Lovely day, Brehon!' He was quite glad to have something to break the monotony of his task. 'Anything wrong?' he enquired.

'Why do you say that?' Mara smiled at him; he was a handsome lad with an open fresh face. Although of the same clan as Ardal, he would only be a very distant relation and yet the family stamp of the red-gold hair and the neat features was upon him too.

'Your young scholar came over to ask about Dalagh the basket maker and now *himself*, the doctor and yourself are all here,' he explained with an engaging grin.

'You don't miss much.' Mara revised her original opinion. In a quiet, out-of-the way spot like this perhaps he would notice any arrivals. His testimony could be valuable.

'The young man from the Aran Islands has been killed over there,' she said with a nod towards the caves.

'Oh!' He was obviously taken aback. 'May the Lord have mercy on his soul,' he muttered.

'Did you see him arrive?' queried Mara. 'Probably some time early this morning.'

'No, I didn't,' he answered readily. 'The first movement in this place was when Dalagh and the wife and children went off about noon and then about an hour ago your scholar arrived with the physician's daughter. I never saw that man – Iarla, is that his name, I never saw him at all today. And yet he would have had to pass me to go down that lane.'

'Would you have seen him, though, Fiachra, if you were busy ploughing?'

'I couldn't have missed him, Brehon,' explained Fiachra. 'You heard yourself how the horses neighed when you arrived. They'd have noticed if I hadn't.'

'And so you're sure that no one else passed this way today?'

'Not a living soul, Brehon.' Fiachra's voice was confident and emphatic.

Three

Do Breitheamhnus for na huile chin doní gach cingcach
(On judgement of every crime which an offender commits)

A Brehon is responsible for ensuring the offender admits responsibility for the crime in front of the people of the kingdom. The Brehon is also responsible for allocating the appropriate fine and checking that it is paid within the allotted time.

Fines are allocated according to the severity of the crime and the extent of the honour price of the victim.

'So you'll be calling a meeting at Poulnabrone on Saturday and declaring this to be *duinethaoide*, a secret and unlawful murder, Brehon,' said Enda.

'I suppose so,' said Mara with a suppressed sigh. Turlough would not be pleased. She had promised him that at noon on Saturday they would walk across to Ballinalacken and spend the weekend there together. She patted Bran's head. He was already nosing at her hand, sensing her distress.

'We'll be having Saturday morning off if we have to spend Saturday afternoon working, won't we?' Fourteen-year-old Aidan tried to insert a note of nonchalant certainty into his voice.

'I think I may need you to do some investigating for me on Saturday morning.' Part of Mara's instruction of these scholars was to share her work as Brehon with them. The boys had to learn how to manage the day-to-day legal business of the kingdom.

'I don't mind that. It's all that Latin and learning judgements and law texts that tires me out,' said Aidan fretfully. 'It's all a muddle to me. I feel like that old king who kept saying *ba gó* (it is false) to everything that the judge Caratnia told him. He probably just got fed up at the judge telling him about all of these laws. Sometimes I feel that my head is going to split open if I put anything else into it.'

Mara shot a quick concerned glance at him. There was no doubt that there was a very heavy burden of study before someone could

become a Brehon; even boys like Enda and Shane who were natur-
ally quick learners had to work hard. Aidan and Hugh, who were of
a more average intelligence, were finding the work difficult at the
moment. She would talk to Brigid about Aidan; perhaps he could
have some herbal drink or some special food. His skin was bad and
he was growing almost visibly. He was a worry to her at the moment.
Moylan, though not as clever as Enda, had a natural sharpness and
would probably do well now that he was settling down to work. And
Hugh, at barely thirteen, had more time ahead of him.

'Let's talk about the case and plan our work,' she said now, and
watched affectionately as Aidan shut his Latin grammar with a
relieved sigh.

'Who are the suspects, Brehon?' asked Enda in a businesslike way.

'And we do remember our oath to say nothing outside the law
school about any matter discussed here,' added Hugh with a smile.

Mara laughed. She enjoyed the company of her scholars.

'I'm not sure whether you heard the tale told on Monday when
Iarla turned up from the Aran Islands?' she began.

'It was all over the place,' said Moylan. 'Donogh Óg O'Lochlainn
was there when Iarla spoke to the *taoiseach*. He was fighting mad.'
Moylan gave a long, low whistle.

'Who? Donogh Óg? Why was he annoyed?' asked Hugh in a
puzzled tone.

'Well, what would you expect, birdbrain? Donogh Óg's father is
the O'Lochlainn's *tánaiste*.'

'So if the O'Lochlainn dies,' said Shane in a practical manner,
'then Donogh O'Lochlainn becomes *taoiseach* and probably Donogh
Óg would be his *tánaiste*.'

'And,' said Moylan impressively, 'the O'Lochlainns of Glenslade
would be very, very rich, then.'

'Even as it is, they benefit,' said Enda shrewdly. 'Ardal O'Lochlainn
is always giving presents to them all. Every horse that Donogh Óg
and his brothers own came from Ardal.'

'What would Iarla's honour price be, Brehon?' asked Hugh.

'Well, I suppose he would have to be counted as a blacksmith,
that's if he did finish his training. I suspect he was more of a fisherman than a blacksmith, but I suppose we would have to give him
the benefit of the doubt, or rather his family,' she amended. There
was no need to explain to her scholars that the family of the murdered
victim, once one twelfth had been deducted for the Brehon's fee,
received the fine.

'So, the honour price of a blacksmith is seven *séts* . . . and the fine for a secret and unlawful killing is eighty-four *séts* . . . that means that the whole fine is ninety-one *séts* or . . . forty-five and a half ounces of silver, or forty-six cows,' said Hugh slowly.

'Oh, well done!' Moylan had a look of exaggerated admiration on his face and Mara hastened to divert their thoughts before Hugh had worked out the true meaning of his fellow scholar's praise.

'Let's go back to the sons of Donogh O'Lochlainn,' she said hurriedly. 'So you think that they resented Iarla's claim that he was the son of the O'Lochlainn. And that caused the fight, then, did it?' And as they looked at her in surprise, she added, 'Liam, the O'Lochlainn's steward, mentioned that there was a fight between Iarla from Aran and some of the young people.'

Enda and Moylan exchanged glances and then looked for help from Fachtnan. He was usually the diplomatic one who soothed the way between Mara and the younger boys whenever there was trouble brewing.

'That fight was about something else.' Fachtnan's voice was hesitant and then when Mara raised her eyebrows, he said to Enda resolutely, 'I think we must tell. This could be important. Iarla has been murdered and everything that happened to him in the last few days is significant.'

Mara turned her eyes towards Enda. After a moment he nodded. He paused for a moment, marshalling his thoughts and then rose to his feet. He is going to make a very impressive lawyer when his time comes, thought Mara admiringly. He has brains and presence, a good voice and perfect sense of timing and of drama.

'Well, this was how it happened,' said Enda slowly and impressively. 'It was quite late, but the moon was full, the fires were warm and the drink flowed freely, so everyone, except the old people, was still dancing in the courtyard.'

'I see,' said Mara, biting back a smile.

'Iarla from Aran was drinking – to be honest, we were all drinking – but he was probably drinking more than the rest of us,' continued Enda. 'And then the drink gave him courage and he went off to have his wicked way with a girl.'

'How bright was it?' Aidan sounded much more alert now than he had done while coping with the gerundival attraction in his Latin grammar.

Enda bowed. 'I'm glad that my learned friend brought that up,' he said graciously. 'As my learned friend will remember, it was the first night of the full moon and there were fires, but between the pools of light there were black shadows.'

Mara leaned back with a smile, one hand stroking Bran's harsh coat. Enda, she thought, certainly could paint a picture with words.

'And in one of the cabins over by the stables, the girls had a little place of their own,' continued Enda. 'They had a curtain hanging over the window opening, but you could see shadows passing the curtain as they had a lantern inside and when the door opened, you could see the girl for the moment and then when the door closed she was in the shadows. So Iarla from Aran must have waited over there in the shadows near the door and when a girl came out, he put his hand over her mouth and dragged her into the stables.'

'What!' Mara sat up abruptly.

'Luckily for that girl, another girl came out after her.' Enda's voice was low and full of drama.

'Mairéad O'Lochlainn,' supplemented Moylan.

Enda looked irritated. Mairéad O'Lochlainn was the sister of Donogh Óg O'Lochlainn, a beautiful girl with a mass of red-gold curls. Enda was very attracted to her, though Mara had, she hoped successfully, persuaded him not to take love matters seriously until he passed his final examinations.

'Are you going to tell it, or am I?' he demanded fiercely of Moylan.

'*Pax, pax.*' Moylan spread his hands widely in a gesture of peace.

'Well, the girl couldn't scream because Iarla had his hand over her mouth, but Mairéad could and . . .' Another dramatic pause. 'And she let out a shriek that woke up all the horses in the stable. They began to neigh and to stamp and Mairéad kept screaming all the time while she kicked and thumped him.' Enda had an admiring grin on his face.

'I see,' said Mara. 'And then help arrived!'

'Myself and the O'Lochlainn lads,' admitted Enda.

'And me!' said Moylan proudly.

'We didn't do too much to him,' Enda informed Mara.

'Because the O'Brien steward came down and broke it up,' said Aidan smartly.

'I see,' said Mara. 'You've just left one thing out of the story, Enda. Who was the girl that Iarla dragged into the stables?'

Enda and Moylan exchanged glances. 'The O'Brien steward told us not to say,' said Moylan virtuously.

'I think we should tell the Brehon,' said Enda rapidly. 'I think that Fachtnan is right. Anything to do with Iarla from Aran is of significance. No one here −' he cast a stern eye over the junior members of the school − 'is going to say a word about it outside this room.'

Mara waited patiently. Who was the girl? Obviously it wasn't Mairéad O'Lochlainn, who had come rather well out of this episode, she thought admiringly. Was it the younger O'Lochlainn girl? No, she would have been too young and was going home with her mother at the time that Mara herself, with the two younger scholars, had been leaving.

'It was Saoirse O'Brien,' said Enda after a moment.

'What Teige's daughter, Donal's sister?'

Enda nodded.

'And did her parents know?'

Enda nodded again. 'Yes, Saoirse was in a terrible state. Her gown was torn. Mairéad grabbed a cloak from inside the front door and then took her upstairs to her mother. Mairéad told me that Saoirse's father was furious, but he didn't like to say anything to Iarla. He thought it wouldn't be polite to the O'Lochlainn, Mairéad said. She thought the O'Brien was stupid and she went and shouted at Iarla herself when she came down.'

'We heard her from inside the kitchen,' said Moylan.

'And what were you doing in the kitchen?' asked Mara.

'Liam took us into the kitchen house − he said that he wanted to have a word with us, but −' Enda grinned, his strong teeth startlingly white by contrast with his tanned skin − 'he just gave us all a wacking great cup of mead and some cinnamon bread to go with it. When he heard Mairéad, he went out and brought her in too. Gave her a little bit of mead too. He was in grand form. We all had great *craic* inside there in the kitchen.'

'And what happened to Iarla of Aran then?' asked Mara.

Moylan shrugged. 'Nothing, he just went off and got himself another girl.'

'Would anyone like to ride over to Doolin and meet the ferry?' asked Mara when afternoon school had finished. 'I'm expecting Becan from Aran and I would like to talk to him before he goes over to Lissylisheen.' No doubt, Ardal, in his efficient way, had already made arrangements, but Cumhal could send a man over with a message to forestall him.

'Me!'

'Me!'

'Us,' amended Moylan. As so often he and Aidan had spoken simultaneously.

'Take a spare horse with you for him to ride. Oh, and you could take Bran with you too. He'll enjoy running beside the horses and I am not giving him enough exercise these days.' Mara turned her attention to Hugh and Shane. 'Would you like to walk over to Kilcorney with me? I want to speak to Dalagh the basket maker. I think you two would be useful to me in cross-questioning his children. I seem to remember that they are very shy. They won't be so tongue-tied with you as with me.'

'Is there anything you would like Enda and me to do, Brehon?' asked Fachtnan politely.

'I was wondering if there were some way that I could chat to Saoirse O'Brien without making any big fuss about it. Can you think of anything, Enda?' Mara's face was bland as she saw Enda grow slightly pink under his tanned skin.

'Perhaps I could call for Mairéad and then she, Fachtnan and I could ask Saoirse to come for a ride and we could come back here to have supper at Cahermacnaghten,' suggested Enda, with the virtuous air of one who is willing to do anything to help.

'Perfect,' said Mara. The O'Briens were probably being very careful of Saoirse at the moment, but everyone on the Burren liked and trusted Fachtnan. He would be regarded as the ideal companion to escort the girl. 'Just pop into the kitchen before you go and ask Brigid if it would be all right. Tell her that Hugh, Shane and I are just walking across to Kilcorney to see Dalagh the basket maker.'

The sally garden, as it was known, was full of beauty when they arrived. The sky was very blue; the sun was fairly low in the sky, but it still formed a bright backdrop to the willow rods which were lit up by its light until they shone like jewels, some fire-red, others yellow, a few smoky-purple and some a plain green.

Dalagh was out in the swampy ground cutting last year's growth of yellow rods from the stump of an old willow. Dalagh's eldest son was doing the same with some purple rods and two other boys were vigorously attacking the green shoots. The youngest, a boy of about seven, was cutting some slender, finger-thick red twigs. Mara stopped to admire. These would be used for small, light baskets, suitable for sewing silks and cottons, whereas the heavy baskets would be used to carry a weight of turf sods or even stones.

The boys and their father worked with huge energy and the pile of rods at their feet grew by the minute. Dalagh's family was large, but it looked as if that was an asset to him; his baskets were very sought after and even the poorest kitchen had one or two for storing either vegetables or sods of turf to be put on the fire.

'God bless the work,' said Mara as Dalagh came courteously over to her. 'You have a hard-working family.'

'I have indeed,' he replied, but his eyes were wary.

'You were out yesterday selling your baskets. Did it go well for you?'

The wary expression increased. 'That's right, Brehon, we did very well with the basket selling yesterday. We were out all day and we sold every last one of them.'

'All day?' queried Mara. 'I understood from Fiachra that you left about noon.'

He grew flustered, dropped an armful of rods, and bent to pick them up before answering.

'That's right, Brehon. I just meant that we spent the morning loading the cart and trimming up the few baskets that needed it, and then we went from farm to farm selling them.'

'It was about yesterday morning, about the killing of Iarla from Aran, that I wanted to talk to you,' said Mara, noticing that Shane and Hugh had gone over to the boy nearest to them in age and were helping him to tie the rods into neat bundles.

'We didn't see a thing,' said Dalagh guardedly. 'It must have happened after we were gone.'

Mara shook her head. 'No, the man was killed fairly early in the morning.'

'We still didn't hear or see a thing.' Dalagh's voice was firm. He glanced uneasily over to where Shane and Hugh were engaging his son in talk. The glance was enough; the boy instantly turned his back on the two law-school scholars and resumed the work of slashing the rods and piling them into bundles, each bound with a flexible withy.

'But didn't you see Iarla from Aran come along the lane?' asked Mara, feeling puzzled. 'You'd know him to see, wouldn't you?' she added. 'I remember seeing you at Lemeanah on Monday night. You, your children and your wife were there, weren't you?' She recollected noting the family – no doubt they had made the colourful baskets for the display of the wedding guests. Teige O'Brien, like his cousin Turlough, was not a man to forget the humblest, so, though they were of the O'Lochlainn clan, the basket maker and his family were included in the wedding invitations.

'No, I'd know him all right, Brehon. I do remember someone pointing him out to me on Monday, but I'm sure he didn't pass this way while we were here yesterday.' Dalagh's voice was oddly reserved. 'It was a good night on Monday, wasn't it?' He spoke the words as one who wanted to change the conversation.

Mara agreed and spent a few minutes chatting about the fun at Lemeanah, but she felt quite puzzled. Surely Dalagh would have seen Iarla arrive at Balor's Cave.

'And what about your children? Did any of them play around the caves yesterday morning?'

'No, they didn't, Brehon. I don't allow any of them to go near there. The O'Lochlainn is a brave man, and that steward of his, but I would never go near Balor's Cave myself and I make sure that none of my children go either. I frightened them when they are little and that was enough to keep them away.'

Doesn't always work, thought Mara, but aloud she asked, 'And your wife, she saw or heard nothing either, did she?'

'You can ask her yourself, Brehon.' Dalagh's eyes had gone back to his work and Mara took the hint.

'I'll leave you in peace then, Dalagh,' she said in an easy-going way. 'I'll just pop into the cottage for a few minutes to have a word with your wife and then I'll be on my way.'

Dalagh's wife and her three eldest daughters were all sitting on the floor of the little cottage weaving the pliable, freshly cut willow stems into tall-sided baskets, one of the younger girls was feeding the fire with the chopped off pieces and another rocked a willow cradle where a small baby slept peacefully.

They all smiled a welcome as Mara came in, the mother speaking in hushed tones with a quick glance at the baby. Mara tiptoed across and admired the round-cheeked infant in a whisper and then took the proffered seat by the fire.

'She's well asleep,' said the little girl, abandoning the cradle after another few rocks. 'She won't wake up now.'

'Will you have something to eat, something to drink, Brehon?' The woman seemed friendlier and more open than her husband.

'No, I won't. I'll just sit and watch you for a few minutes before walking back. Do you know, I don't think I've ever watched a basket being woven before? It's one of those things that we just take for granted.' Mara smiled happily as the woman resumed her work with no show of embarrassment or resentment of the visit. She would do better talking to her than to the husband, she thought as she settled down to watch.

The first part of the basket had already been made. It was a circular bottom woven from an interlaced cross-work of rods evenly spaced like wheel spokes.

'You see we weave the other withies in and out of these rods until the base is formed.' Dalagh's wife did not slow the rapid movements of her hands as she gave this explanation.

'And then you build up the sides, the same way.' To her amusement, Mara noticed that the child feeding the fire gave her a look in which incredulity was mixed with a little scorn. No doubt, to a child brought up to this work, her comment had seemed quite stupid. She watched quietly as the extra rods were attached and bent upwards to form the sides. Fine rods were then woven between the uprights working from top to bottom.

'From time to time we close up the weave to the basket with a driving iron.' Again it was the women who spoke. The children all seemed rather wary of the Brehon, thought Mara. That was strange: normally she got on well with children.

'It's wonderful. I wish I could do something like that. I think I would enjoy producing something beautiful and being able to think my own thoughts as I do so.' Mara found it easy to praise.

'Normally we work as a team, I do the bases, my eldest daughter, Orlaith, attaches the uprights and puts in the first few rows of weaving and then the two younger ones carry on until the basket is complete. We're just all working together this morning for a change and that's good because it will show you how the basket is done from start to finish. It's quite simple, really. Anyone could do it.'

Mara picked up a basket woven from purple and yellow rods and turned it around admiringly in her hand, before saying carelessly: 'I just wanted to ask you whether you saw anything of that young man from Aran yesterday morning. Or did you see anyone else?'

A wary look came over their faces. Mother and daughters looked at each other and then resumed work.

'No, we didn't, Brehon. We didn't see a soul.'

'I see.' Mara made her voice sound easy. 'And what do you all do to pass the time while you are so busy in here?'

'Orlaith tells us stories sometimes while we work.' One of the youngest girls indicated her eldest sister.

'Does she? What kind of stories?'

'About a prince coming from across the sea, things like that.'

The child was matter-of-fact, but a tide of red colour swept across the delicate white skin of her eldest sister's face. Tears began to well up in the blue eyes. Orlaith got to her feet rapidly; her tawny plait of hair swung over her shoulder as she sought to hide the tears that had suddenly sprung into her eyes. She rushed out of the small room, knocking over a small stool as she did so. Her mother, with a quick glance of apology at Mara, followed her rapidly. Glancing through the unshuttered window, Mara saw, first daughter, and then mother pass. They were not going in the direction of the sally gardens, she noticed, but did not know whether there was any significance in that. The interesting thing was that this window gave a perfect view of the laneway. There would have been no possibility of one or two people passing down there in the morning without being seen by at least one of this hard-working family.

'Orlaith's upset about the fellow that the wicked Balor killed,' confided one of the young girls.

'She's scared he'll get her too.' The youngest gave a dramatic shiver.

'Are you scared?' Mara addressed Caitlin, who looked about fourteen. The girl didn't answer, but gave her a hesitant, sideways glance.

'I heered him howl last night.' The youngest of the girls was chatty; all seemed less shy now that their mother was out of the room.

'Really?' Mara threw a slight note of scepticism mixed with awe into her voice. It was a potent inducement for further information and the young voices tumbled over each other to supply it.

'We hear him sometimes . . .'

'When the moon is full . . .'

'And if he looks at you with his one eye, it burns through you and then you drop dead . . .'

'Orlaith is frightened that he might get her now, just like he got the lad from Aran.'

'That's not what Orlaith is crying about.' Caitlin's voice was sharp and knowing. 'It's because of—'

'Shh, she's coming back.' In a moment they all had heads down and eyes intent on work.

'Sorry, Brehon, you know what girls of that age are like. Giggles one minute and tears the next.' The mother resumed her seat with a quick glance around.

Mara got to her feet.

'I must go now and leave you to get on with your work. I'd love six of those purple willow baskets when you have them made. I'd like to use them to plant my summer lilies. Bring them over to Cahermacnaghten and I'll have some silver ready for you.'

She cast a quick smile around as the woman murmured her thanks and then went out. There was no sign of Orlaith so she walked back into the sally garden and collected her two youngest scholars.

'They think that it was the god Balor who killed Iarla from Aran,' said Shane when they were walking back up the laneway towards Kilcorney. There was a note of amused scorn in his voice.

'We tried to ask a few questions, but it didn't really work,' said Hugh.

'Never mind,' said Mara with a sigh. Her back was aching and she did not seem to be getting very far with this enquiry. It seemed very strange that neither Iarla, nor his murderer, had been seen on Thursday morning. Perhaps both Malachy and Nuala were wrong and he was killed the night before.

They saw Ardal and Liam, holding their horses, standing outside the church when they reached the top of the laneway. Mara hesitated for a moment. She wanted to get home, but hers was the responsibility. She had to make sure that all the arrangements were in place for the burial of the corpse.

As soon as he saw her, Ardal walked rapidly towards her.

'Everything is arranged, Brehon,' he said reassuringly. 'I've seen Father O'Byrne and he'll hold the funeral as soon as the boy's uncle arrives. We thought we wouldn't have a wake. Is that all right?'

'There isn't any point, I'd say,' agreed Mara. 'No one really knew him.'

'I've asked Father O'Byrne to say a mass for his soul the night before the funeral,' continued Ardal.

He had a satisfied look on his face. He was a man who loved to organize and to have everything neat and tidy, in his life as well as his property.

'We were just talking about how we could spare you trouble in this affair, Brehon.' Liam cast a quick surreptitious glance at Mara's waistline; no doubt the news of her pregnancy was all over the Burren by this stage. 'As soon as we get back, we'll gather everyone who would have been working around the house and on the fields between here and Kilcorney and if any of them have anything of interest to say or have seen anything, then we'll send them over to you at Cahermacnaghten. Is there anything else that we can do for you, Brehon?'

'Perhaps while you're here, Ardal, and you, Liam, you could just give me an idea of what you were both doing this morning. Neither of you saw Iarla, that's right, isn't it?'

'That's right, Brehon. I was in the barn for a while first thing in the morning. I was just checking on the empty barrels there – making sure that they were all sound before the Bealtaine tribute and then I went over to Ballymurphy to join *himself.*'

'I had gone over there as soon as I had my breakfast,' explained Ardal. 'I wanted to see how the young colts were getting on. Myself and a couple of the men were giving them the spring dose.'

Mara nodded. Both voices were frank and straightforward. It should be easy to check on both statements. Ballymurphy was on the west side of Lissylisheen and Balor's Cave and Kilcorney on the east side. It would have been difficult for either to go across to Balor's Cave without one of the workers noticing their absence. In addition, their presence would have been noted on the way to Kilcorney, especially as O'Lochlainn lands bordered both sides of the road. Ardal had a large amount of workers always busy around his land. It looked, at the moment, as if Ardal was clear of suspicion.

But what about his brother, Donogh O'Lochlainn? And what about Donogh Óg, the nephew and the probable eventual heir to the rich lands and possessions of the O'Lochlainn?

Four

Triad 100

There are three darknesses into which women should not go:
1. *The darkness of mist*
2. *The darkness of a wood*
3. *The darkness of night*

If a man seduces a woman who is drunk, this crime is known as sleth *(rape) and the fine will be the honour price of the victim's father or husband.*

'It wasn't Saoirse's fault.' Mairéad faced Mara with her characteristic sturdy independence. 'She had nothing to do with it. She had hardly even spoken to that Iarla from Aran – just gave him a dance out of politeness. She had forgotten all about him and then he just jumped on her when she came out of the privy. She's not to blame for that.'

'Of course not!' Mara was emphatic and slightly horrified.

After supper had finished she had inveigled the girls upstairs on the grounds of seeking advice as to which gown to wear for an investing ceremony at Thomond. Neither had shown much interest in the array of colours on the bed; both had the air of waiting for something to be said and when Mara had delicately turned the conversation to Saoirse's ordeal on Monday night, Mairéad had immediately rounded on her.

'It's just that Saoirse's mother and father are so furious.' Mairéad allowed a slight note of apology to enter her voice. 'Her father kept on and on at her all of Tuesday and Wednesday, telling her to keep away from that fellow, Iarla. She didn't have a moment's peace. She wasn't allowed out of the house, not even on to the farm. Isn't that right, Saoirse? You weren't even allowed out to groom your horse, were you?'

Saoirse nodded silently, her full-lipped mouth tightening and her heavy-lidded hazel eyes filling with tears. She looked down, shaking her dark-brown hair over her face. She was a plump girl with a large bosom, dark-haired like her father and curly headed like her mother. Normally she had a lovely pink-cheeked colouring, but now she looked pale and there were dark-blue shadows under her brown eyes.

'I don't know what got into Father,' she said in a choked voice, biting her full underlip. 'He was like a madman. He kept on and on. He thought that I had been fooling around with this Iarla. I kept telling him that I hardly spoke to him. It's just like Mairéad said. I just danced with him a bit because he was a stranger and I was sorry for him.'

'Saoirse managed to get a message to me yesterday evening,' said Mairéad. 'I came down to Lemeanah. I brought a bag with my night-gown and everything with me today and I pretended to Saoirse's mother that it had been arranged that I would stay.'

'And what did she say?' Mara smiled. She was beginning to like Mairéad; she thought her a girl of enterprise!

'Oh, she was fine; there was no problem with her.'

There wouldn't be, thought Mara. Ciara O'Brien was very easy-going. In fact, she had always thought Teige was the same, but perhaps his fatherly feelings were outraged by the attack on his daughter.

'And I had a word with Saoirse's father today after he had his dinner,' continued Mairéad. 'He was all right, then. I just chatted, but I made it plain that Saoirse and I had been together all the evening and that we had been dancing with my brother, Donogh Óg and your Enda, Brehon. He seemed to be fine then and when Enda and Fachtnan came and invited us to supper, he didn't mind a bit.'

'Was that the truth – about you and Saoirse being together all the evening?' asked Mara, suppressing a smile. 'No dancing with boys, no flirting in dark corners?'

The two girls exchanged glances. Suddenly Saoirse's eyes filled with tears. A repressed sob escaped her. She got to her feet and walked over to the bedroom window, opening the wooden shutters and peering out. Mairéad looked at her with exasperation.

Mara understood her feelings. It was no good Mairéad valiantly lying to protect her friend if Saoirse did not play her part. What was the truth about that evening, she wondered. Saoirse had a heavy, ripe sexuality about her, though she lacked the glamour of Mairéad. As far as Mara knew, there was no involvement with any young man on the Burren, though Donogh Óg would be a good match for her. However, Donogh Óg had been a familiar figure from the days of her childhood, while Iarla from Aran would perhaps have appeared as a romantic figure that night with the story of his rela-tionship to Ardal, the richest man in the kingdom. Looking from one young girl to another, Mara had little doubt that Teige's suspicions of his daughter had some grounds. There was no need to probe any more now. Most of the kingdom had been present that night at Lemeanah Castle. Sooner or later she would find out the truth.

'Well, I think I'll get the boys to escort you back now,' said Mara, getting up from the bed. 'We must get you home in good time so that he hasn't time to start being anxious about you.' She looked at Saoirse's downcast face and said gently, 'Don't worry, Saoirse, there was no justification for what Iarla did, no matter whether you had been friendly with him or not. No one could blame you. But that's the way with fathers – he was upset, so he became angry. Things will soon be back to normal again.'

When they got downstairs, Enda and Fachtnan were at the gate of the law school gazing down the road. All four ponies were tied to the rail and ready to go.

'I think Aidan and Moylan are coming now, Brehon,' said Fachtnan, politely holding Saoirse's pony while she climbed on to the mounting block. 'I can hear Aidan's voice.'

'Good,' said Mara vaguely. She, too, could hear a loud raucous laugh followed by a joyful bark. Bran would have enjoyed the run to the coast. 'Goodbye, girls. Come again soon. Get back to Lemeanah as quickly as you can, Fachtnan. Don't stop to chat with the boys.'

It was unfortunate that Saoirse should have to meet with Becan, but hopefully Fachtnan would take the hint and quickly pass on. Mara began to walk down the road after them, narrowing her eyes against the setting sun.

But there were only two ponies coming towards her. She stopped and waited. Yes, it was just Aidan and Moylan on their own.

'Becan didn't come with you?' Her voice held a note of query and she waited while they sprang off their ponies with quick lithe movements. She patted Bran who was ecstatic to see her again and looked enquiringly at the two boys. They both looked excited.

'No, Brehon . . .'

'Brehon, we have something very interesting to tell you,' Aidan interrupted his friend.

'You'll never guess.' Moylan's voice was dramatic.

'Tell me about Becan first,' said Mara. 'Is he coming for the funeral?'

'No, he's not,' said Moylan. 'He told us that he would look after himself and that he had enough of the people of the Burren. The ferryman said that he told him that the lad was no blood kin of his.'

'No blood kin,' repeated Mara.

'But that's not the interesting bit.'

'Let me tell it, I'm the eldest.'

'No, I'm going to tell it. I was the one that the ferryman told. You were chatting to that girl at the time.'

Mara gazed at them in exasperation. 'Stop being silly, the two of you! You are both training to be lawyers and perhaps Brehons. You should know by now that the important thing is to establish the truth. Tell me what the ferryman said and try to behave like fifteen-year-olds, not five-year-olds.'

Moylan and Aidan glanced at each, their colour rising.

In a tight voice, Moylan said, 'Go on, then. You tell it.'

'Thank you, Moylan.' Mara felt a little sorry for her impatience. This pregnancy was making her more tired than she would have expected. It was only just after vespers' time; there were a good two hours of daylight still left. Nevertheless, she felt a great longing to go to bed and sleep for twelve hours. She didn't remember this feeling of exhaustion when she was expecting Sorcha. Then she smiled. She had been fifteen then; now she was thirty-six. There was a difference, she told herself with resignation.

'Well, it was like this,' said Aidan. 'When the ferryman had finished giving the message from Becan, he turned away. He was fiddling with the sail on his boat and I went over and I was asking him how the sails worked when there was a headwind and we got talking and he invited me to come over one Saturday and he would teach me to sail.'

Mara nodded and forced a look of encouragement. Aidan would tell the story in his own way.

'And then when he was showing me the mast, he just sort of muttered to me, "Does the Brehon know that, before the two of them left Aran, Becan arranged a marriage between Iarla and his daughter, Emer?" He told me that everyone in the island was talking about it – what with them being cousins and everything. But be that as it may, the match had been made up before witnesses and Iarla had not said no to Emer at the time.'

'What?' Mara exclaimed.

Aidan and Moylan both nodded. The suppressed excitement bubbled up in them.

'That's right, Brehon,' Moylan said, continuing the story. 'And you remember how there was a fight on Monday night when Iarla attacked Saoirse? Well, later on, when we were all going home, as we passed the Lissylisheen road, I heard Becan and Iarla. And Becan was saying something to Iarla, he was sort of hissing it and then Iarla shouted out: "Oh, shut up and leave me alone. I'll choose my own girl." And then he dug his heels into the pony and galloped on ahead of Becan.'

'And we just thought that he was talking about what happened that night,' supplemented Aidan.

'But you see it might have been that Becan was saying to him: "*Fan bomaite*, what about my Emer?" The ferryman said that it just happened on the day before they came across.'

'And,' said Aidan slowly, deliberately and with great drama, 'while we were riding back from Doolin this evening, Moylan and I were saying, "How about Becan for a suspect? They could have had a row, the two of them, and Becan could have killed Iarla with his dagger and then put his body outside Balor's Cave to make it look like it was the god Balor that killed him.

'And then Becan cleared off and went back to Aran. He had his own boat, waiting there at Doolin, so he could go back whenever he liked. Perhaps he expected that Balor would be blamed for the death.'

'Would he know that it was Balor's Cave, though?' asked Mara with interest. 'I know that he would probably have heard the story of Balor, but would he know where Balor's Cave was on the Burren? I think they came in after the storyteller had finished the tale of Balor.'

'That storyteller told the same story about three times that night,' said Moylan triumphantly. 'People kept asking him to tell it again. And Becan could have found out exactly where the cave was just by asking anyone. Even a child could have told him that.'

'I see.' Mara was silent for a moment. 'The only problem is that no one saw either Iarla or anyone else go along the laneway to Balor's Cave. Fiachra O'Lochlainn was ploughing from sunrise in the field opposite the turn-off for the lane and Dalagh the basket maker was there all the morning and so was his wife and his ten children.'

'Perhaps Becan murdered him somewhere else and then threw the body across a horse and took it over to Balor's Cave,' suggested Moylan.

'No, that wouldn't work,' said Aiden. 'Anyone working in the fields would have noticed him leading a horse with a dead body on top of it. I know how it was done.' Aidan's voice rose and then cracked badly with the force of his enthusiasm. 'He could have put the body on one of those turf barrows, you know how low they are, then he could have thrown some old sacks over the body and people meeting him would have thought he was just wheeling along a pile of winter cabbages, He could have bent double over the barrow, bent down lower than the walls, so that he wouldn't have been seen from the fields.'

Mara thought about the idea with as much gravity as she could command. She was always careful to encourage her scholars to think for themselves; throwing too much cold water on their ideas would just make them reluctant to venture an opinion. However, she could not quite see why Becan should go to so much trouble to hide overnight, kill Iarla in the morning and then creep along the roads in that furtive way just so as to place the body by Balor's Cave.

'Thank you, boys,' she said eventually. 'That's an idea worth thinking about and you have brought me some very useful information. You have done very well and have helped me considerably. Now take Bran into the stables and Seán will feed him while you are rubbing down your ponies. Then go in and have your supper. Brigid will have kept something for you.'

After they had gone she stood for a few minutes wearily watching the sun sink down behind the hill. She wished for a moment that she were at Ballinalacken, the castle on the top of the hill near the sea. She could sit on the window seat and watch the sunset colours streak across the sea and perhaps forget about this puzzling murder and wipe her mind clear of the task that had to be done. She shook herself resolutely and turned to go into the schoolhouse. This was her choice to keep working, her choice to do everything: to be a teacher, a Brehon, the king's wife and the bearer of the king's child.

She wanted to have it all; that was her problem.

'Brehon.' Brigid emerged from the kitchen house.

'Ah, Brigid.' Mara forced a smile and straightened her back. 'I told Aidan and Moylan that you would have kept them some supper.'

'Don't worry about them. That will be the day when they starve!' Brigid narrowed her small green eyes against the sun and fixed them on Mara's face. Her sandy-coloured hair was sticking up in spikes – always a sure sign that she was perturbed. 'Don't worry about them,' she repeated. 'What about you? You look very tired. Why don't you go and have an early night? Cumhal and I will see to the lads.'

'I can't,' said Mara. 'I really should go over to Lissylisheen. I was just wishing that I could ride, but I don't suppose that it's a good idea at the moment.'

'What's there that can't wait for the morning?' asked Brigid sharply. 'You should go over to your house now and just get straight into bed.'

'You could be right,' said Mara resignedly.

Brigid had looked after her when she was little and had not got out of the habit of treating her mistress as if she were about five years old. It was usually easier to follow Brigid's commands than to argue with her.

'Though I suppose you'll toss and turn all night unless you get your own way.' It was Brigid's turn to sound resigned. 'I'll tell you what I'll do,' she continued. 'I'll send young Donie over to Lissylisheen to ask the *taoiseach* to come and see you. Will that satisfy you?'

'There's someone coming now.' Mara's quick ear caught the drumming of hoofs on the stone of the roadway outside.

'Well, well, it's himself,' murmured Brigid with satisfaction. She walked quickly to the gate.

'You're very welcome, my lord,' she said as Ardal dismounted with a neat swing of one leg. 'I was just saying to the Brehon that she was looking tired and that she should leave her ·visit to you until the morning.' Her voice had a warning note of emphasis.

'I won't keep her long.'

Ardal had a smile on his attractive face; it was easy to read Brigid.

'I wondered whether Becan had arrived from Aran,' he continued, looking around the courtyard.

'He didn't come. He refused.' Mara told him the fisherman's words – she didn't mention the betrothal between Becan's daughter and Iarla, though. This was something that she would keep to herself, she decided.

'Strange!' Ardal shook his head in disbelief. 'I never heard of such a thing. To allow your own nephew to be buried without a friend or kin to be there to pray for his soul. And yet he seemed fond of the young man to come all the way here with him. Mind you, we didn't see much of him. Liam told me that Becan went off on Tuesday morning to visit relations of his at Kinvarra and he didn't come back until late on Wednesday.'

'Borrowed your horse too, didn't he?' Brigid's tone was sharp. 'Cumhal told me that he met him on one of the Lissylisheen horses.'

'Let's come into the schoolhouse, Ardal,' said Mara. 'Will you have a cup of ale or wine?'

'Nothing at all,' he said firmly. 'I really won't keep you long, Brehon. You've had a tiring day.' Adroitly he had moved ahead of her, opened the heavy door and ushered her into the schoolhouse, placing her chair by the fire and putting a cushion from the window seat at her back. Then he stood by the fireplace, a look of indecision on his handsome face.

'I don't like this, Brehon,' he said after a moment. 'In a way, though I don't honestly think that boy was my son, I still feel a certain responsibility for him. He came here in good faith, on the word of his mother, and he was murdered. I don't like the thought of burying the poor fellow without friend or family near to put the clay over him. I think I'd like to take him back to Aran and bury him beside his mother; that's where he belongs and that's where he should go. Would that meet with your approval, Brehon?'

'I can understand your feeling, Ardal.'

Mara was conscious of a warm feeling. There were times when Ardal annoyed her; he could be tiresome and stubborn, but there were other times, like now, when she had to admire the essential nobility of the man. The wind was strong and it would be no light thing to embark on a journey in this weather on the turbulent seas between the mainland and Aran, but he would undertake that without a thought if he felt it to be the right thing to do. 'However,' she continued, 'I really don't think that would be necessary. After all, if his sisters had any feeling for him they would have crossed over for the funeral. You don't know what they are feeling. Perhaps they regard him as no relation of theirs. Also, we don't really know whether Becan will come after all. He might have got a passage in one of the fishing boats. That would have been cheaper for him. I don't suppose that he has any silver to spare.'

'Anyway, let's go back to the problem of the murder.' Ardal, as always, was efficient and precise. 'We thought it might help, myself and Liam, to get statements from everyone while they all had supper in the barn.' As he spoke, he carried a table over and placed it close to her chair.

'Yes, of course. That was a good idea,' said Mara.

Ardal had the custom, carried on from the days of his father, of supplying a substantial supper for all of his workers at the end of each day. It probably worked out well for him, she thought. It united the men, gave each a feeling of ownership in the O'Lochlainn land and it meant that farming matters could be discussed and work allocated for the morrow in an efficient way.

'So we took the opportunity, while they were all there, to write down where every man was and whom he saw during yesterday morning.' Ardal unrolled the scroll of vellum, columns carefully ruled and all the relevant information written in Liam's small neat hand. He flattened it on the table, placing the inkhorn and a heavy iron ruler on top of two corners and quickly fetching a couple of law tomes for the others. Mara bent over it.

'Of course,' said Ardal delicately, 'you may wish to question these men in private, but we thought this might save you a certain amount of time.'

'This is wonderfully helpful, Ardal.' Mara rapidly scanned the list. She was very sincere in her thanks, but a slight doubt did come into her mind about the value of the testimony of those who asserted that their master and *taoiseach*, the O'Lochlainn, was occupied on the Ballymahony lands, to the west of Lissylisheen, between daybreak and noon. Still, it would be hard for all three men who were with him to have testified to a lie and there would have been little chance that they would not have noticed his absence. His horses and foals were of huge importance to Ardal and the men would have been consulting him every few minutes.

'But nobody saw Iarla after he left the kitchen house, soon after daybreak,' she said in an exasperated tone. 'You're sure that everyone was telling the truth, Ardal? It wasn't that they were holding something back, unsure as to how it might affect someone else.'

This was the problem of not investigating herself, she thought. Over the years she had developed the skill to hear the hesitation behind a statement, to notice how a voice might falter, or how a pair of eyes could glance away from her gaze. Ardal could give her the facts, but not the impressions. Still, it was valuable evidence that he was bringing to her in this neatly collated form.

'I was thinking about that,' said Ardal, taking out another piece of vellum and leaning over her. 'Look, I got Liam to make a little sketch here of the townlands around Lissylisheen and, of course, Lissylisheen itself. You can see that we've put in names of those who were there on Thursday morning.'

'So Fiachra was ploughing on this side of the road to get the land ready for oats.' Mara pointed. The townland of Lissylisheen lay on the north as well as the south side of the road to Kilcorney.

'That's right, and his father was ploughing on the south side of the road.' Ardal indicated the sweep of the townland border, obviously established before the road to Kilcorney was built. 'They were having a bit of a competition to see who would make the best job of it.'

Ardal's voice was amused, easy-going, the voice of a man who has nothing to fear and for whom life is good. 'And here, at Craigaroon,' he continued, pointing to the townland south of Lissylisheen, 'I had five men on this large field forking dung from the carts and spreading it over the land here. These are my best grasslands so we always get the winter dung out on them as soon as we get a good wind and some dry weather in March.'

'And, of course, if Iarla was going towards Balor's Cave, he would either have had to go by the road or else cross the field at Craigaroon.' Mara looked at the little sketch with puzzlement.

'Not a chance of him not being seen,' said Ardal emphatically. 'The men were spread right across the field in a line so as to make sure to cover everything. And then there were the carts coming and going and with the dry weather a couple of men were clearing the ditches on the road between . . .'

'And there were four men working in the courtyard with Liam.'

'That's right. At this time of year we always get out the storage barrels from the barn and the cellars; we check and clean and repair them all. Then they are ready for the tribute at Bealtaine and at Michaelmas.'

'And what about the townland of Ballymurphy? There's no name here.'

Ardal smiled. 'Well, that's exactly what Liam said. This is the only possibility: Iarla came out of the kitchen house, at a moment when Liam and the other men were in the barn. Iarla could have gone over the wall of the courtyard, through Ballymurphy and down south towards Noughaval.'

'But why on earth should he go towards Noughaval? Anyway, it's the wrong direction for Kilcorney and Balor's Cave.' A sudden thought struck Mara. 'Ardal, on Monday night, how did you take Iarla and Becan back from Lemeanah Castle?'

Ardal looked at her with a puzzled expression. 'How? Well, Teige lent us a couple of horses.'

'I don't mean that. I meant what route did you take?'

'Oh, I see. Well, we just went through the fields. Just went direct.'

'Through Noughaval?'

'That's right.'

Ardal looked puzzled, but Mara said no more. An idea had just come to her. Tomorrow, once morning school was over, she would use the Saturday half-day to pay a round of visits. She would take her mare, Brig, she decided. She would not gallop, or even trot; just a slow walk sitting side-saddle on the horse's back could not do her any harm, despite all the old wives' tales.

She had to see Malachy and Nuala at some stage and ask them if they were certain about the time of death. But first of all she would go to Glenslade, the home of Ardal's brother, and heir, Donogh O'Lochlainn. She would see Donogh, and also his son, Donogh Óg, and his daughter Mairéad. And then she would go to Lemeanah Castle. If Iarla had memorized the route on that Monday night and did leave Lissylisheen through the Ballymurphy townland and then down to Noughaval, the most likely possibility was that he was going to visit Lemeanah.

And if the man from Aran had arrived there on Thursday morning, what sort of reception did he get from the outraged father?

Five

Crich Gablach
(Ranks in Society)

Bláthmac, the poet, compares the relationship between a taoiseach (chief-tain) and his clan to that between God and the Jewish people. A taoiseach must care for all members of his clan, especially if old, sick or handicapped, and he must be just in all dealings with them and protect them against any threats.

'I'm just going to use the mare to walk the road between here and Glenslade. I won't even trot, I promise!' said Mara apologet-ically.

She had sent Moylan to tell Seán to saddle Brig, but Brigid, of course, always knew everything that was going on. Now she was gazing at Mara, her thin lips compressed and her green eyes sparkling with annoyance.

'What do you have to go to Glenslade for, when you will have to go to Poulnabrone to make the announcement at vespers?' Brigid's voice was sharp with anger. 'If you want to see anyone there, just send for them. That's what your father would have done. He didn't do all this journeying around. He sat in the schoolhouse and saw people there.'

'Well, I just want to see Donogh O'Lochlainn and, well . . . well, I thought it was better for *me* to go to see him, than . . .'

Brigid nodded resignedly. She had noted the emphasis on the word 'me'. What Mara had not said – and you know how touchy he is – would not be mentioned by Brigid, but they were both aware of the truth.

'The *taoiseach* could have brought the man over for you,' she muttered, 'but I suppose you don't want to cause any more trouble between the two of them. I remember when they were young, there used to be great trouble. Donogh was always fierce jealous of his brother.'

'Brigid, what were they like when they were quite young, the two of them?' asked Mara curiously. 'I didn't know Donogh too well. Ardal was nearer to my age so I knew him better. Donogh had gone off and was farming over in Glenslade by the time that I was growing up.'

'Not too different to the way they are now,' said Brigid thoughtfully. 'Ardal was a beautiful child, big and strong, could talk to anybody. In fact, even though he was four years younger, he could talk before Donogh – used to talk for him, I remember. And when Donogh did talk, nobody much had time to listen to him. He wasn't good-looking, even as a child. There was talk for a while of sending Ardal to the bard school, but I think that Finn always wanted him for his heir.'

There was a silence as Mara turned over the picture of the two brothers in her mind. It was something that most people had forgotten by now – that at the death of the *tánaiste* (heir) to the O'Lochlainn clan, twenty-five years ago, when Ardal was fifteen and Donogh was nineteen, the clan had decided that the younger brother was more fit to be the new *tánaiste* than the elder. Brigid was probably right, suspected Mara; no doubt Finn, himself, had preferred the tall, handsome, fluent and clever Ardal to the unfortunate Donogh and had quietly made his preference known to his clan. There would have been no doubt in anyone's mind that, of the two brothers, Ardal would make the better *tánaiste* and subsequently *taoiseach*. Glenslade, with its extensive lands and tower house, was given to Donogh and with that he had to be content.

Glenslade tower house was built on a square craggy platform of rock overlooking the deeply sunken glen of Slaoide. This was a depression of about two hundred yards wide and two hundred yards long. The stone of the sides of this pit was squared-off, almost as if it were cut stone and the whole hollow resembled a roofless giant's castle whose proportions made the real four-storey-high tower house appear like a child's toy.

As Mara rode at a slow walking pace across the familiar road between the law school and Poulnabrone, she pondered on the man she was about to meet. This would be a difficult interview – not because she really suspected Donogh of having a hand in the murder of the young man who had turned up claiming to be the son of his brother Ardal, but because every interview with Donogh was difficult; a long, drawn-out agony of stuttered words and unfinished sentences.

He was standing at the back of the tower house, gazing down the sheer drop of the glen, when she arrived. An ugly man, she

thought compassionately as he turned at the measured sound of her
mare's feet on the stone road. He had the red hair of the O'Lochlainns,
but where his brother Ardal had a head of crisp, copper curls, Donogh's
hair was faded and hung sparsely around a bare crown. Ardal was
tall and well made. Donogh was small and barrel-shaped with very
long arms and rather short legs.

'B-b-b-rehon,' he said, but said no more when they met together
at the gate into Glenslade.

How we do rely on words to smooth our daily intercourse with
our fellow human beings, thought Mara, hearing her own voice
chattering on, commenting on the weather, expressing hope for the
good health of Donogh's wife, Sadhbh, and of his son, Donogh Óg,
and of the four younger children. Donogh, in comparison with his
brother Ardal, always seemed to be abrupt and ungracious. But if
the fluent, mellifluous speech of Ardal had been granted to Donogh,
who knows what difference this might have made.

'I just want to talk to you, Donogh, and to Donogh Óg, about
this young man from Aran who was murdered. Shall we go inside?'

He opened the door silently and ushered her into a small chamber
just inside the entrance. Mara was surprised. This room would
normally be just used to receive goods from a messenger or to talk
to an unimportant guest. She would have expected Donogh to take
her upstairs to the hall and to offer refreshment. However, this suited
her better. She still had to visit Lemeanah and then go on to
Poulnabrone so the shorter her visit to Glenslade the better. She
seated herself on a hard stool near to the window and turned to
him.

'You were there at Lemeanah for the wedding feast,' she asserted.
No point in any unnecessary questions. He was there; she had seen
him herself. She hardly waited for his nod before she went on. 'Were
you told of the young man's, of Iarla's, claim to be the son of your
brother Ardal?'

He nodded again.

'Who told you about it?' This time she would have to have an
answer from him.

'N-n-not Ardal.' There was a world of resentment in his voice,
but this did not surprise her.

'Liam?' She raised her eyebrows enquiringly, but he shook his
head.

'Who then?' The question was blunt, but she had many more to
ask and could not afford to waste too much time.

He thought about this for what seemed like a long time, almost as if he had actually forgotten who had brought the information to him.

'P-p-porter,' he said eventually.

'I see.' No wonder that he looked angry. Ardal should really have made time to see Donogh himself, but no doubt he was so bowled over by the news that he had not afforded his brother the careful courtesy which marked his normal behaviour.

'Have you heard that Iarla was found dead outside Balor's Cave on Thursday?'

He hesitated for a long time, but that need not have significance. She had noticed on a previous occasion how he often sought for a word that he could pronounce without embarrassment. Eventually, however, he just nodded.

'So what I am doing now is going around and asking everyone if they saw Iarla on that morning from sunrise onwards.' Mara's tone was brisk and businesslike, and when Donogh didn't reply, she continued quickly. 'Did you see him?'

'H-how do you know that he was killed in the morning? Could have b-been the n-night b-before.'

That was a long sentence from Donogh and Mara tried to show that she was giving it her full consideration.

'Malachy did examine that body,' she explained carefully. 'From the degree of stiffening he is sure that the young man was killed that morning.'

'Malachy is a fool.'

The short sentence was rude and ungracious, but Mara persisted.

'Why do you think that Iarla might have been killed the night before? Did you see or hear anything?'

He looked at her shrewdly. He had all his wits about him, thought Mara. He was reputed to be, like his brother Ardal, an excellent farmer. It was a shame that something could not have been done about that terrible stammer while he was still a child. It seemed unfair that this had deprived him of the chance to be *taoiseach* and allowed his younger brother to supersede him.

'I heard him, I heard Iarla, near B . . . near the cave last night. Talking to Ardal.'

'Really? Ardal didn't mention that. I must ask him about it.'

Was he suggesting that Ardal murdered his putative son? She eyed him with sympathy. She could just imagine his life as a child. How galling to be always put in the second place by this gifted younger brother of his. What an insult that Ardal had been elected by the clan as the *tánaiste*, subsequently *taoiseach*, when he, Donogh, was the eldest son.

'So, where were you yesterday morning, Donogh?' Mara purposely made her voice light, yet decisive.

'H-here.' Now his voice was sullen.

'What were you doing?'

'Checking the stock on B–B–Baur South.'

'Was there anyone with you?'

He shook his head wordlessly. Of course, checking stock was a one-man duty, just a leisurely saunter through fields and lanes counting cows. There would have been no one with him. Mara's interest sharpened. Baur South was quite near to the caves at Kilcorney. She was beginning to wonder about Donogh. Perhaps her scholars were right. This unexpected late arrival with a claim on Ardal's fortune might be of consequences to the family at Glenslade.

And then Donogh Óg came in.

He wasn't as handsome as Ardal, but he had the same form, the same crisply curling copper hair, not quite the breadth of shoulder, the height of forehead, nor the charm of Ardal's smile, but nevertheless very much more handsome than his father. Donogh, Mara noticed, was smiling at his son with an air of worship. In her experience parents of adolescent sons often found them quite a trial, but obviously this father adored his fine-looking son.

Donogh Óg greeted Mara with a ready smile; he and his brothers were companions of the older boys at the law school and spent nearly every weekend either at Glenslade or at Cahermacnaghten.

'Eoin MacNamara was telling me that there were some wolves heard in that pine forest between you and *Sliabh* Elva, Brehon,' he said after the opening salutations. 'He's getting a hunting party up for tomorrow afternoon. Do you think that Fachtnan and the others would like to come with us?'

'You can ask them yourself at Poulnabrone this afternoon. That is if you are coming . . .' Mara allowed her sentence to end on an interrogative note.

Donogh looked quickly at his son, but Donogh Óg seemed unperturbed.

'I'll leave that to my father,' he said with an attractive grin. 'I find these things drag a bit. I'll be busy anyway at the quarry. You will ask them, though, won't you, Brehon?'

'I'll have more important things on my mind than hunting this afternoon.' Mara tried to make her voice sound severe, but could not help smiling at his shocked face. Then she relented; after all to an eighteen-year-old boy hunting was important. 'But I will try to remember. Anyway, Donogh, while you're here, you can perhaps help me. I'm trying to trace the movements of Iarla, the man from Aran, on Thursday morning. No one seems to have seen him after he had his breakfast at Lissylisheen.'

Donogh's smiling boyish face hardened a little. It was hard to say exactly how the change came – perhaps a slight tautening of the muscles in the cheeks, a veil over the sparkle in the blue eyes – whatever it was, Mara strongly sensed a quivering alertness from the boy.

'No,' he said in a voice that strove to sound normal. 'No, why should I?'

'I thought perhaps that you might have gone over to ask him to go hunting with you or something. It would be normal behaviour towards someone who was new in the kingdom, someone near to your age . . .' Mara watched him carefully before adding lightly, 'Someone who was perhaps a first cousin to you.'

'T-t-t . . .' Donogh had become even more tongue-tied than usual, but his son, Donogh Óg, interrupted him quickly, a ready smile now back on his face.

'I might have done, Brehon, if there was a hunt in prospect, but on Thursday no one had planned anything. I spent the morning at Lemeanah. The O'Brien has got me building an extension to his gatehouse and the day before, that wet Wednesday afternoon, I was with Malachy as he is thinking of building on to his house and I said that I would be glad to do the work. I'm good at stone cutting. I met him in the quarry, and we spent some time together there talking about his plans.'

'I see.' Mara kept her face bland but her mind was working fast. There would be no doubt about the truth of this story – Donogh Óg would know that she could verify with Teige and also check with Malachy and she had heard before that he was a very good builder. However, the quarry between Kilcorney and Caherconnell was very near to Balor's Cave. If Donogh Óg were carrying stone from there for the building at Lemeanah, it would have been quite easy for the boy to slip over to Balor's Cave. There was a dense thicket of hazel between the two places; it would be almost impossible to see someone moving cautiously through it.

'I didn't kill him, Brehon.' There was a half-smile on his face as if he guessed her thoughts. 'I had no possible reason to kill him. Why should I? I hardly knew him.'

No reference to the fight on Monday night, mused Mara as she sedately rode her mare at a walking pace down the road from Glenslade towards Lemeanah. Still that was understandable: why should he involve himself deliberately in this matter? In fact, he had probably only involved himself because his sister, Mairéad, had championed Saoirse's cause. Boys had fights all the time and often the protagonists were the best of friends the next day.

Mara passed Poulnabrone while she was still deep in thought. She cast a hasty glance upwards, realising from the position of the sun that she would have to be back there quite soon to make the formal announcement of Iarla's death. It would have made more sense to have gone to Lemeanah first, as it was nearer to the law school than Glenslade, she thought, feeling exasperated with herself. The truth was that ever since Turlough had presented her with this wonderful Arab mare, Brig, she had become used to galloping at high speed around the Burren and seldom worried about saving her steps.

'Poor Brig,' she said, patting the pale-gold neck. 'This is as hard on you as on me. This baby is putting us all out.'

And then as she thought about the baby a feeling of warmth crept over her and her lips curled in a small secret smile and she passed the meeting place at Poulnabrone lost in a happy dream.

It was only afterwards that she remembered a dark figure standing there beside the ancient dolmen.

The bawn outside the tower house of Lemeanah was in a state of confusion when Mara arrived in the late afternoon on Saturday. She clicked her tongue with annoyance. She had chosen a bad time to come. Obviously Teige O'Brien had taken his sheep down from Mullaghmore Mountain this morning; the dry weather meant that the rich grass of the valleys would soon be available for them.

But before turning them out, each sheep was being marked with a large B, the mark of the O'Brien clan. In one corner, just where the storyteller had woven his tale of the one-eyed Balor and the caves of the Burren, there was a great cauldron of hot tar bubbling above a roaring fire. One by one the sheep were seized by a shepherd, manhandled over near to the fire, held while the mark was stamped on its fleece and then driven out of the gate. A line of temporary sheep hurdles made a path between the gate and an old enclosure about fifty yards away and a group of small boys and girls were driving the sheep along this.

Teige himself was standing with the enclosure, checking each sheep as it came in. He had a crook in his hand which he used to pull any sheep showing a trace of lameness towards him. Behind Teige, his farm manager was efficiently corralling the sheep into pens and his assistant was doctoring the lame ones. He'd probably manage better without Teige, decided Mara, dismounting carefully and handing over her mare to the harassed-looking porter. She walked circumspectly along the outside of the sheep hurdles. It was strange how careful she was these days, she thought. The consciousness of holding her baby within her had curbed her natural recklessness. Every step she took was calculated and tested.

'Brehon, how are you? You're looking well.' Teige strove to sound welcoming. 'You've come to see Ciara. If you can wait for a moment we'll manage to clear a way for you through the bawn.' There was a hopeful, but not very convinced note in his voice. Mara was not someone who paid too many social visits; her work at the law school, coupled with her function as law enforcer for the whole kingdom, meant that she had little time to spare.

'No, it's you I've come to see, Teige, but there is no rush.' Mara seated herself on a large smooth boulder. Her face was bland, but her eyes were sharp. Teige, she realized, did not want to talk to her. It wasn't just that he was busy with the sheep; normally he was, like his cousin the king, a most sociable person; in any case there was no need for him, a *taoiseach,* to be undertaking work that any seventeen-year-old could do. She watched him carefully. He seemed oddly subdued now, almost as if his heart was no longer in the work. After about five minutes, he abandoned his role and his crook to his farm manager and came out and sat beside her on the boulder.

'It's good, isn't it, how these old enclosures are still used when there are no longer houses inside them? Toin the *briuga* planted a pear orchard in one, Ardal uses another for the lambing ewes on Oughtmama Mountain, Malachy and Nuala live and grow herbs in theirs and you use this one to check your sheep. And of course, I have my law school in another.' Mara purposely kept her tone light and chatty.

Teige smiled and relaxed a little. 'When we were young boys, Turlough and I used to play here. There were the ruins of an old house just here.' He waved his hand towards the centre of the enclosure and then turned back to her with an expectant face.

'I was just wondering if you could help,' she said. 'You see, I have a bit of a problem with this death of Iarla of Aran. The last time he was seen on the day of his death was at breakfast at Lissylisheen. The next time was late afternoon at Balor's Cave in Kilcorney. You didn't see him over here at Lemeanah, did you?'

Teige shook his head wordlessly. He was watching her face carefully, she noticed, but she went ahead in her most confiding manner.

'You can see my problem. If I could account for even an hour of his time it would help me. I just wondered whether he might have come over here. After all this was the first place that he came to on the day that he arrived from Aran. It would be natural that, if he had enjoyed his evening here, he might come to pay you all a visit.'

Teige's face darkened. Like his cousin Turlough, he was no actor. However, he managed to contain himself. She could see the sentences behind his eyes – that the man would not have been welcome here, that if he had turned up he would have been instantly thrown out, that Teige had felt like killing him after the near rape of his very-loved daughter; but somehow he managed to stop the words spilling over.

'No, Brehon,' he said eventually. 'I did not see the man.'

The bell was tolling for vespers by the time that Mara rode slowly up the road towards Poulnabrone. She was dead tired and somewhat worried. If she felt like this when she was only five months pregnant, how was she going to manage during the months to come? Perhaps she should ask Turlough to engage some young *aigne* to look after the kingdom under the supervision of Fergus, the Brehon of Corcomroe. Still, normally it was a peaceful place. This had been a bad year. Making a huge effort, she squared her shoulders, took a deep breath and turned her mare in towards the ancient dolmen of Poulnabrone.

The dolmen of Poulnabrone stood at the eastern edge of the four miles of flat tableland called The High Burren. Four huge upright slabs, each of them the height of a man, supported the soaring capstone of rough lichen-spotted limestone. The field around it was paved with limestone clints, the grykes between them dotted with primroses, and the dolmen stood silhouetted against the sky, towering above the clints.

Standing beside the dolmen, in the place where Mara normally stood, there was a man. He was a dark man, swarthy of face and hair. His hands and arms were huge and he had several burn marks on his face as well as the hands. It was Becan, the blacksmith from Aran.

'Becan, how did you get here?' The words blurted out of her – not like her normal self, she thought critically, and suddenly saw herself as an exhausted and pregnant woman dismounting clumsily from her horse, clutching at the arm of Cumhal and betraying a surprise that the normal cool and collected Mara, Brehon of the Burren, would not have revealed.

He said nothing for a moment and then just shrugged. By this stage, she had herself in hand, had pulled a few potent drops of energy from her indomitable will and she turned a beaming smile on him.

'It's good to see you here,' she said with sincerity, and then turned to her scholars, all looking neat and tidy in their snowy-white *léinte,* their warm cloaks and well-polished boots.

Fachtnan stepped forward and solemnly presented her with a scroll. There was a glint of humour in his brown eyes and she bit back a responding grin. The fact was that she had been too busy and tired to write up this case yet. However, she never faced the crowd at Poulnabrone without a scroll in hand so it had been thoughtful of Fachtnan to bring one along. She sat down for a minute on the edge of the rock that lay beside the dolmen. The bell for vespers had only just ceased. She would give a few minutes so that those who were further away might have time to arrive before she started. It seemed to be mainly those of the O'Lochlainn clan who were already there. Donogh and Donogh Óg were there, the younger man chatting brightly to his uncle Ardal. Finn O'Connor, *taoiseach* of the O'Connors was there with a scattering of his clan members around him. A few of the O'Brien clan, though not their *taoiseach*. Of course, this murder of a stranger to the kingdom did not concern many, except perhaps those of the O'Lochlainn who had known the reason for the arrival of the young man from Aran. In theory each household was supposed to send a representative to these solemn gatherings, but in fact, unless it was one of the four big festivals of the year, most people were content to be represented by their *taoiseach* and a few others. However, the sparse number of people gave Mara an excuse to rest for a few minutes and she availed herself of it gratefully.

There were a few figures moving across the clints coming from Baur South on the other side of the Glenslade road and two men were riding up the road from Lemeanah. Two men looking very alike, both heavily built men – about fifty years old, with the brown hair, the low afternoon sun picking out gleams of grey from both heads. It was Teige O'Brien and his cousin King Turlough Donn.

Instantly Mara's tiredness left her. She was on her feet, smiling a welcome before the two men had dismounted from their horses. A surge of energy flooded through her as she greeted them both, and her voice, as she turned to face the people of the kingdom, was strong and reached easily to the back of the crowd.

'God and Mary be with you,' she said in the traditional greeting and back came the answer, 'God and Mary, and Patrick be with you.'

'I, Mara, Brehon of the Burren, announce to you that a killing took place of Iarla of Aran on Thursday morning.' No need to say anything about the putative relationship between the young man and Ardal O'Lochlainn, she thought. In the corner of her eye she saw several people look in his direction, but Ardal stood impassively, tall and handsome, flanked by his nephew, Donal Óg on one side, and his steward, Liam, on the other.

'I now call on the person who killed Iarla, the man from Aran, to acknowledge the crime and to pay the fine. Iarla's honour price as a fisherman is one yearly heifer which is worth a quarter of an ounce of silver. The *éraic*, or body fine, for an unlawful killing is forty-two *séts*, or twenty-one ounces of silver. As more than forty-eight hours have elapsed since the killing took place then I now declare it to be a case of *duinetháide,* a secret and unlawful killing. The *éraic* will therefore be doubled to eighty-four *séts*. Add to that the victim's honour price of half a *sét* and the fine will then amount to eighty-four and a half *séts*, forty-two and a quarter ounces of silver, or forty-two milch cows. This fine will be paid to Becan from Aran, the uncle of Iarla,' she ended firmly, looking all around the assembled crowd.

That should relieve Ardal, she thought as she waited for the murmur of conversation to die down. Ardal had plenty of money. He worked hard for the joy of achievement, rather than for the love of acquisitions. His lifestyle was plain and simple: his clothing a simple saffron *léine* topped with an undyed, grey woollen mantle, woven from his own sheep. He certainly would not want the fine and the fact that it would be paid to Becan meant that Iarla's claim to be his son had been judged to be unproven.

'I now call on the person who killed Iarla, the man from Aran, to acknowledge the crime and to pay the fine of forty-two cows,' said Mara. Then she paused and waited, looking all around the crowd. This procedure had to be gone through, but she doubted if it had ever yielded the name of the killer. In this war-like society, most murders resulted from fights and were acknowledged immediately; those few, classified as *duineth\áide,* secret and unlawful killings, took a long and meticulous investigation to solve them.

'For the second time I call on the person who killed Iarla, the man from Aran, to acknowledge the crime and to pay the fine of forty-two cows,' said Mara after she had conscientiously given the people sixty seconds to reply.

'For the third time, I call on the person who killed Iarla, the man from Aran, to acknowledge the crime and to pay the fine of forty-two cows,' said Mara, but she knew by now that no one would reply. There was a buzz of conversation and she allowed it to continue for a few minutes. Then she held up her scroll and silence fell again.

'I will now take evidence about this case,' she said.

There was no pause this time. Immediately Becan stepped forward.

'I name the murderers of Iarla of Aran,' he said in a deep husky voice.

He looked around. His voice did not carry very well and those not close by seemed to be straining to hear him. He took another step forward and this time climbed on one of the boulders next to the dolmen. Now every eye was on him. He pointed dramatically across the heads of those nearest.

'I name the murderers of Iarla of Aran.' This time his voice roared like the beating of iron against iron. 'They are Ardal O'Lochlainn, the father of the dead boy, and his steward Liam.'

Oddly enough there was no buzz of conversation after this announcement. It seemed as everyone was suddenly frozen. No eye turned towards Ardal, all were staring at Becan.

'What is your evidence for this accusation?' Mara kept her voice neutral.

'I saw the two of them, early on Thursday morning. Just after dawn. Liam the steward was pushing a turf barrow covered with sacks and the *taoiseach* walked beside him. They were going down the road from Lissylisheen towards Kilcorney. I took no notice at the time.' As he went on, he gained fluency. His voice was now well under his control and everyone looked on him.

'That's a lie.' One of the young O'Lochlainns advanced aggressively. 'I was with the *taoiseach* from the time that we all finished breakfast. Your nephew hadn't even got up then.'

'He was dead by then.' Becan's voice was beginning to lose conviction.

'No he wasn't.' Another clan member pushed himself forward, a huge fat man. 'I'm the cook and I served breakfast to Iarla of Aran, God rest his soul, a full hour after *himself* had gone off about his business. And if he were dead then, well, all I can say is that he ate a great meal.'

'What about Liam?' asked Mara mildly. She knew the answer to this, but she resolved to let Becan say what he wanted to say. It would be best for him to get all his suspicions out in the open rather than to mutter them afterwards in an inn.

While several of the O'Lochlainn clan gave evidence that they were in the company of either Ardal or of Liam, all through the morning, Mara kept an attentive face turned towards them and noted with pleasure that both Enda and Fachtnan had taken it upon themselves to start writing busily on some blank pieces of vellum. Once no one had anything else to say, she took control of the meeting quickly.

'Iarla of Aran will be buried here at Kilcorney, tomorrow morning at noon. He came to us as a stranger and he did not leave us. I, myself, will be present at his burial and I hope that as many people of the Burren as possible will attend to pray for his soul. Now go in peace with your families and your neighbours.'

'There will be no peace for anyone,' said Becan loudly and harshly. 'That poor dead lad will not rest in his grave until his murderer is discovered.' He looked around. The clan members had turned away as Mara's words finished, but then they turned back, their eyes startled.

Becan nodded with satisfaction. 'You can all be sure of one thing.' His voice now was slow and sonorous, ringing like an anvil across the stone-paved field. 'You can be sure of one thing,' he repeated. 'I know who did it. I don't know how it was done, but I will find out. I said that Iarla would not rest in his grave until the murderer is uncovered; but he's not the only one. I won't rest either until I bring his murderer to justice or kill him with my own hands.'

Six

Córus Bésccnoi
(The regulation of proper behaviour)

The audacht *(testimony) before death is the highest and noblest of all spoken utterances, as at that moment it is not known whether the speaker's soul will go to heaven or to hell.*

A person has the right to leave personal to wealth to whomsoever they please, but clan land must stay within the clan.

'I was talking to Teige today,' said Mara idly as she sat on the window seat of Ballynalacken Castle and looked out over the Atlantic. 'He was telling me that he and you used to play in the ruins of that old enclosure near to Lemeanah tower house.'

'That's right, we did.' Turlough's face bore a happy reminiscent look. Boyhood friends were very important to him; he and Teige had been fostered together and had been friends, as well as cousins, ever since.

'There's some sort of ghost story attached to it, isn't there? About a woman with red hair who used to come out of a cave at full moon riding a blind stallion – I seem to remember something like that.'

Turlough laughed uproariously. 'Teige and I used to scare his sisters with that. It wasn't a cave though; it was one of those underground rooms that you find in old enclosures but the passageway off it did lead to a cave. We tried to go along it once, but we scared ourselves. It was quite dangerous with lots of flooded bits and a rockfall while we were in it. We were happy to get out of it with our heads still on our necks, I can tell you.'

'Funny,' said Mara thoughtfully. 'Teige doesn't seem to remember that. He didn't mention it.' She thought for a moment, frowning to herself, and then looked up to find Turlough's eyes on her with a worried expression. She forced a smile and went on rapidly. 'It's a problem,' she said. 'You see no one knows where Iarla went once he had finished his breakfast and there was only one place,

Ballymurphy townland, with none of Ardal's workers in it. Iarla could have gone over the wall of the courtyard, through Ballymurphy and down south towards Noughaval and that would account for the fact that he was not seen after his breakfast.'

'But not for the fact that he was found dead at Balor's Cave at Noughaval, that was the puzzle, wasn't it?' queried Turlough shrewdly.

'That's right.' Mara nodded.

'You're not thinking that Teige had anything to do with it.'

'I have to consider everyone,' said Mara honestly.

Turlough considered this in silence for a few minutes and then shook his head vigorously. 'Not possible,' he said decisively. 'You're trying to say that Teige might be guilty of the murder of the man from Aran just because the fellow stepped over the boundaries with little Saoirse. Not a chance. That's not Teige at all. You don't know Teige as well as I do. He would just give the fellow a wallop that would knock him into the next townland and that would be that.'

'But he didn't,' said Mara quickly. 'He didn't do anything at all, not even shout at Iarla. It was left to the O'Lochlainn boys and my own boys to teach him some manners. The O'Brien steward broke it up, apparently. And then Liam took them all into the kitchen and fed them with mead, on the pretence of lecturing them.' Mara's lips curved in a smile as she thought of the episode, but she quickly sobered. She agreed with Turlough about Teige, but it puzzled her a little that he had said nothing to Iarla at the time and then had apparently lost his temper with his daughter afterwards.

And why didn't he tell the Brehon about that underground passageway?

Unless, of course, that he feared Saoirse herself had had a hand in the murder. She and Mairéad would have made a formidable couple. They were both strong, well-grown girls. They could have hit him over the head and then got hold of a turf cart or something and wheeled the body down the passageway. The addition of the mutilation of the eye could have been to make the murder fit the story of Balor, the one-eyed god, but it could also have been a final act of revenge. Iarla had spied on Saoirse, had ripped her gown, had tried to view her body; perhaps in their eyes the punishment fitted the crime.

'I suppose the fact is that there was one man who would benefit most of all by this murder,' said Turlough, breaking into her thoughts. 'And that must be Ardal. He did not show any feeling for the boy, did he?'

'No.' Mara turned over the memory of Ardal's face during the last few days. 'No,' she repeated thoughtfully. 'No, he seemed puzzled in the beginning.'

'And after the body was found?' queried Turlough.

'He seemed . . .' Mara paused for the right words. 'He suddenly seemed galvanized – full of energy, rushing around getting statements, organizing the burial tomorrow. You know Ardal – everything will be well done.'

Mara's six scholars were all waiting, looking neat and tidy when she arrived at the little church of Kilcorney. Everything was, indeed, well organized. Ardal's carpenter had quickly put together a coffin of pinewood. The wood smelled new and there were drops of resin oozing from the side of it. Nevertheless, it was perfectly adequate for burying the young man with decency. There were even a few bunches of primroses placed on it. Mara was glad that the lid had been closed; it was customary to leave it open until the last minute, but the less that was seen of that appalling injury to the eye, the quicker wild rumours would die down. No, she thought as she crossed herself and muttered a brief prayer, the god Balor was by all accounts responsible for many evil deeds during his lifetime, but she would not lay this case at his doorstep. Sooner or later she would solve this and do justice to a young man who had come to the Burren to seek his fortune and had not left it.

'Not too many people here.' Malachy was at her elbow; accompanied by Caireen, the widow of a physician from Galway, across the bay from the Burren. That woman must be staying at Caherconnell, thought Mara. There was no sign of Nuala. Obviously she could not bear to see her father and what would be her future step-mother together. Something would have to be done about Nuala, thought Mara as she agreed with Malachy and murmured a greeting to Caireen.

It was true that the funeral mass and the burial were not well attended. A sprinkling of people from all the four main clans of the Burren – not too many O'Lochlainns, noticed Mara, glancing around. No doubt, the O'Lochlainn clan had mixed feelings about attending this burial of a man who had claimed to be the *taoiseach's* son. Ardal commanded great loyalty from his clan; that personal popularity would have been one of Finn's reasons for approving of the choice of the younger son rather than the older. Donogh, though respected, was not popular.

Becan was there. He spoke to no one, and made no reply to the condolences that some made to him. After a while, no one approached him. He stood by the graveside, but made no response to the prayers, nor did he throw the first handful of clay on to the coffin. There was an awkward pause while everyone waited for him to perform this customary duty of the nearest relative. Ardal began to step forward, visibly squaring his shoulders, but Mara stopped him with a quick gesture. This would be too public a gesture of relationship. Rumours about his parentage of the young man from Aran would be stirred up again and would be slow to die down. Hopefully Ardal would marry again and have a son who would be the apple of his father's eye and Ardal would live to see him grow up and be a better choice as *taoiseach* for the important O'Lochlainn clan than would the self-obsessed, bitter Donogh.

No, she thought, she, as the king's representative in the Burren, would perform this last service for a stranger to the kingdom. Walking swiftly forward, she bent down, picked up the small handful of clay and dropped it on to the coffin.

'In the name of the Father, the Son and the Holy Ghost,' she said loudly and clearly, and, as she stepped back, thought, not for the first time, that a prayer was always an excellent method of ending a suspenseful situation.

Becan gave her a quick surly look. His face was heavy with suspicion as he turned and scanned the small crowd.

After the priest had finished his prayers and the small crowd had turned away from the grave, Malachy came over to her. 'Come back and have a cup of wine before you walk back to Cahermacnaghten,' he invited. As she began to form a polite refusal, he said quickly and quietly, 'I would really value your advice about Nuala.'

'Wait a minute, then. I'll just have a word with Cumhal about the scholars.'

'Bring them with you,' said Malachy urgently. 'We'll manage Sunday dinner for them all – Brigid and Cumhal will enjoy an afternoon of peace and Nuala will be happy to see them all.'

It sounded as if the problem with Nuala was fairly acute, thought Mara as she went to tell the scholars. They cheered happily. Malachy's housekeeper, though not as good a cook as Brigid, was notoriously free with her home-made cowslip wine and her notions of its valuable strengthening qualities for growing young men.

'You can save the dinner and it will do for their supper,' she said to Brigid. 'They'll be hungry again by the time we come home.'

Her eyes went to Becan, still standing undecidedly by the raw patch of earth where the boy that he had always known as a nephew was now buried.

'I don't like the thought of not offering hospitality to a man who has a long journey across the sea ahead of him,' she said in undertones. 'Could you bear it, Brigid? Would it be all right if I offered him a meal before he returned? You could just serve something to him in the schoolhouse.'

'He doesn't deserve it after that behaviour, shouting out like that at Poulnabrone and then not even bothering to throw a handful of clay on the coffin,' muttered Brigid.

Mara waited for a minute and was not surprised when her housekeeper tossed her head.

'Do what you like, Brehon, it's no problem to me.' Brigid always had to be allowed her grumble, but Mara knew very well that so far as Brigid was concerned her lightest wish had the force of a command. She went across and proffered the invitation, but was not disappointed when Becan shook his head.

'I won't,' he said with a brooding look. 'I've got some other business in hand before I go back. I've got something to eat here.' Then, turning his back on Mara, he seated himself on the low wall that divided the graveyard from the church entrance, took a linen-wrapped package from his pouch and began to eat some coarse oat bread.

'So had Malachy told you that we have fixed the date for the wedding?' began Caireen chattily as they strolled along together watching the six young scholars running ahead, dodging in and out of the tall uprights of the stone circle set near Caherconnell.

Mara turned to look at her with an attentive air as she shook her head in response. She only half-listened to the plans, the wedding day on Easter Sunday, the gown that the best dressmaker in Galway was making, the feast that they would hold where they would introduce Caireen's friends and relations from Galway to her new friends and relations on the Burren. There was something that she could not warm to about this woman. Perhaps it was the very tight mouth, unexpected in a face so dimpled and so full of curves. Or perhaps it was the coldness of the watery blue eyes. From a distance Caireen had a comfortable, motherly look, the ideal woman, perhaps, for Malachy, with his motherless daughter, to marry, and yet it was a strange choice, thought Mara, thinking back to Malachy's first wife, the finely drawn, very beautiful Mór with her red-gold hair, her very white skin and her wonderful gift for poetry. Malachy had worshipped her and had broken his heart when she died of a lump in the breast before her thirtieth birthday.

'Which of these two big boys is Fachtnan?' Caireen was staring with interest at the golden-haired, handsome Enda.

'The dark-haired one,' said Mara briefly.

'Oh, I see.' Caireen didn't seem to be too disappointed. 'A little bird told me that he and my little Nuala have an understanding.'

'Understanding about what?' asked Mara blandly, thinking to herself that she sounded like Aidan in one of his more obtuse moods.

Caireen gave a forced laugh, but didn't seem able to come up with a reply to this.

'Fachtnan, Fachtnan,' she called in her high, shrill voice. 'Fachtnan, come and have a little chat with me. I'll leave you to look after your other charges, Mara,' she said sweetly with a meaningful glance to where Moylan was trying to push Aidan into a muddy puddle.

For such a plump woman she could walk at quite a pace. Mara ignored Aidan and Moylan, but was soon forced by the speed of Caireen's rapid strides to drop back a little. The ground was uneven and her pregnancy made her wary of forcing her pace. She could still hear fairly well though. Caireen was cross-questioning Fachtnan about his father, the size of his father's farm, the number of brothers in the family, and his future hopes as a lawyer. She even knew about Fachtnan's uncle, the Brehon at Oriel. No doubt, she was vetting Fachtnan's suitability as a spouse for Nuala, but Mara felt infuriated. What business was it of Caireen? she asked herself with gritted teeth. She's not even married to Malachy yet.

She looked around. Enda was kicking a stone in an idle way. He had grown beyond the simple horseplay games of the sort that Moylan and Aidan indulged in. He and Fachtnan had paired off very firmly in the last year. At her glance he now came up and joined her.

'Just go and catch up with Fachtnan,' she said to him urgently. 'That woman is giving him a hard time and you know Fachtnan – he'll be too polite to tell her to mind her own business.'

Enda gave her a quick, amused smile and lengthened his stride.

'You don't mind if I join you, mistress?' His tone was of a polished man-about-town. 'The Brehon told us that you lived at Galway with your late husband, the physician. You must have met some very interesting people there.'

Malachy's house, at Caherconnell, was a handsome two-storey house set within the rounded enclosure wall of an old *cathair*. A comfortable house, but not large: certainly not large enough for two families. It was surrounded by a flourishing herb garden, full of all the plants that Malachy used for making his medicines.

Mara looked carefully around to see if Nuala was there. Although the garden was probably centuries old, when she had known it first it had been a ramshackle place where sturdy herbs battled it out with invading weeds. But Nuala had made the place her own, working long hours, weeding, pruning, ordering the beds of trim plants. Mara had expected to find her working here, but the garden was empty.

When they went in, Nuala was lolling listlessly on a window seat, drawing some old scroll through her fingers, but looking fixedly into the distance. When she saw Mara her eyes brightened and she came forward in her usual impulsive way, and then when Caireen stretched out a motherly arm, she took an abrupt step backwards. She was a pretty girl, not yet fifteen, but well grown and tall. Her colouring came from her father, dark-brown eyes, black hair and an olive skin that still bore traces of last summer's tan, but her brains came from her mother's side of the family. Nuala was immensely intelligent, and immensely knowledgeable about all medical matters. Already people of the Burren were beginning to avoid the father and seek out his daughter. There were no signs of Caireen's sons, but that was just as well; Enda, Fachtnan and the others were friendly boys and would have been sociable to them, and Nuala, in her present mood, might have found that hard to bear.

'Are your sons not here today?' asked Mara in a friendly way.

Caireen shook her head. 'You know what boys are like,' she said coyly, peeping at Malachy in a roguish way. 'They like a bit of fun. This place is quiet for them.'

'So they won't live here then when you are married.' Mara kept her voice light and innocent and saw Nuala turn her head and look at Caireen for the first time.

Caireen's voice hardened. 'Certainly they will live here. Where else would they live except with their mother? The youngest is the same age as Nuala here. Now, cheer up, child,' she addressed Nuala in a patronising way. 'I know you miss the lively company, but there are some other friends coming to amuse you, so you won't be alone for the rest of the day. My lads will be back this evening for supper. They promised they would do that.'

'Fachtnan and the others are just coming. Go out and meet them,

Nuala, will you?' suggested Mara hurriedly. She was afraid that Nuala might explode; the quicker she was out of the room, the better.

'Well, I'll go and see how the dinner is getting on.' Caireen took off her elaborate, stiff head covering and examined herself complacently in the silver mirror by the window.

'Come into the stillroom with me, Mara, and we'll leave this room for the youngsters.' Malachy sounded guilty and his bride-to-be, on her way out, sent a suspicious glance from him to Mara, but then smiled sweetly and forgivingly.

'Yes, you entertain your *cousin*, Malachy.' The strong emphasis on the word cousin made Mara tighten her lips to avert an amused grin. The fact that she was actually married to Turlough Donn O'Brien, king of three kingdoms, did not seem enough to stop Caireen being jealous that Malachy would spend time with another woman.

The stillroom was a small, dimly lit room at the back of the house. It was hung with fragrant drying herbs and the shelves, that lined the wall, were filled with flasks and jars all labelled in Malachy's untidy scrawl. Some shavings of a white root were drying in one shallow dish and there were some fat white seeds in another. An iron brazier, burning lumps of charcoal, stood in the middle of the floor and a pot bubbled with some garlic-smelling mixture.

'Sit down,' said Malachy, pulling out a chair. As she sat heavily, her stomach slightly protruding, he added hastily, 'How are you? The child doesn't cause you too much distress, does it? You should probably be resting.'

'I'm fine,' said Mara briefly. And then, being a woman who disliked beating about the bush, she said abruptly, 'What's the problem with Nuala then, Malachy?'

Malachy spread his broad, well-cared-for hands in a gesture that Mara found slightly irritatingly.

'What isn't,' he said with a sigh.

'If she were my daughter,' stated Mara with emphasis, 'I would be extremely proud of her.'

Malachy blinked. He looked quite taken aback. Mara surveyed him with satisfaction. She said no more. It was for him to make the next move.

'You see she and Caireen don't get on as well as I would have hoped. There seems to be some problem between them,' he said in the voice of one who explains everything.

Mara still said nothing. It seemed eminently reasonable to her that there was a problem between the stupid Caireen and the eminently intelligent Nuala. But that was Malachy's affair. After all, he was the one who chose Caireen.

'Caireen is being very good about it all.' His voice was slightly uncertain as he eyed Mara. 'She understands that Nuala is going through a difficult time in her life. But of course there is a limit and I think we have reached it.'

'Oh?' Mara injected a note of query into the monosyllable.

'I must say that I am losing patience with her, also. Nuala could make some effort. She's so, so . . . well, it's a terrible thing for me to say about my own daughter, but there are times when she just seems to be sneering at Caireen.'

'Really!' Mara hoped that Malachy would think that she was shocked, and not recognize the note of amusement in her voice.

Obviously he didn't as he nodded gravely and repeated, 'Yes, just because Caireen told her that if you find a plant that looks like a disease, then that plant will be the cure for the disease . . .' He stopped as if unable to find the words to express his horror at his daughter's conduct.

'But Nuala didn't believe that, did she?' Surely even Malachy, who was not too bright, didn't believe nonsense like that himself. If he did, it was just as well that she had not bothered to consult him about her baby.

Malachy nodded solemnly. 'There's no harm in having opinions,' he said pompously, 'but she should keep those opinions to herself when someone older than she expresses them, but she didn't. Not only that, but she kept sneering at Caireen all day, calling her attention to plants and shouting things like: "Look, Caireen, there's a pimpernel. Do you think it would be good for stopping bleeding since it's coloured red?" and that's another thing too.' Malachy was obviously determined to get everything off his chest. 'She calls her Caireen even though Caireen has invited her to call her *mother*.'

At that last statement, Mara ceased to feel amused and began to feel annoyed. 'I don't think that you realize how much Nuala's mother meant to her, Malachy,' she said evenly. 'I would not say that there was any possibility that Caireen could take Mór's place in Nuala's heart.'

To her surprise, Malachy nodded solemnly. 'You're right, Mara, I've come to the same conclusion, and I think there is only one thing to be done.'

'Oh, yes?' Mara eyed him with interest. Could Malachy be getting tired of that stupid Caireen and was going to use the excuse of Nuala in order to finish the relationship?

'I've been talking to the O'Lochlainn about the problem and he came up with a solution.'

Mara smiled, though she was slightly disappointed. She had hoped that Malachy had been about to say that Caireen and he had decided to part. 'Ardal usually has a solution; he has a neat and tidy mind,' she said amiably.

Did Ardal also have a solution to the arrival of the young man from Aran? she wondered briefly and then turned her attention back to Malachy and his problems.

'Yes, Ardal's been very helpful. He suggested that it was not a good idea for Caireen and Nuala to live in the same house. He offered to take on the guardianship of Nuala. She would live with him until such time as a suitable marriage could be arranged for her.'

'Have you talked to Nuala about this?' It was, thought Mara, a possible solution but not a good one. Malachy was not just Nuala's father, her only parent; he was also her master, her instructor in the profession of medicine. If Nuala were to live with Ardal at Lissylisheen, then she would no longer be involved in to the day-to-day medical problems of the people of the Burren. She would be forced out of her heritage and Caireen's boys would take her place as apprentices to Malachy.

'Not yet.' Malachy's answer was brief and it was obvious that he had more to say. 'You see, it will solve lots of problems. I'm not a well-off man. I've been a bit worried about arranging a marriage for Nuala as I would not have cows, and not much silver to endow her with.'

That was true, thought Mara. Malachy, unlike she herself, did not own a farm. Mostly the people of the Burren would pay for his services with some goods such as a chicken for the pot, milk, a piece of beef, only occasionally would silver change hands.

'So Ardal has promised to take it upon himself to arrange Nuala's marriage and to endow her from his own funds?' asked Mara. In some ways it was a suitable arrangement as Ardal was wealthy and unmarried and Nuala was the daughter of his much-loved, much-mourned sister.

'That's right – but on one condition. She must give up this idea of being a physician.'

'I don't think she will ever want to do that.' Mara's voice hardened.

'I had hoped that you might talk with her, might persuade her.'

'You've chosen the wrong person for that errand.' Mara's voice was blunt. 'Why do you think that I could persuade her of that – even if I wanted to?'

'Well, you have a lot of influence with her – she admires you.'

'She also knows that I have followed my profession, that I allowed nothing to stand in my way.'

There was silence for a moment. Mara could see Malachy turning things over in his head. Eventually he sighed.

'You don't think it will work, do you?'

'No, I don't.' Mara decided to say no more. Surely the man had enough intelligence to see that for himself. She scanned his face carefully. His dark eyes were fixed on the table before him, but his mouth wore a stubborn, tight-lipped expression. His fist opened and closed a few times, and then without warning, he crashed it down on the board.

'I can't help it,' he said explosively. 'I'm not going to give up everything now. I have a right to a little happiness in my life. Nuala has her own life ahead of her. I just can't afford to endower her now. It will have to be Ardal who takes care of that and his price is that Nuala goes to live with him, gives up the idea of being a physician and that he will be responsible for her marriage.'

Was he really that short of silver? thought Mara. He had said nothing about that last year when he was trying to arrange a betrothal between Nuala and Naoise O'Lochlainn. She eyed him closely and saw him flush under her gaze.

'It's just that Caireen feels that we will have to build on to this house,' he said hurriedly. 'It's certainly not big enough for the two of us, and all the boys. And, of course, Caireen will bring her servants with her.'

He had not mentioned his daughter, noticed Mara. It seemed as if Caireen's servants were of more importance to him than his own daughter.

'What about Nuala's inheritance?' she asked suddenly. She had forgotten about that. 'Surely she is well endowed enough of her own right. You do not need to make provision for her.'

Malachy's swarthy complexion reddened. He looked into her enquiring eyes with a show of bravado.

'Nuala is subject to me,' he blustered. 'That property at Rathborney is mine to use for her benefit. Ardal has agreed to take her into his care and in return I plan to sell that property and use the silver to extend my own property here at Caherconnell. I have to make provision, not just for Caireen and myself and for any child which we may have, but also for Caireen's sons whom she has entrusted to my care.'

'What!' Mara stared at him open-mouthed. 'You are going to rob Nuala of her property in order to endow Caireen and her sons!'

'Ardal is happy to look after her and to endow her so she won't need it.' Malachy had turned from belligerent to sullen.

'May I ask when this was discussed between you both?' Her tone was icy and Malachy squirmed uncomfortably, picking up the heavy pestle that he used to crush seeds and weighing it in his hands.

'Three or four weeks ago,' he said eventually.

'I see. Before the man from Aran turned up. Before Iarla came with his claim to be Ardal's son, and thus his heir.'

'Well, of course,' said Malachy hastily, 'if that had turned out to be true, then I would have had to think again.'

'No one knows whether the claim was true or not,' said Mara evenly. 'I may have been able to find out eventually, but Iarla was murdered before I could make my enquiries. Someone could not wait. There was someone who could not run the risk that this young man would take his place as heir to Ardal O'Lochlainn, that's the way that I read this murder.'

Malachy stared at her; his face had suddenly lost its colour and showed sallow by the thin light from his candle. He said nothing though. She waited for a moment, eyeing him sternly. There was a tense silence between them and it was only broken when the door suddenly swung open and in bounced Caireen.

'So there you are,' she scolded. 'What are the two of you up to sitting here in the dark?' There was a thread of insinuation beneath the layer of teasing and Mara stared at her with dislike.

'I'm glad you've come in, Caireen,' she said. 'Just close the door, will you, and come and sit down here?' Mara indicated a stool and waited until Caireen, looking slightly taken aback, had followed her instructions.

'I'd just like to get something straight.' Mara spoke with due solemnity. 'The house and farm at Rathborney does not belong to you, Malachy. I myself drew up the will that gave Nuala her property. The king himself was present on that occasion. This property is for her and for her alone. Malachy's only role is in helping her to manage and safeguard the farm and the house. I feel personally responsible for making sure that the property is passed on, intact, to Nuala on her sixteenth birthday, or on her marriage day, whichever comes first. You must make whatever arrangements you choose for the expansion of your own house and for the conduct of your own business.' She took her eyes away from Caireen and looked directly at Malachy. She could see from his furtive, guilty expression that, while he read the implacable resolution in her eyes, he was still trying to find some way around this dilemma, some means of using Nuala's inheritance to fund his own new lifestyle.

Mara kept her eyes on him for a long minute and then included Caireen in her glance, as she finished, in a firm and resolute voice, with the words: 'Nuala's property must not be touched.'

Seven

Maccslechta
(Son Sections)

On the death of a father, the land and property is divided among his recog-
nized sons, from all of his unions.

To ensure fairness, the rule is ranaid osar agus dogoa inser *(the youngest*
divides and the eldest chooses). As the youngest son gets the last choice he
will be careful to ensure that the shares are equal ones.

'You go on ahead, all of you. I feel like walking slowly.' Mara's
back was aching and her six scholars seemed to be even more
full of life than usual. Enda and Fachtnan were daring each other
to leap from boulder to boulder. The four other boys copied them
for a while, but then tired of the game. When Mara next noticed
them, Aidan had Shane on his back and Moylan had Hugh. The
two younger boys, mounted on their human steeds, were hitting at
each other with the dried stems of giant hogweed in mock semblance
of jousting. So far this game was fairly good-natured, but it could
soon end in bad temper and the trial of strength and agility between
the two elder boys might result in a broken leg for one of them.
All six had brightly flushed cheeks and Mara felt annoyed with
herself that she had not kept a check on how much cowslip wine
they had been fed by Malachy's housekeeper. She had been too
preoccupied with Malachy's and Nuala's affairs to keep her usual
watchful eye on her scholars.

'Just walk sensibly back to Cahermacnaghten and then you can
have the rest of the day to yourselves,' she continued. 'And if you're
hungry by the time that you get there, Brigid will have something
for you to eat.' Hopefully the extra food would mop up the excess
of wine, she thought as they set off. At least they were all on their
feet and on solid ground now.

Mara did not follow them on the most direct route to
Cahermacnaghten, which would be across the clints and grykes of
the stone-paved land of the High Burren. She turned to the left
and made her way down to Green Valley. She would go by the

Kilcorney road, she decided. It would be easier walking on that smooth, solid surface than across the uneven surface of the stone pavements.

Just as she entered Green Valley, she heard a rhythmic clinking of a hammer against stone. She hesitated for a moment. To go to the quarry would take her slightly out of her way. However, it would be a good opportunity and she was never one to allow opportunities to pass her by.

As she came nearer, her leather boots echoing on the limestone road, she heard a pause in the hammering, which then resumed and then stopped again. This time there was no further sound. The hammerer had heard her coming. Perhaps if she passed by the work would recommence but she wasn't going to do that, not after her trouble in taking the road to the east instead of the road to the west. She took another few steps and then moved on to the grass verge where she could walk without sound. Once she had done this, she heard the hammer blows start again.

The opening to the quarry was wide enough to admit carts collecting the cut and dressed stone, so as soon as she reached this he saw her.

'Brehon!' Donogh Óg came forward instantly with a broad smile on his face. 'I thought you were the priest for a moment. You put the heart across me.'

'Why should you worry about the priest, Donogh Óg?' There was no trace of guilt or self-consciousness about him and his eyes were merry and mischievous.

'Oh, Sunday and all that!'

'The better the day, the better the deed. That's what Brigid always says if she finds it necessary to do some mending on a Sunday.' Mara kept her voice light, but she continued to scrutinize the young O'Lochlainn carefully. Would Fiachra, busy with his ploughing, have noticed if Donogh Óg were working in the quarry on the morning of the murder? It may be that he worked there every day and the tapping of chisel against stone would have formed a background to the vehement bursts of birdsong from courting couples of blackbirds and thrushes. She looked around. There were plenty of stones heaped up in piles: good, solid, well-cut, box-shaped stones, carefully sorted by size and shape.

'You're a good workman,' she said with approval, noting the clean edges to the blocks.

'Thank you, Brehon.' He was completely at ease with her. There was not a trace of hesitation, no shadow of worry in those blue eyes. He was the same as he always was.

Could he have been guilty of the murder of Iarla? Somehow, she did not think so. He showed no signs of guilt and the prospect of Iarla inheriting the wealth of Lissylisheen would probably have seemed quite remote to him. After all, Ardal was not yet forty – he could live another twenty or thirty years and that was a very long time to someone of Donogh Óg's age. Iarla from Aran, or even Donogh Óg himself, could be dead before Ardal died. Many of these young men would take part in clan warfare and would not live to see out their futures.

In any case, Donogh Óg had a wildly optimistic nature. Whenever he visited the law school, larking around with Fachtnan and Enda, he was endlessly making plans for the ultimate wolf hunt. Instead of returning tired, happy, soaked in sweat, but empty-handed from their mountain stalk, the next hunt was going to yield such bounty that they would have to summon carts to bring the carcasses home and the following winter they would all be warm in cloaks of wolf fur. There was always the next hunt for Donogh Óg; he was always sanguine that this would bring the booty.

No, thought Mara, unless I am very wrong Donogh Óg is not the murderer of Iarla. She had another man in mind now though, and her gaze went back to the well-cut blocks of stone. If these were all for Malachy, then the work was well advanced on this new extension of the house at Caherconnell.

'I'm thinking of having a new building at the law school,' she said thoughtfully.

'Oh.' He looked immediately interested and then his face fell. 'I suppose you'd get Cumhal and Seán and your other lads to build it for you.'

'Well, I did think of that – then it would be just like the other buildings at the school – just stones piled on top of each other and then fitted together, big thick walls, but seeing the cut stone here made me wonder about asking you to do it. I've seen the horse cabin that you built for Ardal's best stallion. It looks very good.'

'What do you want a new building for?' he enquired. 'Will it be a new guesthouse?'

'No, no, what we have is fine – it sleeps three and that's enough. No, I was wondering about having a girl scholar next year and I would have to have a separate house for her.'

'A girl scholar!' Donogh Óg was open-mouthed with astonishment. Mara gave him a stern glance. This was the sort of attitude that made life so difficult for poor Nuala. No one expected a girl to have a craft or a profession. Nuala's own mother should have been sent to bard school and would probably have risen to the highest grade of *file*, but her father married her off to Malachy at the age of fourteen and that was the end of the dreams for the beautiful and talented Mór O'Lochlainn.

'I was once a girl scholar myself,' she reminded him.

'I know, but that was different. Your father was the Brehon.'

'Well, this girl that I am thinking of is the daughter of a Brehon. Anyway, it would be a small house, just enough for a sleeping place and study place for one or two girls. What would that cost me?'

Immediately a businesslike look came into his amused eyes. Suddenly he looked a lot more like his uncle Ardal. He paced the ground, obviously measuring. 'Round or square?' he asked over his shoulder.

'Round,' said Mara decisively. She didn't care – the new house was just something very much at the back of her mind and she had plenty to do and little time to waste, but there was a piece of information that she needed and this was the best way to get it.

'I could do it for ten ounces of silver if Cumhal and Seán would thatch it for you.'

Mara blinked. That was quite a large sum, far more than she had expected. Ten ounces of silver – ten cows, her mind translated the price automatically. If Malachy wanted to use this boy in order to extend his house to make provision for three extra people – and perhaps an extra room for servants and also stillrooms and perhaps a fancy parlour for Caireen – well, the cost of this piece of work was going to be well outside any savings that he had from the living that he made as a physician.

'And of course, I'd probably have to employ a man to help me. All labour and carriage of stone would be included in that price,' put in Donogh Óg rapidly, disconcerted by her silence.

'Well, I'll think about it and have a chat with Cumhal and see what he feels,' promised Mara. 'I know that you would do a good job. I must be getting back now, so I'll leave you to your work.'

He had resumed whistling happily before she reached the entrance and as she walked down the Kilcorney Road, the melodious dance tune, punctuated by the tapping of a chisel, followed her until she reached the graveyard.

Becan was there, still sitting on the wall. For a moment she was startled, thinking that he had not moved since she had left him several hours ago, but then her eye went to his boots and saw that they were covered with heavy, wet clay.

'You've been back to Balor's Cave, Becan,' she said after greeting him and was absurdly pleased to see a flash of surprise in his eyes. Childish and silly, she told herself severely, but somehow she felt now as if she needed to prove that, even if her body had began to slow up, her brain was as quick as ever. She smiled benignly at him.

'You've got that yellow boulder clay on your boots,' she observed. 'The *dathbuidh*, they call it on the Burren. You don't get it normally on the limestone, but it's around here in parts of this valley and especially around the cave.'

He didn't answer that and she looked at him in a kindly manner. Despite his spirited outburst at Poulnabrone he had a miserable look about him.

'All this has been a terrible shock to you, hasn't it?'

'I suppose so,' he said dully. 'I knew him from the day that he was born, of course. I saw him grow up and now he's dead and it was a sad day for him that his mother opened her mouth at this late stage. She should have done it twenty years ago, or else kept quiet for ever.' He had a heavy brooding look on his face, the look of a man who has something on his mind.

'Had she kept quiet all those years?' Mara asked the question with a certain amount of curiosity. As he said, twenty years was a long time to keep silent. She moved impatiently. If she were not pregnant, she would have waited for a fine day, taken her scholars off to Aran and found some woman who had been friendly with Iarla's mother and probed her way towards the truth.

'Were she and your wife friendly?' she asked. It would have been normal; two women married to the two blacksmith brothers.

'They were sisters, his mother and my wife were sisters,' he said, and then looked surprised at her expression. 'Did I not tell you that? I told you that he was my nephew.'

'Yes, but . . .' She decided not to argue. This was good news. 'They'd have been close then,' she asserted.

He nodded indifferently. Of course, they would have been close: two sisters marrying two brothers. Then she suddenly thought of something else. Aidan's story about Becan wanting Iarla to marry his daughter Emer came to her mind. Of course, marriage between first cousins was not unknown, though frowned upon by the church, but marriage between double first cousins would be a risk that most people would be unlikely to take.

'But you were happy for your daughter Emer to marry Iarla,' she asked bluntly.

He looked surprised at her knowledge, quite taken aback for a while and then he shrugged his shoulders. *What did it matter now?* She could almost hear him say the words.

'Emer was very in love with Iarla and determined to marry him. I saw no harm in it.' The explanation was given quickly and without any apprehension.

'So you did not believe that Iarla was your brother's son.'

He said nothing, but it had been a statement, rather than a question, so she followed it by asking: 'Did your wife believe that story about the O'Lochlainn being the father of Iarla?'

Becan looked at her angrily, but that was understandable. He had done his best for young Iarla; it would have been a splendid thing for all of the family if his future son-in-law had been accepted as the only son and heir to the wealthy Ardal, but now that prospect was in ruins.

Mara waited quietly, her eyes on his boots. Why had he gone to Balor's Cave, again? Was he intent on finding out what happened to Iarla and perhaps felt that the secret lay in the place of his death?

Eventually he answered her. 'I don't listen to women's chatter,' he said loftily.

'So your wife believed that Iarla was truly the son of your brother, the blacksmith's son. And you were not worried about Emer marrying a double first cousin.'

He turned a surprised eye on her. 'I didn't say that.' His tone was alarmed more than angry.

'No, but you implied it. That was the meaning that I took from your words. If there was no talk about it to her own sister; then it was unlikely to be true.'

'Well, you took the wrong meaning then. There was plenty of talk.'

Mara waited. Becan bore the expression of one who wanted to say more. On the other hand, he didn't want to leave her with an impression that he had no interest in the dangers to his grandchildren from a union where the parents were so closely linked by blood, but on the other, he was reluctant to open his mind fully to hers.

'My brother never believed the boy to be his,' he said after a moment.

'Really, but he accepted him.'

'Life is hard for us,' he retorted bitterly. 'The lad was a strong lad. From the start he looked as if he would be a help to him. He was well made, stout, healthy and after him came a string of girls. My brother had no choice, you could say. Just the one to choose from and if he were a cuckoo in the nest, well, he was a fine strong fellow.'

'I see,' said Mara. It was true that life was hard for the people on that barren island. Even the sparse earth in their fields of oats or of vegetables had to be built up, painstakingly, year by year, gathering any little scraps for soil from among the rocks, pounding boulders of limestone until they were reduced to fertile dust, and above all by carrying tons of dripping seaweed in baskets on their backs from the rocky shores up to the small wall-enclosed fields. Without that fertilizer there would have been no possibility of growing oats or vegetables. No doubt Iarla and been hard at work from an early age. It slightly disgusted her that a human child should be regarded as a possible beast of burden, rather like a donkey or a mule, rather than a member of the family, a son to be cherished. However, her task now was to establish the truth of Iarla's death so she carried on with her questioning.

'You must have heard the rumours though. Your wife would have told you. Don't ask me to believe, even if she were sworn to secrecy, that there wasn't an exchange of information when you were both in your sleeping place and there was none nearby to hear.'

He hesitated, looking down and then furtively peeping at her from the corner of his eye. They both sat so still that two young hares shot out of the hedge almost at their feet, bounded across the road with fast jerky, rocking movements from their over-long legs and then fled up the steeply sloping field opposite. Mara waited patiently, her eyes fixed on the pale-green, heart-shaped leaves of the lords and ladies plant at her feet. The coiled centre was still tightly closed but soon it would open and show its golden heart. Another spring would flower in the Burren and on the islands, but the young man, Iarla from Aran, would never see it. She wondered if those thoughts had been going through Becan's head when she had accosted him.

And then, just as Becan seemed about to open his lips, there was a sound of horse hoofs drumming. There was no sign of them yet – the strengthening westerly wind blew the sound to them – but it was enough to break the mood.

'I'd better be going,' said Becan, getting to his feet. 'I have things to do, people to see, places to visit.'

'Could I offer you any hospitality? You're welcome to a meal and a bed overnight in my guesthouse.'

He hesitated a little at that and then shook his head firmly.

'No, Brehon, I'd best be on my way.'

And with that, he was off, striding determinedly down the road back towards Caherconnell.

Mara almost called him back, but the horse hoofs were coming nearer. This would be no time for a delicate conversation, where silences had to be allowed to stretch to their limit and nothing could be forced, just waited for and patiently coaxed. Moreover she guessed who was coming, that loud laugh was unmistakable.

Mara was on her feet and striding vigorously along the road by the time that they met. She could not afford to show any signs of fatigue in front of Turlough. She had no intention of allowing him to dictate to her as to whether she should work or not, but it seemed easier not to have an argument about it.

'So there you are!' Turlough had spotted her as soon as they rounded the corner. He was riding ahead of his bodyguards as usual. Mara smiled as she remembered his indignation when Fergal had once hesitantly suggested that it would be best if he led the way, that Turlough should come next and Conall, the second bodyguard, should guard the rear. Like his kingly ancestors, Turlough led from the front and would never condescend to hide behind any man. He rode and the bodyguards followed, anxiously scanning the hedgerows and the fields.

'Don't tell me, you were getting hungry,' she teased, spotting her servant, Cumhal, following the bodyguards, leading her golden-skinned mare, Brig.

'We were getting worried about you, weren't we, Cumhal?' said Turlough. 'Brigid sent me,' he added defensively.

'Oh, well, in that case . . .' said Mara sweetly.

Cumhal had already dismounted and throwing his own reins to Fergal, walked the mare over towards the bank.

'Hold my hand,' said Turlough protectively. 'That's it, carefully now. Let me do it.'

'You're strong for a man of your age,' she commented as soon as she was safely on the side-saddle. As she had intended, this diverted him from anxious inquiries and while he blustered she quietly turned over the implications of her conversation with Becan in her mind. It seemed to imply, she thought, that the secret of young Iarla's parentage was certainly known to his wife, Iarla's aunt, and probably also known to Becan himself. But if it were, in fact, Ardal who was named as the father on the deathbed, why did Becan not reiterate the claim?

And if it were someone else, then why not name that person and have done with it? There could not be any reason against that at present – Iarla was dead; there was no hope now that some of the wealth of the *taoiseach* of the powerful O'Lochlainn family would be diverted into the hungry mouths of the blacksmith family on the island of Aran.

'Turlough, tell me some more about that visit to the Aran Islands – that time when you, Ardal and Teige went across twenty years ago.'

Mara and Turlough were sitting by the quietly burning turf fire in the Brehon's house. Brigid had cleared away the remains of the meal and then left them alone. There would be another fire burning upstairs in the bedroom, but for the moment Mara was content to sit there quietly, nursing the wooden cup of hot milk that Brigid insisted she drink every evening.

The night was stormy with sudden gusts of wind rattling the outside shutters of the windows and causing the fire to flicker orange and then subside back to a dull red. Somehow the gale outside made the warm cosiness of the little room seem even more enticing.

'There goes a tree,' said Turlough, rising to his feet and trying to peer out of the window. 'Did you hear that crack?'

'You'll see nothing – the night is too dark,' said Mara peacefully. She wasn't worried. Cumhal always made sure that no tree could threaten any building and a fallen tree would be quickly and easily chopped up for next winter's firewood.

'Why do you drink that stuff?' Turlough abandoned the window and came back to his seat by the fire. The chair had been a gift to the married pair from Mara's daughter, Sorcha, who knew her mother well enough to know that, while the law school was in session, Mara would spend little time at Ballinalacken Castle. Oisín, Sorcha's husband, had gone to a lot of trouble to get it made in Galway. It was a large, sturdy chair, well crafted from fine Irish oak and uphol- stered in a royal purple with carved arms and a scrolled headrest and Turlough settled back into it with a sigh of contentment.

'Fit for a king,' Sorcha had said when they brought it over and it had become 'King Turlough's chair', dusted daily with great reverence by Brigid.

Mara smiled now. 'Brigid makes me,' she said in answer to his query. 'She tells me that it's good for the baby. She doesn't like me to drink much wine either. Her reasoning is that cows and horses don't drink wine and they have fine babies, able to get up and look after themselves as soon as they are born.'

'Well, our boy will be better than any calf,' he said boastfully.

He knelt on the floor by her side and put his arms around her affectionately, laying a large, warm hand on her stomach and bending her head with his other until their lips met. She slipped off the floor and lay on the sheepskin rug by the fire, her head propped against the settle bench. He stretched out beside her, holding her tightly.

'Have you heard that the Pope doesn't want anyone to make love during Lent?' he asked teasingly.

'Not even married couples!' Mara raised a delicate eyebrow in amazement.

Turlough chuckled. 'I don't suppose that he would even like to contemplate the prospect of anyone other than a married couple making love,' he said.

'Why not during Lent? Anyway, why didn't you tell me of His Holiness's decree last night?'

'Just went right out of my mind. I was too busy.' Turlough leaned over and began kissing her again.

After a moment, she struggled out of his grip and sat up. The bodyguards were out in the kitchen and an alarm might send them in with only a perfunctory knock.

'I wonder who he will look like, our baby, I mean?' she said. 'Or she, of course! Brown haired and light-eyed like you, or black-haired and dark-eyed like me?' Reminded of her thoughts about Iarla of Aran, Mara tore herself away from this pleasant musing and came back to her question, sitting up a little straighter and smoothing her hair.

'Well, go on, tell me about that visit to the Aran Islands.'

'It was probably about this time of the year, a little later, perhaps.' Turlough mused over the past, adding, 'I was a fine figure of a man then.'

'Just like now.' Mara smiled affectionately at him, but inwardly she was impatient. Her mind was very active and would remain like that until she had solved the mystery of the brutal murder of Iarla from Aran.

'It was stormy, too, just like tonight.' Turlough got up, poured himself another cup of wine and threw a few more sods of turf on to the fire from the basket at his feet. 'I remember we were stuck at Doolin for a couple of nights – no boat could cross the sound in that weather. The alehouse keeper there kept apologising every few minutes and we kept telling him not to worry as he was bringing us more of his *uisce beatha* all the time and telling us that it was made from the best oats. Strong stuff too.' Turlough gave a long, low whistle.

'So you were fairly merry by the time that you arrived at the island. Now tell me about the blacksmith's wife. When did she arrive on the scene? Try to remember her. She had red hair and grey eyes. Ardal told me that.'

'I remember her all right,' said Turlough with a chuckle. 'They had a big party for us that first evening. It was in the alehouse because that was before the tower house on that island was built. She got pretty wild as the night went on! The blacksmith was snoring happily in the corner so she was enjoying herself. I can just see her there in front of the fire – they have a custom over there that when they lay the flagstones on the floor of an alehouse, they bury an old cracked iron cauldron under the flag near the fire and that's the place for the best dancer in the room. It makes a great echo and her feet must have been as hard as iron because I can still hear them tapping the tune out as she danced to the music of the fiddle.'

'Dancing by herself?'

'In the beginning – that's right. She was wearing that red petticoat that all the island women wear, you know they have that custom, there, of dyeing the women's *léinte* with the madder plant – they say it is so that the men, out fishing, can spot their womenfolk against the grey of the stone, but it's a lovely colour and she was a lovely girl. Her hair wasn't the colour of Ardal's, not that sort of coppery colour. Her hair was the colour of her petticoat. No, not that either, you know that garnet ring that I have? Well, her hair was that colour. And she wore a bunch of yellow primroses, just tucked behind one ear.'

'And what were you all doing? Were you dancing?'

'No, we were just standing around the walls of the room, clapping. Everyone was clapping. Clapping in time to the sound of her feet. And then, fool that I am, I finally realized what everyone was waiting for. They were waiting for me to start the dancing so I went out and took her hand and we danced a few reels and jigs. Everyone joined in then.'

'And Ardal?'

'Well, when I got winded, Ardal took my place – or was it Teige? I can't remember. I know that the girl never tired.'

'And then Ardal slipped outside with her? Out to the barn?'

'To be honest,' said Turlough with a grin, 'there was a lot of slipping outside that night. The storm had completely died down by that time and the weather had turned suddenly very hot. And there were plenty of places to go to. Not me,' he added, quickly seeing the inquisitive look on her face. 'I couldn't afford to do that. There had been enough fuss about a girl in Thomond . . . remember I was reliant on my uncle King Conor na Srona and he'd have flayed my hide open if there was any trouble between me and one of the island girls – especially a married woman like that blacksmith's wife. It was always a tricky sort of place, Aran. They resented Thomond. I don't think that they even liked being ruled over by the O'Lochlainns of Burren, but once the O'Briens came on the scene, well, that started a rebellion. It caused big problems that took quite a while to settle down. Even at this stage things were quite edgy. No one wanted any difficulties with Aran. And I certainly didn't want any problems with Conor na Srona. As well as having a big nose, he had a terrible temper. So that boy was nothing to do with me, I can assure you. To me, at that stage, hoping to be Conor's and the clan's choice of *tánaiste*, no woman would have been worth sending him into a rage with me. Not even the beautiful wife of the blacksmith.'

'I believe you,' said Mara thoughtfully. 'But somehow I can't believe that young Iarla is Ardal's son. They're just too unalike and from what you and Ardal say, Iarla doesn't resemble the mother either. Anyway, the fire is dying down, let's go up to bed now.'

Turlough took the candle from the table beside the fireplace, lit it and walked out through the doorway. Mara covered the fire with some damp sods of turf and then followed him. He had only gone three steps up the stairway when he paused suddenly, giving the candle in his hand a sudden jerk and dropping a winding sheet of hot wax down its creamy sides.

'Étain, that was her name. I've just suddenly remembered.'

'Étain the beautiful,' said Mara thoughtfully, remembering the old legends.

It was a pity, she thought, as she followed Turlough and the candle up the steep stairs to the bedroom, that Iarla of Aran had not inherited the grace, beauty and charm of his mother; no doubt, he looked like his father.

Eight

Cáin Lánamna
(The Law of Marriage)

A woman has a right to bear a child and she may divorce her husband if any failing on his part impedes that right.

Divorce may be obtained if the husband is:

1. *Impotent*
2. *Too fat for intercourse*
3. *If he spurns the marriage bed and prefers to lie with boys*
4. *If he is sterile (and his wife has been fruitful in an earlier marriage)*

In the case of sterility, if the husband wishes to retain his wife, she has the right to conceive a child with another man and then to return to her husband. The child must be reared by the husband with all rights and privileges as if it were his own.

'I'd like us to think about a woman's right to have a baby under Brehon Law,' said Mara.

It was eight o'clock, the beginning of the school day and the boys looked, as usual on a Monday morning, slightly sleepy and very disinclined for work.

They sat up very straight as her words penetrated to their drowsy brains. Aidan shot a quick glance at Mara's waistline before looking with an air of deep thought at the blazing logs of pine in the fireplace.

'I was thinking about this when I was considering the case of the blacksmith's wife and her son, Iarla.'

They gazed at her in an interested way, even Aidan abandoning the fireplace to give her a startled glance. She looked back at them blandly and added, 'Étain was her name. And I understand that she was a very beautiful girl with red hair and grey eyes back in the dim and distant days of 1489 before any of you were born.'

'Twenty years ago,' said Hugh brightly.

Moylan gave him a pitying glance, but stopped short of saying anything as he saw Mara's gaze rest upon him.

'You see,' went on Mara, 'the blacksmith's wife swore on her deathbed that Iarla was the son of Ardal O'Lochlainn, _taoiseach_ of the O'Lochlainn clan.'

'What if he swears that he isn't?' asked Aidan.

'Let's go back to the law, shall we?' said Mara. 'Fachtnan, could you hand me _Trencheng Brétha Féne._'

Fachtnan carefully carried over the huge tome of Triads of Irish Law and placed it carefully on the table in front of Mara. She placed her hand on the cover and then looked around enquiringly.

'Triad 165, I'd say,' said Enda quickly.

Mara concealed a triumphant smile. He was certainly one of the best pupils that she had taught. He was gifted with brains and a good memory, but he also had a sense of fun, and an appreciation of the drama of the law. She felt proud of him and sorry to think that she would probably lose him at the end of the year.

'Let's see,' she said, though she knew that he was right. She opened the page and read solemnly from the triad: 'The oath of a woman on her death bed is one of three oaths which cannot be counter-sworn.'

'Not fair,' muttered Aidan. 'The O'Lochlainn should have a chance to deny it. I wouldn't like all the dying women of the countryside going around saying that I was the father of their child.'

'You have a hope!' scoffed Moylan.

'Do you believe it, Brehon?' asked Enda. 'I mean that Iarla from Aran is Ardal O'Lochlainn's son.'

'I find I am puzzled about the subject,' admitted Mara. 'I have a feeling that there is some mystery about Iarla's parentage. Why was she, this Étain, so sure that the blacksmith could not be the father? After all, she was a married woman at the time. I met Becan yesterday and I talked with him and I got the impression that Étain had named, to her sister, Becan's wife, someone else, not Ardal, but not the blacksmith, either, as the father of this young man. I'm inclined to believe that whoever the father was, it was not the blacksmith.'

'Why not the blacksmith, Brehon?' asked Fachtnan with interest.

'If it were the blacksmith,' said Mara, 'then Emer and Iarla would have been double first cousins. Becan – in fact, no father – would want a daughter of his to marry a double first cousin. The risk to the children would be too great. You can ask any farmer – none would risk a mating like this for their cattle. And yet Becan had betrothed his daughter to Iarla.'

'So why was this Étain so sure that the blacksmith was not the father of her son?' Enda asked the question gravely, seemingly of himself, because, without looking at anyone else, he suddenly said, 'Of course, I've got it! Because the blacksmith was impotent. That must be it!'

'That won't work,' said Mara, ignoring the sniggers from Aidan and Moylan. 'They had other children, all girls.' Then she thought of something. 'But there may be something in what you say, Enda. I remember that Ardal told me that the blacksmith was drunk for the whole three days that they were there.'

'So if he were drinking very heavily, he might have been impotent during drinking binges.' Enda seized on her words with enthusiasm. 'I remember that Donogh Óg told me . . .' Then he stopped, thinking, no doubt, that Donogh Óg's words were not fit to be aired in the schoolhouse.

'If . . .' Mara was suddenly conscious that Shane, and perhaps Hugh, might be a little young for this discussion, but she was determined to pursue the line of thought. 'If,' she continued, 'this young wife, Étain, was being denied the right to have a baby by her husband's continual drunkenness, then she might seize upon any opportunity to become pregnant.'

'And if her husband did not . . . well, you know,' said Moylan enthusiastically.

'Have intercourse with her,' supplemented Enda, with the indifferent air of one who has these sorts of discussions all the time.

'And if he had not had intercourse for the previous or ensuing four weeks, or whatever time that her monthly flux was due,' said Mara gravely, determined that, now the subject was aired, she might as well deal with it fully, 'Étain would be certain that he was not the father of her child.'

'What if Étain had intercourse with a few men,' said Enda enthusiastically. He blushed a little and tried to hide his embarrassment under a show of judicial equanimity. 'What would happen then, Brehon? How could she determine which one of them was the father?' He smiled then. 'I know. There has to be an answer in the law!'

'Any ideas?' Mara looked around at her scholars, in particular at Fachtnan. He was a nice, amiable boy, but he would have to take his final examination this year and she was worried about his memory problems. She had noticed recently that he was rather inclined to sit back and allow Enda to take over the position of senior scholar in the law school. He shook his head now as she looked at him questioningly.

'*Fineguth, finechruth, finebés,*' said Shane suddenly, his slate-blue eyes blazing with enthusiasm.

'Well done,' said Mara warmly. 'Very well done indeed.'

Moylan threw Shane a jealous glance. 'Family voice, family appearance, family behaviour. Well, if that is proof of paternity, then Shane is no son of his father. The last time that I saw Brehon Mac Brethany he had a big deep voice, a bald head and a beard, and he wasn't running around playing hurling in every spare moment so I don't think that you could say that Shane passes the test of *fineguth, finechruth, finebés.*'

Mara sighed, but said nothing as Shane just looked amused, his white teeth flashing in the grin which set off his olive skin and very black hair. In any case, she had noticed that her scholars seldom forgot any law which could be turned into a joke. They were all word-perfect in the little-known laws of bee trespass since Enda had drawn up a list of fines against Eoin MacNamara whenever they spotted any of his bees feeding on flowers at Cahermacnaghten.

'So we now have to ask ourselves whether Iarla of Aran, who was, unlike my junior friend here, a man grown, in any way resembled Ardal O'Lochlainn,' said Enda grandly.

'And the answer is no,' said Moylan.

'What did the blacksmith look like, Brehon?' asked Fachtnan.

'Do you know, Fachtnan, I forgot to ask. That was stupid of me; I could have enquired of Becan when I was talking to him.'

'Iarla certainly looked as if he might be related to Becan,' said Fachtnan thoughtfully. 'That is,' he corrected himself, 'he was darkhaired, but otherwise I'm not so sure. You know the way that you meet someone and you can see a family look about them . . .' He thought for a moment, gave a half-deprecating glance at Moylan who was inclined to tease and then said hastily, 'I always think that Nuala is more like how I remember her mother even though her hair and eyes are dark like Malachy's.'

'You're quite right, Fachtnan,' said Mara enthusiastically. 'That's a very good example. I've often thought that myself. Nuala has the same way of talking, the same way of moving and even the same way of thinking as her mother had.'

What a good Brehon that boy could make eventually if he could only pass his examinations, she thought. He had an understanding and an interest in people and this was something which could not be taught.

'It's not going to work for Iarla though,' said Enda. 'Both Étain and Ardal were redheaded. I vote that we stop thinking about Ardal as a possible father.'

'Then it could have been anyone on Aran that Easter,' said Moylan. 'You could send us over there, Brehon. We'd like that. We could go around checking for *fineguth*, *finechruth*, *finebés*.'

'I'll think about it,' promised Mara. 'Now, you'd better get out your Latin exercises.'

Was the father of Iarla to be found on Aran? she wondered as the scholars opened their books. Her mind went to the enchanting picture that Turlough had painted last night of the gorgeous redheaded girl dancing there on the hollow flagstone in front of the fire.

'Visitors,' said Aidan. He stretched himself, yawned, his hands behind his head, and then rubbed his tired eyes with ink-spattered knuckles.

'Just one visitor,' said Shane, whose seat was nearer to the window. 'It's a girl.'

'Probably Mairéad for Enda,' said Moylan with a smirk.

'No, it's the O'Brien girl, the eldest one,' said Shane.

'Saoirse!' exclaimed Enda. He looked enquiringly at Mara.

'What time is it?' asked Aidan fretfully. 'It must be time for vespers at least.'

'Not yet,' said Mara with a quick glance at the candle clock. 'However, it is nearly three o'clock so I think we can stop now. Fachtnan, would you bring our visitor in, please. Off you go, the rest of you. Don't pester Brigid for food before she is ready for you.'

'We can have a game of hurling.' Aidan sprang to his feet with all signs of fatigue rapidly vanishing.

Saoirse came in timidly. It was a pity that Mairéad was not here, thought Mara; that might have given the girl more confidence. Enda, sent by Brigid, followed on Fachtnan's footsteps with two cups of mild ale and a plate of honey cakes. They were both well-mannered boys, easy in company, but Saoirse seemed strangely shy of them and sat with downcast eyes until they had left the room.

'How are things at home with you?' asked Mara solicitously.

Saoirse was paler than usual and Mara noticed the bluish trace of a mark on her face below the left eye.

'All right.' Saoirse, looking up, saw Mara's eyes on her cheekbone and then blushed heavily. 'Nothing has happened since that night,' she said.

'Your father hit you there?' Mara laid a light hand on the bruise and Saoirse flinched and then nodded.

'That wasn't like him,' said Mara.

She was astonished. Teige had always seemed such an equable, good-tempered man. Turlough, she remembered, had spoken of his cousin giving young Donal everything that he asked for.

'No, it wasn't.' Tears welled up in Saoirse's eyes. 'I don't know what got into him. He's never like that. He doesn't even beat the boys no matter what they do. Mother is always complaining about that.'

'Perhaps he didn't like the thought of you kissing and cuddling with a young man. Was that it, do you think? Perhaps he thinks you're still a little girl and should be playing with your dolls.' Mara kept her tone light.

'No, it wasn't that.' Saoirse shook her head. She looked a little embarrassed, but then blurted out, 'At the festival of Imbolc, Donogh Óg and I . . . well, we were hiding in the window embrasure and we were . . . well, Father just pulled the curtain away and laughed and laughed. He just kept on teasing me about Donogh Óg for days after, even though I told him that it wasn't serious and we had been just playing about. And when we visited the O'Connor once at Ballyganner Castle, Father got up a game of hide-and-seek and he was the one that paired me off with Tomás O'Connor. Well, you know what it's like with hide-and-seek games . . . we ended up at the top of the hot press in the kitchen. . . .' She gave a quick giggle at the memory.

'I see,' said Mara. This was puzzling. Of course, Donogh Óg, the son of one of the wealthiest farmers on the Burren, would be a better match for Saoirse than an unknown from the Aran Islands, as would young Tomás, but on the other hand, by that hour of the night of St Patrick, everyone present, and certainly Teige, at Lemeanah Castle had known that Iarla came with a very good claim to be Ardal O'Lochlainn's son. Why had Teige been so furious with his daughter's dalliance with Iarla and yet so amused and easy-going about the same behaviour with Donogh Óg and the O'Connor boy?

'What did he actually say?' Words spoken in the heat of the moment were often very revealing.

Saoirse frowned, compressing her lips. 'He yelled at me,' she said, tears beginning to well up into her dark eyes.

'About your behaviour? He thought you were the one who led Iarla into making the attack.' It still didn't make sense if Teige had been happy to see her kissing and cuddling with Donogh Óg and with the young O'Connor on another occasion.

'No, I don't think so. I don't think it was that at all.' Saoirse's frown deepened, her very black brows meeting on the top of her rather fleshy nose. She had quite a look of her father, thought Mara. Only youth lent her a certain beauty; Teige would be well advised to allow her to marry as soon as an offer came forward. She would be a heavy, swarthy-looking girl within a few years. 'He shouted at me to keep away from that fellow from Aran – almost as if he disliked Iarla for some reason, as if he knew something really terrible about him. And yet . . .'

'And yet he had never met him,' finished Mara. There was no doubt that Teige's behaviour was quite puzzling. 'But everything is all right between you and your father now, is it?' Mara was a little worried. She did not approve of this habit of hitting girls that some fathers indulged in. She would have a firm word with Teige if it continued to happen.

'Oh, yes, Brehon,' said Saoirse reassuringly. 'He was very sorry that he did it. He even bought me a present of some lovely thick double-dyed red woollen cloth from Galway. He told me to make a gown for myself out of it.'

'That's good.'

Mara waited. Saoirse had not ridden over in order to tell her this. And it probably wasn't to see any of the boys either. Moylan and Aidan were too young for her; Enda was her friend Mairéad's property; and the whole of the Burren knew about Nuala's infatuation for Fachtnan.

'It's just that I thought you might like to know something that Iarla told me.' Saoirse hesitated.

'Yes, I would.' Mara looked at her with interest.

'It was my father that told me to come and tell you about it.'

Saoirse was still hesitant, not worried in any way, noted Mara, but, like all the young, afraid of making a fool of herself or making too much of some words spoken casually. 'Father was asking me what Iarla was talking to me about when we were together. He told me to tell him everything that Iarla had said.'

She would have been frightened by her father's unaccustomed severity and willing to spill out everything said – apart from words of love, of course, surmised Mara.

'And then today when he came back from Galway and gave me the present, he said that he had been thinking about what Iarla said and he felt that I should come and see you.'

'Your father was quite right,' Mara assured her. 'The more I know about Iarla from Aran, the easier it will be for me to solve the problem of his murder.'

'It's just that when we were dancing together, Becan, his uncle, came up to him and tapped him on the shoulder. Iarla shrugged him off; he didn't want to go with him. So I said something like: "Go on, he wants you, he's waiting for you. You'd better go." And he just shook his head and said: "Let him wait. I'm tired of him bossing me around, telling me what to do. He's always like that. He was even bossing my mother on her deathbed."'

'And that was all?' asked Mara, looking keenly at the girl.

'No, that wasn't all. You see it's difficult to remember exactly because he was drunk and he'd say something and it wouldn't make sense and then he would finish saying it later on . . . But, anyway, I got the feeling that he was furious with Becan because he felt that Becan was keeping a secret from him and that he was the one that persuaded Iarla's mother not to tell him the truth.'

'Not to tell him the truth about Ardal O'Lochlainn being Iarla's father?'

'No, it wasn't that. I asked about that and he just laughed. I thought,' said Saoirse, a shrewd expression on her plump face, 'that he didn't really believe, himself, that he was the son of the O'Lochlainn. But then he was very drunk.'

All the more reason for him to tell the truth, thought Mara. As Enda was prone to declaring in a superior manner to the younger boys: '*in vino veritas*'.

'Thank you very much for taking the trouble to come to see me and tell me all of this, Saoirse,' she said aloud. 'Would you like me to get one of the boys to escort you back to Lemeanah?'

Saoirse cast a regretful glance at Enda and Fachtnan vigorously battling on the hurling field, but then shook her head.

'No, I'll be all right, Brehon. It won't take me long. My pony is a very fast one.'

She climbed up on the mounting block, vaulted on to the back of the sleek pony and clattered off down the road at a smart pace. It was only when she had rounded the corner leading to Kilcorney that something just came into Mara's head. What was it that one of the scholars had remarked when telling her about Mairéad's dramatic rescue of Saoirse? *And then he went off and got himself another girl.*

Who was that other girl? She had a fair idea, but she went over to the edge of the field and called the hurlers so that she could verify her suspicions. How lucky, she thought, as she crossed back the courtyard towards the kitchen house, that on the impulse of the moment, she had ordered those purple baskets from Dalagh the basket maker.

'Now, Brigid, don't make a fuss,' she said, peering around the door of the kitchen house. 'I'm just going for a very quiet slow walk down the road towards Kilcorney. It will do me good; fresh air and moderate exercise are both important when a dog is having puppies and I'm sure that the same thing applies to humans.'

Brigid looked at her suspiciously. 'Just a walk?'

'Just a walk,' repeated Mara. 'I'll drop into the basket maker's cottage and enquire about my lily baskets, have a little rest and then walk back again just in time for supper. The king won't be coming tonight; he'll be in Thomond so I'll just have a light supper and an early bedtime.'

'Well, I suppose that can't do you too much harm,' said Brigid grudgingly. 'Should someone go with you? What about Seán?'

'Brigid, I have another four months to go before this baby is born,' said Mara in exasperated tones. 'I can't wrap myself in sheeps' wool and sit by the fire for all of that time. I must lead a normal life.' With that she marched out of the kitchen house. Between Turlough and Brigid she felt like a stalled cow.

'These look lovely, just the right size and shape,' said Mara with genuine admiration, looking at the four baskets that were already made. 'Do you think that I could possibly take these with me? I'm longing to start planting my lilies in them.' She picked up two of the baskets, stacked them together and made a show of slightly sticking out her stomach as one who is bearing too heavy a load.

'No, no, Brehon, one of the boys will carry them for you. Wait a minute and I'll see if one of them has just finished a task.' The basket maker's wife looked horrified, got up and glanced hurriedly out of the open door. Mara came and stood behind her. All boys were busy cutting rods.

'Could Orlaith come with me?' asked Mara. 'Would that be all right, Orlaith?'

By a piece of good luck, Orlaith had just been finishing off the fourth basket when Mara arrived at the door. She looked up now at her mother with an expression of hope on her small-featured face. These children probably led a life of such unremitting toil that even a walk along the road was a treat for them.

'Yes, of course she will. Give them all to her, Brehon. They'll be nothing to Orlaith. You help the Brehon with her lilies, Orlaith, and then you can come back when she has no further use for you.'

And then Orlaith was out the door and walking demurely by Mara's side with no questions asked, no worries, no apprehension on the part of daughter or parents. There is a lot to be said for doing things in a tactful way, thought Mara, feeling rather pleased with herself. If she had followed Brigid's advice, or her father's practice, and sent for Orlaith, no doubt both parents would have been counselling her to say nothing, not to interfere in other people's business and would have given her a hoard of instructions which would probably have resulted in a silence from the girl.

'That was fun at Lemeanah on St Patrick's Day, wasn't it?' said Mara chattily as they turned out of the gate and began to walk along the little lane.

Orlaith didn't reply. She was gazing apprehensively over her shoulder. Mara quickly followed her gaze. Orlaith wasn't looking at the sally garden; that was in the opposite direction and they had not come to it yet; she was gazing back towards Balor's Cave. The air was full of harsh cawing noises. Great tattered crowds of ravens circled and swooped and then rose again into the air. Mara frowned with puzzlement. What could be there to catch the attention of the birds? She stopped and stood very still looking back. Orlaith took a few steps forward and then she, also, stopped, resting the baskets on the stone wall. The day was breezy and the sudden squalls of wind blew the ravens, scattering them, and then subsiding and allowing them to coalesce again in one black, untidy mass.

'What's attracting the birds, Dalagh?' called Mara, seeing that he and his sons had stopped work and were looking at her.

'Just the wind exciting them, Brehon,' he called back. 'There's nothing there for them. They just get wound up when the weather is stormy.'

Mara raised a hand to show that she understood. The wind was getting up to gale force, bending the bare branches of the trees and almost blowing her off balance. The sooner she and Orlaith got to the sheltered garden of Cahermacnaghten the quicker she would be able to talk to the girl. No conversation could be heard in this wind.

Once they got out on the Green Valley road, though, the wind did not seem so strong. Mara admired the baskets again, getting Orlaith to explain how they were made and praising the workmanship. And then she turned the conversation.

'I thought that you were very upset about the death of Iarla from

Aran when I was in your house the other day. Did you know him well?' she asked, looking solicitously into the girl's face.

'No!' Orlaith's exclamation sounded startled and almost frightened.

'You see,' went on Mara, 'I am anxious to hear anything he said that night, no matter how trivial it might seem. It's not right that someone should come here as a stranger for a night of fun on St Patrick's Day and end up dead three days later. I've talked to Saoirse O'Brien and she told me what he said to her and then someone told me that Iarla had danced with you, also. Don't worry,' she finished hastily as she saw the girl glance anxiously over her shoulder, 'anything you say to me will be private. I won't tell your parents.'

'He didn't say much; we just danced.' Orlaith's eyes were cautious. 'Don't tell my father. He and my mother and the younger ones had gone home; I was going to stay the night with my aunt. She's the cook at Lemeanah.'

'Saoirse spoke of a secret,' said Mara. 'She said that Becan, Iarla's uncle, was keeping a secret from him. Did he speak of Becan at all to you?'

Orlaith stopped in the middle of the road. She looked at Mara solemnly, almost appraisingly.

Mara stayed very still, looking back. 'Trust me,' she said quietly. 'I won't let you down.'

'He did mention him,' admitted Orlaith. 'It was just when he saw Becan drinking some *uisce beatha*, he said: "I hope he doesn't take too much of that stuff and start spilling secrets. Else we might both end up in the ditch with our throats cut." That was all he said and I don't think that he meant to say it – he had been drinking a lot too. The next minute he was just joking and laughing and teasing me.'

'*End up in the ditch with our throats cut.*' Mara repeated the words and then she turned swiftly, saying over her shoulder, 'You carry on, Orlaith. Take the baskets to Cahermacnaghten. You can give them to Brigid, she'll know what to do with them. I must go back. There's something that I must see. Don't worry; I'll say nothing to your parents about you and Iarla.'

There was a song that Mara's father used to sing. She had forgotten most of it. Stanza by stanza, it went through all of the birds and described their sweet singing, but each verse ended with the ominous words: *But the raven, the black raven, he sings of naught but death.*

Nine

Brecha Comaichchesa
(Judgements of Neighbourhoods)

A man who preserves the carcass of a dead animal from the depredations of ravens and grey crows is entitled to one quarter of its value. Even though it is the property of another man, his action will have saved the skin and sometimes the meat of the animal.

Becan was there. Lying in almost the very same spot as his nephew. Stretched out on the damp, pale-brown clay in front of Balor's Cave. Once again the upturned roots of the willow half concealed the body, but this time the ravens had been bolder. Becan's face was covered with peck marks where pieces of flesh had been gouged out by sharp beaks. One eye had been removed by the ravens, but only one; the other had been dug out with a sharp knife.

I could have prevented this, thought Mara, bending down to look closely at the disfigured eye. I should have made more time to talk to him. I should have known that he came back from Aran for a purpose, that he wanted to investigate his nephew's death, that perhaps he guessed the murderer. Why didn't I insist that he came back with me to Cahermacnaghten? I must do my job properly. Just because I was tired, I didn't press him on where he was going to spend the night and now this has happened. I must not allow my marriage and my pregnancy to get in the way of the position that I hold. The law must be upheld in this kingdom.

And now there had been another killing beside Balor's Cave. More rumours would be spreading, more superstitious unease and more half-recollected stories about the evil god. Ardal would find it hard to get men to work for him here at this spot after these two murders.

Wearily Mara straightened her back, using one of the roots of the upturned willow to assist her. She had to do her best now for Becan and for Iarla. The truth of these deaths had to be uncovered and the murderer exposed as soon as possible for everybody's sake. Slaughter could not be allowed to happen here on the Burren. She turned to go back, her mind sorting through the tasks ahead of her. She would have to find a few messengers – it was lucky that Dalagh and his industrious children were working so close by.

It was strange though, thought Mara, thinking of the basket maker as she picked her way down the muddy lane. Why had Dalagh not shown any curiosity about the behaviour of the ravens? Even now, as Mara moved away from the body, they were flocking back, shrieking and circling just above her head. Mara bent down and automatically turned to throw a stone at them, but her mind was still busily considering the problem of Dalagh. He was not a farmer; but he would, doubtless, have been the son of a farmer, have lived amongst farmers all of his life. Even the carefully brought up daughter of a physician had immediately thought to turn aside from her path once she saw the ravens hovering. Too many young lambs and even calves had fallen victim to these blood-hungry birds.

The wind from the west was very strong and Mara had difficulty in forcing her way along the small lane, staggering against its invisible force. It seemed to her almost perverse the way that Dalagh continued to ignore her while still chopping against the willow rods with his long sharp knife. There was no point in calling to him until she got a little nearer; the force of the wind would just sweep her words away so she struggled on until she came near enough to attract his attention.

'Dalagh,' she shouted when she reached the stone wall just opposite to him.

For a moment he did not show any signs of hearing her and in exasperation she thought of throwing a stone at him. Then one of the boys timidly touched his shoulder and Dalagh swung around, a passing streak of sunshine glinting on the knife in his hand, and then he came across to her, moving with the sureness of long custom through the closely set willow rods. The boy followed and his brothers all ceased work and stood looking across at her.

'Brehon?' Dalagh's voice sounded a query. He looked down at the knife in his hand and then hastily slotted it into its leather scabbard at his waist.

'Dalagh, Becan, the uncle of the boy from Aran, is dead.' Mara spoke the words firmly and unemotionally and for a moment he did not react. He just stared at her as if wondering what to say.

'Jesus, Mary and Joseph,' said the boy beside him. 'Another one dead!' He was a young boy, probably younger than Shane.

Mara was sorry for his distress, but at the same time she did not allow her eyes to move from Dalagh's face. Why did the man not say something? Surely it was unnatural that he should just stand there eyeing her in that uncertain way as if he were in some social situation where he was unsure of the correct response.

'May the Lord have mercy on his soul,' he muttered eventually, rather as if he were attending the wake of the dead man.

'What happened, Brehon?' asked the boy. 'Was he killed by Balor?'

Suddenly Dalagh seemed to come to life.

'Another killing?' he asked. Now there was a correct measure of horror in his eyes.

'That's right,' said Mara evenly. 'And I don't think that Balor is responsible. Dalagh, could you send one of your older boys for Malachy the physician and another one of them for your *taoiseach*, the O'Lochlainn. We'll need to move the body quickly before the storm breaks.' She cast a quick, worried glance at the dark grey clouds.

'I'll do that, Brehon.' Suddenly Dalagh was galvanized into action. 'I'll get my lads to bring our own cart over. That will save time a bit. We'll be able to move the body to the church as soon as the physician is finished with it. I'll go for the *taoiseach* myself. This lad here is a good shot with the stones. He'll go back with you and keep those ravens off the body.'

'My name is Dathi,' said the boy chattily as they walked back side by side. From time to time, he picked up a stone and flung it with deadly accuracy at the ravens, causing a squawk and a flutter from amongst the bunch with his third stone. A cluster of black feathers floated down, whirling vigorously in the wind. The ravens flew off exclaiming loudly and the boy smiled with delight.

'I told Father that they were up to no good!' he shouted in her ear. Now that they had passed from beyond the shelter of the sally gardens the wind's force was unchecked.

Mara held on to her cloak, wrapping it tightly around her body. She wished that the boy had something warm; the short leather jerkin that he wore over his *léine* seemed inadequate in a wind like this and his legs were bare apart from a pair of laced sandals. However, he seemed cheerful and unperturbed by the weather. Children do seem to have this ability, she thought, almost as if their own bodies regulated the heat for them, irrespective of clothing.

'So you guessed that something was wrong when you saw the ravens?' she asked as they turned into the comparative shelter of the old misshapen willows that lined the entrance to Balor's Cave.

'That's right.'

He aimed a sharp-edged stone at the ravens and gave a victory shout as another few feathers tumbled down. The ravens, however, were now desperate for their prey. It had probably taken a long time before they had got up enough courage to actually attack and they were determined not to relinquish their booty. Mara began to be sorry that she had not taken a bigger boy with her. There was something very frightening and inhuman about the ravens' determination; from time to time one of them flew near enough for her to see its cold, grey eye and she felt like joining Daithi in his assault against the birds.

Still, his father was right, Daithi was a good shot; she could leave it to him. In the meantime, there was something else to be ascertained before Dalagh came back. She had noticed how silent and inhibited all of the children were in front of their parents – perhaps this quelling of their natural talkativeness was an inevitable consequence of a large family who were all trained to work hard from an early age; a pity, thought Mara, but she didn't feel that she could interfere. There was affection there and no cruelty as far as she could see. Dalagh could only make a good living out of basket-making if he had the assistance of all of his large family. It was nothing to do with her really. In the meantime, in Dalagh's absence, she could use her opportunity to find out how long Becan's body had been lying there.

'When did you first notice the ravens?' she asked after the boy had successfully dispersed the next assault from the swooping birds of prey.

'Saw them in the morning, first thing, a few of them.' He was searching around the ground for a well-shaped stone with the concentration of a craftsman selecting the right tool.

'Just a few,' she echoed.

'Yes, just a few. They kept coming and flying over and then going away and flying back with a few friends and going off again.'

Mara nodded. It seemed as if Becan's body had been there all day. It would have taken quite some time before the ravens had gathered enough courage to attack, especially as the body, like Iarla's before him, was half sheltered by the willow twigs. 'Perhaps we'll wait here,' she said. 'The ravens have attacked the body and you might not like to see it.'

'Nah, I don't care,' he said nonchalantly. 'I'd like to see it. I'll be the first, after you and I can tell everyone about it. I didn't see the other fellow from Aran and the others did.'

And then he strode out in front of her determinedly, waving a challenging stone-filled fist at the ravens. She followed him with a half smile lifting the corners of her lips. *Boys will be boys*, Brigid would say. She guessed that he wouldn't like the sight of Becan's body, on the other hand, these country children were realistic and they lived with death. It might actually be better for him to see the body, than to imagine what might have happened to it.

They had come to the body now and the child gulped a little, averted his eyes and then looked back with as nonchalant an air as he could assume.

'Made a fine mess of him, didn't they?' He frowned, came a little nearer and peered down into the disfigured face.

'Do you believe in Balor?' he asked then, trying to steady his young voice.

'No,' said Mara. She didn't add any reasons. He had not asked for that and she was interested to know what he would say.

'Neither do I,' he said surprisingly. 'My father and mother do, but sometimes we, us boys, think they are just putting it on, trying to keep us away from the cave.'

'Why would they want to do that?' Mara watched his face with amusement.

'They might think it's dangerous for us,' he replied shrewdly. 'You can't trust caves, you know. They collapse on top of you, or else they can flood and drown you. We went in there once, three of us, it goes back a long way. And then we heard a weird sort of noise. The others were frightened and they ran. I wasn't scared,' he boasted, 'but I thought I might as well go back too. My sandals were in a mess with the clay. Listen to that wind! We'll have some more trees down tonight.'

'See if Malachy the physician is coming, will, you, Daithi? I'll be all right here for a few minutes. I think that you've frightened the ravens away for good now.'

'They'll be back,' he said wisely, and then he was off, running energetically down the road.

Mara moved forward once he was out of sight. The cave entrance was small and low, but she thought she would just be able to fit into it. The boy's conversation had awakened her curiosity. Were they murdered, both uncle and nephew, at this spot? And if so, what had attracted them here?

'Mara!' The clear voice rose high against the noise of the wind and Mara turned around guiltily. It was a silly idea anyway, she thought; the clay was wet and slippery and she might fall and damage her baby. Carefully she moved back and went down the path to meet Nuala accompanied by the basket maker's boy.

'Father's not in, he's gone to Galway,' said Nuala when she came within earshot. 'I thought I would come straight away. I think it will rain soon. You shouldn't be out in this weather in your condition,' she scolded with a grin.

'Don't you start. Brigid is bad enough.' Mara returned the grin and then sobered. 'Have you heard the details?' She looked at the tall boy, the eldest son of the basket maker who was surveying the body with feigned indifference.

Nuala nodded. She had her medical bag with her and now she advanced and knelt beside what was left of Becan the blacksmith from Aran.

'Could you two go back and tell us when the *taoiseach* is coming? I think the ravens are keeping their distance now.' Mara didn't want to have the two boys around while she was talking to Nuala.

'Come on, Daithi.' The eldest boy took him by the shoulder and hauled him away.

'We'll keep pelting them with stones as we go along, Brehon,' shouted back Daithi, wriggling free from his brother's grasp.

Mara nodded, but her eyes were on Nuala. What a piece of luck that Malachy was out, she thought. There was no doubt in her mind that Nuala, despite her age, was the better physician of the two. Her knowledge was probably, after all the intense study that she had undertaken, superior to Malachy's and she was definitely far more intelligent.

'What do you think?' Mara could distinguish the deep rumble of a cart's wheels from below the high whining of willow branches bending and creaking in the wind. The sky was getting so black that it felt as if nightfall would soon occur. The quicker this body was placed in Kilcorney church and she and Nuala indoors, the better.

'I think that you have the very same situation here as we had last week,' replied Nuala briefly. 'To my mind this man, Becan, was killed at around the same time as Iarla. They were both killed in the same way, by being struck on the back of the head and their skull smashed inwards. I would say a very heavy stick or something like that. Both had a knife poked into the eye, and in this case, as in the last, the eye was mutilated after death. Probably the murder was done by the same person.'

'I suspected it would prove to be a copy of the first murder,' said Mara thoughtfully. 'Done by the same person, why do you say that?'

Nuala hesitated. 'I just think it was,' she said eventually. 'It feels as if it were the same hand behind both murders. I remember once hearing a shepherd saying to another one, "It was you that put the mark on those sheered sheep belonging to Donogh O'Lochlainn, wasn't it?" He knew by the way the mark was pressed on, the position on the sheep's back and probably a few other things too. When a man strikes a blow like this, a blow that is meant to kill, then the probability is that the second blow will land in the very same place as the first blow.'

'And that is the case here?' Mara made the query, but she understood very well what Nuala was telling her.

'That's it,' asserted Nuala. She hesitated for a minute. 'There's another thing too, I didn't like to push it too much the last time as Father was there and I don't want to set myself up against him too much – we always seem to be fighting these days . . .' She heaved a sigh.

'Tell me now,' said Mara. She cast an anxious eye down the road. The cart was coming, but luckily there was no sign of Ardal yet.

'I think I could swear that the man was not killed here. And neither was the other man, Iarla. There just isn't enough blood on the ground. Any man in the world would fall instantly after a blow like that and the blood would have poured out from that wound. But you can see for yourself.' Nuala bent down again, and half lifted the body. The back of the cloak was stained with yellow clay, but the neck and shoulders clearly showed the dark patches of blood. 'There you are,' she said, replacing the body on the ground, 'though there is blood on the clothing, there is none on the ground. Any head wound bleeds profusely, even the slightest scratch; a blow like this would have felled the man to ground, but the blood would have continued pouring out for a couple of minutes at least.'

'So what you are saying is that Becan and Iarla were probably killed by the same man and that both were killed elsewhere and their bodies carried, in some way, perhaps on some sort of barrow or cart and laid down in this spot just by Balor's Cave.' Ardal was coming now, following the heavy cart led by the basket maker. Mara could see both he and Liam riding down the road.

'Yes, outside Balor's Cave,' repeated Nuala. 'And in each case, someone cut out the right eye after death.'

Liam's face bore its usual look of avid curiosity, lightly overlaid

by a placid exterior, Ardal's face showed intense gravity with perhaps
an edge of anger below the surface: a conventional veneer of horror
at the offence and sorrow for the two murdered men, but why the
anger?

'This is a terrible affair, Brehon. It seems as if the world has gone
mad. What on earth can be the reason for this?'

Mara left this unanswered. It was fairly obvious, she thought, that
Becan had been murdered, because he was on the trail of Iarla's
killer. Or else was it because both of them knew a secret which put
them both at risk – however, Ardal couldn't be expected to know
about this.

And what part did Iarla's dubious paternity play in the tragic
affairs of the week?

'We had better get the body moved to the church as quickly as
possible, Ardal,' said Nuala impatiently. 'The ravens have been attacking
it and it's going to rain at any minute.'

Ardal gave her an irritated look which Mara noticed. Her mind
went back to her conversation with Malachy and she resolved to
do something about Nuala as soon as possible. Moving her from
Malachy and Caireen and sending her to Ardal would solve nothing.
Ardal disliked the idea of Nuala becoming a physician and would
want to arrange a suitable marriage for her as soon as possible. Uncle
and niece clashed too often to make Ardal's offer of a home and a
dowry to be a suitable one for the child without some conditions
being agreed first of all. Nuala would have to be assured that her
future as a physician would be safeguarded and that any marriage
arranged had to be one that she wished for.

'Yes, you can move him now,' she said. 'Nuala has finished her
examination and has told me all that I need to know.'

Mara noticed the half-smile on Liam's face at her words, which
pointed to her belief in Nuala's medical knowledge. He was a clever
man, she had often thought. He was certainly picking up on all the
undercurrents in these few brief exchanges. Quickly and efficiently,
he now began to give orders to the basket maker and his sons; the
body was lifted on to the cart which went trundling down the road.
Ardal, Malachy had said to her once, could never have achieved so
much with his lands and his animals if he hadn't had Liam as his
right-hand man. 'The first to rise and the last to go to bed' was
the way that Malachy had put it and Mara had heard the same praise
from others. Now she could see that he was glancing around the
scene, thinking of the next task to be done.

'I'll go and inform the priest, my lord,' he said to Ardal, and then he went cantering after the cart, his horse snorting and flicking his tail.

'Thunder in the air,' said Nuala knowledgeably. 'You'd better get home, Mara, before it starts to rain. You don't want to catch a cold.'

'I brought a horse for you,' said Ardal turning from his niece to Mara. 'I thought you could just sit on it and I could lead it. We won't go quickly, but it will be faster than walking pace and less tiring for you.'

'Thank you, Ardal,' said Mara gratefully.

She accepted his help in mounting the sturdy horse and then looked at Nuala's downcast face. Poor child, she would go back to an empty house and then there would be nothing to look forward to; just the arrival of her father who she felt did not understand her, and of Caireen and her sons whom she disliked. 'Would you like to come back with me and spend the night in the guesthouse, Nuala? I think I probably need a physician on hand. Just joking,' she added hastily, seeing alarm in both faces.

'Yes, I'd like that,' said Nuala after a moment's consideration. 'It's Sive's day off so she won't worry about me and when Father comes home he'll probably guess I've gone to Cahermacnaghten.' She sounded indifferent as to whether her father would worry about her or not – the housekeeper's feelings were of more importance to Nuala and Mara found it hard to blame her.

'She can get up behind me, can't she, Ardal?' asked Mara.

'Yes, of course,' he said readily. 'Liam uses this gelding often and he'd make double both your weights added together.' He looked at his niece with a certain amount of disfavour as she climbed lithely on to the back of the horse. 'You should try and put on some weight, Nuala. You're far too thin. Try having some cream on your porridge every day.'

'He wants me to be as fat as Caireen,' whispered Nuala in Mara's ear as Ardal turned away to climb on his own horse.

Mara couldn't help a quick smile, but didn't reply. Her mind was on Becan, picturing his cloak and his clay-encrusted boots.

'Becan didn't stay with you last night, Ardal?' she asked.

'No.' Ardal sounded startled. 'No, I haven't seen sight or sound of him since the day of the burial.' He was silent for a moment, perhaps reviewing his own conduct. Ardal was always the soul of hospitality. 'I didn't feel like inviting him after his accusation, at Poulnabrone, that I had murdered his nephew.'

'No, no, I didn't really think that you should have,' said Mara hastily. 'The thing is that I wondered where he did stay the night. I invited him, but he refused and when I left him, daylight was fading fast. He wouldn't have had time to get to his relations in Kinvarra before dark and even if he did go there, he was back here again in early morning. It looks as if he spent the night somewhere near here. It couldn't have been with the basket maker; he would have mentioned it – so where did he go?'

'Well, I'll make enquiries, Brehon, and send over to Cahermacnaghten if I find out anything.'

'If you could do that, Ardal, I would be very grateful,' said Mara, wondering whether this would be a good way to get rid of him. She couldn't stand being led along the road like a flighty heifer. 'Do you think it would be possible for you to do this now, before the men go home for the night?'

'Well,' said Ardal with a hesitant glance at the clouds. 'I'm—'

'Why don't you gallop on ahead?' interrupted Mara. 'I'll be fine here with Nuala to help me. I really would be so grateful if you could do that for me.'

'Well, if you're sure.' That was the good thing about Ardal. Her word was always law to him.

'Yes, of course, I'm sure.' Mara made her voice brisk and author-itative.

'Well, I'll do that then. To be honest, I would like to be back for the men's supper. Liam's been telling that there is a lot of unrest. It's time for the spring sowing of vegetables and none of the men want to do it. They don't want to go near Balor's Cave. And, of course, this second death will make things worse. I'll have to try to clamp down on the rumours before they go too far.' And with that, Ardal clapped his feet to the sides of his horse raising his hand in a brief salute.

'Where do you think that Becan stayed last night?' asked Nuala curiously as Ardal shot away down the road, his thoroughbred stal-lion carrying him at more than double the speed that Liam's gelding would have been capable of.

'I think I know,' said Mara thinking of the clay-stained boots and the besmirched cloak. 'I think I know, but it would be good to be sure. In any case, it got rid of Ardal. I'm sure that I can manage without him since I have you to take care of me.'

Her voice was affectionate and she thought from the quick intake of breath from the girl behind her that Nuala repressed a sob.

'Thanks for inviting me, Mara,' she said after a minute. 'Things are very bad between Father and me at the moment. Has he told you that Ardal wants me to come and live with him?'

'Yes, he has.' Mara said no more. Let Nuala talk, she thought. This slow journey back to Cahermacnaghten at walking pace was the ideal opportunity for the girl to unburden herself.

'That was Ardal's idea.' From the sound of her voice, Mara could tell that Nuala was frowning. 'Well, perhaps not his idea from the start. The strange thing is that I think it was big, fat Liam who dreamed it up. I don't know what business of his it was, but I suppose he thought he was being useful. He's the greatest busybody in the kingdom, always sticking his nose into everyone's business.'

'You wouldn't think about living with Ardal, would you?' asked Mara mildly. 'He's a very generous man; he would treat you well. You would want for nothing when you were with him. I wouldn't be surprised if he would give you your own way about a marriage. I'd say that, if you put your mind to it, you would be able to handle him well. If not, I would do it for you.'

'But you don't understand, Mara.' Nuala's voice was almost a wail. 'If I go to live with Ardal I lose all chance of becoming a physician. I know that Father doesn't bother teaching me much, but I'm there and I can use his stillroom, I can grow the herbs, I can experiment with medicines, and if anyone comes looking for a physician I can go with him. I make sure that I do that no matter what he says and no matter what hour of the day or night it is. And, of course,' she added with a note of deep satisfaction in her voice, 'if he is off in Galway, dancing attendance on Caireen, letting her spend all of his silver, then I can manage the case myself.'

'I see. Well, leave it to me. Don't you worry about it any more. I'll think of something.'

The rain had begun as they turned into Cahermacnaghten, but Mara hardly noticed it as she left Nuala with Brigid and hastened over to the Brehon's house. Her mind was busy with worries about Nuala. Briefly she thought of Turlough, but the sky had turned as black as soot with ominous rumbles of thunder, and, as she stood at the doorway of her house, the rain began to fall in long slanting lines, hopping silver on the flagstoned path. It would be unfair to send any of her men out in this. Turlough, she knew, was staying at Inchiquin with his son Conor, but even so the ride might take about two hours in this weather. The news could wait until the morning.

Mara closed the door, lit her candle and went into the kitchen.

Brigid had left her supper – succulent meat pie – keeping warm in
one of the three-legged pots to the side of the fire. She would eat
it now and then go to bed, she decided. There was no point in
worrying about Becan tonight. Tomorrow she would deal with the
consequences of this second and unexpected death. Tonight she
would consider the plight of Nuala, who was as dear to Mara as
her own daughter, Sorcha, over in Galway.

There was only one solution as far as Mara could see, but she
felt she had to inform Malachy before saying any more to the girl.

Whatever the consequences to the father, she thought the daughter
of her best friend, the brilliant Mór O'Lochlainn, was not going to
be allowed to waste her potential and to go on suffering like this.

Ten

Brecha Comaichchesa
(Judgements of Neighbourhoods)

Trees are classified, according to their value, in four categories:

These are the Class Two Trees:
  Alder: useful for its hard, water-resistant wood.
  Willow (Sally): its rods are used for boat-building and basket weaving.
  Whitethorn: used for cooking spits.
  Rowan: its berries are valuable for food and its wood makes cooking spits.
  Birch: valuable firewood.
  Elm: wood is used for making stools and its bark is used in rope-making.
  Wild Cherry: the fruit is eaten and the bark is used to dye wool.

Damage to any of those trees is punishable by a fine related to the extent of the damage.
  1. Breaking of branch: one yearling heifer.
  2. Destruction of the tree: five séts or two and a half ounces of silver, or three milch cows.

' *I didn't see the other fellow from Aran and the others did.*' Mara woke with a start, the words as clear in her head as if they had just been spoken at that instant.

But of course they hadn't been spoken then. It had been yesterday that she had heard them and she had been so perturbed by the sight of Becan's body and the macabre threat to it by the hovering ravens that she had not picked up on them. It was the boy, the youngest boy of Dalagh the basket maker, who had said that.

And who were the *others*? For a boy like that, the youngest of the family, the others would have had only one meaning. It was of his brothers that he spoke. There had been something about that family that had made her uneasy. She had worried that the parents were unkind to their children, that the constraint that she had felt from all of them was the result of ill treatment.

But that had not been true, she thought, recalling the basket maker's cottage and the sally gardens. These children were chatty and open when their parents were not around. They were not damaged, frightened children, normally; she was sure of that. Something had happened, something in connection with this secret and unlawful killing of Iarla from Aran, and this event had some connection with this hard-working family of the basket maker. The children had been warned to keep their mouths shut and were now showing an uncharacteristic silence.

Dalagh and his wife knew of the death of Iarla from Aran before Nuala and Fachtnan had discovered the body. They had all been there that morning, parents and children, loading up the cart with baskets to be sold in the surrounding farms. What could be more natural than for one of the children to notice the ravens and to sneak over to the cave to see what was interesting the birds so much?

And if it were true that one, or all of these older boys, saw the dead body on that Thursday morning, then why were they all told to say nothing.

Was that the reason why the basket maker and his wife had taken all of the children with them when they went off to sell the baskets? Now that she thought about the matter, Mara realized that it was strange behaviour on their part. Surely the older ones could, and would, in normal circumstances, have been left behind to get on with their work.

Deep in thought, Mara got out of bed, gathered up her clothes and went down to her bathhouse. Her father had built that when she was a child. There was a big pump there and she rapidly half-filled the wooden bathtub with icy water from the hundred-foot-deep well. Brigid had already been in and had lit the charcoal in the iron brazier. The room was warm and there was a large pot of almost boiling water ready to be ladled into the cold water.

She was tempted to linger in the bath for some time, admiring the curved mound of her stomach where her baby kicked happily inside the encircling walls of the womb. However, she had a busy day ahead of her so soon she forced herself out of the warm water and began to dress, her mind busy with her plans for the day.

'Some nice hot milk for you and some honey on your porridge. Now eat it up.' Brigid hovered over her like an anxious mother.

'I can manage, Brigid,' said Mara cheerfully. She couldn't stand honey, but it was quicker to get rid of Brigid than to argue about it. 'Are the boys up yet?' She cast a meaningful eye out of the window towards the law school.

'Don't you worry about them,' scolded Brigid. 'Young Nessa is giving them their breakfast.'

'Hope they're not teasing her and being silly.' Mara kept her tone nonchalant, but she noticed that Brigid in her turn looked out of the window as if alert for any signs of riotous behaviour.

'Nuala is there and that might make them a bit more sensible.' Despite her words, Brigid sounded unsure and after a few fidgety minutes, said, 'Well, if you're sure you've got everything, Brehon, then I'll go back over. It's a lovely morning after all that rain last night.'

'Thanks, Brigid. Oh, and tell Seán to saddle the cob, will you? I want to send him on a message over to the king. He's at Inchiquin Castle.'

Brigid was right. It was, indeed, a lovely March morning. On her way across to the law school, Mara lingered a few minutes in her garden. The sun was warm and illuminated the dark purple of the violets with its light, making a lovely contrast with the pale faces of the primroses. There were still some remaining sudden gusts of wind and the small trumpets of the daffodils swivelled happily in its breeze, their golden colour rivalling the bright sunshine.

The boys were still eating their breakfast as she came through the gates, and Nuala was standing, the picture of gloom, by the door of the kitchen house.

'I know,' she said as Mara approached. 'I'd better get back.'

'Just in case your father is worried about you,' said Mara gently. 'Otherwise you'd be welcome to stay.'

'He probably spent the night in Galway and never gave me a thought,' said Nuala bitterly. 'Still, I'd better get back before they arrive. Will you be able to return the gelding to Ardal, Mara? I don't want to go over there. I'd only get a lecture from him.'

'Yes, if you're sure that you don't want to borrow it to get back to Caherconnell.'

'I'd prefer to walk,' said Nuala, and then she was off, her cloak swinging as her long legs moved rapidly down the road.

Mara watched her go for a moment and then turned her thoughts back to work. Her mind was fully made up now. She had to find out the truth of what really happened to Iarla from Aran in that hour or so between his breakfast as Lissylisheen and the moment of his death. But, first, Turlough had to be notified about this second death. She remembered his words about Aran. If there was still a certain amount of unrest at being ruled from the mainland, then two deaths in rapid succession was going to cause trouble. She would not send news of Becan's demise across to the island until Turlough was informed. Quickly she went into the schoolhouse and wrote a short note to Turlough on a piece of vellum, coiled it into a scroll and tied it. Then she lit a candle, melted the top of a stick of sealing wax, dropped a blob of wax on to the knot and pressed her ring into it. It had been her father's ring before her and she wore it on her thumb, a feeling of pride within her every time that she used it and remembered the long line of lawyers from whom she was descended.

'I'm ready now, Brehon.' Seán's rather vacant face peeped in through the door. 'Brigid said you need me to ride over to Inchiquin. Some sort of message, she said.'

Seán's voice held an inquiring note, but Mara did not respond. There was no real secret about Becan's death, but if Seán felt that he had a piece of interesting news to impart he would stop at every farm on his route and the message would not get to Turlough before noon.

'That's right,' she said briefly, handing him the scroll and watching carefully until he had stored it safely into his satchel. 'Make as good time as you can, won't you? I may have another errand for you.' That, hopefully, would get him back quickly. He was easily bored by routine farm work and loved to ride out on the Brehon's business. 'Send the scholars into me, Seán, will you, if they've finished their breakfast?'

'I'll need you all to do a task for me this morning,' she said as they crowded into the schoolhouse, jostling against each other playfully. 'It was something that we should have done before now, but this case has been confusing. We'll take a look at this map that the O'Lochlainn got Liam to draw out for me.'

She went to the top shelf of the wooden press and took out the piece of vellum. 'You see, from the evidence taken from Ardal's men, who were all working in those fields here –' she pointed with a long finger, before continuing – 'you can see there was no possibility of Iarla going the direct route from Lissylisheen as he would undoubtedly have been seen, therefore he must have gone back towards Lemeanah through the Ballymurphy lands and then come from Lemeanah back up through Shesmore, Carron, Poulawack and then turned down towards Kilcorney. Now I want you boys to visit every house on that route and enquire whether they saw any sign of the stranger from Aran on the early morning of Thursday the twentieth of March. Take your pens, inkhorns and some vellum in your satchels. It's a wide area to cover so I am going to trust you to work quickly and bring back the results to me as soon as possible.'

'So who's doing what?' Aidan sat up very straight with an air of energy that was quite alien to his usual lethargic attitude.

None of the scholars had mentioned Becan so Nuala must have kept quiet about this second murder. This showed an unusual degree of maturity in a girl of only fourteen, thought Mara, musing on the puzzle of how a father could not see what an exceptional daughter he possessed.

'What about Kilcorney itself?' asked Enda, studying the sketch map with interest.

'I'll do that,' said Mara, turning her mind back to business. 'At least,' she amended, 'I had planned to see the basket maker and his family, but thank you for reminding me, Enda; there are also the priest and his housekeeper at Kilcorney. It's possible that they may have seen something. I hadn't thought about the priest.'

'Probably because he is as old as the hills and as blind as a bat,' muttered Moylan under his breath.

Mara ignored this. She had long ago decided to allow her scholars to give vent to their witticisms and complaints as long as they did not force her to acknowledge that she had heard them.

'So Fachtnan and Hugh, I'd like you to go to Lemeanah. Ask questions of the guard in the gatehouse, or the porter, or anyone that you see around, but if they offer to fetch the *taoiseach* or any member of his family, just say that the Brehon will be seeing them herself.'

This was a slightly delicate errand and that was why she had chosen this pair for it. Fachtnan was tactful and very well liked by all on the Burren, and Hugh was a nephew to Teige O'Brien and his red curls and innocent blue eyes made him a favourite with all the womenfolk.

Moylan and Aidan were standing side by side looking eager and she gave them a considering glance. They were at a silly age and if partnered would probably enjoy being out of school too much to be wholly in earnest about their task.

'Enda,' she continued. 'I'd like you and Aidan to start at Shesmore and work your way right up to Kilcorney. Do see the priest and his housekeeper.' That would work out well, she thought with satisfaction. Enda was too tough to take any nonsense from Aidan and he was such a well-mannered, good-looking young man that he would be the ideal person to interview the priest.

'So I have Shane?' Moylan didn't look too disappointed.

It was the first time that he had been trusted to look after one of the younger boys. Shane, Mara privately thought, had far more brains and far more sense of responsibility than had Moylan. However, the thought of being in charge was obviously enticing to Moylan so she nodded solemnly.

'Yes,' she said. 'You're fifteen now, so I can trust you. You and Shane have the hardest job. You'll have to start at Ballymurphy, the townland just behind Lissyslisheen. Go right through to Noughaval, make sure that you enquire at all the houses there and then go through the churchyard, right down through Ballyganner and then come back the same way. Do you think that you can manage all of that?'

'Sure,' said Moylan nonchalantly.

Shane nodded vigorously.

'We've got the least to do.' Hugh sounded disappointed.

'Yes, but I want you back quickly. I may have another task for you then.'

Mara noticed Cumhal hovering outside the window. He and Brigid always seemed to have an instinct that alerted them when anything was wrong. They would have realized that, since Turlough was expected to ride over to Cahermacnaghten tomorrow, that something must have occurred since Mara wanted to send him a message today.

'Take your pens, ink and vellum and store them carefully in your satchels and then go and saddle your ponies,' she said. 'Fachtnan, could you just ask Cumhal if he can spare me a minute?'

Mara's summonses to Cumhal were always carefully couched in terms of a request. She was always conscious that the scholars should be aware of Cumhal's position of authority over them when she was absent and she never missed an opportunity to give him the respect that his post as farm manager entitled him to.

He was with her a minute later, but Mara waited until the boys had ridden out of the law-school gates in a noisy, cheerful cluster before turning to him.

'Cumhal, something very sad and very worrying happened yesterday,' she said, carefully watching him to see whether he had any knowledge of what she was about to tell him.

Yesterday afternoon he had planned to visit Donogh O'Lochlainn's farm at Glenslade. The Cahermacnaghten farm kept a few sheep, mainly for meat purposes, and this year Cumhal had planned to exchange their ram for one from Donogh's herd. As far as she knew he had gone over to Glenslade as intended.

He looked at her inquiringly now, but there was no sign of any flash of comprehension in his eyes. If the family of Glenslade knew anything of this second death, they, like the basket maker's family, were not speaking about it.

'Becan, the uncle of Iarla from Aran, has been murdered, and in just the same way as his nephew. I think he was killed some time early yesterday morning and I want to question the basket maker's boys. I have a feeling that they did see the body of Iarla long before it was discovered by Fachtnan and Nuala. It's possible that the same thing happened yesterday and that they were the first to see the body of Becan.'

Cumhal nodded. He was a man of few words, but she saw a slight look of puzzlement in his eyes. He was wondering what this was to do with him.

'I think that I would like to question those boys, but they are uneasy and silent while their father is around. So I thought I would send you over to fetch them and bring them over here so that I could talk to them away from the parents. What do you think?'

Cumhal considered the matter for a moment. 'Just have one of them over here, Brehon, I'd say. If you question two or three of them, they'll be looking at each other and if one of them tells you something, he will be wondering whether the others will report back to their father.'

'You're right,' said Mara enthusiastically. 'We'll just have the eldest then. What can we use as an excuse?'

'Excuse?' Brigid had come across, full of curiosity to see what was happening. She had probably guessed that something was wrong from Nuala's gloomy face.

'I'm doing what you suggested, Brigid. I'm getting my witnesses to come over to me, rather than me going to them. So what can I use for an excuse to summon the basket maker's eldest son over here?'

Brigid sniffed. 'Your father wouldn't have bothered looking for an excuse. He'd have just sent a message. Still –' she couldn't resist the appeal to her inventiveness – 'I suppose you could pretend that we need some more apple baskets. And there's not a word of a lie about that, so help me, God! The ones we have are all breaking up. It's the fault of the lads. They will overload them and then dump them down on the floor of the cabin with no care, just showing off to each other how strong they are.'

'That's a good idea.' Mara seized on this enthusiastically. 'That would make a good excuse to bring him over. We'll have some smaller baskets made from heavier materials. Take the cob for him to ride on, Cumhal, so that we don't have to delay him too long. He could look at all of our baskets, the turf ones, also. And he could advise about thickness and everything like that. The only problem is that Dalagh might wonder why I haven't asked him.'

'I'll say that you wanted this boy to come. I don't need to give any explanations.'

Cumhal, like Brigid, was very conscious of Mara's status in the community and now he sounded quite confident that the approach would work. In his view it would be outrageous for the basket maker to question the Brehon's wish in any way. She watched him with affection as he went instantly to the stable shouting for Séan as he went. He probably already had a myriad of other tasks lined up for the day, but her word was always law to him.

Ardal O'Lochlainn came in the gate soon after Cumhal, leading the cob, had disappeared around the corner to the Kilcorney road.

'I met Cumhal,' he said as he dismounted, handing the reins of his handsome stallion to Donie who looked honoured to have such a fine horse under his care.

Mara smiled a welcome. 'Come inside, Ardal, come into the schoolhouse. I've sent all of my scholars out on errands so we will have it to ourselves.' She did not answer his unspoken question.

'I was wondering if you wanted me to go and see the king and tell him about the latest death.' He followed her into the schoolhouse.

'That's been already done, thank you, Ardal.'

'So Cumhal is going to Kilcorney. What about . . .?' He looked at her inquisitively, and then finished by saying, 'What about the burial?'

Mara had a feeling that was not the question that he intended to ask, but she answered readily.

'I'm waiting until I hear from the king, but my feeling is that the body has to be sent back to Aran. This man has a wife and family over there. It was different with Iarla.'

'Well, if you need anyone to escort the body, Brehon, I would be at your service.'

'Thank you, Ardal; I'm very grateful to you. And thank you for lending your gelding yesterday. Would it be possible for you to lead it back with you or would you prefer if I sent a man over with it later on?'

He took the hint, rising immediately. He had not asked after his niece, Mara noticed, and she was determined not to mention Nuala's name unless he did.

Cumhal was back quite soon afterwards. He must have ridden at a fine speed along the road to Kilcorney and negotiations had been conducted with the basket maker at quite a quick, decisive pace.

The eldest son of the basket maker was a fine boy, thought Mara as she came out to meet and greet him. He had an intelligent face with finely moulded bones – no sign of lack of feeding or lack of care in his well-formed body and bold eyes.

'This is Danann, Brehon,' said Cumhal, carefully polite. His eyes showed an appreciation of this youth and of his bearing.

'Perhaps Danann would like a cup of ale and some honey cakes before you bring him to see your requirements for apple baskets?' queried Mara.

Cumhal immediately nodded and with a quick, 'I'll see to that, Brehon,' he left her alone with Danann.

'Come in,' said Mara, walking directly into the schoolhouse. He followed her; she knew he would do so. He would have been trained to automatic obedience from a very early age.

'What passes between us now, Danann, will stay between us.' Mara's tone was confident and matter-of-fact and she kept her eyes fixed on the boy and a friendly smile on her face. 'You are old enough to know that there are certain things that adults feel that children can't handle. I can understand and I'm sure that you also can understand that your father did not want you, or any of your brothers, involved in this affair of the murder of the man from Aran.'

He kept his eyes fixed upon her. He did not answer – not even to nod, but she felt that he understood her point and that he was not afraid.

'I think last Thursday, you, or perhaps it was one of your brothers, saw the ravens hovering over the spot where the dead body of Iarla, the young man from Aran, lay murdered.'

She stopped there and eyed him in a friendly, straightforward way. He said nothing for a moment, but then, eventually, nodded.

'I was the one that noticed them,' he said.

'And went over there?' Purposely her question came quickly – she wanted to catch him off-guard, to jerk him into telling the matter as it really occurred, to give him no time to consider his father's attitude.

'Yes,' he said, the word spurting from him as if beyond his control.

'And then you went back and told your father?'

'Yes.' This time the word was steadier. He was an intelligent boy. He knew that he had gone too far now. He had to see the matter out.

'And he was alarmed?'

Danann took his time to think about this, to turn the matter around, to explain the situation to someone like the Brehon, who could not be expected to understand the life of someone like his father.

'He was worried,' he said eventually. He looked at her and his gaze was very direct, very honest. 'He wasn't worried because he had anything to do with it, but he was worried because of . . .'

And then he was silent and she got the impression that he was searching for words, searching to explain something to her that he had never formulated even in the secret depths of his own mind.

'You see, Brehon,' he said eventually. 'We are very poor. And we depend on goodwill to make a living.' He stopped again and Mara nodded gently.

'I understand,' she said. 'You are dependent on the O'Lochlainn for the lease of the sally gardens and of your cottage.'

'Not just that.' He frowned a little as if she had failed to understand him. 'We are dependent on everyone. People could make their own baskets, you know. There is no great skill in it, just a lot of hard work. But people say, "Look at Dalagh and his wife and their family, they have no farm, no land, no cattle. Those children will starve if they can't sell the baskets." And then they decide: "We'll buy the baskets from them and this will save us the trouble of making our own and we will feel that we have done a good deed."' He frowned again. 'It's not that they actually say this, Brehon, but that's what is behind it.'

'I understand,' said Mara again. She felt a quick rush of admiration for this boy. In a different circumstance he could have made a fine scholar. That had been very well expressed. 'Your father felt that he didn't want to cause any trouble. He knew that Iarla of Aran had come on a very unpopular errand and that many people would have been glad that he had disappeared.' Her mind went quickly to the sullen, disappointed Donogh of Glenslade and his bright happy son, Donogh Óg, and then strayed over to Ardal at Lissylisheen, contented in his work, in his relationship with his brother and his brother's children. And then her mind went back to Teige, blazing with anger at the insult to his daughter.

'And of course, there was another reason to avoid drawing any connection between the dead man and the basket maker's family.' She eyed him very closely, uncertain as to the extent of the family's knowledge on this subject. 'On St Patrick's Night, when he arrived from Aran, Iarla danced for a long time with your sister Orlaith. This was after your parents had left, but people do gossip . . .' Purposely she allowed her sentence to tail out into silence and she watched him closely. There was no doubt that he was dismayed at her acquaintance with this matter. He thought for a moment and then raised his chin.

'The word was that it was the daughter of the O'Brien who was being courted by Iarla of Aran,' he said courageously, and she warmed to him even more because of that courage and his family loyalty.

'I know all about that,' she said brusquely. 'But I also know that when Mairéad O'Lochlainn took Saoirse up to her mother, Iarla turned his attentions towards another girl and that this girl was your sister Orlaith.'

Now he looked alarmed. He didn't challenge her statement, just looked worried and suddenly rather young and out of his depth.

'Don't worry.' Mara put a hand on his arm. 'I mean no harm to any of you, but I must have the truth. Sit down here by the fire.'

She went to the door and opened it. It was as if she had sent a signal. Brigid immediately appeared at the door of the kitchen house, a tray in her hand. Mara waited as Brigid crossed the cobbled yard with her quick footsteps and then took the tray from her. Brigid, she knew, would tell Cumhal that young Danann would not be joining him yet. I'm blessed with such tactful servants, thought Mara as, with a quick smile at Brigid, she closed the door behind her.

'Have some ale,' she said solicitously. 'And a honey cake.'

Danann ate and drank heartily and seemed glad of the break in the questioning and she allowed a comfortable silence to develop between them until she saw the wary look go from his eyes. He looked around the schoolhouse with interest, eyeing the solid oaken benches and tables, the ink horns and the trays of well-sharpened quills, and the shelves of the wooden press filled with scrolls and leather-bound books. It must seem a strange life to him, the life that her boys led, with their clean, smooth hands and their carefree shouts as they galloped over the Burren on their ponies. Their study of books, memorizing of law texts and continual sharpening of their wits would seem, perhaps, a luxurious existence to him.

'Can you read, Danann?' Mara asked the question with interest. There was something about the way that his eyes scanned the books that aroused her curiosity.

He smiled reminiscently. 'A little, Brehon. When I was serving on the altar as a seven-year-old the priest here at Kilcorney taught me my letters. I can read a bit, but I never progressed.' He paused for a moment, then added with dignity, 'Myself and the priest of that time fell out.'

'I'm not surprised.' Mara said no more. She had vivid memories of the former priest of Kilcorney and she would not wish any vulnerable child to have fallen into his clutches. It was a shame that his studies had been interrupted, but she applauded his spirit and his courage. Perhaps there was something that she could do she thought, but then dismissed the matter. What she needed to concentrate on now was the issue of these two deaths. She gave a quick nod and then turned back to him.

'So Iarla came up to Kilcorney to see your sister, Orlaith, was that?' Mara made her voice sound casual.

Outside there was a sudden, heavy shower, sweeping in from the Atlantic. She got up and closed the shutters, threw another log of pinewood on to the fire, but all the time, she kept an unobtrusive eye on the boy's face.

'No,' he said when she had resumed her seat, 'that was not the way of it at all. Not that morning. The first I saw of him that Thursday morning –' he paused looking suddenly rather appalled – 'well, he was already dead when I saw him that time and it was not long after sunrise then – about an hour perhaps, but no more.'

Not that morning, noted Mara, but there were other questions to ask first.

'You were the one who found the body. Is that right?'

'Me and two of my brothers.' His reply was brief; his face tense and worried.

'Did you touch him?'

This time he just nodded.

'Was he stiff?' Mara asked.

Again he nodded.

'And his eye had been gouged out?'

He flinched at that as he nodded and then took a large bite

from a honey cake to hide his reaction. Mara also took one of the tempting small cakes from the wooden platter and crunched it in unison.

'Nice,' he said, and she returned his grin.

'Brigid is a great cook,' she remarked nonchalantly. And then she carelessly added, 'Did you go for your father straight away?'

'That's right. He had gone in to the cottage to talk to my mother about the size of some of the red willow rods. When he came out we told him. We waited because we thought he wouldn't want the girls to know.'

He was relaxed and at ease with her now. Danann could not be much more than Moylan's age, she thought, but his life had been a hard one and it had given him a spurious maturity.

'And why did he tell you all to say nothing? To leave the body lying there on the earth! Why did he do that? I wonder.'

'We kept the ravens away.' This time Danann sounded uncomfortable.

'But why not send someone to me, or to the physician, or to your *taoiseach*? The O'Lochlainn would have come instantly.'

'Father said that it was Balor who had killed him and we shouldn't meddle.' His voice held a slight hint of amusement in it.

Mara smiled broadly. 'But you didn't believe that, did you? Not at your age!'

Danann put the remains of the honey cake into his mouth and swallowed it down with a large gulp of ale.

'Have another.' Mara pushed the platter towards him, saying rapidly, almost to herself, 'I suppose your father didn't want to get mixed up in the affair. After all, everyone knew that this Iarla from Aran had claimed to be the *taoiseach*'s son and that the *taoiseach* wasn't happy about it.'

'No one believed that he was the son of *himself*.' His answer was brief and slightly muffled by a mouthful of cake. 'It's like Liam the steward was saying . . . There was no way that the man from Aran was an O'Lochlainn. He hadn't the look of them, nor the way of them . . .'

Fineguth, finechruth, finebés, thought Mara. The clansmen of the Burren were not lawyers, but a knowledge of the law lay deep in their bones; it was the rule by which their lives were led in peace with their families and their neighbours.

'So your father thought that his *taoiseach* might be annoyed if he interfered in this matter?'

Danann fidgeted slightly, breaking his cake into crumbs, but he did not deny this.

'And, of course,' continued Mara, 'Iarla had come to see Orlaith on Wednesday and your father was cross about that. Most people knew by then what had happened to the O'Brien's daughter on St Patrick's Night and no father would want a man who behaved as Iarla did to come courting his daughter. He sent him away then, I suppose, and told Orlaith to have nothing to do with him. That was the way with it, wasn't it?'

'That's right.' Danann said the words with a cheerful recklessness. No doubt he had decided that he might as well make a full confession. He glanced over to the door as if wondering when he would do the job that he had been asked here to do.

'Just one more thing.' Mara followed the direction of his gaze and smiled reassuringly at him. 'I just wondered why no one discovered the body of Becan yesterday. You couldn't have failed to see the ravens. Did any of you go over to Balor's Cave?'

'No, we didn't,' said Danann. 'My father told us not to, to mind our own business. He got the notion that the body of Iarla had been dug up in the night by Balor and put back outside the cave. I don't know whether he thought that would frighten us, but none of us argued with him anyway. Sooner or later someone would come, that's what I said to myself. And of course, it was yourself, Brehon.'

'That was all very helpful to me, Danann,' said Mara, rising to her feet and rummaging along the shelf of the press. 'Here, take this bag, put the rest of the cakes in it. There should be enough for one for each of your brothers and sisters.'

'I promise not to eat them on the way home.'

He had an easy grin on his face and she responded by saying, 'And I promise that everything you have told me will remain a secret between us both.'

He looked grateful for that and she took the opportunity, as they walked towards the door together, of saying, 'I'd say that it's all nonsense about Balor and that cave being owned by him, wouldn't you?'

He shrugged, but, boy-like, could not resist a boast. 'It's just a cave like any other cave, Brehon. My brothers and I took candles in one night and explored it. We went back quite a long way and found no Balor!'

Eleven

Crích Gablach
(Ranks in Society)

The lowest grade of king has an honour price of 42 séts and he has direct control only over his own kingdom. A king who has control over three kingdoms has an honour price of 48 séts and can be called a great king.

The highest king in the land has an honour price of 84 séts. He rules over a province and can be described as a king of great kings.

Fachtnan and Hugh arrived soon after Cumhal had taken Danann back to Kilcorney. They clattered into the courtyard as Mara was searching through her law scrolls. There was no doubt that Turlough would be seriously worried about this second death of a man from Aran. Aran had been part of the kingdom of the Burren for a long time, but it had been an uneasy relationship. In the past before new methods of boat building had become the norm, Aran, with its cockleshell-like *currach* boats made of a wicker frame covered with skins, could be inaccessible for many months of the winter. The small island communities had become accustomed to relying on their own *taoiseach* for government.

'Well, how did you get on?' she asked, turning around.

'Not well,' said Hugh with a disappointed look. 'Though we tried our best,' he added.

''I think it was probably all right, Hugh,' said Fachtnan quietly. 'We probably found out what the Brehon had guessed.'

'And what was that?'

Despite her worries about Aran, Mara smiled. She enjoyed her boys, watching and guiding their growing personalities and their active minds was one of the chief pleasures of her position. Fachtnan never disappointed her when it came to an understanding of people.

'Well, no one had seen any sign of Iarla from Aran, on that Thursday morning,' Fachtnan told her.

Mara nodded and a quick smile flickered over Fachtnan's face.

'We questioned everyone we could find,' he continued. 'Even the man who went out to the fields in Ballyganner south to check on the cows. He went out there just after sunset and spent about half an hour going from field to field.'

'And he would definitely have seen Iarla if he had come down from Noughaval,' said Hugh. 'So we can be almost certain that Iarla did not come to Lemeanah that morning. We've checked as much as possible.' Hugh sounded more cheerful.

'Well done, boys. A good lawyer always checks facts as painstakingly as possible and that is what you've been doing this morning.'

'And that's not all,' said Fachtnan generously. 'You'll be very pleased with Hugh because he found out something very interesting from one of the serving girls.'

'I had to give her a kiss before she'd tell me.' Hugh was half laughing, but half embarrassed. Mara was glad that neither Moylan nor Aidan were present.

'She heard us asking questions of the guardsmen in the gatehouse so she called Hugh out to look at the new foal,' explained Fachtnan.

'Anyway,' said Hugh, his cheeks turning slightly pink, 'she told me that Teige O'Brien had given orders to the guardsmen and the porter that Iarla was not to be allowed in the gates of Lemeanah on any account.'

'And what's interesting,' broke in Fachtnan, 'is Teige told them that they were to tell no one that he had given that order.'

'He threatened the guardsmen – this is what they told her – that he would string them up if they disobeyed his instructions in any way.' Hugh finished his story with a dramatic flourish.

'Did he give the men any reason why they should not say that he gave that order?' asked Mara. She rather discounted the threat to string up the men, but the very fact that Teige had uttered it showed that he was taking this matter seriously.

'He just said that he didn't want to offend the O'Lochlainn, but he was not going to have that *ambue* put even a big toe inside the gate to Lemeanah.'

'I see,' said Mara thoughtfully. That word, *ambue*, had been an interesting word to use, she thought. It was not often heard these days, but it meant alien or outsider. Why did Teige use that expression and why was he, despite his wish not to offend Ardal O'Lochlainn in any way, so anxious to ensure that Iarla from Aran did not come near his house again? Saoirse had been kept in close captivity – not even allowed out to groom her horse, Mairéad had said that – not until Iarla had been murdered and then relationships between father and daughter were restored to their normal friendliness. Saoirse had been allowed to gallop out with Fachtnan and Enda and to ride unescorted over to the law school, with Teige's full blessing, last Monday.

'That's excellent work, boys.' Mara picked up the notes and made a pretence of scanning through them, though her mind was too active to take in everything. 'Now go and see Brigid. She'll give you something to eat, or perhaps you can have your dinner a little early.'

'Enda and Aidan are coming now,' said Hugh. 'That was quick. I suppose there are not many houses on their route. May we stay and listen?'

'Of course,' said Mara warmly. She had caught a glimpse of Enda's and Aidan's faces as they dismounted from their ponies and she could tell from the subdued looks that they, also, had found no trace of their quarry.

'Did you pick up the trail?' Hugh asked the question almost as if he had read her mind.

'Not a sign of him anywhere,' said Aidan in an annoyed way. 'We stopped at every house and questioned them. We made a list for you, Brehon. No one had seen him on that morning. In fact, no one had seen him since St Patrick's Night at Lemeanah.'

'We did just get one piece of information for you, Brehon,' said Enda, delving into his satchel and producing a roll of vellum. 'I questioned the priest's housekeeper quite a bit as it seemed to me, with just one man to look after, that she would have a lot of spare time on her hands.'

'Well done,' said Mara approvingly. 'I should have thought of that myself. She's a gossiping sort of woman too. I've often noticed her if I go to Mass at Kilcorney. She always seems to be in a huddle with some other women and she's always whispering very loudly. So there you are, boys,' she ended lightly. 'That's a valuable piece of legal information for you: women in a cluster, whispering, and looking over their shoulders, usually mean that a juicy piece of gossip is being exchanged.'

Fachtnan, she noticed with amusement, was regarding her with a quiet smile while Aidan and Hugh stared, their mouths slightly open. Enda gave a quick, matter-of-fact, businesslike nod before inscrolling his vellum.

'Unfortunately, it's not about Iarla, but about Becan,' he began.

'Go on,' said Mara, her interest sharpened.

'Well, apparently, as far as she could tell, by continually strolling down the road between the church, the sally gardens and Balor's Cave, Becan never left that area for the whole of Sunday.'

'The day before he was killed.' Fachtnan sounded thoughtful.

Enda nodded. 'That's right. And he wasn't saying his prayers either, those are her words,' he said, reading from his vellum sheet.

'What did she think that he was doing, Enda?'

'She didn't know, Brehon. He just seemed to be wandering around. He would be missing for a while and then he would turn up again and then he would disappear again, but never for long enough to go anywhere in particular. In the end, she invited him to come in and have a cup of buttermilk, but he refused.'

'Wanted to get it out of him what he was up to, I suppose,' Aidan commented with an air of satisfaction at his own sharpness.

'Well, it didn't work. He just went on appearing and disappearing.'

'That's very interesting.' Mara said no more, but the picture of Becan's boots came to her mind's eye.

'Here come Moylan and Shane.' Aidan made a dash for the doorway and then came back in a moment, announcing with satisfaction, 'I bet that they haven't found anything either. They don't look too pleased.'

Moylan and Shane had done good, thorough work with every house and farm on their route methodically checked off and clear, well-written notes of the names of all who had been questioned. Mara went through the vellum carefully and praised the script and the careful methodical layout of the notes, but Aidan was right. They had found no sign of Iarla on the fields and the back lanes leading from Lissylisheen to Lemeanah.

It looked as if the young man from Aran had eaten his breakfast on that fateful morning of the Thursday the twentieth of March and had then disappeared into thin air.

Mara brooded over it for a minute and then lifted her head to find that the six boys were watching her expectantly.

'You've all done extremely well,' she said warmly. 'I'm lucky to have you. Now I think that you should all go and have your dinner. Brigid will be waiting for you.'

When they were gone, she stood very still for a moment. Things had not been going well with this investigation, she thought, and the fault had been hers. This pregnancy was hampering her, slowing her movements, making her cautious, filling her with unaccustomed doubts and fears. She straightened herself, feeling the baby kick vigorously and then she smiled, a warm feeling flowing through her body. This baby, this boy – she allowed herself, in private, the certainty that it was a little boy – he would be a son of warriors. There was no need for her to hunch over him, to cosset him. She would be sensible, but she would be herself.

She knew now what she must do. The last strands had to be woven into place and then she could solve the case of this double murder that had stained the honour of the Burren. The culprit had to be brought to justice and made to declare his sin at Poulnabrone.

Energetically she strode across the room and pulled open the door, feeling the vigour coursing through her as she closed it behind her.

'Cumhal,' she called. 'What do you think that the weather is going to do for the next few days?'

Cumhal put down his axe and cast a glance at the sky above, then turned his gaze towards the Aran Islands.

'It promises fine, Brehon,' he said eventually. He licked a calloused finger and held it up, turning it slowly around. 'Not much of a wind,' he said with satisfaction, 'but what wind there is comes from the east. I wouldn't be surprised if we'd have three or four days of fine weather ahead of us.'

'Two days will do me,' said Mara merrily. 'I'm relying on you, Cumhal, mind.'

He smiled in return. He was a noted weather prophet and men came from miles around to consult him at haymaking time. He looked a bit curious; no doubt puzzling over the reason for her question, but Mara did not enlighten him. She would have to talk to Turlough first.

Turlough did not arrive until the end of afternoon school for the boys. Mara was relieved at that as she liked to make sure that she did not interrupt their teaching hours too often. When he did arrive, she saw the reason for the delay. He was followed by a small troop of men-at-arms.

'You can go now, boys,' she said quietly. Through the open shutter of the window she studied Turlough's face. It had a grim look, she decided. No doubt he was worried about his relationship with the Aran Island people after this double murder. She would have to take this burden from him. As soon as the guilty person was named and the fine paid, then the islanders could settle back again into their happy relationship with their king.

'The O'Lochlainn, *himself*, is here too.' Shane's dark head popped back in through the door, with Hugh's red head peering over his shoulder. They both looked excited as they stood aside to allow her out. The sight of those armed men, with their swords by their sides, their shields on their backs and their jackcoats made from boiled leather, shining in the sunshine, thrilled all of the boys. Despite tempting smells from the kitchen house, none of them had yet gone in for supper.

Mara stood back for a moment. Ardal had jumped off his horse, thrown the reins to Liam and approached Turlough, standing in front of him with bended head, as one who pays homage to his chieftain. Their conversation was low and she did not move nearer in order to hear what was been said. She glanced again up at the blue March sky with its strengthening sun that was bringing back a glow of green to the browns of winter and then she walked over towards the kitchen house.

'The king will be having supper with me tonight, Brigid,' she said. 'Have you got something nice for him? He'll need a good meal. It's always good for him to eat well when he's worried.'

'There's some venison in the north cabin there that is just ready for eating up.' Brigid had obviously decided on this matter already. 'I'll make a wine sauce to go with it. Or would a plain cream sauce be best for you?'

'Tonight,' said Mara gaily, 'I'm going to drink wine. I'm going to celebrate being pregnant at thirty-six, and I'm going to celebrate being married to the King of Thomond, Corcomroe and Burren, and tomorrow, Brigid –' she eyed her housekeeper in a way she tried to make seem commanding – 'tomorrow, Brigid, I am going to the Aran Islands with the king.'

Well, that went well, she thought with an amused grin as she walked across to the two men. Turlough leaped from his horse when he saw her coming and wrapped her in a warm hug. She smiled, her face against his bulky chest, thinking how, for such a large, rather clumsy man, he was so careful and gentle with his hugs these days. This child in her womb had made their relationship very close and very real.

'I was saying to my lord, Brehon,' said Ardal as soon as she had disentangled herself. 'I was saying that there is no need at all for him to go to Aran. I and Liam will accompany the body of Becan back to his home place.'

'I think that both men should be returned home,' said Mara, casting a quick look at Turlough.

'I agree,' he said immediately. 'Both men should go back. Aran was their birthplace and, the Lord have mercy on them, Aran should be their final resting place.'

'Very well,' said Ardal. Immediately his practical, organizing mind took over. 'You'll be able to see to that, Liam, won't you?'

'Of course, my lord, there'll be no problem. The man has only been in the ground for a few days. Two men with picks and we'll have him up in a few minutes.' Liam, like his master, was matter-of-fact and sensible about this. He could have been talking about a clump of turnips, thought Mara.

'We'll take the two bodies on the ferry,' continued Ardal. 'That's the largest boat.'

'No,' said Turlough stubbornly. 'I want to go. You're welcome to come too, Ardal, if that's the way that you want it. But I must go myself.'

He glared around as if expecting opposition and then gave a slight start when Mara said firmly, 'You're quite right, my lord, you should go yourself. This is an important matter.' She looked carefully at the two men and then said mildly, 'On the other hand, Ardal, I don't think that you should go. You've been too connected with this matter. Too many accusations have been made against you. For you to arrive at Aran with two dead bodies, one of a man who claimed to be your son, and the other of a man who accused you of the murder of that man – well, that would be bound to inflame tempers.' She held up one hand solemnly – although he had said nothing – and continued. 'No, Ardal. You must not go. It is right and fitting that the king go and it is right and fitting that I, as King's Brehon and his representative of all matters concerning law and order, here in the Burren, should go.'

Turlough's craggy face broke into a smile while Ardal looked uncertain and Liam horrified.

'But, Brehon . . .' he said, breaking into the conversation and then abruptly ceasing, having decided, no doubt, that it was not his place to interfere.

'There will be no problems,' said Mara firmly. 'I have taken advice about the weather and I have heard from a very reliable source . . .' Here her eyes slid across the courtyard to where Cumhal had just emerged from the cool cabin with a haunch of venison in his hand. 'From an extremely reliable source,' she repeated, 'that it is promised fine with very little wind for the next few days. The king and I will make the crossing tomorrow morning with the two bodies and his men-at-arms and we will spend the following night on the island and return on Thursday.'

'Are you sure?' asked Turlough quietly.

'Of course I am sure.' Mara nodded happily. 'I will enjoy seeing the island again. I'm feeling so well these days,' she went on. 'I'm full of energy and I will enjoy a day out. This visit is overdue. The islanders should meet your new wife as soon as possible.'

'It wouldn't be wiser to postpone your visit until after the birth?'

Ardal put the question with such deference and such genuine concern on his handsome face that Mara could not feel offended.

'You forget,' she said quietly, 'that I am Brehon of Aran as much as Brehon of the Burren. I owe them my presence now at this time. The king and I must go.'

'I wish there was something that I could do.'

There was a regretful look in his blue eyes and Mara took pity on him.

'There is much that you can do,' she said immediately. 'We will leave all arrangements for the bodies in your hands and there is also another matter. We have no accommodation here at Cahermacnaghten for the men-at-arms and the night will probably be frosty. If you could take them back to Lissylisheen and put them up for the night in your hall or guardroom then we will be very grateful to you.'

'If you're sure that it is no trouble, Ardal.' Turlough bestowed a warm smile on Ardal who responded immediately with his usual courtesy.

'It will be a pleasure, my lord. And you can rely on me to make all arrangements. I will send a messenger to Doolin to the ferryman and ask him to have another boat ready for the coffins.'

Mara did not argue. She did not believe the old superstition that it was bad luck to travel across the sea with a dead man, but this would mean that there was plenty of room on board the ferry.

She joined her thanks to Turlough's and watched Ardal leave, while looking speculatively at her six scholars still clustered around the men-at-arms. Enda had persuaded one to lend him a sword and he was gracefully fighting his own shadow on the whitewashed wall of the enclosure. Shane was holding a shield almost as big as himself and Aidan was running his finger along the blade of the battleaxe slung across the back of a brawny soldier. Turlough followed the direction of her eyes with an amused, indulgent look.

'I suppose you want those boys of yours to come too.' He heaved an exaggerated sigh, but she was not deceived. Turlough loved a crowd and he had fun with her scholars.

'I think it would be good for their legal training, if you have no objection, my lord,' she said demurely.

'Oh, well, if it's a question of their legal training . . .' Turlough's light-green eyes were amused. He raised his voice in a bellow that would have done credit to any battlefield.

'Boys, come over here.'

They came instantly. None looked alarmed. They knew him well.

'My lord.' Enda had handed back the sword and crossed the court-yard in the blink of an eye.

'The Brehon thinks that it is essential for your legal training to cross over to Aran tomorrow. Do you think she's right? Surely you'd be better off staying here and studying your books – isn't that right?'

Enda bowed low. 'My lord, Fithail says "to walk a land is to know that land".'

Turlough tried to keep a serious face, but the tips of his warlike moustache twitched. Mara cast a sceptical eye in Enda's direction. Personally she had not heard of that particular saying of Fithail, though the sage had been a very prolific hander-out of pithy axioms a few hundred years previously.

'Well, in that case,' said Turlough eventually, 'since Fithail advises that, perhaps we will take you all.'

'Thank you, my lord.' The young voices tumbled over each other.

'And thank you, Brehon,' said Fachtnan.

'Let's go and tell Brigid,' suggested Hugh. 'Shall I ask her to get ready some baskets of food for us for tomorrow, Brehon?'

'That's a good idea,' said Mara approvingly.

There was an inn at Doolin but it probably served more liquid than solid refreshments. The boys would have keen appetites with the sea breeze and Brigid's food would fill the empty stomachs until they found their night's lodgings.

'Let's hope that they're not all seasick,' said Turlough with pretend gloom as the boys ran off towards the kitchen house.

'No one is seasick if they believe they won't be,' said Mara in absent-minded tones. She was thinking about the island people. There had been a secret and unlawful killing there about six years ago, and the O'Brien, a distant relative of Turlough's, had come to seek her assistance. A body had been washed up on the rocks; an islander and the man had been one of his own workers. No one had admitted to the crime. She had gone across and had done her

best to solve the mystery, but she had been met with a blank wall
of silence. Neighbour had stood by neighbour; nothing was divulged
and nothing could be proved. She had not been summoned since,
though it was against reason to suppose that there had been no
crimes. It seemed as if the people of the eastern island, the smallest
of the Aran Islands, felt able to deal with their own crimes, or else
the O'Brien ruled them with fear of his vengeance.

'Turlough,' she said hesitantly, 'were you thinking of staying with
the O'Brien of Aran?'

'Yes, of course,' he said readily. 'The man owes me *cuid oiche*. I
haven't been there for over a year.'

Mara nodded reluctantly. *Cuid oiche*, a night's lodging, was owed
by all clients to their overlord. Turlough was scrupulously careful to
exact this, not from any meanness, or desire to save his silver, but
because this was one of the lynchpins in the relationship that a king
had with his most noble subjects. A feast would be held, harpers
and bards would attend, and entertain the guests, the talk would go
on late into the night and relationships would be cemented. It was,
she supposed, inevitable that Turlough should stay with his distant
cousin. Aran was a poor place and the inn would find it hard to
provide more than one bedroom for guests. The O'Brien tower
house would be more suitable. And, of course, her boys would thoroughly enjoy the experience – the feasting, the singing, the telling
of tales, the wit and boasting. This was what thrilled adolescent boys.
She listened to their excited voices fondly and then thought of
another young person on the Burren.

'Turlough,' she said thoughtfully, 'do you think that I should take
a physician with me?'

Ardal would have found this alarming, but Turlough, who knew
her well, just grinned. 'You want to take Nuala as well, I suppose,'
he said in tones that he tried to make sound resigned.

'I thought it might be prudent. Do you want to go over to the
Brehon's house now and I'll follow you over after a few minutes.'
Mara didn't wait for an answer, but went across the yard and beck-
oned her farm manager.

'Cumhal, could Seán or one of the other men take a note over
to Caherconnell?'

'Seán can go, Brehon,' said Cumhal firmly.

Seán was presently carrying a basket-load of turf into the kitchen
house, dropping some on the path and, judging from the high-
pitched scolding way that Brigid had just shouted his name, Seán

was also dropping the sods on the freshly washed kitchen-house floor.

'I'll just write the note, then.' Mara repressed a smile.

I really must try to get someone else to help Cumhal, she thought. Seán is just so useless; he's more trouble than he is worth to poor Cumhal. He would have to be retained, of course; his father and his grandfather before him had been employed at Cahermacnaghten. However, perhaps one of the sons of Daniel O'Connor, an ocaire, of Caheridoola on the High Burren, would be old enough now to be employed as extra help. She would see about this as soon as she came back from Aran. She went into the schoolhouse and took down a piece of vellum, a horn of ink and a pen from the shelf of the press.

Cousin Malachy, she wrote in her square italic hand, *'I have to take a journey to Aran with my lord, King Turlough. He feels it would be best if I were to be accompanied by Nuala in case I need any attention on the journey and while at the island.*

I would be grateful if she could be here at Cahermacnaghten shortly after sunrise.

Your affectionate cousin,
Mara, Brehon of the Burren.

That should do it, she thought. It doesn't really give him any option of refusing. After all, who could refuse a king's desire? Not even Caireen with her dislike of Nuala could interfere in this. She rolled up the scroll and went out in high good humour. Seán was taking the cob out of the stables, Brigid was shouting merrily in the kitchen and the boys were responding with guffaws of raucous laughter. Cumhal was smiling to himself as he dipped his bristle brush into a pot of limewash and began the spring work of whitewashing the schoolhouse. He was a quick, neat worker and Mara knew that by the time she came back from Aran each of the five buildings, the schoolhouse, the scholars' house, the kitchen house, the guesthouse and his own house, as well as all of the small cabins, would be shining an immaculate white.

'Don't stop, Cumhal,' Mara said hastily as she saw him about to put down his brush. 'I'll talk while you paint.' She waited until he resumed his even strokes of the brush before continuing. 'It was just that I was thinking that perhaps Seán could drive myself and the six scholars, and young Nuala, to Doolin shortly after sunrise tomorrow morning.

'The king, and the men-at-arms, will have their horses, of course,

and these will take up most of the space in the hold of the ferry-
boat and I don't want to leave my mare and the boys' ponies at
Doolin.' She didn't bother informing Cumhal that she was going to
Aran. He would know that already. He would have overheard everything that passed between Ardal, Turlough and herself, though, like
a good servant, he would have not appeared to hear.

'I'd prefer to drive you myself, Brehon,' he said respectfully but
firmly.

'Whatever you think best, Cumhal,' said Mara meekly. 'Could you
tell Brigid that I am going over to the Brehon's house now? There's
no hurry about supper for the king. She can serve it whenever it
suits her.' She would avoid Brigid for the moment, she decided. The
surprise announcement that she was going on the sea journey to
Aran had momentarily robbed Brigid of speech, but, no doubt, by
now she would have recovered. 'King Turlough and I have matters
to discuss,' she ended grandly, though at the moment her plan was
to lie on her bed for a half an hour or so and recover her energies
enough to enjoy her meal with Turlough.

'What are we going to tell the people of Aran?' asked Turlough,
draining his wine and leaning back in his splendid chair. He replaced
her precious Venetian glass on the white linen cloth with a slight
bang to give his words emphasis.

Mara cast a quick, worried glance at him. Turlough was the soul
of honour and he hated the feeling that there would be resentment
in Aran, that there would be a feeling that they, his island subjects,
were of less importance than the people of Burren, Corcomroe and
Thomond.

'Here comes the venison.' Mara found that her sense of smell was
much stronger since her pregnancy. Turlough turned towards the
door with an air of anticipation and then the kitchen door opened
and the quick, light footsteps of Brigid came down the passageway
followed by the heavier tread of Cumhal.

'Well, Brigid, a man would die for a meal like that,' he said enthusiastically, eyeing the slices of venison, crusty on the outside and
pink on the inside. Cumhal had two dishes of roasted roots and
Turlough made the appreciative noises of a man who had been
starving for days.

Mara waited patiently while Brigid heaped up both platters and
placed an extra dollop of a cream sauce on hers. Even after Cumhal
and Brigid had left the room, she delayed answering until Turlough

had almost emptied his plate. She poured herself a very small amount of extra wine into her glass and then passed him the rest of her food.

'You eat this. I don't want to get too fat,' she said. And then while his mouth was full, she said quietly, 'I don't think you should say anything. I think we should let the two funerals take place, show the utmost respect during them, have your men-at-arms line the roadway to the graveyard, both of us will attend, walking behind the mourners and then we will ask your relation to call a meeting and I will speak to the people. You say nothing; I will say it all for you.'

Twelve

Críth Gablach
(Ranks in Society)

A king has many clients. These clients hold the land for the king and swear:
1. *to pay rent and tribute to their overlord,*
2. *to escort him in public assemblies, to offer hospitality to the king and his household,*
3. *to bring his own warriors to each slógad and, in the last hour of the king, to assist in digging the grave mound and to contribute to the death feast.*

Cumhal had been right with his weather forecast, thought Mara happily. The sun rose steadily from an azure sky on that Wednesday morning. There was a very slight wind, more a current of air than the usual winds so common here on the western Atlantic coast and the grey-blue smoke from the chimney of the kitchen house drifted gently like a plume from a helmet. Despite the light wind, the air was still crisp with the overnight frost still silvering the new blades of grass.

'Here come my men,' said Turlough, joining her at the gate to the law school. His ear was acute; it was only after he had spoken that she heard the clatter of horse hoofs.

'Have you had breakfast?' she asked when they arrived and dismounted hastily, bowing to the king and to her.

'Yes, Brehon,' said the leader respectfully. 'The O'Lochlainn gave us a fine breakfast.'

'Poor Ardal, he would have liked to come. I'd say that he is very disappointed,' said Turlough, turning to walk by Mara's side as she made her way towards the kitchen house. 'He was telling Teige how much he would have liked to come. Liam told me that.'

The scholars were up early, dressed in snowy-white *léinte*, well-brushed cloaks, each fastened at the neck with a brooch and boots polished to high shine.

'I wouldn't eat all that breakfast, if I were you,' said Turlough, surveying them with a look of mock ferocity. 'I don't want to see bowlfuls of porridge and honey and slices of dried apple being vomited over the railings at some stage during the next few hours.'

'None of my scholars will be seasick,' said Mara serenely. 'It is forbidden to any scholar from Cahermacnaghten to suffer from this silly sensation.'

'I suppose I was about the age of young Moylan when I first went to Aran. Teige and I went over together,' said Turlough, smiling at the memory as he and Mara strolled across the yard to where Cumhal was checking the seats of the wagon.

It was not often used, but every autumn Cumhal painted it with a dark-red lead paint and now it gleamed in the early spring sunshine. Mara put her hand on it. Although it was only March, the sun had already warmed the timber.

'I've put a cushion on the seat for you, Brehon. I hope it will be comfortable enough for you.' Cumhal sounded concerned.

Mara hastened to reassure him. However, only half her mind was on the soothing phrases because the other half was busy thinking about what Turlough had said.

Ardal had been disappointed not to be able to accompany his king to Aran, but what about Teige? Why had Teige not offered to be one of the party? He, after all, was Turlough's cousin.

'Mara, is there anything you can tell the Aran Islanders about your investigations into these two murders?' Turlough had waited until Cumhal had gone over to the stables and they were standing outside the gate of the law school. His voice had changed from the playful, light-hearted tones of a few minutes earlier and now there was a deep note of anxiety in it.

Mara made no reply. She stretched up and touched a small bunch of yellow catkins that swung above her head. Her touch was light but a shower of golden dust sprinkled down on to the back of her hand.

'Brigid would say that is good luck,' she said lightly, showing him her hand.

'You haven't answered my question,' he said.

'Only because I was thinking that a belief in good luck is a very useful thing. It can help you to sail through difficult situations when too much thought can weigh you down.'

'I was thinking –' Turlough eyed her tentatively – 'Well, I was just wondering if you could say that you had someone in mind.'

Mara frowned. 'Give a name to them?'

'No, no, not that.' He was taken aback. 'You could say that you are not at liberty to disclose the name until the matter is dealt with at Poulnabrone. You could just imply, not say anything . . . just imply . . .'

'I don't think that I would do that.' Her tone was decisive. He was the king, but she was the Brehon. The law was her business and the law said that no suspect should be named in public until he or she had been given a chance to admit to the crime and to promise to pay the fine. As Brehon she was not going to play games with the islanders and allow wrong conclusions to be drawn.

Turlough said nothing. He did not look angry, just disappointed and her heart melted.

'Turlough,' she said, 'at this moment there is probably only one name on the lips of every islander. If the people of Aran think that I am certain of the truth and that I am not naming this man because he is a friend and ally of yours, then things may get violent. I would not like to encourage any private vengeance or any public outcry for a blood feud.'

'You mean Ardal.'

Mara nodded. 'Yes, of course.'

'But that's ridiculous.'

'You say that only because you know Ardal and you trust him. Otherwise it is not ridiculous. Look at the facts. This young man from Aran turns up claiming to be Ardal's son. Ardal does not believe that Iarla is his son; does not believe the mother's sworn deathbed statement. He does not want this lad. What is more probable, to anyone that does not know the man, than that Ardal is the murderer of Iarla.'

'And of the uncle.'

'And of Becan,' agreed Mara. 'It would be very easy to make the case, as we say at the law school. Becan could have seen something, could have known something, could perhaps have confronted Ardal with his suspicions and then he in turn was murdered.'

'But you can't believe that.'

Turlough sounded so aghast that Mara found it difficult not to smile.

'As soon as I am certain of the murderer, I will talk to that person, ask for an admission of guilt. Whether I obtain that confession or not, I will then go to Poulnabrone and tell the people of Burren the truth.'

'And then?'

'And then go, or send a messenger, to Aran to tell the islanders the truth.'

Turlough nodded resignedly and she gave him a quick kiss while no one was looking. For a man who ruled three kingdoms, he was a very easy-going, pleasant husband, she thought.

'Tell me about your cousin Brian,' she said. 'How do you get on with him?'

'Not exactly a cousin. He's just one of the Mac Teiges.'

'Which Teige?' The O'Brien family seemed to lack imagination when it came to picking out names. Down through the generations there were Teiges, Turloughs, Diarmuids, Murroughs and Conors, with the occasional Brian thrown in. No wonder there were so many nicknames among them.

'Teige the bonesplitter,' said Turlough with a grin. 'They all took after him too. No one messes about with any of the Mac Teiges.'

'A very dark man, isn't he, this Brian?' Mara's voice was thoughtful. On her visit to the island she had not formed any great liking for the Lord of Aran. He had been dark of hair, eye and skin, but there had been something dark about his personality too.

'Mother was Spanish,' said Turlough, signalling to his bodyguard, Fergal, to bring over his horse. The soldiers immediately leaped on to their horses and formed a line on the road outside the law school.

'Really? I thought his father was married to one of the MacNamaras.'

'He was, but this Brian is the result of a marriage of the fourth degree. His mother was originally the wife of the captain of a Spanish ship that Brian captured. He took the cargo off the ship and then gave the captain the choice between having his ship back and leaving his wife, or of losing everything. The Spanish captain decided that he'd prefer his ship and the lady herself was quite willing to stay on Aran apparently, so that's where Brian comes from. Brian the Spaniard, as he's known, but not to his face. He doesn't like the name.'

'I see,' said Mara.

She wanted to ask whether Brian the Spaniard was, like his father, a pirate, but Seán had just pushed the wagon so that was drawn up by the gate and Donie was harnessing two horses to it.

'Run down to the crossroads, Aidan,' she called as he and Fachtnan emerged from the kitchen house, wiping their mouths. 'See if Nuala is coming.'

'Here's a bite for the boys to eat.' Brigid came bustling out with a basket full of honey cakes and flat slabs of oatmeal bread. Hugh and Shane followed with some leather flasks of buttermilk and Moylan had a string bag of wrinkled apples. Brigid was not going to allow any of them to go hungry, thought Mara with an amused smile. She was about to get into the wagon when she saw Cumhal had drawn away from the busy scene around the gate and was standing at some distance with his eyes fixed on her.

Immediately Mara went over to him. She knew from his expression that he had something to tell her.

'I just thought you might like to know that the O'Lochlainn and Liam the steward passed here about an hour ago, Brehon,' he said. 'They had the two coffins on the cart.'

'Thank you, Cumhal.'

Mara was glad that he had not said that in front of the boys. Their spirits were high and she loved to see them like this, laughing and joking. The real purpose of their visit would come when they arrived, but she knew that she could trust them to behave decorously at the burial of the two islanders. It was good to know that there had been no problems with the lifting of Iarla's coffin from the graveyard.

'You go first, my lord,' she called to Turlough. 'We'll wait for Nuala and follow you.' Just as well, she thought, to have the boat with the two coffins go first. This would announce their arrival to the islanders and give Brian the Spaniard time to prepare for their arrival. She felt sorry that she was not there to break the news to Becan's widow, but no doubt the Aran man with the boat would be able to do it better. These islanders were very close-knit, reserved people; to them she would be just an outsider.

Nuala arrived just as Mara was beginning to think that they would have to go without her. Despite the sun, it still was only March and the journey would take at least four hours. It would be essential for them to arrive in time for the burial and that would have to take place before daylight ended.

'Sorry,' Nuala said briefly as the eager shouts summoned her to the wagon. She handed her pony to Donie and clambered into the wagon, stepping over the boys' satchels and seating herself between Fachtnan and Shane. Mara cast a quick concerned glance at her. Nuala's dark-brown eyes were deeply shadowed and she looked as though she had slept badly. I'm glad I thought of inviting her, thought Mara, she isn't having a very pleasant life these days. A day out in the boisterous company of the law scholars would do the girl good.

'What do you think will happen at Aran, when we have to tell them that Becan was murdered, as well as Iarla, Brehon?' asked Enda.

'I'm not sure, Enda.' Mara always liked to be frank with her scholars. If they, in their turn, became Brehons they would have to deal with situations where they would have to probe to find the perpetrators of crimes. They would have to cope with doubt and uncertainty and still hold fast to the principles in which they were educated. 'I've prepared a few things to say in my mind,' she added, 'but I will have to wait until I see what their attitude is before I finally decide what I am going to do. Whatever happens, the more information that I can gain about Iarla and Becan, the better my chances are of solving this murder.'

'You remember we did wonder about Becan,' mused Enda. 'Well, it's unlikely that he murdered Iarla now, isn't it?'

'I'd say that Becan was murdered because he found out something about the murder of Iarla, perhaps even found the murderer and accused him.' Moylan leaned over to join in the conversation.

'Could be.' Mara's tone was reserved and she said no more. Enda and she had been speaking in low murmurs, but once Moylan with his loud, adolescent, uncontrolled voice joined in the conversation, everyone would hear. Discussing suspects in the privacy of the school-house was one thing; here on the open road with Cumhal and Nuala listening was another.

'What about a song?' she enquired after a few minutes.

Fachtnan, always a sensitive boy who could interpret silences as well as words, immediately raised his voice in the words of *Is Trua Gan Peata Mhaoir Agam* (*'Tis a pity I haven't the Steward's pet*).

The blackthorn is out here earlier than it is in the Burren, Mara thought, listening to the singing as the wagon trundled its way along the muddy roads of Corcomroe. Nearer the sea, of course. She admired the tiny snow-white blossoms that almost completely masked the black twigs of the bushes. When the wagon paused to allow a man on horseback to cross the road in front of them, she reached out and pulled a cluster off and held it close to her nose. The scent was very faint, quite elusive, but it smelled of a promise of spring. The petals were soft and immaculately white. Unlike the hawthorn, where the cream was mixed with tiny antlers of red powder, these were pure and velvet soft. And then her mind went back to the subject of Becan. Undoubtedly he was killed because he knew too much. But how was it that he had spotted the murderer when she herself was still uncertain. Her mind went back to Enda's evidence from the priest's housekeeper. What had Becan discovered from the cave on that day, she wondered? Judging by the clay on his boots, it was obvious that he had gone into it.

'I see the sea,' shouted Shane as they rounded the corner.

They were back on the limestone land now, with the fields paved with the huge slabs of dark-grey stone and the grykes between the clints crammed with frilly yellow primroses and a few dark-purple violets. The wind was to their backs; nevertheless, the salt tang of the seashore was unmistakable. Even the birds were different; instead of blackbirds and thrushes there were the soaring pale-grey seabirds and the red-legged choughs shouted greetings at each other.

'They've got sail up,' shouted Shane. He lived near to the shores of the Great Lake in the north of Ireland and his summer holidays seemed to be mostly spent in a boat.

That would be the coffin boat, decided Mara. It skimmed lightly across the waves, making little of the weight of the two well-built bodies that lay on its deck. She was glad that it was well ahead of their boat.

'Sit down all of ye.' Cumhal's order was sharp and the boys all obeyed him instantly. 'They've got the king's flag up and flying on the ferry, Brehon.'

'So they have!' Mara smiled as she saw the three lions stretch and snap in the fresh sea breeze. That would have been Ardal's idea, she guessed; Turlough, the most unassuming of men, would not have bothered.

Ardal was still there on the seafront when Cumhal pulled the wagon to a halt. He was talking to Turlough while Liam walked his mare, and Liam's own cob, up and down the path. The men-at-arms and all of the horses had already been loaded on to the boat. They both turned at the rumble of the wagon's wheel and came over towards her.

'You're going to have a great day for your trip, Brehon,' said Ardal as Turlough carefully handed her down from the wagon. She smiled at him, noting the regret in his voice, but she did not speak. There was nothing to be said; Ardal was an intelligent man and she was sure that he had understood her reasons for refusing his offer last night. She stood for a moment, looking around at the busy pier where men loaded baskets and seagulls cried overhead, conscious that feelings of pleasure and of excitement were buoying her up and swamping the tiredness which had so often engulfed her in the last week or so.

'It looks a fine ship,' said Mara.

'It's a caravel,' said Aidan.

'Looks more like a cog to me,' said Shane. 'That's what we call them on the Great Lake. Look, it has only one sail.'

'It's a cog, all right,' said Ardal, smiling at Shane. 'I'm thinking of buying one and getting into the fishing business myself. Liam and I have been talking about it. He's not as keen as I am, but I plan to make a few enquiries.'

'Let's go on board,' said Mara.

Aidan was muttering something uncomplimentary about Liam and his weight to Moylan, but they would be distracted once they were on board. Apart from Shane they were all from inland homes and this was going to be a rare treat for them.

'We'll hoist the sail once we are out of the harbour, my lord,' said the ship's captain to Turlough. He bowed to Mara. 'We could rig up a shelter for you on deck, Brehon,' he said. 'We've got a spare sail here.'

'No, no,' said Mara. 'I'd prefer to be out in the open. I'll just sit here on the sail locker and I'll be quite comfortable.'

Turlough eased himself down beside her cautiously. Fergal and Conall took up their guarding positions right behind him, each with a hand on their swords.

'Oh, go and look after those boys and stop them falling overboard,' said Turlough irritably. 'These are my own people in this boat. Do you expect one of the O'Kellys or the Great Earl himself to land on the deck disguised as a seabird?'

From the corner of her eye, Mara could see Conall grin at Fergal, but they both chorused a 'Yes, my lord,' and took themselves off to the other side of the ship.

'Hope I'm not sick,' said Turlough apprehensively.

'We're still in the harbour,' pointed out Mara, eyeing him with amusement. 'And it's a very calm day.'

'There's always a swell in these parts,' grumbled Turlough. 'Look at those rocks over there. Imagine being thrown up against them! That group over there is called Hell's Kitchen. Imagine being caught among them.'

'Oh, for goodness' sake,' said Mara, exasperated, 'let's just take pleasure in the journey. Look, they're putting the sail up now. The boys are enjoying this.'

The captain had given each boy a rope and they were all pulling lustily, Shane shouting orders at the others and revelling in the unusual position of being the most knowledgeable of the scholars.

The sail had originally been a dark colour, but rain and strong sunlight had leached the colour from it and now it was as white as the tops of the waves. Mara could see the places where it had been patched and mended. The salt waters and the strong winds would give these linen sails a short life.

'I never get used to this journey,' muttered Turlough.

Mara gave him another amused glance.

'Brehon, look at the currach over there.' Shane was pointing out to the distant horizon.

'What's wrong with it?' shouted back Turlough. He stood up, almost lost his balance and then sat down quickly again as the boat lurched and then slipped over the top of a wave.

'Nothing's wrong, it's just that they've stopped fishing and gone over to that other cog, the one that went ahead of us, the one with the brown sail. Look, they've left their fishing nets and they've gone speeding over.'

'Wanted to find out the news from Corcomroe,' suggested Enda as Mara and Turlough made their way to the prow of the ship.

'That's what it will be.' Turlough's ruddy colour was beginning to return to his cheeks, Mara was glad to notice. It reinforced her belief that seasickness didn't occur if people kept their mind on something else.

'Is that the ship that is carrying the coffins, my lord?' asked Fachtnan. He had taken off his cloak and draped it around Nuala who was looking pale and cold.

'That's it,' said Turlough briefly.

'They'll know why we're coming then,' said Aidan alertly. 'Look, someone on board is leaning over the rail, shouting down to them.'

'He's pointing back at us,' chimed in Enda.

'The currach is hoisting a sail now.' Nuala had a little flush in her cheeks and was looking a little better now and she, like the boys, was leaning over the rail.

'Funny little square sail,' said Shane disapprovingly.

'You'll be surprised to see how fast that little currach can go,' said Mara.

'That's right. They're just made from hazel boughs covered in ox skin, so they're really light.' Aidan obviously felt that Shane should be put in his place as the youngest scholar.

'Bet we can go faster,' said Shane. 'Look at the size of our sail.'

'Can we go any faster?' appealed Enda as the captain came up to the prow.

'Well, you hang on to the rudder there, keep the currach in your sights and you won't go far wrong. The rest of us will spread the sail a bit wider.' The captain was willing to entertain the boys, but Mara doubted that he would overtake the coffin ship, and certainly not the light little currach that was skimming across the waves towards the distant bulk of Inisheer Island. Still, it was keeping them all occupied and excited with their eyes fixed on the horizon. Already they had begun to adapt themselves to the rise and fall of the boat as it climbed each wave and then went down into a trough before climbing up again. Even Turlough was looking a little better with the excitement of the race.

'The currach is turning again,' shouted Nuala.

'It's not going to the island after all. It's heading for that ship out there.' Aidan's eyesight was keen.

'That's a galley,' yelled Shane.

'A galley, eh.' Turlough leaned over the rail, narrowing his eyes. 'I can't see it very well, but I'd say, by the flag, that is my relation, the O'Brien of Aran. That's the man who's going to put us all up, that's if we arrive safely. Please God,' he added piously.

'Is he out fishing, then?' Shane climbed up on the rail and stood fearlessly with one hand on the rope that led from the mast to the rudder.

'I'd say that he's patrolling.'

'Get down, Shane,' said Mara. 'Patrolling?' she queried with a lift of her eyebrow towards Turlough.

'He gets paid by Galway merchants to stop pirates attacking their ships,' explained Turlough.

There was a twinkle in his eye and Mara smiled to herself. This Brian O'Brien would probably indulge in a spot of piracy himself, she guessed. However, unless a complaint were made, it was not anything that she had to investigate.

'Pirates!' exclaimed Shane, open-mouthed. 'Hugh, did you hear that? The man that we are going to stay with fights pirates!'

'The currach has turned around and is going back towards the island,' yelled Enda.

'We'll never catch up with it now,' said Moylan in disgusted tones.

'We'll bet which one of them gets to the island first – the O'Brien of Aran or the men in the currach,' said Enda, always one to abandon a useless cause. 'Do you want to have a go at the rudder, Fachtnan, while I get out a piece of vellum and take the bets?'

'Come what may, they'll be ready for us on the island when we arrive,' said Mara softly, looking out across the waves.

And one family will know that they have now lost two of its members, she added silently to herself as she watched the busy and animated crowd, Turlough and his two bodyguards amongst them, shouting and cheering for their choice.

The news had certainly spread by the time that their boat had docked. A group of women, keening gently, knelt by the two salt-stained coffins on the massive stone pier. As far as the eye could see, other women in their red *léinte* knelt on the white sand and the men, in their brown cloaks, stood in small groups on the beach or the dunes. From the boat they looked like statues but once she stepped ashore Mara could hear the rhythmic sound of the prayers of the rosary. The faces of her scholars were now solemn and the men-at-arms shuffled their feet uneasily on the pier as they waited for directions from their king.

Then the priest came down the hill. He was a young man and his walk had the springing agility of one born to these rocky places. His face was fresh but his bearing was pompous and self-satisfied and he trod with the assurance of a man who knew his worth was above that of those around. Mara watched him with disfavour as he pushed a small child out of his way and did not look back when the little boy stumbled and cried. The mother snatched up the child and stilled its wailing against her shoulder but no one else seemed to take notice.

One by one they came forward and took up places around the coffin. No one looked at the new arrivals from the mainland or greeted them; all of the concentration was on the two coffins. Eight men came forward, four for each coffin. Others helped and soon the coffins were placed on the shoulders, Becan first, and then the coffin of Iarla. Mara knew that because the second coffin, despite Ardal and Liam's efforts, still bore traces of having been in the ground for days. Turlough spoke a few words to his men-at-arms and they came forward and formed a guard of honour on either side of the coffin.

And then the crowd hesitated. Another man was coming down the hill, walking at fast pace, leaping from rock to rock. He was followed by some men-at-arms, the sunlight glinting on the swords by their sides.

'There's Brian the Spaniard,' whispered Turlough as the dark-faced man, bronzed by the winds of the Atlantic, came through the crowd that parted for him.

The *taoiseach* looked older, thought Mara. It was six years since she had seen him at Thomond and the very black hair was now streaked with grey. His dark-brown eyes swept over the crowd and landed on Turlough and Mara. After a brief prayer at the coffins he made his way over to them.

'You're welcome, you're welcome both of you.' Brian's words were warm, but his face retained its proud, aloof expression. He was much darker than any of the O'Brien clan that Mara knew, but his high-bridged fleshy nose reminded her of Teige and he had the O'Brien domed forehead. 'We've a room prepared for you and we'll feed you a bit of fish for your supper. There's my place up there.'

It was impossible to miss the castle, among all the small, thatched cottages. It was built within the sheltering walls of an old fort on top of the hill on the south-eastern flank above them. It was quite a small castle, only two stories high but it dominated the inhabited part of the island and the harbour below.

'I'll see you later then.' Brian gave a quick inclination of his head, first to Turlough, then to Mara, and then went forward and began to talk to a tall, grey-haired woman. This was Becan's wife, thought Mara, and the three young women standing behind her were, no doubt, Iarla's sisters, the daughters of Étain. They probably looked like their mother, though perhaps her spirit, thought Mara, glancing surreptitiously at the red-gold hair that hung around the shoulders of each of the pale-faced, silent girls. Becan's wife, Babhinn, had probably once been red-haired, but now her beauty had faded. Would Étain, if she were still alive, have looked like her sister? thought Mara sadly. Would her red hair, hair as red as the precious garnet in Turlough's ring, have turned grey, her exquisite fair skin have been roughened and coarsened to a blotchy red by the salt winds and the fierce light on this barren island? Would her straight back now be bowed by incessant labour and her nimble feet turned swollen and clumsy? These island women worked hard – it was a life of incessant toil for them and a life of danger and early death for their husbands, brothers and sons who tried to snatch the fruits of the sea from the mountainous waves.

There seemed to be little curiosity about the king and the Brehon from the islanders; this was an island funeral and it would be carried out according to their own ancient rituals. The crowd parted for the priest who shook holy water over the coffins and then stood back while the mourners and their families formed into a long line behind the coffin; only then did friends and neighbours join the procession.

Mara gestured to her own scholars to stand apart. When the last person was in place, she and Turlough took up their position and the bodyguards, the law-school scholars and Nuala lined up behind them.

Little by little the people began to move, following the men bearing the coffin. Even without a weight to carry, it was slow going as the sand was very deep and powder fine. The islanders, in their bare feet or with soft goatskins bound around their feet, walked more easily than those from the mainland in their heavy boots, but even for them the ground was difficult with ankle-wrenching stones buried here and there beneath the sand.

The island, thought Mara as she struggled on through the sand, looked rather like a lower version of the mountain of Mullaghmore. The limestone rock was terraced in exactly the same way, though the terraces here were not barren and deserted except for a few goats or sheep, but lined with small, white-washed, thatched cottages, each with a neat garden of vegetables beside or in front of it. There was an extraordinary amount of stone taken out of the ground in order to have these small patches of fertility. From a distance the place looked like a giant tilted chessboard with thousands of walls outlining small squares. In the past when she had come here, either by herself or with her father, there had been a constant movement of figures carrying baskets of seaweed or of sand, both of which, when mixed, eventually formed the soil in the small fields and gardens where they grew their vegetables or small crops of rye. These small, fertile places were treasured; elsewhere, as on the high Burren, grass only grew in the grykes between the limestone rock slabs and the men and women spared no effort to add to their fertility and to shelter them with high walls against the Atlantic winds.

But today no one was working; everyone on the island was at the funeral. Prayers rose up, deep and fervent, the keening women cried out like seagulls and the chains of rough, hand-made rosary beads were busily moved, bead by bead, through work-roughened hands.

'They'll stop here,' whispered Turlough, taking Mara's arm as she half-stumbled on a buried stone. She waited and looked with puzzlement at the mourners. They were nowhere near to the graveyard yet.

Ahead of them was a flat slab of stone and beside it a large cairn or pile of loose stones. The coffins were laid on the slab and then the entire funeral procession searched in the sand and the nearby field until they found a stone and placed it on top of the cairn with a muttered prayer for the souls of the deceased. After that they formed up in a solemn procession going sunwise around the cairn. Around and around the red *léinte* and the black cloaks went, like some vast wheel turning endlessly in the grip of a fast-flowing river.

No one looked around at the visitors; the islanders were all caught up in their sad ritual, swaying and muttering prayers while waiting their turn to add a stone to the strange wayside cairn. The scholars waited respectfully and then they in their turn placed a stone on the cairn. How long had this ritual been going on for? wondered Mara, looking at the height of the mound and then frowning at Aidan who was about to pick up the largest stone that he could find – everyone else, she noticed, was seeking out small round stones. Fachtnan muttered something in Aidan's ear and he, in his turn, found a similar pebble.

The midday sun was in their eyes as they moved on again, up the hill towards the graveyard. The intensity of light that bounced off the white limestone and off the pale gold of the sand was almost painful. Mara kept her eyes fixed on the ground as she trudged up the hill at the back of the funeral procession. For a moment she hardly noticed that a small, red-haired boy had fallen back and was walking beside her, looking intently into her face. Then she smiled at him.

'The priest wants to talk to you after the service is over,' he said softly, and then he was off, burrowing his way back through the crowd like a small eel through wet sand, before Mara could reply.

Turlough looked down. It was obvious that he had caught the boy's words.

'Well, his reverence can seek me out then.' Mara gave a shrug. She had other things on her mind, other people to talk to. She did not care for the look of that complacent young man.

'Another stop here,' whispered Turlough as the head of the procession drew level with another cairn. This would be a welcome rest for the coffin bearers as they had started to climb the steep hill. Once again the stones were gathered and once again the mourners encircled the cairn in the sunwise direction, murmuring their prayers.

The grave had been dug, but only just, when the funeral procession reached the small church of St Caomhain. The diggers were still leaning on their shovels and pickaxes, sweat pouring down their faces and soaking their *léinte*. Every man had laid his cloak on a small bank at the side. There was little soil here; the huge pile of stones showed the difficulties. The coffins were lowered down with ropes and then the widow, children and the sisters of the dead men threw their handfuls of soil and by the time everyone else of the family – most of the islanders – had added their handful there was very little to be shovelled over the graves. The stones that had been taken out were now piled on top of the grave, heaviest first and by the time that the work was finished there was a mound like a cairn on top of the two coffins.

'That will sink down in a few weeks,' murmured Turlough, watching with interest the ceremony of these far-flung people of his kingdom.

Mara nodded. She could see how the other stone-covered graves had fallen down to almost the level of the ground around. The priest gave his last blessing and then looked over towards the Brehon. She looked blandly back. Now was not the moment for any public announcement she decided. That would have to wait until tomorrow when the grief was less raw-edged and the people were receptive to her words. Perhaps Brian the Spaniard would be useful in interpreting the mood of his island people. For now she would behave as an ordinary mourner and just quietly offer her condolences and then leave. Turning away from the graveside, she made her way over to where Becan's wife, Bebhinn stood, surrounded by her children and her three nieces.

'I'm sorry for your trouble.' Mara repeated the words that she had heard murmured over and over again during the past quarter of an hour.

Bebhinn nodded mechanically and then suddenly her grey eyes were alert and she held out her hand to stop Mara moving on.

'I must speak to you, Brehon,' she muttered.

The grip on Mara's wrist was almost painful and the woman's grey eyes were suddenly alert and focussed.

'Yes,' murmured Mara. 'I want to speak to you too. Not now, perhaps. Tomorrow.'

'You'll be staying at the castle.' It was more an assertion than a question, but Mara nodded.

'Do you see that field up there, to the left of the castle, the one with the black and white cow and calf?' Bebhinn didn't wait for Mara's assent, but hurried on. 'I'll be there tomorrow morning as soon as the sun comes up. I'll have to milk the cow.'

'I'll be there,' said Mara quietly, and she moved on to allow the scholars to mutter their expressions of sorrow before joining Turlough.

'Do you want to see the priest?' he asked. 'He's over there, talking to one of Iarla's sisters.'

Mara studied the young priest attentively for a few minutes. Unlike most of the islanders he was plump, his sand-coloured hair glossy and his skin pale. He saw her looking but turned away with a slow deliberation, continuing his conversation in a leisurely manner. She shrugged; no doubt he was used to the islanders responding instantly to him, but she owed him no allegiance. He had meddled with the truth; she would be surprised if he had not been aware of the correct paternity of Iarla.

'Let's go up to the castle,' she said impatiently. 'I can do no more here until tomorrow.'

Thirteen

Ɱuirbrecha
(Sea-judgements)

All judges should be well-versed in the matter of sea-judgements and great depths.

1. *Owners of flotsam are free of claim in sea-judgements.*
2. *Owners of jetsam are free from claim in sea-judgements.*
3. *Owners of goods carried off by a stream and deposited in the sea are also free from claim in sea-judgements.*
4. *Goods may not be taken from ships or boats unless these have been abandoned.*

'Bother,' said Mara in a low voice.

'What's the matter?' Turlough joined her at the window.

'That relation of yours has asked the priest to supper tonight.'

'Well,' said Turlough judicially, 'what did you expect? He probably dines at the castle most nights by the look of him. Brian likes an audience and he would regard most of the islanders as beneath him in status. What do you think of the chamber?'

'Very opulent.' Mara swept a quick glance across the room before turning back to the window again. There was something about this priest that puzzled her – something familiar about his features. She shook her head angrily, but no enlightenment came, so she turned back to Turlough.

'Your cousin certainly is a man of wealth,' she said, looking at the hanging carpets, the carved chairs, and the elaborately sculpted bed head. 'How does he afford all this from a set of three barren islands?' She walked forward and inspected a painted leather hanging. 'Spanish,' she remarked with a nod, frowning at Turlough's grin. 'It's just thievery,' she added. 'He'd better not expect any mercy from me if one of these ship masters brings a case against him.'

'They won't.' Turlough sounded confident. 'Think of it as a fee for a service. Brian escorts them in safety into Galway harbour – even puts one of his own men on board if they are unsure of the way through the rocks. Then he relieves them of a little of their cargo. It happens all over the place. O'Malley of the Boats, up there in Mayo, he takes much more.'

'Well, O'Malley of the Boats is not under my jurisdiction; Brian the Spaniard is,' said Mara firmly, but she guessed that the tradition was too long-standing for her to be able to do anything about it. Unless a complaint was made then Brehon law had no powers to interfere. She was about to suggest that Turlough had a word with his cousin when a respectful knock sounded at the door.

Turlough eagerly crossed the room and flung the door open, glad to be finished with the subject of piracy, guessed Mara. Turlough was always easy to read. Shane was standing there.

Turlough greeted him boisterously. 'Well, what have you been doing with yourself, young Shane? Getting up to mischief?'

'No, my lord.' Shane was quite at his ease, used to the king and his teasing. 'We've all been helping with putting up the trestle tables in the hall – all of us except Enda and he went off into the kitchen to help there.'

Probably hungry, surmised Mara, fastening the neck of her gown with her best brooch of silver and gold wires twisted together and then slinging her fur-lined cloak over her shoulders. The air was colder on this exposed island and the inhabitants of the castle would be used to an outdoor life; she doubted whether the hall was as warm as her own sitting room back at Cahermacnaghten.

'Some of the trestle boards were taken from wrecked Spanish ships, but we put the best ones on the side of the table where you will be sitting, my lord, and you, Brehon, and we covered them with linen cloths so you would never know that they are riddled with holes from the sea worm.' Shane chatted on happily as they went down the winding stairway.

Fachtnan and Nuala were coming in through the open door; Nuala's cheeks were flushed with the combination of wind and sun. She looked very happy and very relaxed. Mara was glad that she had brought her. She gazed at the boy and girl with satisfaction and then her eyes left them and went to the young priest who was just behind them. Now was the moment that he could approach her, but he had decided that this opportunity was not the right one because he passed them both with a bowed head and a murmured greeting.

'Come in, my lord, and you, Brehon, come in, come in and be very welcome. It's wonderful to have you both. I wish I had known sometime ahead and I would have been able to offer you a decent meal. You'll just have to have what we have ourselves.' Brian the Spaniard was playing the part of an affable host.

'Then you must live well, judging by the look of your table,' said Mara with a smile.

Not many guests were expected; there was just one table, the long trestle boards on their trestles arranged with four chairs at the top, the sides lined with benches and a few stools at the bottom, but the snowy linen cloths were covered with dishes. The centre-piece was a dish of pickled salmon, its pink and silver sides dotted with fresh thyme from the stony hillsides, there were pots of what looked like pâté, pink shrimps piled up in dishes, lifelike crabs appeared to wave tentacles from the bed of green leaves and scarlet lobsters were lined up, right down the centre of the table, resting on huge platters of beaten silver.

'Do you know what those brown things are on that dish over there?' asked Shane eagerly. 'They are dates and they come from Spain. They preserve them in sugar. The *taoiseach* gave us one each to thank us for helping with the tables. Do you want to taste one?'

'I think I'll wait . . .' began Mara, but then stopped as a very beautiful woman entered by the door from the back of the hall.

The woman was not young; her dark hair was streaked with white, but her eyes were dazzling, huge eyes of the darkest brown, as dark as pools in a peat bog with specks of amber, like sunshine, warming their depths. Her face was beautifully formed with a delicate aquiline nose, high cheekbones, a rounded chin and perfectly moulded mouth with full lips.

'My mother,' explained Brian, leading her forward. 'She speaks no Gaelic,' he added to Mara as Turlough bowed courteously but silently over the stately lady's hand.

After all those years, thought Mara. Her son, however, spoke to his mother in fluent Spanish and presumably her dead husband, Brian's father, the descendent of Teige the bonesplitter, had also spoken Spanish. Mara listened carefully as Brian explained the reason for the visit of the king and the bishop. She could make out the name of Iarla and of Becan. Then there seemed to be something about the priest. Both sets of dark-brown eyes moved towards the dapper red-headed figure at the bottom of the hall where the priest was engaging Fachtnan and Nuala in conversation. Mara had a good ability with languages; she could speak fluent English, French, Latin and when her father had returned from his journey to Italy he had taught her Italian. Spanish did not seem too difficult; some of what had been said was comprehensible.

'You'll have to teach me to speak Spanish,' she said to the dark-eyed

lady. Her words were a mangled mixture of Spanish, Italian and
Latin, but they brought a smile to the woman's face and at the sight
of that smile, with the still-white teeth just showing through the
exquisite curve of the lips, Mara understood why Brian's father had
wanted this woman for his own and perhaps why the son of this
marriage of the fourth degree was the one chosen to succeed him
as lord of the isles.

'Come and sit down.' Brian ushered both women to their places
on the elaborately cushioned chairs at the top of the table. Turlough
was on one side of him and Mara on the other. The priest came
forward and Brian introduced him as Father Petrus. He had acquired
that name in Rome, or in some monastery, guessed Mara, smiling
politely and then joining her hands as Father Petrus blessed the feast
laid out before them.

Enda only arrived as Mara was helping herself from a chicken
pie with almonds. She had chosen that over a dish of porpoise –
something she had never eaten and felt that she would probably
not like – when he sauntered in, holding a large lump of marzipan
in his hand and then ostentatiously licking his fingers as his fellow
scholars eyed him enviously. He smirked at them and then looked
up the table. His face changed when he caught Mara's eye. She
knew him well and knew that expression that he wore. Enda had
something to tell her, something that he found hard to keep to
himself.

Mara thought about it for a moment and then curiosity got the
better of her. She raised one finger and beckoned.

Enda was by her side in a moment, kneeling gracefully on the
floor by her chair. Turlough was talking loudly about old times with
Brian and the noise of their laughter was enough to drown out
even normal speech. Others watching would simply think that Mara
was reproving the boy for his late arrival.

'Yes, Enda.' Mara bent her head until it was near to his ear.

'Sorry for being late, Brehon,' said the quick-witted Enda in his
usual tone and then he lowered his voice. 'I've been in the kitchen,
Brehon, and the cook told me something interesting.'

'Oh, yes.' Mara reached down and picked up her linen napkin
from her lap and opened it with a flourish, dabbing her mouth delicately as she bent a little nearer to Enda.

'Apparently his reverence over there is the brother of Iarla.'

'Really!' Mara's voice rose slightly with amazement. She took
good care not to look over at the priest, but glanced under her

eyelashes at her companions at the upper table. Neither Turlough nor Brian looked at her, though, and the Spanish mother was immersed in her roasted porpoise.

'That's right. He's the brother of Iarla; Étain was his mother,' whispered Enda.

'So how did he get to be a priest?' hissed Mara. The education and profession of a priest would have been a long and expensive business and the family would have not been able to afford the training. 'I wouldn't think that the father could earn much as a blacksmith,' she continued. There was no iron here on these islands and probably not much demand for iron, she guessed.

Enda smiled and took another bite of his piece of marzipan. He rose to his full height and then bent down towards her ear. 'According to the cook, the blacksmith wasn't his father,' he whispered, and with that he sauntered back to his place beside Fachtnan.

Mara looked after him with exasperation. She was dying to know the full story. She looked across at the young priest. Of course that was where the resemblance lay. He was not like Iarla, but he was like the pale-faced girls that she had seen at the funeral, like Iarla's sisters and presumably Iarla's mother. He would be older than Iarla, probably nearer to thirty than to twenty – an older brother then, but not mentioned by anyone before now. Hopefully, Enda had obtained the full story and she would be able to get it out of him before the end of the day. With a shrug she pushed the matter to the back of her mind and concentrated on her food and on learning Spanish from the lady beside her.

By the end of the meal Mara had begun to make excellent progress. It had occurred to her that the lady of the house, the beautiful Spaniard, would doubtless know the whole story of this young priest. Quickly she learned the terms for man, woman, boy, girl, king and then priest. As she had suspected, her knowledge of Italian and Latin was proving very helpful and the Signora as everyone seemed to call her was excited at the prospect of being able to communicate properly with one of her son's guests and she bent all of her energies to the task.

'*Mater,*' queried Mara pointing first to her hostess and then to Brian.

'*Madre,*' was the immediate response.

'*Padre,*' Mara outlined a moustache and beard and was rewarded with a vigorous nod and a hearty laugh.

'Who?' she asked tapping herself on the chest.

That took a minute, but then the Signora responded: 'Brehon Mara' and then supplied the word.

Mara went all around the table asking the simple question, 'Who is . . .?' and receiving answers which included extra information such as relationships, by inserting questions using *padre* or *madre* – by now she was reasonably sure of understanding her hostess, but to her disappointment, the priest was only named for his office with no other details added and a shrug and a shaking of the head was the only response to a question about paternity. It was, she silently conceded, quite possible that the Signora did not actually know any of the details. If she had not bothered to learn Gaelic, then she probably had no interest in her neighbours. Oh, for Brigid, she thought longingly; if she had only brought her housekeeper with her by now she would know all of the gossip. Her eyes went to the bottom of the table where Enda was joking with one of the waiting women who were starting to serve the sweet course. Hopefully he had all the details; he had spent quite a while in the kitchen before the meal was served and she could see that he was on very friendly terms, indeed, with the dark-haired girl who was serving the dishes of sweetmeats. He was holding up his platter with a pleading look and making kissing motions with his lips. However, the sweet course was obviously just meant for the chief guests and the girl passed the scholars with an apologetic glance as well as a few appreciative giggles.

'You'll enjoy this, I hope,' said Brian to Mara as the elaborate silver dish approached the top of the table.

It was the first sentence that he had addressed to her and she gave him a half nod. She would bide her time, she thought grimly, but she planned to enjoy herself even more, after the meal, cross-questioning him about affairs in this watery kingdom of his.

It was not surprising that this course would be considered too good for any except the special guests at the top table. The dish was covered with ridges of blue marzipan, each topped with a white foam of spun sugar. On this sea was set numerous boats, everyone of them made from differently dyed pieces of pliable marzipan and at the side, the tower house of Brian the Spaniard rose up, built from blocks of marzipan and decorated by windows of spun sugar marked into diamond shapes by strips of marzipan. On the cobbled yard in front of the tower were various little figures also made from marzipan.

'Very good,' she said in what she hoped was Spanish and the

Signora nodded silently while packing a huge piece of marzipan shaped like a Spanish ship into her mouth.

Mara took a little, but she was not very keen on sweet food and this tasted overwhelmingly sweet. Soon the meal would be over, she hoped.

'Come with me to my solar,' said the Signora, signalling to the door at the back of the hall.

'I must see to my boys,' said Mara in a mixture of Spanish and Latin. She gestured towards the six at the bottom of the table.

'Your sons?' The Signora's very black eyebrows rose as she looked from nineteen-year-old Fachtnan to ten-year-old Shane.

'No.' Mara smiled. 'Scholars,' she added in Latin.

'Give them some,' said the Signora generously, pointing to the sweetmeats. She crammed another large boat into her mouth and then rose to her feet, acknowledging the bows of the rest of the guests who all got to their feet while she was making her way in a stately manner towards her own quarters.

Mara did not stand, but took the opportunity to remove some of the waves, seven of the boats and all of the figures from the scene in front of her. By the time that everyone had sat down again she was sauntering, platter in hand, down the room towards where the boys were sitting.

'One boat each and one figure each and then we'll divide up the rest,' she said as Fachtnan made room for her between Nuala and Enda. He immediately went to the top of the room and carried her chair down. She smiled her thanks and gave a sidelong glance at Brian, but he did not appear to notice the action. In any case the room was beginning to empty out now. The priest, she noticed with annoyance, had moved his position so that now he had become part of the conversation between Brian and Turlough. However, this meant that he was completely out of earshot as Mara turned expectantly towards Enda.

'So, the priest, what did you find out?' she asked in Latin. The maidservants and the steward were busy around the table so she took this precaution. Even the youngest of her scholars were fluent in that tongue so the conversation could be carried out with ease. Nuala had also learned Latin, although she would not have the same opportunities as the law-school boys to practise the language.

'The cook is a relation of Étain's – a cousin, I think,' mumbled Enda, chewing vigorously on a ship's sail made from marzipan coated with spun sugar. He swallowed it down and then said more clearly and with the beginnings of a grin lifting the corners of his mouth, 'The cook says that Étain was always wild. She was very pretty as a child and the priest here on this island apparently took quite a fancy to her. He even brought her some stuff for a cloak from Galway when she was about ten.'

'How old was the priest?' asked Moylan, popping one of the little figures into his mouth.

'Quite old,' said Enda impatiently. 'Anyway, that's nothing to do with the story.'

'Yes, it is,' contradicted Fachtnan mildly. 'The Brehon always tells us to find out as much as possible about every person connected with the case.'

'*Vae.*' Enda had been impressed by Fachtnan's uncharacteristic intervention so he shrugged his shoulders and continued. 'Yes, he was an old man and a very jolly one, according to the cook – liked his mead and playing jokes and that sort of thing. Anyway, when Étain was thirteen years old she became pregnant and he, the priest, immediately admitted that he was the father. When the baby was born he took the little boy away and told her that the boy was going to be dedicated to God. He brought it to a monastery – the cook didn't know where the monastery was – and the boy was brought up there and when he was a priest he came back to the island as an assistant to the old priest.'

'And did everyone know who he was?' Mara was fairly sure of the answer to this question.

'They guessed immediately. Apparently he was the image of Étain herself. And of course, once they had counted up the years it made sense. Apparently, also, Étain was very proud of him and couldn't stop whispering the secret to various people.'

'What a girl, that Étain!' whistled Aidan. 'The priest, her husband and then Ardal, or whoever was the father of Iarla. She certainly did put . . .' He stopped, unsure of his Latin, and contented himself with repeating, 'What a girl!'

'Would you like to borrow my knife to divide up the waves, Brehon?' asked Hugh politely, more interested in the sweetmeats than in the long-ago tale of romance and loss.

'So the elderly, jolly priest died,' guessed Mara, giving Hugh's knife a quick wipe with her napkin and slicing up the waves into fairly equal pieces.

'Yes, he died and before he died he arranged with the bishop that this Father Petrus would be appointed in his place to administer the parish and to receive all the dues.' Enda's Latin, as usual, was concise, fluent and well constructed.

'I wonder what Étain would have called her first-born child if she had been allowed to keep him. Not Petrus, I'm sure.'

Mara's mind was full of pity for the dead woman as her eyes watched the young priest nodding vigorously as Brian the Spaniard held forth in loud, harsh tones. Turlough was pushing a piece of marzipan around on his plate, a sure sign that he felt uneasy as Turlough was a man who loved his food, especially sweetmeats. I must go back and join them, thought Mara, but first she had to find out the end of the story.

'And what was Father Petrus's attitude towards Étain and her family?' she asked. 'Did he help to support them? Did they get anything from him? Contribute to his half-sisters' dowries? Lend a hand to Iarla to set himself up in the fishing business?'

Enda shrugged his shoulders. '*Nihil,*' he said succinctly and helped himself to another slice of marzipan wave.

Mara gave a satisfied nod. 'Fachtnan,' she said, 'would you bring my chair back up to the top of the table? No, place it beside the fire,' she amended with an eye on the priest who was still holding forth fluently. 'Ask the king would he and his cousin join me when they have finished their conversation.' That, she thought, was quite neatly planned. Turlough, at any rate, would now understand that she did not wish the priest to be present during their discussion. She got to her feet and followed Fachtnan as he carried her chair in stately fashion up the hall, bowing his head graciously at the servants and the few remaining guests who stood back to allow them to go through.

Mara stood by the fireside for a moment, warming her hands from the glowing sods of peat while Fachtnan went to deliver her message to Turlough. The heat of the fire was welcome as the wind from the Atlantic swept through the mullions of the unshuttered windows and lowered the temperature of the hall. Turlough, she noticed, gave her a startled glance and, waiting for him to under- stand the meaning of her request, she tapped her foot impatiently. There was a slight booming sound from beneath her foot and then another as she repeated the action. The floor was hollow here, she realised – like the alehouse where the beautiful Étain danced alone that night over twenty years ago, this flagstone in front of the fire- place had probably been laid over a damaged iron cauldron. She was beginning to understand Étain and she could guess what had led to the naming of Ardal as the father of Iarla. Her first son had been totally supported by his father, the jolly priest, so it was time that the father of her second son took care of the young man's welfare. Did she speak the truth on her deathbed, though, or was she persuaded by her priestly son, and possibly by Becan, her brother-in-law, to name a different man?

'Nice and warm here by the fire.' Turlough gave a quick glance at her determined face and then moved closer to the fire, rubbing his hands vigorously. He looked a little nervous so Mara gave him a reassuring smile.

Brian the Spaniard escorted Father Petrus to the door and then turned back towards them, beckoning to a servant to bring forward chairs and position them around the fire.

'I wanted to consult you, Brian, about addressing the people of the island tomorrow.' Mara had decided against talking about piracy. After all, her only evidence came from Turlough's unguarded speech and she couldn't betray her husband to his cousin.

'About the killing?' His tone was guarded.

'About the two cases of secret and unlawful killing,' contradicted Mara, smiling sweetly at him. 'I think it is important that I, as the king's Brehon, should talk to the people about what has happened and what steps I am taking to solve these deaths and how the fine will be paid and to whom – matters like that.'

'I see.' His Gaelic was perfect, but sometimes it seemed as if he were a man of few words, almost as if he hesitated to commit himself in a language that was foreign to him. Perhaps as a child he had spoken Spanish with his parents and had kept that slight hesitancy through to adulthood.

'So I wondered whether you have a chosen place where the people of the island would meet for judgement day. On the sands, by the harbour, perhaps?'

'No.' The word was abrupt and he seemed conscious of that as he immediately rushed into an explanation. 'These days we normally meet on the courtyard in front of the castle. It's easier for everyone like that – the noise of the waves can drown voices down there.'

'Very well.' Mara nodded graciously. 'If you can call the people together at noon, at the time of the angelus bells, will that give us enough time for our return journey?'

'Should do. The wind is going around to the north-west. You'll make Doolin in three or four hours. You'll be home before sundown.'

'Good. Well, if you can arrange the meeting for noon then that will give us enough time for our return journey.' And give me enough time to meet Becan's widow tomorrow morning, she added silently to herself.

Brian seemed ill at ease. 'I must apologise for the poor reception that you received, my lord, and you, Brehon, and your scholars,' he said after a moment. 'It just seemed to me . . . well, to be honest, the priest, Father Petrus, felt that we could not have a big party when it followed the funeral of the two men of Aran. I would like to have had some more merriment, but you understand that I had to defer to the priest on this matter.'

'Yes, of course. No, you could not have done any more. Everything was excellent.' Turlough was loud in his reassurance.

Mara said nothing. The door had been closed; she had been sure of that, but now there seemed to be quite a draught coming from it. Rapidly she stood up, gathering her cloak about her and pretending to shiver. She crossed the floor and jerked the door by its latch.

'Ah, Father Petrus,' she said, 'were you coming to join us?'

He was very taken aback by this, but he rallied quickly. 'I just wanted a word with you, Brehon,' he said. 'I was puzzled as to why Iarla was not considered to be the son and heir of Ardal O'Lochlainn. Did he give the letter that I wrote to you?'

'Yes, of course, it was given to Ardal and he showed it to me.' Mara kept her voice neutral.

Why was the priest so concerned about this matter? she wondered. Was there perhaps some feeling on the island that he should do something to aid the other children of his mother? Was he, perhaps, the one who had suggested Ardal as a father for Iarla? And if so, who was the real father of the boy?

'Nothing was proved before the unfortunate death of Iarla,' Mara said. She waited for a moment, eyeing him appraisingly and standing determinedly in the centre of the doorway.

'Thank you, Brehon,' he said eventually, and backed away awkwardly.

Mara was up early next morning, but by the time she arrived at the field in front of the castle the woman, Bebhinn, was already in the field, milking the black and white cow. Mara stood for a moment watching her; she had a strong determined face, intelligent, but careworn. She was extremely thin, almost as if there had not been enough food to go around and her large family had taken most of it. The farms on these islands were tiny and since there were no trees and no bogs, much of their produce would have to be bartered for winter fuel from the mainland. And now she was left without a husband and still with young children to care for. Mara made a silent vow that whoever was responsible for the killing of Becan would be forced to pay the rightful fine to this poor woman.

'I need your help, Bebhinn, if I am to find the man or woman who robbed you of your husband.' Mara did not waste time with any greetings or expressions of sorrow. The field was tiny and soon others would pass by on their way to milk and tend the cows scattered on the hillside.

Bebhinn gave a last few tugs of the cow's udder and then straightened her back. There was pitifully little milk in the small wooden cask. She saw Mara look at it and smiled grimly.

'Enough to flavour the porridge.' Her voice was harsh and husky, the voice of someone who lived most of her life in the open air among the rains and mists of this offshore island. 'Ask your questions and I will answer them with the truth, so help me God.'

Mara nodded. 'Becan came back here after his visit to the Burren. He was here when the news came of the killing of Iarla, your sister's boy.'

'That's right.' Bebhinn gave a quick nod. She seated herself on one of the great slabs of stone that paved the little field. The wind was cold and she wore no cloak over her *léinte* but she did not shiver or wrap her arms around herself but kept her eyes fixed on Mara.

'Was he surprised when the news came?' Mara sat down beside the woman. She wished that she could offer Bebhinn the shelter of her fur-lined cloak, which had enough folds to wrap around both women, but the unyielding pride in the face beside her made her hesitate to make the offer.

'No, he wasn't.' Mara allowed a silence to hang after this short sentence until the woman reluctantly added, 'He was angry.'

'What did he say?'

'He said that he should have stayed.'

'And what did you say to that?'

'I told him that he shouldn't have meddled in the first place. I knew that nothing would come of the plan. Why did he have to involve himself? It was nothing to us. We would get nothing by it – he was a selfish boy, Iarla. Étain spoiled him. She always treated him as if he were something special.'

'So why do you think Becan did come over with Iarla? I must

say that I thought at the time,' said Mara with a show of frankness, 'that it was surprising that Becan came to support Iarla. After all, his support was enough to declare to the people of Aran and of the Burren that he knew his own brother to be a cuckold.'

Bebhinn considered this while a contemptuous smile twisted her lips. 'Not surprising at all if you had known Étain. She could always get any man to do what she wanted.'

'From the parish priest down,' commented Mara.

Bebhinn gave her a grudging smile. 'So you've picked that up,' she commented. She looked curious, but Mara had no time to waste. Already the smoke was rising from cottage chimneys, doors were slammed and commands shouted. They would have little more private time together.

'So your husband wanted to put Étain's mind at rest by making provision for her son. Was he the one that thought of Ardal O'Lochlainn, the O'Lochlainn *taoiseach*?'

'He and the priest together. They cooked it up between them and put it to her.' Bebhinn's voice held a note of distaste.

'And Étain went along with it?'

'She didn't care as long as Iarla was cared for. She would tell any lie if it benefited Iarla. There was nothing here for him. The blacksmith's business was hardly enough for one and Iarla had no boat. All he could do was help when an extra man was needed and that was not often.'

'But of course she and you knew that Ardal O'Lochlainn was not the man who had fathered Iarla.' Mara's voice was so confident that Bebhinn, after a startled glance, did not contradict her. In fact, Mara thought she could discern a slight nod of the woman's head. 'Would you tell me the name of the man who actually was the father?' she continued.

Bebhinn met her eyes. There was a troubled look on her careworn face. 'I can't do that, Brehon. I swore on the gospel to Étain when she was on her deathbed, I swore to keep her secret. Ask me anything else you like, but I can't give you that name.'

Mara thought for a moment. There was a deep note of sincerity in the woman's voice. There was no doubt that she would keep the secrets of her dead sister so any further questions on this would not be useful. A statement, however, might work.

'I suppose Becan thought that Iarla had been murdered by the man that had fathered him.' Mara kept her eyes fixed on Bebhinn's face and did not miss the quick flash from those grey eyes. She said nothing, however, so Mara continued: 'Anything that you can tell me will help in finding the murderer of your husband and of your nephew.' Then she waited watching the struggle that took place in the woman's face.

'I think that you will find the man that did the deed, both deeds, Brehon,' Bebhinn said eventually. 'You're a great woman to make a good guess,' she added casually, rising to her feet.

Mara rose too. 'The *éraic* will be forty-five cows if I do find the man or the woman,' she said nonchalantly. 'I will be announcing that at the meeting outside the castle at noon, but I want you to know the position now.'

A tide of red colour poured across the woman's face. It started at her forehead, engulfed her cheeks, and then swept down over her neck. She looked up at the tiny fields on the hillside, almost as if she could imagine them peopled by that vast amount of cows. And then she looked down at her own careworn hands – the hands of an old woman with their broken thickened nails, distorted fingers and calloused palms. Then her glance went up into the grey sky where the clouds were beginning to gather over the sea. It was almost as if she had linked for a moment with the heaven that was supposed to lie above those clouds where she hoped that her sister had found a resting place. The light went abruptly from her eyes and the colour died out of her face, leaving it an ugly grey.

'I can't do it, Brehon,' she said hoarsely, and for the first time on that chilly morning she shivered. 'I can't do it,' she repeated. 'I can't break my sacred oath.'

'Don't worry, Bebhinn.' Mara smiled serenely. 'I won't ask you to endanger your immortal soul.'

Étain, she thought, had shown more courage.

Fourteen

Din Cechtugad

(On legal entry)

Where there is dispute as to the rightful inheritor of land, this procedure must be followed.

To claim land as his own, a man must enter the land, holding two horses and he must be accompanied by two witnesses and sureties. He must make sure that he crosses the boundary mound of the property. Then he must withdraw and the occupant has five days to decide to submit to arbitration.

If that is not done the whole procedure is repeated up to three times with double the number of horses, witnesses and sureties each time.

'Anyone arrive while I was away, Brigid?' The question was a perfunctory one. After the sea journey across from Aran and the jolting ride home from Doolin, Mara was ready for her bed. It was very unlikely that anyone would have visited the law school; news travelled fast around the small kingdom of the Burren; everyone would know of her journey.

'Well . . .' Mara had been on her way out of the kitchen when an uncertain note in Brigid's voice had made her turn. She said nothing, just waited, an inquiring look on her face. Turlough had gone back to Thomond with his men-at-arms so she had decided to have an early night. However, she had the time to spare to allow Brigid to unburden herself.

'Well, I was going to tell you tomorrow morning. I didn't want to be bothering you tonight.' Brigid's face bore a look of annoyance, almost of anger.

'Tell me tonight or I'll be wondering.' Mara's voice was light-hearted.

Brigid was a great worrier about things. This, doubtless, would prove to be something small – a careless word spoken, something that she and Cumhal might regard as threatening the dignity of the Brehon's office. Or perhaps some problem in the neighbourhood that would require a legal decision.

'It's just that Seán . . .' began Brigid.

Mara went back into the kitchen and sat on a stool to drink her

milk. Her housekeeper didn't often complain to her about household matters and if the problem about Seán was as serious as it
seemed from the angry look on Brigid's face, then Mara would give
her full attention.

'You see,' said Brigid guiltily, 'with you and the lads away for a
couple of days I thought I would go over and see my cousin in
Kinvarra.'

'Good idea,' said Mara heartily. Brigid took very few hours for
herself out of the whole year.

'Well, while I was away, and Cumhal was out seeing to a cow
calving, that Caireen turned up with her eldest son.'

Mara had only been half listening; her mind was running on a
conversation in Aran; as usual, she was well able to pay outward
attention to Brigid while thinking her own thoughts. Now, however,
she put down the milk and looked startled.

'Caireen!' she exclaimed. 'But she must have known that I was
away. Malachy would have told her; after all we took Nuala with
us.'

'Oh, she knew you were away all right.' Brigid's voice was rough
with anger. Brigid was whole-hearted in everything. She adored
Nuala and therefore she detested Caireen who was threatening the
child's happiness.

'So?' Mara spoke the word softly, giving Brigid her full attention.
There would be more to come; she knew that. But what was Seán's
part in all of this?

'So what does my brave Seán do but put the two of them into
the schoolhouse to wait. To wait!' Brigid's voice rose to a note of
pure fury. 'To wait for what? I asked him that. The *amadán*! What
did he think they were going to wait for? You had only gone an
hour! Did he think that you were a sea eagle and that you would
fly over to Aran and be back before dinner.'

'Never mind, Brigid.' Mara's voice was soothing. 'I don't suppose
they stayed long.'

'They stayed long enough. And that's not the worst of it.' Brigid's
pale, freckled face turned red with shame. 'I can hardly bring myself
to tell you this, Brehon, but when Cumhal came back from the
calving and he was out there in the yard, washing his hands under
the pump, he saw them in there. And he saw what they were up
to. He rushed over to the door. And then in comes Seán, puffing
and panting, he was, the way he is when he's pretending to do
some work. "Oh, Cumhal," he says —' Brigid lifted her voice into

a strange falsetto that yet had an uncanny resemblance to Seán's rather moronic tones – '"Oh, Cumhal, I've been all the way up to the Moher, and back, looking for you to tell you that the Brehon has visitors."'

'They were a long time there then.' Mara felt even more puzzled. The Moher was a small field, enclosed with tall flagstones, and it would have taken Seán a good twenty minutes walk from the law school.

'And, of course, with all that hee-hawing from Seán, the two of them came to the door then, but Cumhal had already seen what they had been up to.'

'Up to?' Mara put a note of query into her voice.

'The son it was – the woman probably can't read.' Brigid injected a strong note of scorn into her voice before continuing dramatically. 'And you'll never guess, Brehon. He was looking through your books.'

'Perhaps he got bored waiting.' Mara was annoyed, though. 'But I locked it,' she said as memory came back to her. 'I locked it before I went.' These days, when the schoolhouse was not occupied that wooden press was always kept shut and securely fastened.

'And so you did,' said Brigid triumphantly. 'I know you locked it because the first thing that I did after you all disappeared down the road was to give the schoolhouse a good clean out. I scrubbed the flagstones and then when they were dry I gave your table and the press a good polish. It was definitely locked. But I'll tell you something else, Brehon, when Cumhal went into the schoolhouse after the two of them had gone, what do you think that he found?' Brigid didn't wait for a comment from Mara before finishing dramatically, 'That very same key, that had been lying in your drawer, was left stuck in the keyhole of the press.'

'Let's go and have a look.' Mara put down her milk and rose to her feet, all tiredness gone.

'I knew you'd be furious.' Brigid's expression was torn between curiosity and concern. 'Shouldn't you go to bed though?'

'Come on,' said Mara, 'let's go and see what the lady was up to. If they took the key from the drawer then they must have been looking for something.'

'And she took the son along so that he could do the reading for her. She can't read; I'd wager you that, Brehon.' Brigid's voice held the scorn of one who, though she couldn't read herself, worked for someone who had been able to read since the age of four.

I wonder could it be anything to do with Fachtnan, thought Mara as they both hurried along the road between the Brehon's house and Cahermacnaghten. Caireen had seemed to be very interested in Fachtnan on that Sunday when they had all gone for dinner at Caherconnell. Perhaps she wanted to find out his marks in law examinations or something like that. The thought made her rigid with anger, but then she remembered that all documents to do with the scholars were locked up in a box with the Burren law judgements and the key to that box was in her own pouch.

The schoolhouse was dim with a small fire of banked turf just smouldering in the brazier. Brigid took a candle from a box on the window seat and thrust it into the small glow.

'How lovely everything looks!' Mara forced her voice to sound sincere in her praise. Brigid worked so hard and always treasured a few words of praise. In reality, though, Mara's whole attention was focussed on the huge oaken press that took up much of the space against one wall. Mostly the doors were kept hooked back against the whitewashed walls, but before leaving for Aran she had closed and locked them, more to protect the precious books than for any reason of secrecy; all private documents were kept securely locked in the box.

'Here's the key. I put it back in the drawer.' Brigid pulled out the large key and handed it to her.

'Odd.' Mara had unlocked the door and stood staring at the books. There they all stood, these large tomes, heavily bound in leather and bearing the sheen of the many hands that leafed through them on almost a daily basis. She knew the order in which they stood as well as she knew the placement of the different sized fingers on her own hand. Each scholar was trained into replacing a book back into its correct situation. Her eyes immediately went to the left hand side, but *Bretha Déin Chécht*, the book that dealt with matters of interest to a physician, had not been moved. She was sure of that. It was a week or so since that it had been consulted and an opportunistic spider had woven the first few strands of web between it and the top of the next shelf. There was one book that had been moved, though, and that had been replaced so carelessly that one of the leaves had been slightly twisted. Mara took it down from the shelf, automatically smoothing out the page. Its title was inscribed boldly on the spine of the book – there could have been no mistake. *Din Techtugad:* on legal entry. Why on earth were Caireen and her son, the medical apprentice, so interested in a book that dealt with the legal procedure for taking possession of a disputed property?

Mara was refreshed by her early night and was already in the schoolhouse when the scholars entered. She had thought of going over the duties and privileges of an over-lord, in order to reinforce what they had learned in Aran, but the discovery of last night had made her change her mind.

'I think today, we'll talk about *Techtugad*,' she said. 'Hugh, fetch down the right book for me, will you?'

He went straight to the shelf and she saw him give a slight start. The book had been left where it had been put when she was away and for a moment Hugh could not see it. She watched him carefully. Hugh had been in charge of keeping the press neat and tidy last week and he would instantly see if anything was amiss. He picked up the book, frowned hesitantly and his colour rose. He was a very sensitive boy, always anxious to do the right thing and to please, so she hastened to put him at ease.

'It's a bit of mystery,' she said lightly. 'Someone came into the schoolhouse when we were in Aran and took the key from my drawer and opened the press. Which book do you think this person looked at?'

'*Din Techtugad*,' said Hugh hesitantly, and she rewarded him with a beaming smile.

'Well, done,' she said. 'A good piece of deduction. I also think that.'

'It's out of place, isn't it?' Aidan tried for his bit of glory and Mara didn't disappoint him.

'That's right,' she said. 'Now why would anyone come into my schoolhouse, open my press and take out *Din Techtugad*?'

'Was he a lawyer?' asked Enda alertly.

Mara shook her head. 'No, he was a physician.'

'But there is a lawyer coming across the yard just now.' Aidan, as usual, was keeping an eye on the comings and goings out the window.

'That's Cavan, the fellow who used to be at MacClancy's law school,' said Moylan, twisting his body around and balancing precariously on two legs of his stool. 'He used to be a great man with a hurley.'

'He qualified as an *aigne* last year,' supplemented Enda.

'And went off to Thomond,' added Fachtnan. 'He's about my age.'

'Open the door, Shane,' said Mara.

Large heavy footsteps sounded outside. It was obvious that this young *aigne* was coming to see her. Perhaps Turlough had sent him with a message, she thought.

Mara remembered the young man once he was inside the door. Quite a bright lad; she remembered Fergus MacClancy saying that he was sorry Cavan had not got a position in some household or as an assistant to some Brehon, but he had preferred to take a chance wandering the countryside and giving his services to any who needed them. She welcomed him and went through the usual greetings and enquiries.

'So where are you living now, Cavan?' she asked in the end.

'Mostly in Arra and in Galway, Brehon.' His voice was reserved and she wondered what had brought him here. He did not seem interested in his former opponents at the hurling matches that took place every few months between the MacClancy Law School in Corcomroe and the O'Davoren Law School in the Burren. He kept his eyes firmly fixed on her and ignored the scholars.

'So you're on your way over to see Brehon MacClancy,' she continued, wishing that he had timed his arrival better. He should know that the boys would be hard at work at this hour of the morning, she thought impatiently. Presumably he came to impress them with his experiences and to talk over former days.

'No, I came to see you, Brehon, on a private . . . well, a legal matter.' He had said the words bluntly and she sensed unease within him.

'A private matter?' she queried. 'Is it private to you, personally?'

Cavan shook his head. 'No,' he said.

'Here's Nuala,' said Aidan suddenly.

On this occasion there had been little need for him to be gazing out of the window. The clatter of pony feet on the flagstoned yard had made every head turn.

A minute later the door was flung open and Nuala burst into the room.

'So there you are.' Her voice was quivering with fury. She marched straight up to the young *aigne* and stared aggressively into his face. 'Why didn't you tell me to my face and not sneak behind my back?'

Cavan blinked and then recovered. 'Because your father is your legal guardian,' he said in a voice that he strove to make authoritative.

Suddenly Mara understood everything, the surreptitious visit of

Caireen and her son, Ronan; no doubt a plausible reason would have been found to consult *Din Techtugad* even if they had encountered a less gullible member of her household, the arrival of Cavan, a young *aigne* practising in Galway, in the same area as the dwelling place of Caireen and her sons. And then there was the relationship between Nuala's benefactor, Toin, the man who had bequeathed his house and farm to the girl, and Caireen's late husband; it all added up.

'Sit down, Nuala,' she said crisply. 'Yes, sit down there beside Hugh. Just let me do the talking. Yes, Cavan, say what you've come to say.'

Cavan bowed respectfully. He had acquired a certain polish and self-assurance since she had last seen him on a muddy hurling field. Now he took a scroll from his leather satchel and unrolled it with a flourish.

'On behalf of my *céile*, Ronan O'Luinin, I give notice, to you, Mara O'Davoren, Brehon of the Kingdom of the Burren, that my said *céile*, Ronan O'Luininn . . .' He hesitated and then continued impatiently, 'But, you know all the procedure, Brehon. There is no point in me going through it.' He broke off, conscious of eight pairs of eyes fixed on him intently. A slight flush rose to his cheeks still marred by some late adolescent skin problems.

'No, no.' Mara's voice was mild and judicial. 'Let's stick to the proper procedure. I never like to skip any of the correct legal process. Fachtnan, would you like to check? Hugh, give him *Din Techtugad* and Fachtnan, you can check, just in case my memory is defective. This is an important matter, and it is essential that all the steps be gone through correctly. You say that your client has already taken the first step. Tell us about it.'

'The claimant, Ronan O'Luinin, has entered the property at Rathborney, formerly owned by Toin the *briuga*, declaring this property to be his by right of law, and relationship and he . . .'

'He has crossed the boundary mound of the property, is that correct?' interrupted Fachtnan.

Mara was surprised. This sharp cross-questioning sounded more like Enda than Fachtnan, she thought, but no doubt he was moved from his usual easy-going, amiable manner by the sight of Nuala's eyes filled with tears.

'He has gone through the entrance gate – the property does not possess a mound,' retorted Cavan. 'He has brought two horses with him – as laid down in the judgement texts,' he added with heavy emphasis.

Fachtnan nodded gravely and waved his hand.

Mara gave a quick glance and a slight inclination of her head to Shane who seemed to be at bursting point from the strain of restraining himself, his hand waving like a flag in stormy weather.

'What about sureties?' His question startled Cavan who had returned to his scroll.

'His sureties are his knife and his physician's bag.'

'He's not yet a physician,' muttered Nuala angrily.

'So therefore his bag is of no value.' Enda took up the cudgels with enthusiasm. Nuala was like a sister to the law-school scholars.

'And a knife isn't valuable unless it is made from silver,' said Hugh, the son of a silversmith.

'What about witnesses?' queried Fachtnan.

'I was the witness,' said Cavan grandly.

'You're only one, *Din Techtugad* says *witnesses.*' Fachtnan laid heavy emphasis on the plural form of the word.

'And the physician Malachy, as present owner of the property, has gone down there now.'

'Guardian of the present owner of the property,' corrected Mara.

Nuala gave a loud snort, but said nothing.

'So what is your message to me then?' queried Mara.

'I want to give due notice that we are asking for arbitration,' said Cavan solemnly.

'I think,' said Mara with a sigh, 'we all need to go down there to Rathborney. Please go and saddle your ponies, everyone. Fachtnan, would you ask Cumhal whether Seán or Donie could see about my mare for me?'

When the door closed behind them all, she looked at Cavan appraisingly.

'Have you satisfied yourself that your client has a just claim?' She kept her voice neutral. After all, he hadn't been a scholar of hers and it was not any of her business. However, he was a young man at the onset of his career and perhaps a quiet word of advice would be valuable to him. It was important that her profession only numbered those of high integrity amongst its ranks.

He flushed angrily. 'I take the word of my client, Brehon,' he said stiffly. 'I can assure you that I am perfectly capable of handling my own affairs.'

'I see,' she said, and then she waited quietly until her mare was ready and all of the boys were seated on their ponies. She would say no more until she reached Rathborney, she decided, and then she would explain the position to all who were there, including her scholars. After all her duty was to them, not to this opinionated young man. Brigid, she noticed with amusement, made no attempt to persuade her not to ride down to Rathborney. The housekeeper looked with concern at Nuala's tear-stained face and then cast a look of deep suspicion at the young lawyer.

Malachy was already there at Rathborney. He looked deeply uncomfortable when he saw Mara and his daughter, but said nothing. Mara gave him a quick nod and greeted Ronan, the son of Caireen, gravely inspecting the two horses, the battered medical bag, probably belonging to the boy's father, she thought, and the plain knife with its blade of steel and its handle of smooth alder wood and directed Fachtnan to make a note of the animals and the articles. There was no sign of Ronan's mother, of course, she noticed: Caireen was a woman who worked from behind the scenes. She wheeled her horse around and faced Malachy and his future son-in-law, including Cavan and her scholars in her glance.

'The procedure for *tellach*, legal entry, has been correctly carried out,' she said. 'This is classed as *céttellach*, first entry. The claimant must now withdraw and the person who is occupying the land, that is Nuala, through her father Malachy, may now consent to submit to arbitration after five days.'

'And what if I refuse,' said Nuala, chin in the air.

'Then the claimant may make a second entry and then a final entry, twenty days after the first entry, which is today.' Mara kept her voice neutral but felt annoyed with herself that she had not told Nuala what to do while they were back in Cahermacnaghten. She moved her horse and all eyes followed her. To her pleasure, she saw that Fachtnan took the opportunity to whisper in Nuala's ear. It didn't take long, just a minute, but Nuala was quick and clever.

'I submit to arbitration,' she said.

'And so do I,' said Malachy, earning a scowl from his daughter.

'Let me fill you all in on the background of this case, then, before we proceed to arbitration,' Mara said gravely. 'Toin, the now deceased owner of this property, was the son of the royal harpist. He was apprenticed to a physician at an early age and he received no kin lands from his father or any member of his family. His wealth, which enabled him to buy the property at Rathborney, was acquired solely through his own professional works, through his dedication and his excellence as a physician. Now if he had direct kin, son, grandsons, first cousins, nephews; *derbh-fine*, in other words, he would still have had the right to dispose of two-thirds of the property, but he did not. In any case, as it is, Ronan's father was not even a first cousin, so not of the *derbh*-fine, therefore Toin had a perfect right to make the will as he did and to leave the entire property at Rathborney to Nuala, daughter of Malachy the physician, in the kingdom of the Burren.'

There was silence when she had finished. Mara purposely did not look at Cavan; he would be humiliated and she was sorry about that. However, this had to be stopped as soon as possible and it was better that he should be humiliated here than in the presence of the king and kingdom at Poulnabrone. She had given him a chance back in Cahermacnaghten and he had not accepted it. In future he would be more circumspect and remember to consult his law texts more thoroughly. She dismissed him from his mind and turned her eyes to Malachy. He had a dark skin, as she did herself, and that skin did not easily show pallor, but now he looked sallow and suddenly older than he normally appeared. He said nothing, did not look at his daughter. He moved towards Ronan and there was something in his bearing that reminded Mara of a dog who knew it had done wrong and that it was going to be scolded. No doubt Caireen would have much to say about this. It would have been a good solution for her large family if they could have seized the farm and house at Rathborney, but it was not going to happen while Mara was Brehon of the Burren.

'So what do you want to do?' Mara asked Ronan briskly. 'Give up this claim or go for arbitration in five days' time at Poulnabrone? Talk it over with your lawyer but remember it's your decision. I'll walk my horse down the lane while you are making up your mind.'

'No need,' said Ronan bitterly. 'I withdraw my claim. There is no point in going to arbitration if that is the case. I was misled.' He shared a glare impartially between Malachy and the unfortunate Cavan and then hooking the bridle of one horse over his arm, and mounting the other, he rode away without a backward glance.

More brains than his mother, thought Mara and then said aloud, 'Well, we'd better be getting back. What about you, Nuala? Would you like me to keep her for tonight, Malachy?'

'You can keep her for as long as you like,' said Malachy bitterly, 'and then she can go and stay with her uncle at Lissylisheen. She's no longer welcome in my house.'

And with that he mounted his horse and followed his future stepson at a slow pace up the hill.

Nuala, to Mara's surprise, did not seem to be upset by her father's outburst. Perhaps it wasn't the first time that she had heard sentiments like that. Mara watched as she rode ahead. She appeared quite normal, joking and laughing with the boys. Mara turned to Cavan.

'Well, I'm not sure that you are going to get paid for your trouble on that case,' she said with a friendly grin. 'If you don't mind me giving you a little advice, it's good to check all the facts before you take something on. Did you know the family well?'

'I just met them a couple of times when I was at Galway.' Cavan didn't seem too bothered. His voice was careless and quite cheerful. 'As a matter of fact,' he said with a burst of frankness, 'I only took that case on this morning. I called in at Caherconnell this morning; I half-hoped I would be invited to a meal and Caireen asked me to help.'

'I see.' Mara was amused. 'Well, what about coming and having dinner with us before you go on your way? I wouldn't waste time demanding a fee. Now why don't you go ahead and ride with Fachtnan and the others? I'm taking everything at walking pace these days.'

Well, that was just a piece of opportunism to get hold of the young lawyer this morning, thought Mara. No doubt Caireen and her son would have waited for a while before staging the dramatic bid for the Rathborney property if Cavan hadn't turned up. He seemed cheerful and resigned now, riding ahead with Fachtnan. Nuala had fallen back and was joking with Aidan. Their voices floated back to Mara.

'Well, I suppose you wanted me to lose my property just so that you had the pleasure of getting out of school,' she said.

'You'd have got it back in the end. They had no case,' said Aidan cheerfully, 'but it would have been fun seeing him doubling up his horses and his witnesses every time and seeing what sureties he managed to find.'

It wasn't fun to everyone though, thought Mara, thinking of Malachy's face. To him it was deadly serious. He was a man of very strong passions; she had known that about him for a long time. It worried her to think what measures this infatuation for that stupid woman, Caireen, might have driven him to. Something would have to be done about Nuala; she had to be safeguarded. Let her enjoy the fun and the teasing for the rest of the short ride back to Cahermacnaghten, but then a serious talk would have to be had.

'You go in and have your dinner now, all of you,' said Mara when they reached the gates of Cahermacnaghten. She wondered whether she had the strength left within her to make the effort to ride over to Lissylisheen, but decided reluctantly that all she wanted to do now was to lie on her bed for half an hour before afternoon school. Still, the problem about Nuala would have to be solved immediately. She would have to rely on Ardal's good nature and understanding of her condition. Slowly she walked her mare into the courtyard of the law school and sat on her mare for a moment. Bran came up, his tail wagging and his eyes inquisitive; he was wondering why she did not dismount. She looked at him affectionately, envying his vigour and good health. I must get this case solved, she thought, I must get it all settled before Easter, and Easter is at the beginning of April. All of the boys were going back to their homes for a week's break before the start of the Trinity Term. She would have a rest then; hopefully there would be no urgent legal or political matters to deal with; she and Turlough would be together at Ballinalacken Castle. She imagined herself stretched out on the cushions in the big, three-mullioned window seat overlooking the sea and gave a deep sigh.

'Are you well, Brehon?' Cumhal sounded startled.

He was standing beside her, patiently waiting for her to dismount. He must have heard her sigh. Quickly she straightened her back and took his outstretched hand and climbed awkwardly from the mare on to the mounting block.

'I'm fine, Cumhal,' she lied, sitting on the block for a moment. 'As well as can be expected,' she amended. 'I was just wishing that I had Bran's energy. I really need to go over to Lissylisheen and at the same time I want to have a rest.'

'If it's the O'Lochlainn you want, Brehon, I'll fetch him for you,' said Cumhal firmly.

Mara bowed her head in acquiescence.

'Tell him that there is no hurry, Cumhal. Some time today, if he can manage it.'

Mara had just begun to rise from the mounting block after a last caress of Bran who was anxiously licking her hand when the sound of lightly galloping horse feet rose from the road between Lissylisheen and Cahermacnaghten. Cumhal came back out of the stable.

'That sounds like the O'Lochlainn,' he said. 'He has a new mare.

He's trying out her paces. I've seen him go up and down past here a few times this morning.'

Ardal's new horse was enjoying the ride and its hooves danced on the hard stone road. Mara came to the gate of Cahermacnaghten to admire.

'What a beautiful mare!' she exclaimed, admiring the picture of the copper-haired man and the strawberry-blond mare.

'I came down to find how everything went at Aran.' Ardal dismounted from the mare in one fluid movement.

'Very well,' said Mara firmly.

He nodded, but asked no questions about the reactions from the islanders. Ardal would not push for details. He was a man of very delicate feelings.

'And you didn't find the journey too much for you? You are well?'

Mara looked at him affectionately. He looked well himself. He had a glow of happiness about him.

'Could you spare me a few minutes, Ardal? Cumhal will get one of the men to walk your mare up and down, will that be all right? We'll just go down to my house; I won't delay you too long.'

'Of course, Brehon.' He handed over the mare to Cumhal instantly and followed her down the road and up the path to the Brehon's house.

'You had good weather for your trip,' he remarked as he held the door open.

'Perfect for the trip; it was quite misty on the island, but the sea was calm coming and going. The wind even changed direction just to suit us.' Brigid had a fire burning and the room was warm and comforting. Mara sat on a cushioned seat beside the fireplace, bending down to throw some aromatic pinecones on to the blaze and Ardal sat opposite to her.

'Yes, I saw the mist over the islands . . . I saw it from Galway . . .'

There was a note of hesitancy in Ardal's voice and Mara turned to look at him inquiringly. He had a slight smile on his lips and his very blue eyes seemed to sparkle with pleasure at some inner thought.

'You look very happy today,' she said impulsively.

His smile broadened. He tugged at the copper curls of his moustache.

'My child was born early this morning, soon after midnight,' he said quietly. 'A little boy.'

'Ardal, how wonderful!' Mara beamed a smile of immense delight at him. For years there had been rumours that Ardal had a wife of the fourth degree, a fisherman's daughter, somewhere on the Atlantic coastline beyond Galway, but Ardal himself had never spoken of the matter to Mara.

'What have you both decided on as a name for the little fellow?'

'Marta would like to call him Finn, after my father.' Ardal's face bore a tender brooding look. 'He's a red-head, like me,' he added.

'A good name for him: Finn the golden-haired.'

Mara hesitated. Ardal was a very private man and she was uncertain whether what she was going to say would be welcome, but she felt that it needed to be said. She stretched across, put her hand on his arm and looked intently into his face. 'Ardal, shouldn't this little boy, this new Finn, shouldn't he be brought up in Lissylisheen as your son and your heir?'

She expected him to turn away, but he didn't. He took her hand in his and squeezed it. With a feeling of shock she realized that he was near to tears. The birth of a son seemed to have pierced his armour. She had known him since her childhood, but had never seen him like this before.

'It won't be altogether my decision,' he said eventually. 'Marta does not want to leave her family. She can't bear not to live within sight and sound of the sea.'

'Then, I shall just pray that together you come to the right decision for you and for your son.' Mara got to her feet, went to the press in the corner of the room and took down a silver goblet. 'This is for the baby; give it to him with my love, and my love also to his mother. When my baby is born then you must bring your son and his mother to see me. The children will be of almost the same age.' She felt very moved by this news of a successful birth and her spirits rose. She blinked the tears from her eyes and saw him pass his hand across his face.

Ardal was the first to recover. 'You said that you wanted to see me about something, Brehon,' he said, his tone holding its normal polite, efficient note.

'I was going to ask a favour of you.' Mara smiled at him. She hesitated for a moment, rearranging matters in her mind and then decided to tell him the whole story of the morning, finishing with Malachy's angry words.

It would not be Ardal's style to break out in a torrent of abuse against his brother-in-law, but Mara expected him, at least, to express a cold disapproval of such conduct. He did not, however, and Mara was intrigued to recognize almost a look of pity on the neat-featured face in front of her.

'You're not surprised,' she commented.

'No.' There was such a long gap after the monosyllable that she thought he would say no more. He tugged his moustache and frowned slightly.

'You see, Malachy is a man of strong passions . . .' He began fluently enough and then tailed off looking at her appraisingly as if trying to decide whether she would understand.

'Yes, I believe you are right,' she said in a manner which she tried to make matter-of-fact as well as encouraging.

'You remember, of course,' he said, 'that Mór had child after child and that all of them, except for Nuala, the first-born, were born dead.' Mara nodded again. It was something that she could hardly bear to think of. The small, grey bodies and the beautiful, distraught young mother. 'Well, then Malachy discovered that Mór was ill, that she had a large lump in her breast. He knew from one of his medical texts that to be pregnant was the worst possible thing for a disease like this so from that day onwards Malachy forewent the pleasures of his wife's bed – that was two years of abstinence and then there were another two years after her death . . .'

'And then he meets Caireen.' Mara nodded her head. 'I understand what you are telling me, Ardal. Caireen now means the world to Malachy, and his daughter's needs are very much second place. But you can see why I don't think that Nuala should go back into that household for the moment. She is very unhappy. I would have her myself, but she would have to stay in the guesthouse and I really need to keep that for guests and for Turlough's men when he is living at Cahermacnaghten. In any case, this isn't a suitable place for her with all those boys around. She's growing up and she needs someone to care for her. It should be her father, but if he is occupied with different responsibilities . . .' She allowed her voice to trail away. Despite Ardal's explanation, the thought of Malachy still filled her with fury, but she was too diplomatic to allow it to show.

'Of course, she can come.' Ardal's response was immediate and vigorous. 'I told Malachy that. Caherconnell is no place for her at the moment.'

'I have another favour to ask.' Mara studied his face and sought to find the right words. 'I ask this favour, not just for myself not just for Nuala, but also in memory of your sister Mór. Mór had all the gifts that nature could bestow on her,' she went on carefully. 'You remember her burning intelligence, her desire to study, to learn, her wish to go to bard school, but she was not allowed to bring those gifts to fulfilment. I think her daughter should be given the chance that Mór was denied: I think that she should finish her training as a physician.'

'Stay with Malachy?' Ardal looked puzzled.

'No, that won't work, not with his new marriage. I was wondering if we could find a tutor for her, someone who could live for a while at Lissylisheen, perhaps some physician who is now too old for the hard life of journeying out to distant farms in bad weather and during the night, but who would be willing to take on a pupil. I was thinking that the king could perhaps find someone like that in Thomond. The income from Nuala's property at Rathborney will easily cover the expenses. But the question is, would you be willing to do that, Ardal? To house both?'

He was taken aback; she could see that, but she waited quietly. After a moment, he bowed his head.

'I can refuse you nothing, Brehon,' he said, and a small triumphant smile crept to his finely formed lips. 'I can refuse nothing today, on the day of the birth of my son and my heir.'

'I'll talk to Nuala,' said Mara. She rose to her feet and went to the door with him. She looked after him as he strode down the road to where Donie stood patiently walking the mare up and down. There was a spring to Ardal's step and a buoyancy about the way that his arms swung from side to side. She had never seen him in such high spirits before.

So, she thought, as she watched him; a little baby had been ready to be born from within the body of a woman that Ardal had loved for years when Iarla had arrived with his claim to be Ardal's son. What a disastrous moment for the young man from Aran to choose after twenty years of silence.

Fifteen

Cáin Adomnáin
(The Law of Adomnán)

A man must not touch a woman against her will. Even if rape does not occur, there are still penalties to be paid:

1. *For touching a woman inside her girdle: ten ounces of silver or ten milch cows*
2. *For kissing a woman against her will: the full honour-price of her father or husband*
3. *For shaming a woman by lifting her dress: six ounces of silver or six milch cows*

Mara was up early the following morning, but she wasn't the first to rise. The mist of the grey dawn still hung around the fields and that, oddly enough, seemed to create a greater emptiness in the landscape than if the usual, far-reaching view had stretched out before her eyes. The cows in their meadows were hidden, the hedges cloaked by the grey vapour and nothing was visible except one figure.

'You're out early, Nuala.' Mara approached the girl as she sat on the mounting block beside the Cahermacnaghten gates.

'I couldn't sleep well,' said the girl. Her eyes were deeply shadowed. Mara felt regretful that she had not sought her out the night before. She had been deceived by the bold front that Nuala had put on as she joked and laughed with the law-school boys. I should have realized, she reproached herself. The girl was heart-broken by her father's rejection and sick with worry about her future.

'I spoke with Ardal last night, Nuala, and I think that between us we have worked out a temporary solution to your future.' Mara's tone was matter-of-fact and businesslike. Nuala was no child and would not relish being treated as one. 'The first thing I have to say is that you need not worry about your inheritance; that is yours and yours alone. No one can take it from you. Toin's will was perfectly valid and he had a complete right to leave the house and farm at Rathborney to you.'

Nuala said nothing, but she heaved a sigh of relief. Her eyes were still troubled though.

'Secondly,' said Mara briskly. 'It may be beneficial for you to study under someone other than your father and I intend to ask the king to look out for a suitable tutor for you – perhaps someone who wishes to give up the practice of medicine, but is happy, and capable, to pass on the results of his experience and knowledge to a young pupil.'

'What! A school!' Nuala was open-mouthed.

'A school would be good, but, as yet, I don't know of one,' admitted Mara. 'However, Ardal has promised that he will house you and your tutor and I think that will work out very well.'

'Live with Ardal.' Nuala's tone was thoughtful. She was very still. Mara also did not move. The girl had to be given time to absorb the arrangements for her future. A missel thrush flew down on to the bush near the gate, cocked his head to look at them and then broke out into a melodious song. Nuala waited until he had finished and flown away before she spoke again.

'Ardal's happy for me to go on studying?' she queried.

'Yes,' said Mara with conviction. 'He is happy to do that.' She waited for a moment watching the downcast face in front of her. Fachtnan was right; despite the difference of colouring, Nuala's face was the face of her mother Mór. Like Mór, who never rushed into speech, Nuala was now taking her time, turning the matter over in her mind.

Mara watched her affectionately. 'Nuala,' she said eventually. 'I think you should take this as a great opportunity. Ardal is a man of importance and he has many distinguished and interesting visitors from all over Ireland. You go to live with him, be his hostess, learn to greet his guests, to make conversation with them and your confidence will grow and you will become a woman. You've been trying to pretend to be a boy; you've sensed, rightly or wrongly, that your father would have preferred to have a boy, but there is nothing superior about being a boy. You be yourself, a beautiful woman with brains and knowledge, and be glad to be yourself. Then you will have a happy life. Does this all make sense to you?'

For a moment Mara wondered whether she had been too frank. Nuala, after all, was only fourteen years old. Perhaps it was too much to expect that she would understand all that Mara had been saying to her; perhaps it would have been better to have approached the matter from a simpler line, said that Ardal was lonely, that he would like his niece to live with him, promised her that all would soon blow over and that she would be reinstated as her father's daughter and apprentice.

Suddenly and quite unexpectedly, Nuala laughed. She reached forward and impulsively kissed Mara on the cheek.

'You're trying to make me like yourself, fit to be a wife to a king,' she said with a humorous quirk to the side of her mouth. 'Well, I think I'll ride around to Lissylisheen now and give big, fat Liam a surprise when I turn up for breakfast. It will probably all be rather fun.'

And with those brave words, she strode off to the stables and Mara heard her talking cheerfully to her pony as she saddled her.

'Only five more days to go to the end of the Hilary Term,' said Aidan boisterously, slapping Bran on the side of the wolfhound's lean shoulder as he came into the schoolhouse on Saturday morning. 'You'll miss us, old fellow, won't you?'

'Do you think that we will solve the secret and unlawful killing before we go home, Brehon?' asked Shane with a worried air, as he in turn stroked Bran whose long, whipcord tail was wagging as vigorously as if he had not seen the boys for a whole year, rather than for just one night.

'I think we should,' said Mara cheerfully. 'Everything seems a lot clearer now.'

'What made it clearer, Brehon?' asked Enda curiously. 'Was it going to Aran?'

'That and other things,' said Mara. 'You see, solving a murder is a matter of clear, logical thinking and a lot of hard work. I'm lucky to have you all because you have helped me very much. We've managed to eliminate a lot of people and that just leaves some possibilities on the list still.'

'I've got a *taoiseach* on my list,' said Enda, smiling mischievously.

'And so have I.' Moylan was not to be outdone.

'Is it the same one?' asked Hugh with interest while Mara cast a hasty glance to make sure that the door to the yard was closed. The shutters were open, but the window was screened by a heavy piece of sacking.

'Speak quietly when you mention names,' she said.

'I don't think it was a *taoiseach*; I think it was the basket maker,' said Aidan suddenly. 'He's got a turf barrow that he uses for his willow rods. I saw it there. And Iarla was messing about with Orlaith . . .'

'Well, I don't believe that the basket maker had anything to do with it,' said Enda with a scornful glance at Aidan. 'For one thing, the man has ten children hanging around. It would be hard for him to sneak off and go over to Lissylisheen and murder Iarla and find some way of bringing the body back to the cave. It's silly to say that he would just crouch down so that he couldn't be seen from the fields – the hedges aren't that high and he would just attract attention to himself.'

'Go on then,' said Aidan truculently, 'if you're so clever, say who did it and how.'

'Ah, well, there you have me. I don't know how it was done, but I still think that Ardal O'Lochlainn did it. He is the only one who has a real reason. Anyone could see that he didn't like a son aged twenty suddenly turning up. But I haven't managed to work out how he could have done it.'

'And what about you, Moylan?' Mara turned to the younger boy. 'Is your *taoiseach* also Ardal O'Lochlainn?'

'I think it was Teige O'Brien.' Moylan's tone was nonchalant.

'But he's my uncle!' Hugh sounded outraged.

'Doesn't mean that he couldn't kill someone.'

'But why?' Hugh was still indignant.

'Because of what Iarla did to Saoirse, birdbrain. That was a deadly insult and Teige avenged his family's honour.'

'And how did he get the body to Balor's Cave, Moylan?' asked Mara.

'Well, you know that Donogh Óg was building the new gatehouse at Lemeanah. There was a cart coming and going all the morning with stone from the quarry near Kilcorney; perhaps something could have been managed with that, couldn't it? The body could have been put into the cart and then taken out and hidden in the quarry.'

'That's quite clever,' said Enda enthusiastically. 'But it makes it more likely that it was Donogh Óg. I vote that we put him back on the list. He would have had much more opportunity to do it. Shall we go over to Lemeanah, Brehon, and make enquiries.'

'I think not.' Mara looked regretfully at the eager faces, but shook her head. 'We're going to have to work now. We've lost two days from your studies by going to Aran and we are almost at the end of the Hilary Term. Fachtnan and Enda, you have important examinations at the end of the Trinity Term. I'll see on Monday afternoon, but for now we must study.'

★   ★   ★

Mara waited until the boys had eaten their dinner and disappeared in the direction of Doolin – sailing and rowing were now huge interests with them all and she guessed that she would not see them for the rest of the afternoon. Once the sound of the ponies' feet departing down the road had vanished, she quietly ordered Seán to saddle her horse. Brigid was scrubbing out the kitchen house and was now resigned to seeing Mara going out at a walking pace on the back of her mare.

The blackthorn was beginning to unfurl, she noticed as she ambled down the lane. There was not the profusion that she had seen on her way to Doolin, but the black twigs with their pointed ivory-coloured buds, each emerging from a small, pale-green sheaf, were almost more beautiful than their full-blown cousins in the warmer air near to the Atlantic. As she neared Lemeanah she could see how the grass was beginning to take on that deeper hue of spring green in the well-drained pastures around the castle, and beneath the grey stones walls a few purple and yellow gilly flowers sent out their sweet fragrance.

'Is the *taoiseach* at home today?' she said to the porter. She half hoped that Teige would be bustling around the courtyard, or somewhere nearby but the answer came instantly.

'Yes, Brehon, he's in the hall.' With his other hand, the man set the bell jangling. Mara dismounted from her horse and allowed the porter to take it away to the stable, and then turned to greet the steward who had hastened down the pathway to the gatehouse.

'The O'Brien is on his way down, Brehon. He saw you from the window. Here he comes now.'

No hope for a quiet word in the courtyard then, thought Mara. She would have to go through with a social visit now. 'Ah, Teige,' she said when he arrived. 'I hope I'm not disturbing you.'

'Come in, Brehon, come in.' He was surprised and slightly worried by her visit, she thought. She would have to be quick-thinking and inventive if he were to be in the relaxed state that she needed before she cross-questioned him.

'You are all well?' She paused by the first embrasure and made the usual enquiry before they got too far up the steeply winding staircase. Soon she would be completely out of breath and her silence might be taken as ominous.

'Yes, indeed we are, and you, you're keeping well?'

'Never better!' The heroic lie was becoming second nature to her now and she rattled it off without hesitation.

'That's good.' Teige was definitely uneasy. She could hear it in his voice and see it in the furtive glances that he threw over his shoulder at her. 'Come in.' He positively galloped up the last section of the stairway and stood above her with the light flowing out from the hall. He cast a look over his shoulder and said loudly, 'Ciara, the Brehon is here.'

Ciara, Mara decided, was her usual cordial self. Whatever was causing Teige's uneasiness had not affected her. She was full of questions about Mara's health, exclamations of admiration at her bravery in attempting the journey to Aran and comfortable horror at the two deaths that had happened in the Burren.

'And how is Saoirse these days?' asked Mara, after answering queries about her own daughter, Sorcha, in Galway. Her question was addressed to Ciara, but she kept a sharp eye on Teige and noticed that he winced at the mention of his daughter. Her suspicions hardened to a near certainty as she studied his florid complexion, his dark hair and eyes, his fleshy nose. It was odd, how, after having known him for all her life, that she was now studying his face for resemblances as if it were that of a stranger.

'So we're hoping it might be a match,' finished Ciara. Mara had heard very little of the woman's flow of words, but gathered that she had been talking of Saoirse and the eldest O'Connor boy. It would be a very suitable match and would unite the clans, according to Ciara.

'That would be wonderful,' Mara said warmly, endeavouring to conceal a smile as she remembered Moylan's, and Aidan's, whispered words about Saoirse. There was no doubt that it would be a good idea to get Saoirse married off as soon as possible. 'You would be pleased about that, wouldn't you?' She addressed the remark to Teige and saw a broad smile spread over his face. Pleasure? Yes, that, but also a shade of relief, she thought.

'Such a pretty girl.' Mara allowed a silence to elapse after this remark and saw the gratified smiles on both parents' faces fade into a slight bewilderment. The Brehon had already declined all offers of refreshment; now should be the moment that she would approach the reason for her visit, but Mara just sat there, smiling gently. After another few moments, Ciara rose to her feet.

'I'll leave you then, Brehon, if you'll excuse me. I have some household duties and I'm sure that you have messages from the king to talk over with Teige.'

For a large woman she got herself out of the room very gracefully and Teige was left alone with Mara, looking as if he wanted to follow his wife.

'So you found the visit to Aran useful, Brehon, did you?' Eventually Teige broke the silence between them.

'Yes, I did,' said Mara thoughtfully.

Teige had run out of conversation now, so he just sat on his chair staring at her uneasily.

'You see murder is a terrible thing. In order to find the reason for murder, I have to look into the heart of the murderer and find what has provoked the deed.' Mara's voice was bland and conversational. She allowed the pause to grow until Teige became uneasy and then she looked at him inquiringly as one who expects an answer.

'So you found a reason for the murder when you were at Aran, is that right?' He said the words awkwardly and his eyes did not meet hers. Mara allowed another few moments of silence to elapse and then nodded, slowly and sadly.

'Yes, Teige,' she said. 'Yes, I did find a possible motive for the murder of Iarla when I was at Aran.'

He paled then; his florid skin suddenly looking sallow. How alike these two young people, with their fleshy noses and heavy jaws, were to him, thought Mara. The newly married Donal took his better-cut features from his mother's side of the family and so did the younger members of the family at Lemeanah.

'I spoke with the widow of the man Becan,' she added. 'Did you know that she was the sister of Iarla's mother, the girl that you, Turlough and Ardal danced with in those far-off days in Aran twenty years ago?'

'Yes,' he muttered. 'Yes, I think that I did know that.'

'Of course, you've been backwards and forwards quite a few times during the last few years, haven't you?'

He didn't deny that. He just sat like a man who is waiting for a blow to fall and is powerless to avert it.

'Did you see Iarla then when you went over?' Mara questioned. Suddenly she felt curious about that. Teige, she remembered, had been quite carefree on that evening of the wedding. He had shown no signs of recognizing this young man from Aran.

Teige shook his head. 'No, I had never seen him.'

'But his mother, the blacksmith's wife, told you that he was your son?'

He didn't look surprised at her knowledge – the blow had fallen and he almost looked relieved. 'No, I never saw him, but the mother told me that he was the image of me. It was just bad luck that she was by the shore when I went over there to collect the rents for Turlough a couple of years ago. She came right up to me and said that now she had seen me again she was sure that her son was of my begetting.'

Fineguth, finechruth, finebés, kin voice, kin appearance, kin behaviour, thought Mara. Aloud she asked, 'Did she blackmail you?'

'I sent her some silver from time to time. They were very poor.'

'So why didn't you acknowledge him when he turned up with the story that he was the son of Ardal O'Lochlainn?'

Teige gave a weary shrug. 'How was I to know the truth of the matter? We had both lain with her. He could be the seed of either. Or even of the blacksmith.' His voice lacked conviction.

Mara paused. So far the conversation had been about issues that were of private concern only. The parenthood of Iarla was a matter between him, his mother and his father. But there were larger issues of concern. The young man had come to the Burren with a letter from his mother swearing to his paternity and he had not left the kingdom, but had been secretly and unlawfully killed. What had triggered that fatal blow?

Mara turned her mind back to that evening of the wedding. She looked gravely at the man opposite her and tried to imagine his feelings when he heard the news. He had looked very alarmed; she remembered the look on his face then.

'Why do you think that the blacksmith's wife, Étain, that was her name, wasn't it? Why do you think that Étain named Ardal as the father rather than you? She had recognized that Iarla was your son as soon as she saw you again a few years ago.'

Teige shrugged his heavy shoulders. 'She was a woman of sense. She knew that there was no more to be got from me. I told her that plainly. I would not acknowledge him; I refused that. I have enough children of my own.'

Teige stopped. Mara nodded solemnly, looking at him with a blank face, but her mind was working busily. *End up in the ditch with our throats cut,* that was what the boy Iarla had said to Orlaith when he had feared that drink would loosen his uncle's tongue. Had Teige threatened Étain? Hinted, perhaps, that if she persisted he would turn violent?

'She had no proof either,' continued Teige bitterly. 'Who knows who was the father of that boy? It could have been anyone, as far

as I knew. And then, I suppose, she changed her plans. She had heard
that Ardal was rich and that he had no children, so she decided to
name him. God have mercy on her,' he added with a sudden real-
ization of the heroism of this mother who had put her eternal soul
in danger by her deathbed perjury.

Étain knew she was approaching death so she sent Becan over
to check on the reputed wealth and childlessness of Ardal
O'Lochlainn, thought Mara, feeling a surge of pity for this woman
who had made the ultimate sacrifice for the sake of the welfare of
her child.

'Jesus and his Blessed Mother will have mercy on her,' she said
with conviction. No matter what the Church would say about this
sin, it was one that any mother could understand and forgive. Mara's
resolve to find the truth about the killing of Iarla and to punish the
murderer hardened. Cost what it may, she would do that last service
for Étain of Aran, the beautiful girl who had danced by the firelight that night twenty years ago; the woman who had loved many
men, and for whom, ultimately, mother love overpowered all else,
even the fear of eternal damnation.

'Who was responsible for Iarla's birth may never be known,' she
said eventually. 'The question now is –' she said the words quietly
and steadily, looking at him intently – 'who was responsible for his
death here in the kingdom of the Burren.' Teige didn't answer so
she added bluntly, 'Were you?'

He sat up very straight, his mouth open with an expression of
astonishment on his face. Mara was sceptical though. Surely it must
have occurred to him by now that he was under suspicion.

'Me?' he said. 'Why would I do a thing like that?'

'I think,' said Mara, 'that if you truly believed that Iarla was your
son, you would have had a very good reason. If you even suspected
that he was your son, you would still have had good reason.'

The room was very quiet as Mara and Teige looked at each other
across the table. A smouldering log tumbled in the fireplace, then
crashed on to the flagstone, a small black-headed bird flew in between
the stone mullions and hit its beak with a sharp tap against one of
the small diamond-shaped panes of glass and a heavy velvet curtain
moved with the draught from the door. Neither spoke nor moved.

Suddenly a shout of laughter came from below. A door slammed,
flying feet clattered against the stone of the staircase. Ciara called
out a protest, but the feet continued. The door burst open and a
crowd of young people exploded into the room. They were an

attractive sight: the dark-haired O'Brien youngsters and two blond-haired O'Connors.

'Excuse me, Brehon.'

'Sorry to interrupt, Brehon.'

'Father we just wanted to ask you . . .'

'Mother says we may, if you say yes . . .'

'It's the races.'

'The horse races.'

'They're on today.'

'The races at Coad.'

The young voices tumbled over each other and Mara smiled. Saoirse had her arm around her father's neck and Teige's heavy moustache was lifted by a huge grin. Though he then pretended to frown and to shoo them away, they were not deceived.

'Now then, now then, if your mother says that you may go; then you may go. What are you coming bothering me for when I am busy?'

One of the younger girls giggled. 'We want some silver.' Her hands reached around Saoirse, who was now ensconced on her father's knee, and fumbled in his pouch.

'I'm being robbed,' said Teige with relish. 'Help, I'm being robbed. Save me, Brehon!'

Mara laughed. 'I think you'll just have to pay up, Teige. You're outnumbered.'

'You'll have me ruined all of you,' he grumbled. 'Stop kissing me now, Saoirse. Come on, let me stand up. Now remember that's your lot; nothing else this week or I'll have you all out cleaning the stables from morning to night.' He winked at the two O'Connor boys and produced a bundle of small pieces of silver from his pouch, handing them out one by one to his daughters and sons with a teasing remark or a quick kiss. Saoirse, Mara noticed, got an extra large piece of silver and a very warm hug. Obviously relationships between father and daughter were back to their usual affectionate terms.

'You have a very loving family,' she said as the door closed behind the last of the young people. Then, when he didn't reply, she added, 'And, of course, you are a very loving father to them all.'

He faced her then, his eyes hardening.

'Let's go back to the St Patrick's Night, the night of the wedding,' she said softly. 'You remember it, I'm sure. Iarla danced most of the time with Saoirse. He had been drinking heavily. It had all gone to his head, I suppose, the new place, the new company, the thought of being son and heir to someone of Ardal O'Lochlainn's standing and wealth.'

Teige compressed his lips: his grey eyes were angry and she realized that he was not capable of understanding the feelings of a young lad, such as Iarla, fresh from the Aran Islands and facing the glittering prospects of wealth and security. His thoughts were completely centred on his daughter.

'And then Iarla went too far. It had been a case of kissing and cuddling up to then and Saoirse had been as keen as he.' She didn't allow him to reply to this, but hurried on. 'But then he tried to attack her, possibly to rape her. It might have happened too if her friend Mairéad O'Lochlainn had not been brave and resourceful.'

Mara gave him time to reply to this, but he said nothing. He understood where she was leading.

'And, of course, if Iarla had raped Saoirse and she had conceived as a result of that rape, then the child would have been a child of incest. Saoirse would have lain with her own brother. That was something that you could not afford to allow to happen. You dealt with Saoirse severely, scolded her, even struck her – and I'm sure that was not your normal practice. You knew that she was a passionate young girl and you were afraid that she might forgive and forget and go back to the man who had wooed her so roughly. You told her to have no more to do with the young man from Aran, you warned the guards not to allow Iarla to put foot inside the gates of Lemeanah . . .'

Mara paused here. Teige said nothing so she continued. 'But what if that were not enough to set your mind at rest? What if you still feared that they would seek out each other behind your back? Saoirse is attractive, and she is attracted to young men – just as a girl of her age should be. As I said, she is a passionate girl and you must have known that quite well. You could not take any risk of this relationship developing, could you?'

Still he did not answer so she finished with the words: 'Was Iarla's death a small price to pay to keep your daughter safe? Were you the one who killed him, Teige?'

He denied it, of course. Bitterly, vehemently, swearing every possible oath, Teige denied murdering Iarla. Mara listened, nodding her head and making some notes and then she left him, an angry, fearful man. She had another errand to do before her energy ran out.

★   ★   ★

Donogh Óg was working away at the quarry, as she had guessed. He had told her boys that he couldn't do any hunting that weekend as he had to get some more blocks cut. The gatehouse at Lemeanah had used up a lot of the stock that he kept in order to tempt prospective clients, he had explained to Enda. When Mara arrived he was chipping away and there was a satisfactorily long line of newly cut blocks lined up at the front of the entrance.

'I'll wait until you take a break,' said Mara, seeing that the block he was working on was almost finished. He was a good craftsman, she thought and she admired his industry. He could so easily have just accepted his way of life as his father's eldest son, helped with the farm and hoped to inherit his share of the lands after the death of his father. He was more like Ardal than Donogh, she thought. He had recognized that with the large number of brothers in the family, his share, according to Brehon law which allowed the youngest brother to inherit as much as the eldest, would be a small one so he had gone ahead and built up a new business for himself.

'Have you thought any more about that house you wanted me to build at Cahermacnaghten?' He had laid down his chisel and hammer, and then placed the finished block, very precisely, in line with the others. He came over and sat beside her.

She smiled at him, admiring his enterprise and confidence. 'Not yet,' she said firmly. 'I've had too much on my mind.'

'Ah, the murders, yes.' He seemed quite cheerful about it. Death didn't appear to be of much consequence to the young; it was the middle-aged who had begun to value life and to shudder at its untimely loss.

'You did a very good job at Lemeanah,' said Mara. His business-like look came back again. The extension to the gatehouse was a building to be proud of. 'I just wanted to ask you about that day when the body of Iarla was found at Balor's Cave,' she went on.

'That would have been the Thursday, wouldn't it?' he mused. 'That's right, isn't it? The wedding was on Monday, not much done on Tuesday, I remember, everybody had too much to drink and the bargain was that Teige's men were to do some of the work for me – mixing the mortar and that sort of thing – none of them were fit on the Tuesday. Wednesday was a very wet day, so I took the opportunity to talk to Malachy so when Thursday came I started work as soon as it dawned.'

'You started here?' Mara looked around the quarry.

'That's right, Brehon. I filled up the cart with blocks and drove it over there and began work immediately.'

'Any sign of Iarla, the man from Aran?'

'Not a sign.' There was an air of distaste in the way that he had said the words. That was understandable. Donogh Óg, according to Enda's story, was one of the party of youths that had punished Iarla for his behaviour to Saoirse.

'And were you the one that drove the cart to and fro for new blocks?'

Donogh Óg shook his head. 'No, Brehon,' he said with the air of one who knows his own value. 'That would have been a waste of my time. I was doing the building, laying the blocks, supervising the mortar making.'

'So who drove the cart?'

Donogh Óg hesitated. 'To be honest with you, Brehon, I wouldn't be too sure. It could have been anyone. It seemed to be a different person each time. These are very heavy blocks – you couldn't take too many at one time – so the cart was going and coming continually over the morning. Sometimes it was one of the guardsmen, sometimes a servant from the house, a farm worker, sometimes one of the O'Briens themselves . . .'

'What about Teige?' asked Mara. 'Could he have taken a turn?'

Donogh Óg wrinkled his forehead in an effort to remember. 'Could have done,' he said eventually. 'I don't remember. I was working very hard, getting the walls up. We were hoping to have it thatched before night. The thatchers were standing by with their bundles of reeds and their thatching tools and they were putting pressure on me. It could have been Saint Patrick himself that drove that cart and I wouldn't have noticed as long as the supply of blocks kept coming.'

Sixteen

Crích Gablach
(Ranks in Society)

A Brehon has responsibility to the king to maintain good order in his kingdom. No crime should be allowed to go unpunished. If there is a puzzle over the author of the crime, the Brehon must use all knowledge and experience to solve that mystery.

The mist was gathering by the time Mara walked her mare down the lane towards Balor's Cave. The sky was a silver-grey, the bright yellow of the willow catkins was silvered by the moisture and drops of water nestled between the blue-green crisp curls of lichen.

In the sally gardens, Dalagh the basket maker was sorting out the rods of purple willow, grading them according to size and thickness. Mara could see that he had been up since dawn. Already the green, yellow and red rods had been sorted and were securely tied with withies into neat bundles.

'God bless the work, Dalagh,' called Mara cheerfully. 'You haven't the family helping you today.'

'No, I don't, Brehon.' He came over to the wall, carrying a set of beautiful purple twigs with him. 'The O'Lochlainn sent a wagon and they all piled in. I'm having a fine peaceful afternoon to myself. I won't see any of them before sundown. It's Coad,' he explained, seeing her puzzled expression.

'Of course,' said Mara.

Coad Horse Races was a big day for Ardal. He bred some very fine horses and always liked to match them against other horses from Corcomroe, Thomond and other kingdoms. Everyone who worked for him had the day off. This part of the Burren would be very quiet today. Dalagh would be one of the few people still working on O'Lochlainn land. Mara stood still for a moment mentally rearranging her schedule. An opportunity like this might not come again.

'I'll leave you in peace then, Dalagh,' she said good-humouredly. 'Could I tie up my mare here against your willow tree? I'm just going to go for a little walk down here.' He looked surprised and then a little alarmed and she quickly added, with a bright smile, 'I need to say a few prayers.' And if that left him thinking that she was going to spend half an hour on her knees in front of the altar at Kilcorney Church, well, that was his affair.

Balor's Cave looked ominous: a gaping mouth in a hillside of green. The clean neat black rows of earth piled into ridges outside the cave, waiting for their spring sowing of vegetables, seemed incongruous in that setting. Mara could see that Ardal would have a problem in persuading his men to work there again, even if they had overcome their fears in the first place. The picture was still in her mind of the dead man, of the two dead men, each with an eye gouged out, lying in front of the cave while the ominous ravens hovered overhead. Even the upturned willow tree, still not cleared away, gave the impression that a force stronger than man was at work here.

Unhesitatingly, Mara turned her back on the tree and went towards the cave. She would never get such a good opportunity to do this again. This afternoon most of the Burren would be at the races in Coad. At the entrance she bowed her head, pausing once she was inside. It was unexpectedly dark; of course it faced north. She fumbled in her pouch and took out a box of sulphur sticks. Standing near to the light she counted them. Ten altogether; that should last her well enough.

Oddly enough there was a neat, tidy look about this cave that reminded her of Ardal. The floor seemed to have been swept clean of the rocks and small stones that usually littered the floor of any other cave that she had been in. Perhaps Balor, despite his wicked ways and ferocious reputation, was of an orderly and tidy disposition. She grinned at the thought.

By the wavering light of her first sulphur stick Mara could actually see the back of the cave as she advanced. She frowned, puzzled, but continued walking until she could actually touch the dripping limestone wall. Odd, she thought. She clearly remembered the words spoken by Danann, the basket maker's boy.

'*It's just a cave like any other cave, Brehon. My brothers and I took candles in one night and explored it. We went back quite a long way and found no Balor!*'

She had only come about six feet; no one could have called this 'a long way'. She looked around, holding the sulphur stick aloft. It was burning steadily, she was glad to see. Cumhal had always impressed upon the boys that air in a cave should always be tested with a flame. *Not enough air for fire; not enough air for people*, she had heard him say again and again.

And then, as she turned slowly around, she saw it. At first she thought that it was a shadow, but then she realized that it was a narrow slit in the rocky wall of the cave. The young slim boys had probably slipped through there easily but it was difficult for a woman five months pregnant. Eventually she was through, however, and then her sulphur stick wavered and went out.

Mara stayed very close to the entrance while she lit the second one. Her hands shook for an instant. Was the air here bad air? Being pregnant had robbed her a little of her courage and her optimism; now she was not just risking herself, but the baby: her and Turlough's unborn child. It will be all right, she told herself. This is the perfect afternoon for the exploration with everyone at Coad Races and then I will know the truth and can tackle the murderer with all the weight of the law and of my position.

Once the second sulphur stick flared up, Mara could see that there was another way between the two caves, a much wider portal. She went over and examined it curiously. '*There used to be lots of under-ground rivers once in the Burren,*' her father told her when she was a child, '*and these rivers carved out passages through the limestone.*' She didn't know whether that was true or not, but this opening was made by a man, she guessed, holding up the sulphur stick and examining the chisel marks in the limestone rock. It was very low; a person would have to bend almost double to get through it, but it was quite wide.

With an eye on her sulphur stick, still burning steadily, but at a rather alarming rate, Mara left the intriguing man-made opening and went down to the end of this cave. Going south in the direc-tion of Lemeanah, she thought to herself, picturing the Burren above her head. This was a bigger cave than the last one and she guessed that it was probably as far as the basket maker's boys had gone. They would have had the fear of discovery by their father in their minds and would not have wanted to spend too long out of their beds.

This cave, too, seemed to end in a blank wall, but now Mara was sure that her guess was a correct one, so she painstakingly searched for another exit in the craggy dripping walls around her. It was diffi-cult to see by the very small thin flame of the sulphur stick. It was burning down perilously near to her hand and then her foot slipped on the smooth, wet boulder clay underfoot and the flame went out. Mara drew in a deep breath. She was no longer sure of where she was and whether she would be able to retrace her steps. The dark made everything seem disorientating. Added to that, the whole cave was dripping wet. Already her hair was soaked and the wool surface of her cloak shed water when she passed her hand over it. Even the air that she breathed in was damp, with the sensation of being out in a heavy mist. The sulphur sticks in her pouch might get wet and then she should have no light. Common sense told her that she should now go back and return with Cumhal and perhaps another few men and certainly with a couple of reliable closed lanterns.

But which was the way back? As Mara groped her way around the wall she could not seem to find any break in the stone. There must be, she told herself. And yet, she was sure that she had already knocked her hand a few minutes ago on the protruding spike of lime-encrusted rock. Quickly she reached inside her cloak and unthreaded a ribbon from the bodice of her gown. She would tie this ribbon on to the jagged point and then go on feeling her way around.

There was something about the steady drip, drip, drip of the limey water falling from the ceiling that began to make her feel nervous. It did not seem particularly colder than it had been on the March day out of doors, but the damp made her hands feel numb. She stood still for a minute, rubbing them together, twisting her long fingers over and around each other. And then, to keep the blood coursing through them, she began to clap her hands, first in a steady, measured stroke and then faster in the rhythmic beat as played on the drum at those *céilí* dances in the cottages and halls of the Burren. The sound brought back the picture of Iarla's mother, the lovely red-headed Étain, with her feet slapping out the rhythm on the hollow flagstone and the firelight striking glints of gold from her hair.

The thought steadied her and she resolved that she would solve this murder of the boy who meant so much to Étain, probably all the more since her first-born son had been taken away from her as soon as he was born.

Steadily Mara went on, moving her way down the wall, feeling the rough surfaces of some stones and the smoother ones of other. Here and there she encountered a protruding spike where some harder piece of stone had resisted the water, but none of them bore her cluster of silk ribbon. She knew that she was being stupid, but she could not help a surge of triumph. She was about to discover how Iarla and Becan could have been murdered.

Mara almost missed the opening. Only the slight draught that stirred the hem of her cloak warned her that there was something different about this part of the wall. She lowered her hand and there was nothing there, just a gap.

Was this the way back or the way forward? She would have to take the risk. Everything in life was a risk, Mara told herself. If she missed this opportunity, she might not get another one like it. Once she was certain, she would go straight back, retrieve her mare from the basket maker, ride home and then come to a decision about what to do next. She hesitated about whether to light a sulphur stick but decided to go right through first. There undoubtedly was a movement of air so there was probably little danger of poisonous fumes. Putting down her hand to feel her way, as she bent down as low as she could manage, she noted that these stones did not have the encrusted powdery lime clinging to them; no doubt this way through was also man-made.

A series of caves: that's what it was. A series of caves and someone had the enterprise to make the links between them. But why? This was not done in the last few days; weeks and weeks, perhaps done over a space of few years, no doubt many months of patient, secretive cautious hammering and chiselling would have gone in to the construction of these passages.

Once Mara was standing upright, she rubbed her hands once more, slotted each hand far up the opposing sleeve of her *léine* in order to make sure it was dry, then unloosened the string of her pouch and counted the sulphur sticks. Yes, there were still seven of them. This time she would immediately look for the exit; she planned, as she struck the soft pink head against the ridged steel of the container.

This cave was taller than the others. Mara raised the sulphur stick and looked around. The ceiling was hung with rods of petrified lime, but it was the walls that took her attention. Almost straight in front of her there was another exit, this time a natural one, she thought, though it may have been slightly widened at one spot at the bottom. She could walk straight through this and she did so carefully, holding the precious sulphur stick high out of the reach of the persistent air current that still moved on ground level.

Mara wondered how far she had come – possibly a hundred yards, though probably less, but the thought left her head as she saw something standing in the centre of this cave. She stopped and stared at it and then a smile curved her lips. It was a low vehicle with four wooden wheels, very long and very wide, with two shafts at hand height on the back of it. In her mind she apologised to Aidan: this was a turf barrow and that was what he had said. She remembered his words clearly: '*He could have put the body on one of those turf barrows, you know how low they are, then he could have thrown some old sacks over the body and people meeting him would have thought he was just wheeling along a pile of winter cabbages. He could have bent double over the barrow, bent down lower than the walls, so that he would haven't been seen from the fields.*'

Aidan had been right about the turf barrow; this was what had been used to convey the body. But he had been wrong about the old sacks: here in these secret caves they had not been needed, nor had the murderer needed to bend double.

And Aidan had been wrong about accusing Becan of the murder; Becan had been the accuser, had been the one who had stumbled upon the truth before she had arrived at the correct conclusion.

Suddenly Mara's elation died away. She was not the first person to make this journey in the last week. Becan had been there before her. He probably had the foresight to bring a lantern with him, but he had been there; she was sure of that now. He had seen the turf barrow. What had he done next?

Recklessly Mara lit another sulphur stick and went forward in the footsteps of the man whose body she had recently committed to the sparse soil of Aran. She went forward to find full evidence against the murderer.

Mara saw him immediately. She had not expected to meet him, but her courage was high and she showed no sign of dismay at the sight of him as she stepped through yet another arched opening and into a room-like cave filled with the light of a large lantern. This was far less damp than the others that she had passed through. It was higher, of course; she had been aware that the passages between the individual caves had become upward slopes – always slopes, never steps or stairways. The way for the turf barrow had been made smooth. This room was a storeroom; its walls were lined with barrels and casks and large wooden boxes.

Mara's eyes went rapidly to the far side of the room. There was a ramp there, and beyond it was the O'Lochlainn's barn. A tall heavy press in the barn had been moved aside. She noticed immediately that it had small wooden wheels underneath it; from the back they were visible, but from the front the wheels would have been hidden by the carved flange of wood attached to the bottom of the press. Once back in place, the wooden press would have completely concealed the entrance to anyone in the barn. Mara remembered

Turlough's words about how most of the old enclosures had an underground room beneath their buildings. The barn at Lissylisheen had probably once been the main living place before the tower house had been built and this room that she was in now would have been the underground storage place.

'Brehon!' He had given such a violent start that the barrel, filled with springy sheep wool, which he had been wheeling through the entrance, spun out of his hand and crashed to the floor at Mara's feet. She didn't look at it and neither did he. The small, enclosed space was filled by the sound of his heavy breathing. He looked over his shoulder hastily and then back at her. She could see the thoughts rushing through his mind and then his ready tongue came to the rescue.

'Lord save us, Brehon, you gave me a shock, turning up like that. Where in God's name did you spring from?' Once again he looked up at the unblocked entrance to the barn, but he knew that she had not come from there.

I am the third person that has appeared in the caves before this man, thought Mara. And the first lost his life instantly, possibly even before he knew that he had been seen. And the second had lost his life too. Perhaps Becan had been bending over the turf barrow, searching for traces of blood that would betray the cargo that it had carried on that Thursday after St Patrick's Day. Perhaps he had been examining the soft clay on the floor for telltale wheel marks, just as she had done herself, and the murderer had picked up a heavy club and had bludgeoned him to death.

He had no staff here, as far as she could see, but like everyone else he carried a knife at his belt. Instantly she took control.

'I must have got lost,' she said carelessly. 'I should have taken the advice of the basket maker when I was talking to him an hour ago. He told me not to explore that cave, some nonsense about Balor.' She looked at him intently as she said these words and noted the change in his face. A stranger, two strangers, to be killed and their bodies wheeled down on the turf barrow and deposited outside Balor's Cave – that was a much easier matter than getting rid of the Brehon of the Burren, not just the king's appointed judge, but also the king's wife. And now there was mention of the basket maker knowing where she had gone. Mara smiled at him gently and moved forward.

'I can get out through here, can't I?' As she spoke the words, she had swiftly walked across to the wooden ramp that covered the original steps and led out of the storage room.

'Up here?' she queried putting her foot on the ramp.

He had followed her and was just behind her. She could hear his breathing and it took all of her courage not to glance behind as she went nonchalantly up a wooden ramp and into the barn.

'Well, I never knew that you had this underground storage room at Lissylisheen.' She steered her way through the barrels of salted lamb in the barn, praying that someone else would be around and quickened her step until she was at the door of the barn. The fresh breeze smelled wonderful after the smell of old decay in the damp slimy caves and the gleaming white of the limestone walls was pleasantly cheerful after the darkness.

'Is there anyone that you could send down to Kilcorney to collect my mare?' She asked the question with a slight laugh, which, to her pleased amazement, sounded quite genuine.

'There's no one here but ourselves, Brehon,' he replied.

She could tell from his tone that he was uncertain as to how to handle the situation.

'Walk down the road with me then,' she said in a voice which, she was pleased to hear, came out as authoritative and brisk.

He didn't know how to handle the situation; she was relying on that. I am the Brehon of the Burren, she recited silently to herself. She dared not think of anything else, not of the baby, not of Turlough, not of Brigid and Cumhal, nor of her scholars. To her enormous relief there was a great bellowing in the distance, growing louder every second. Then shouts of men were intermingled with the cattle noises and around the corner came a local farmer, Niall MacNamara, wildly waving a stick and shouting.

'Better step back inside the gate, Brehon,' said the man. 'That bull of Niall's is a nasty one and now he's got his herd of cows with him, he's in no biddable mood.'

Mara did as she was told in a nonchalant way. She was immensely cheered by the sight of Niall. His farm was at Noughaval, but he also owned a mill and some land on the other side of the kingdom. By some fortunate chance he had chosen this afternoon to move cattle from Oughtmama to Noughaval and there he was, passing Lissylisheen, flourishing his stick at the bull and calling out a breathless greeting to her.

Behind the cattle came Niall's brother; though classified as a *druth*, a man lacking in full wits, he was an enormously strong and amiable fellow. Mara greeted them both cheerfully and once they had passed she immediately stepped out into the road after the two brothers and the herd of cattle, neatly avoiding the plentiful blobs and spatters of cow manure all over its surface.

'We can go now,' she said, raising her voice above the cattle chorus. 'Just walk with me as far as Cahermacnaghten and Cumhal will send one of the men to fetch the mare.'

She wasn't sure whether he would obey her; he hesitated for a long moment, but then, perhaps reassured by her casual manner, he joined her. Nothing needed to be said for the moment; she was glad of that. She kept her eyes fixed on the comforting bulk of Niall's brother and walked as closely to him as she could. The noise of the cattle was too loud to make conversation comfortable so they continued to march down the road without a word being exchanged until they came to the crossroads where the two men departed towards Rusheen, still driving the cattle along the road.

'Lovely to see the flowers coming back again.' Mara turned determinedly in the direction of Cahermacnaghten. 'I love these bugle flowers, don't you?'

She watched him from the corner of her eye while lightly touching a slender finger to the furry, half-opened buds of purple-blue blossoms and realized that he was being torn by two emotions. One was the hope that she had not come to the correct conclusion about the murder of the two men from Aran, and the other was the fear that she was just inveigling him into her net. On the one hand lay continued safety and the trust of the community and on the other hand was nothing but disgrace, ruin and destitution. He would take the chance, she guessed and was confirmed in her guess as he continued to walk by her side, his face bland and his eyes stony.

'Seán,' said Mara as they reached the gates of Cahermacnaghten law school, where her servant was doing a little desultory sweeping of the courtyard, 'could you please go and fetch my mare from the basket maker at Kilcorney. Cumhal,' she called, noting with satisfaction that he, also, was working in the yard, sharpening all of his tools, 'is it all right if I send Seán over to Kilcorney, to the basket maker's place, to fetch my mare?'

She barely heard Cumhal's reply, but noted that words had registered with the man by her side. Donie was cleaning the harness outside the stables and another of the servants was milking in the cow cabin. With alacrity, Seán fetched the cob out of the stable and threw a long leg over his back.

Mara surveyed the scene; yes there was plenty of aid within call if she needed any. She bent down and caressed her enormous wolfhound and then turned back to the silent man at her side.

'Come in, Liam,' she said, clicking her fingers to Bran to order him to accompany her. 'Come into the schoolhouse. We will be quite private in here.'

Seventeen

Bretha im Gata
(Judgements about Theft)

Every Brehon has to distinguish between gat *(theft by stealth) and* brat
(theft with violence).

*If bees are stolen from a house or yard, it is a more serious offence than
if they are stolen from a field. An animal stolen from a field near to the
house is a more serious offence than if the theft takes place in a field at a
far distance from the house. This is because violence is more likely to occur
if the owner is nearby.*

*The penalty for theft is the payment of the value of the object and the
honour price of its owner.*

A big, genial man, large and affable, Liam had been steward to
the O'Lochlainn family since before Mara was born. Finn
had relied completely on him, and when Ardal succeeded Finn,
he in turn had trusted everything to Liam. Mara gazed at him
thoughtfully, as she ushered him into the schoolhouse. She was
remembering the words spoken by her neighbour, Diarmuid
O'Connor, at the time of the Michaelmas tribute at the end of
September. Mara was blessed by a wonderful memory and
Diarmuid's words were as clear in her mind as if she had just
heard them that morning.

'*Only the birds in the air know how much he has salted away for
himself,*' Diarmuid had said. '*He's been steward to the O'Lochlainn clan
for the last forty years. Never took too much off anyone, mind you. It was
just a matter of a little present here and little present there, a sheaf of oats,
a flagon of ale, a bit of silver, but over the years it has all been mounting
up. Of course it helps that Ardal O'Lochlainn and his father Finn before
him were not the types to be counting . . .*'

'So, how many years has this been going on, this stealing from
the O'Lochlainn?' she asked crisply, seating herself behind her table
and nodding to him to sit on one of the stools. Diarmuid, of course,
had not known the full truth of the matter. Liam, she reckoned now,
had been stealing large quantities from the O'Lochlainn.

Liam looked at her. His large face was bland and impassive but the small grey eyes were narrowed and concentrated. This would be a fight for his life.

'I don't know what you mean, Brehon?' Liam's tone was that of an honest man, worried by an unjust accusation.

'Don't pretend to me.' Her voice was sharp. 'Remember I have seen that underground chamber below the barn. Does anyone other than you know of its existence? Not your *taoiseach* certainly. Remember the O'Lochlainn and I grew up as friends; as a child I played games of hide-and-go-seek in that barn with Ardal and his sisters. No one knew of that chamber then and I would definitely have heard if there had been a new discovery. So why is it full of goods?'

'I don't bother the O'Lochlainn with small details; that room is useful for extra storage.' Liam muttered the words and Mara sensed from his tone that he knew his position was weak.

'That will be for the O'Lochlainn to decide.' Mara's voice was grave. 'But it is for me, as King Turlough Donn's representative here on the Burren, to decide the two cases of secret and unlawful killing. The murders of the two men from Aran – Iarla and Becan.'

He went very white then. She had never seen him look like this. She remembered that she had been surprised when she heard his age a few months ago, but now he looked every year of it. She hardened her heart, remembering the poor widow, with the large family, left bereft on the barren land of Aran and the beautiful Étain who had put her eternal rest in jeopardy for the sake of a very loved son only to have him murdered days after his arrival in the Burren.

'I don't know what you are talking about, Brehon,' he said, his voice shaking. He clenched the fist of his right hand and tightened his mouth.

'Let me tell you the story the way that I see it,' said Mara calmly. 'You have been stealing from the O'Lochlainn for years.' He made a hasty gesture and she shook her head at him. 'No, don't trouble to deny it. Anyone other than O'Lochlainn would have heard the rumours and would have kept a stricter eye on you. Your *taoiseach* is a man of such honour himself that he could never bring himself to doubt the honour of a man who worked for him.'

Mara thought Liam would flush with shame as she said those words, but he didn't. If anything his colour became more normal and there was an expression of cool contempt in his eyes which angered her. Her voice became harder as she went on.

'I'm not sure how long this has being going on for, though I will probably find out when I question the other workers.' He looked taken aback at that, she noticed. He probably expected Ardal to forgive him and no more to be said. He certainly hadn't expected that she would involve herself.

'However, the first matter to be heard at Poulnabrone is going to be the secret and unlawful killing of the two men from Aran.'

'I had nothing whatsoever to do with that.' His voice was truculent. He half rose and then, as a shouted order from Cumhal to Donie came through the open window, he sat down again. Bran raised his head from his paws and looked at the man thoughtfully.

'Let me tell you how it happened,' said Mara.

She thought she could see a glint of regret in his eye. He was probably sorry that he didn't take the chance, while it was available. No doubt, if he had been able to make up his mind as to whether she knew the truth or not, she would now be lying dead, with one eye gouged out – another pretended victim of the one-eyed god Balor. She walked across the room and opened the shutter of the small window a little wider and then came back to her chair.

'The problem lay in the excess drink swallowed by Iarla on that St Patrick's Night,' she said calmly. 'Because he had insulted Saoirse, the daughter of the O'Brien *taoiseach,* very few people on the Burren wanted to have anything to do with him. This meant that for the next few days he was at a loose end. Everyone at Lissylisheen works hard; the work is allocated to them the night before – by you, of course. All have their tasks. This means that you could pick your time for transferring some of the goods from the barn to the storeroom below and thence, when the time was ripe, by the turf barrow to Balor's Cave. You could pick them up at the same time as the vegetables and sell them at markets in Kinvarra and in Galway. This was a duty which you reserved for yourself and yourself only.'

'You tell a good story, Brehon.' Liam's voice strove to sound light and teasing, but his eyes were hard.

Mara gave him a cold glance. 'As I say,' she continued, 'Iarla was at leisure and he was curious. Possibly he was anxious to understand and to estimate the extent of the O'Lochlainn's wealth so he kept an eye on you. I guess he saw you go into the barn from an upper window perhaps, came down, followed you in and found that you were not there. However it happened, I suspect that he discovered your secret. He slipped into the barn on that Thursday morning after breakfast, when you were busy with the men in the courtyard. He slid back the press and went down the ramp. You saw him go into the barn, followed him, and when there was no sign of him in the barn you realized that he had found your secret.'

There was a long silence. Mara did not break it. She could see that Liam was searching through the possible options available to him. He had been the O'Lochlainn steward for forty years. He had hoped to retire, perhaps to become a *briuga*, a hospitaller, one who entertains guests at his own expense and thereby attain noble status. He had had the complete trust of his *taoiseach*, both Finn and Ardal O'Lochlainn. Now this lifetime of hard work, these hopes and ambitions, had been destroyed by this woman standing in front of him; he would be poor and he would be disgraced. Knife in hand, he leaped to his feet with an inarticulate, half-smothered cry of rage.

And Bran sprang at him, seizing him by the right arm.

And then there was a clatter of horses in the courtyard outside and the loud cheerful voice of King Turlough Donn calling out a greeting to Cumhal. This was followed by the quieter tones of Ardal O'Lochlainn.

'Let go, Bran,' said Mara serenely. 'Put that away, Liam. The time for violence is over. Now you must be prepared to make payment for your crimes.'

Without a second glance at him she went to the door and looked out.

'We've come to take you back to Lissylisheen for supper,' called out Turlough boisterously. 'Ardal has had a great triumph. His horses beat horses from all over the country. There were even some there from the lands of the Great Earl himself.'

Instantly Liam was on his feet. 'You'll not shame me in front of the king, Brehon,' he said with some of his usual easy assurance. 'I'll talk to *himself* tonight about the whole business.'

'You'll stay there and I'll do the talking,' snapped Mara, infuriated by his apparent belief that he could talk himself out of this situation. 'On guard, Bran.'

Bran looked up at her and then went to stand by Liam. The boys had taught Bran this command so that he could guard the baskets of apples from the crows at apple harvest time. It seemed as though he understood that it was this human who was the offender because his brown eyes, normally so soft, were hard as he fixed them on Liam.

Nevertheless, Mara kept the door open and an eye on Liam as she called to the two men to come in. She would not risk a knife in her beloved dog.

'We had a great day – you should have come.' Turlough was flushed with excitement and even Ardal leapt from his horse in an exuberant fashion.

'Come in both of you,' repeated Mara. She waited until they were both inside, then beckoned the king's two bodyguards to come to the doorway. 'Stand here, Fergus and Conall,' she said quietly, 'we won't be long.' As she turned back, she saw Liam's eyes go quickly to the two bodyguards and then fall before hers. She shut the door before saying quietly, 'Please give your knife to your *taoiseach*, Liam.'

Turlough looked puzzled and so did Ardal, but after a glance at her face, the smile died from the face of the O'Lochlainn chieftain. He held out his hand quietly and Liam took his knife from his belt and handed it over to his master.

'What's wrong?' asked Turlough, but Ardal said nothing. He continued to study the face in front of him.

I wonder whether Ardal had some suspicions, guessed Mara with a sudden flash of insight. After all the two men had worked side by side for the last twenty years. No man can commit murder twice in two weeks and not betray something to those who lived and worked with him. Ardal, like his sister Mór, had a fine intelligence.

'I wonder, Ardal,' she said quietly, 'whether you suspected that Liam was the man who killed both Iarla and Becan from Aran.'

Ardal looked uneasily at Liam and then went to sit on one of the scholars' tables. Turlough lowered his bulk on to the window seat. His face was alert as he looked from Ardal to Liam. No one spoke.

'Did you?' Mara repeated her question.

Ardal stirred uneasily, his finger tracing an etched line of a Latin word carved on the table by some scholar of the past.

'No,' he said eventually, but his voice lacked conviction. He seemed to hear this himself because he turned and looked at her apologetically. 'At least it may have crossed my mind, but I put it from me.'

'Well, Liam was the man who committed these two secret and unlawful killings,' said Mara crisply. She was disconcerted by the look of deep sorrow and sympathy on Ardal's face. Liam, she noticed, was beginning to look more hopeful. He sat up a little straighter and looked from Mara to Ardal. A slight tinge of colour came back into his pallid cheeks.

'What!' Turlough was open-mouthed. 'Why on earth did you do that, man?'

Liam turned a face of deep sadness towards his master and *taoiseach*. He opened his mouth and then closed it again. He sighed deeply.

'He did it for me.' Ardal's voice was choked with sorrow.

Bran turned his narrow head and looked at him in a puzzled way. He was a dog who was always very sensitive to emotion. Then Mara saw his eyes leave Ardal and go to Liam and they hardened. Mara smiled to herself. Bran, she thought, was a better judge of character than was Ardal.

'What do you mean?' Turlough sounded puzzled and a little incredulous. He looked over towards Mara, but she avoided his gaze and fixed her eyes on Liam.

Liam was not a man to allow the moment to pass without seizing it. 'I did it for my lord,' he said without a blush.

Turlough frowned sceptically but Ardal looked moved. A faint colour rose to cover his prominent cheekbones. 'Liam, that is not anything that I would have asked of any man,' he said hurriedly.

'I know that, my lord.' Liam's voice was unctuous and confident. 'But I swore to my late lord, your father Finn, may God reward him, that I would care for you as if you were my own son. I couldn't allow your life to be upset by that false lie. I knew that this man was not your son. He didn't have the look of you nor the cut of you.'

'You shouldn't have done it, Liam.' Ardal's tone was broken.

'I think,' said Mara, her voice practical and assured, 'that you are making a mistake here, Ardal. You seem to think that Liam committed these two murders out of some sort of mistaken loyalty to you.'

She suddenly stopped and looked, startled, at Bran, who was emitting a long, low growl. His eyes were fixed on Liam's face and his lips were slightly stripped back from his teeth. She had never seen him like that except at times when he was confronted by a wolf. She smiled confidently.

'Bran doesn't believe this lie,' she said lightly, 'and neither do I. Ardal, Liam's motive for murdering that boy and his uncle were nothing to do with his loyalty to you for the simple reason that he has no loyalty to you.'

An expression of pain and disbelief flickered across Ardal's sensitive features. He stirred uneasily and half raised a hand, almost like one in pain. Turlough frowned uneasily, looking from one face to another. Liam assumed an expression of gentle sorrow.

Mara looked at Ardal impatiently. 'He has been using you in order to feather his own nest,' she pointed out. 'Down below the barn at Lissylisheen, Liam has made himself a storage room for all the goods that he robs from you every year from the tribute paid by your clan at Michaelmas in September and at *Bealtaine* in the month of May. He has carved out some linking passages between that storage room and Balor's Cave.'

She stopped. This was pointless, she felt. Liam would talk his way out of everything with Ardal. Now was the time to stamp her authority on the scene.

'Liam O'Lochlainn,' she said solemnly. 'I charge you with the secret and unlawful killing of two men – Iarla and Becan from Aran. I will hear the case at Poulnabrone at twelve noon on Saturday April seventeenth. Any defence or repudiation should be uttered then in front of the people of the kingdom. If you are not present on that day and hour, then you will be declared an outlaw and you will not be allowed back into the kingdom.'

And then Mara put her hand on the king's arm and turned away from the two men. Not once did she look back, but as she and Turlough went through the door of the Brehon's house, she heard the slow steady beat of two horses walking soberly down the road towards the south.

Liam was following his wronged chieftain back to Lissylisheen, the place that had been his home for more than sixty years.

Eighteen

Heptad 35

There are seven circumstances when the killing of a person may be justified:

1. *The accidental killing of an unrecognised clan member in a battle situation will carry no penalty*
2. *A physician who kills during an attempt to relieve pain will not be found guilty of murder*
3. *It is lawful to kill in battle*
4. *It is lawful for a wronged person to kill an unransomed captive*
5. *It is lawful to kill in defence of a woman or child*
6. *It is lawful to kill in self-defence as the law states that 'every counter-wounding' is free from liability*
7. *It is lawful to kill a thief who is caught in the act of stealing from your taoiseach*

The weather on that mid-April day was good. There was little wind and the noonday sunshine felt warm on Mara's back as she walked slowly down the road towards Kilcorney and then turned up towards Poulnabrone. She looked quickly around as soon as she had taken her position beside the ancient dolmen. For a moment she feared that Liam, the unjust steward, had not come, but he was there, not next to his master Ardal, where she had looked to see him, but over to the north of the field, talking earnestly to his companion. Mara narrowed her eyes, but she could not see the face of the second man as he wore the hood of his *brat* pulled forward around his face. Ardal, himself, accompanied by his niece Nuala, looked uneasy and kept sending glances across at Liam.

There was a large crowd of people present. Although her summons had not mentioned any names, rumours had obviously being flying around and many heads turned to look across at Liam. Almost the entire O'Lochlainn clan was present and a fair sprinkling of the O'Connor and MacNamara clans. Teige O'Brien, however, was not there and very few of his clansmen attended. Mara felt annoyed at his absence – he should have trusted her not to mention his name without prior warning, she thought as she took the scroll from

Fachtnan's hand and moved forward to greet the people, wishing them a benediction from God and his blessed mother.

An expectant silence ensued once the murmurs of 'and Patrick' died down and Mara immediately raised her voice, pacing the delivery of the words as the cliff-face to the east of the townland of Poulnabrone picked up her words and echoed them back to the crowd grouped around the ancient dolmen.

'Over four weeks ago a stranger from Aran came here to this kingdom of the Burren,' she began, watching to see comprehension in the faces of those furthest from her in order to be sure that her voice carried. There were nods from all and a strange sigh went up from the assembled clansmen, almost as if they were children hearing a story of which the beginning was familiar, but the ending was still unknown.

'He came here in good faith with a message from his mother on her death bed,' went on Mara. 'He came, he spoke, he lived among us for three days, from the feast day of the blessed Saint Patrick to the following Thursday and then he died, brutally murdered.'

The murmur began again, rose and swelled and then quite suddenly died away as everyone looked at their Brehon with expectant eyes.

'And then,' continued Mara, making a pretence of consulting her scroll, 'four days later, on Monday March twenty-fourth, another man, the uncle of Iarla from Aran, a man named Becan, was also found murdered.' She paused again, but this time there was no sound from the people and no one moved.

'I now name the killer of both men,' Mara said, her voice firm and unemotional. 'It was Liam O'Lochlainn, steward to the O'Lochlainn. He committed the first murder because Iarla from Aran had detected him in the act of stealing from his *taoiseach*.'

Now every head turned, but there were no gasps, no murmurs, just curiosity and interest on all faces. I wonder, speculated Mara as she glanced at her scroll, whether everyone on the Burren, except Ardal O'Lochlainn, suspected the truth about Liam.

'The second crime,' she said firmly, 'was committed because Becan had suspected what had happened to his nephew and was bold enough to investigate the cave, known as Balor's Cave, which led back underground to Lissylisheen and provided the means for the steward Liam to remove goods in secret from the O'Lochlainn barn. He met his death there.'

Now the sound of a hundred voices swelled up into the warm, still air. Everyone was interested in this, and to Mara, listening carefully, shocked indignation seemed to be the prevailing note. As she had thought, people had surmised that Liam had been stealing, but had not known how he could do it. The implications of the possible extent of his thievery had now dawned on this quick-witted people and over a hundred alert and interested faces turned once more towards her. With a slight feeling of amusement, she noticed that Nuala, her cheeks crimson with fury, had slipped her hand into her uncle's hand. Ardal glanced down at her with a smile and patted her arm with his other hand.

'I now call upon Liam O'Lochlainn, steward, to come forward to admit to his two crimes of secret and unlawful killing.' Mara's voice rang out as clear as the bell from the abbey.

And Liam did come forward, but not alone. The figure beside him pushed the hood back from his face and as he advanced Mara recognized him. It was the young man, Cavan, who used to be a law-scholar at MacClancy's Law School before he qualified as an *aigne*. Mara looked at him with interest, wondering whether he was better briefed now than he had been at Malachy's abortive attempt to take Nuala's property for himself.

Cavan bowed to her and she bowed back gravely. It was the first time for many, many years that an accused person had bothered having legal representation at her court. The people of the Burren seemed mainly resigned to the sentences that she passed, or else her reputation as a lawyer of great knowledge made other lawyers reluctant to take on the task of sparring with her.

'You speak on behalf of Liam O'Lochlainn?' Mara addressed him with formal courtesy.

He bowed again. 'My client, Liam O'Lochlainn, denies the charge of murder.' His voice, though loud and emphatic at close quarters, did not carry as well as hers and Mara could see the people on the outskirts of the crowd pressing closer in order to hear better. This young man would need to practise his delivery, she thought critically. All courts in Ireland were held in the open air so he would be unsuccessful in his pleading if he did not improve.

'Cavan the *aigne*, formally a scholar at the MacClancy Law School in Corcomroe, will represent the accused man,' she said to the crowd, and saw the nods that showed her words had reached them all. 'Speak for your client,' she said to Cavan.

'My client, Liam O'Lochlainn, admits the killing of Becan, uncle of Iarla, but says that it was done in self-defence as Becan tried to strangle my client. Becan accused my client of the murder of Iarla

and attempted to kill him in revenge. The cook at Lissylisheen is
available to give testimony that he observed marks on my client's
throat the following day.'

'Why was the matter not reported to me?' Mara kept her voice
confident and slightly scornful, but she was taken aback. She had not
expected this. It might even be true, she thought. Becan and Liam
might have come to blows, though if they had it seemed surprising
that a man of Liam's age and sedentary occupation would have been
able to overcome the blacksmith in a fight. Still, if the cook had
noticed marks on Liam's throat, it may well have been the way this
happened.

'My client regrets this now,' said Cavan blandly. His voice still did
not carry to the back of the crowd, but Mara decided not to waste
time interpreting for him. She had other matters to think of. Suddenly
she was filled with a sense of panic. She felt her breath come quickly
and her hands began to sweat. She could not think for a moment.
What was the law on the subject? For the first time in her career,
she felt as if all her knowledge of the law was sliding away from her.

Deliberately, Mara moved her eyes away from the crowd and
looked towards the west. She concentrated on taking long, deep
breaths of the soft air. She could not see the law school at
Cahermacnaghten from where she stood, but she could visualise it.
The schoolroom was as vivid to her as if she were present. Her
mind's eye wandered along the shelves of the wooden press, lingering
over each leather-bound volume until it stopped at the oldest and
most worn book, the book that she had handled thousands of times.
Her panic subsided and she turned towards Cavan with a slight smile
on her lips.

Enda, she now saw, was writing a note on a piece of vellum. She
waited until he slid it over, then glanced at it and gave him an appreciative nod. It had been unnecessary though. Her mind had cleared
from the fog of pregnancy and tiredness and the correct law was
on the tip of her tongue. Nevertheless, she would give Enda his due
praise.

'My young colleague here reminds me that if a killing is unre-
ported and the body left in an unfrequented place then the crime
has to be classified as *duinethaide,*' she said clearly and added in a
low voice to the young *aigne*, 'See *Cáin Adomnáin,* page 128.' She
did not care that, even to her own ears, her voice held a patron-
izing note. She had had a bad fright for a moment and, rather meanly,
was not sorry to take her revenge.

'Let us turn now to the first murder, the murder of the young man Iarla,' she said in clear, carrying tones. 'What is your client's explanation of that? Does he also plead not guilty to this charge?'

Cavan raised his voice. 'Not guilty,' he said and this time his tones rang out against the cliff face. He looked confident and happy now, but Mara waited without apprehension. Liam was guilty; she was certain of that and she was also certain of her own ability to remember the ancient laws better than this callow young man.

'Not guilty because . . .?' she queried.

'Because he acted in defence of the property of his *taoiseach*, the O'Lochlainn,' shouted Cavan. He was now determined to be heard by everyone in the moment of his glory and was bellowing as if he were on a hurling field.

'Go on,' said Mara.

'Let me speak.' Suddenly Liam elbowed Cavan back and climbed, with great agility for a man of his age, on to one of the large boulders scattered around the dolmen. Ardal O'Lochlainn took a quick step forward, his eyes fixed on his steward's face.

'Brehon, my lord, fellow clansmen, people of the kingdom . . .' Liam's rich, confident voice was easily reaching to the back of the crowd. Every eye was upon him. 'This is the truth of what happened on that Thursday after the feast of St Patrick. I was working in the barn and in the courtyard at Lissylisheen. I saw Iarla from Aran go into the barn. I took no notice of that; I was used to him going in and out of the barn ever since he had arrived to stay with us. But –' Liam made his voice low and dramatic and his glance swept the crowd like that of a practised orator – 'when I went into the barn a few minutes later there wasn't sight or sound of him. He had disappeared. Then I noticed something. There's an old press in the barn – something I had never taken much notice of before and it was pulled out from the wall and there was a gap beyond it. And beyond the gap was a passageway. I had lived all of my life at Lissylisheen and my father before me, but I had never known of this place. It was a cave and the passageway led all the way underground.'

'And Iarla?' interrupted Mara. She didn't like the way that Ardal had his eyes fixed so admiringly on his steward's face and the way that the crowd hung on his words as if they were, to them, as real and as true as the Gospel read at Mass on Sundays.

'And there he was!' shouted Liam triumphantly. 'There he was wheeling an old turf barrow that we keep in the barn for moving

heavy barrels. And it was full of the most valuable goods that he
could find, thief that he was, in the barn. I followed him, Brehon.
I followed him silently. I didn't know what he was up to until we
had come a long distance and then I saw that the underground
passageway ended at Balor's Cave.' He paused to look around the
crowd. Every face was turned towards him, mouths slightly ajar.
Mara noticed a slight smile twitched at the corner of Liam's lips. It
was gone in a second and then he continued his tale. 'And then I
saw it all!' he said dramatically. 'Iarla was going to stay as long as he
could, imposing on my lord, himself, and he was going to steal as
much as he could manage and the other fellow, that uncle of his,
Becan, was going to pick up the goods late at night and take them
to Kinvarra.'

'And you killed him?' Mara's voice was icy but her mind was
working quickly. Was there any way of refuting this?

'I killed him because he stole from my lord,' said Liam firmly.
His voice was full of confidence. 'And the law says that we can
do this. I learned that from your own father, Brehon.' He bowed
his head humbly as if he waited for her acquiescence before
continuing.

'*Ba gó,*' called out a clear, young voice.

'Who gives me the lie?' Liam's head snapped up and his eyes
burned with fury.

'*Ba gó,*' repeated the voice.

Now Mara knew who it was. He was in the centre of the large
group of his brothers and sisters, his father and his mother, but she
knew that voice.

And then something strange happened. Suddenly it seemed as if
the eyes of everyone had been opened to the truth. '*Ba gó,* '*Ba gó,*
'*Ba gó,*' came from every corner of the large field. Every voice took
up the chant. It became rhythmic, almost like the accompaniment
to dance music. Even the harsh voices of the grey crows that circled
overhead were hushed by the sound.

Mara waited, her eyes fixed on Liam. Something had happened
to the large self-confident, fat man. Like an inflated bladder that has
been pricked by a sharp stone while being passed among a crowd
of boys, he climbed down from the boulder and turned his back
upon the crowd. It was as Mara had surmised earlier. Everyone had
known or guessed that Liam was cheating his master and now they
saw how. They were quick-witted enough to see how he had
condemned himself out of his own mouth, how likely it was that

the trusted steward had made this passageway and how impossible it was that he had not known of its existence. How he could have arranged for the heavy wooden press to block it and how unlikely that a stranger could discover in a day what Liam had not discovered in a lifetime.

'*Ba gó,* '*Ba gó,* '*Ba gó,*' chanted the crowd until Mara raised her hand for silence. She obtained it instantly; each person wanted to know more.

'Danann, will you come forward?' she said mildly.

Every neck twisted as the basket maker's eldest son came forward. He didn't look at his father or his mother as he left them and his mien was confident and assured.

'I'm here, Brehon,' he said when he arrived at the foot of the dolmen.

'You say that the words of Liam the steward are false?' She put the query to him with no preliminary reassurance and his answer came as quickly as her question.

'I know that they are false, Brehon.'

'Why?'

'Because I and my brothers watched Liam come out of Balor's Cave on one moonlit night last year, before ever the man from Aran arrived in this kingdom. We saw him come out, look all around and when he went back in, we followed him and we came to the barn at Lissylisheen. We saw all the goods piled inside the cave and we found more goods on the turf barrow just inside the passageway at the entrance to the barn.'

'And you did not think to tell anyone of this?'

'No, Brehon, we thought it best to say nothing.' His words were dignified, but his eyes pleaded with her not to question him further.

Mara nodded. 'Could you call one of your brothers who was also present that night?'

The younger boy was not as confident as Danann but he said enough to corroborate his brother's evidence. When he had finished, Mara looked over at Cavan.

'Have you or your client anything more to say?' she asked courteously.

Both men shook their heads.

'In that case I pass sentence.' She took a step forward and waited until complete silence had descended on the crowd.

'Liam O'Lochlainn, I find you guilty of the crime of *duinetháide,* the secret and unlawful murder, of two men, Iarla from Aran and his uncle Becan. Becan's honour price as a blacksmith was seven *sét*s and the fine for his secret and unlawful killing is eighty-four *sét*s. This makes a fine of eighty-nine *sét*s, that is forty-five cows or forty-five ounces of silver. Iarla's honour price as a fisherman was only half a *sét* so the fine for his murder would be forty-two cows or forty-two ounces of silver. These sums are to be paid to the victim's families within ten days.'

She waited, but Liam said nothing. He had turned away and was staring at the cliff, meeting no one's eyes, so she finished in her customary fashion: 'Now go in peace with your families and your neighbours.'

Epilogue

It was the last day of April when Turlough returned from the Aran Islands. Mara was waiting at the gate of the Brehon's house. She had seen the king and his retinue go past while she was still teaching in the law school and had guessed that he was going to Lissylisheen to give Ardal an account of his journey. He would leave all of his men, except for his two bodyguards, at Lissylisheen, she guessed. School was over now for the day and they would have supper together and then she would hear everything and tomorrow they would have one of their precious weekends together at Ballinalacken Castle.

Turlough's face bore a look of shock when he dismounted. He hardly waited to kiss her hastily before saying dramatically: 'You'll never guess what sound I heard as I rode into the courtyard at Lissylisheen.'

'Not Liam giving orders, anyway,' said Mara. She had her own news about Liam, but that could wait until they were inside and having their supper cosily seated by the fire.

'I heard,' said Turlough slowly and dramatically, 'a child cry.'

'Oh, that.' Mara smiled dismissively. 'That was just little Finn.'

'Finn,' he repeated.

'Yes, Ardal's son. I've been down three times this week to see him. He's a beautiful baby. Ardal and Marta are so proud of him.'

'Marta,' repeated Turlough.

'Well, never mind that now,' said Mara, taking his arm and walking up the path towards the open front door of her house. 'Tell me all about Aran,' she said as soon as they were inside. 'Did you put the bunch of primroses on Étain's grave for me?'

'I did,' said Turlough wincing slightly at the memory as he sank down on the big cushioned chair and stretched out his long legs, 'and I had to do it with all the men-at-arms standing there and trying not to laugh. I also paid over the fine money to Bebhinn and to Iarla's sisters. I think that was very welcome. I just went down to tell Ardal about that. I still feel bad about Ardal paying the fine when that scoundrel, Liam, absconded. Any sign of the villain, by the way? I'll put him in chains as soon as I catch up with him. I have men looking for him all over the three kingdoms.'

'I don't think that you will catch up with him,' said Mara quietly. 'My son-in-law, Oisín, brought me some wine from Galway today. He brought some news as well. Liam is apparently the owner of a prosperous inn in Galway, right in the centre of the city. He has owned it for years. People often wondered about it because there was always new building going on there – and nothing but the best of furnishings and hangings. All the rich merchants from overseas countries stay there.'

'Well!' Turlough was speechless, staring angrily into the fire.

'Did you meet Ardal's new steward?' she asked lightly to distract his thoughts from Liam.

It worked. Turlough was always endlessly curious about people. 'No, who has he found? I was going to offer to spare one of my men to him for a while.'

'I don't think he'll need anything; the new steward has taken to the work very well. He's a clever boy. Do you remember I told you about Danann, the basket maker's eldest son? Well, Ardal is training him in the business and the boy is doing very well. His writing and adding up is almost as good as Liam's and I would stake my honour that he is honest.'

That had been a mistake. Turlough stared at her, a flush of fury mounting to his forehead. 'I'm glad Ardal's suited, but it doesn't alter the fact that Liam has defied the authority of the laws of this kingdom. I'll get him back if it's the last thing that I do,' he blustered.

'You won't,' said Mara quietly. 'You know very well that you have no jurisdiction over the city of Galway. That is ruled by English law. Liam knew that well when he bought an inn there all of those years ago. If anything ever happened to let Ardal know what he was up to, then he had only less than half a day's gallop to put himself beyond the reach of our law. He's a rich man there and you can do nothing. Ardal knows that. I don't think he cares.' Mara smiled when she thought of Ardal. 'All Ardal is concerned about now is watching his son and planning for his future; I love to see him with that child. Next June or July, you and I will be the same. We will have our own child to watch over and to bring up in this kingdom.'

'Hm.' He was only half-appeased; she could see that. The whole business with Liam had reminded him of the close proximity of English rule and the dangers to the Gaelic kingdoms even here on the Atlantic fringe.

'You must be tired after your sea-crossing,' she said solicitously. 'Sit by the fire while I finish writing up my casebook. Brigid will be in with our supper in a minute.' And then, as he continued to drum his fingers on the windowsill, she took a glass from the court cupboard in the corner of the room. 'Have this glass of wine while you're waiting. It's good, this one. We just opened the little barrel in your honour today. It's been two years in my cellar.' She poured some dark red wine into the glass from the flagon on the table by the fire.

Turlough sipped the wine with appreciative noises, but was restless and would not sit by the fire. He paced the room and then came to stand behind her, watching as her pen moved swiftly over the vellum leaf.

'To think of all the worry and trouble this case has been to you, and all for nothing,' he burst out as she paused to trim the quill with her knife. 'I can't bear to think how that villain escaped after all your hard work, and poor Ardal left to bear the burden of paying for his crime!'

'I don't look at it like that at all.' Mara put her pen down carefully on the penholder and looked up at him. She was surprised at so much vehemence from such a tolerant man. 'As for Ardal,' she said thoughtfully, 'I have a suspicion that he was aware of what Liam was doing, not precisely how and to what extent, but he didn't want to challenge him. Paying the fine helped him to make reparation for two crimes which were partly caused by his own weakness and dependency on Liam.'

'He was lonely, poor fellow,' said Turlough compassionately.

'That's true, I suppose.' Even now Mara could still be surprised at the compassion and understanding of this warlike man that she had married. 'Ardal *was* lonely. I can see the huge change in him since Marta and the baby have come to live at Lissylisheen. As for me, what was important to me was achieved.' And, then, before he could question her, she drew a line under the entry in her casebook and in her square minuscule handwriting she wrote:

THE WISE SAYINGS OF THE BREHON
FITHAIL NUMBER 353
IT IS THE DUTY OF EACH BREHON TO
SEEK THE TRUTH FOR TRUTH IS THE
MOST SACRED OF ALL THINGS.

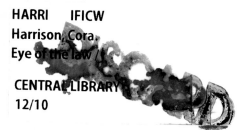